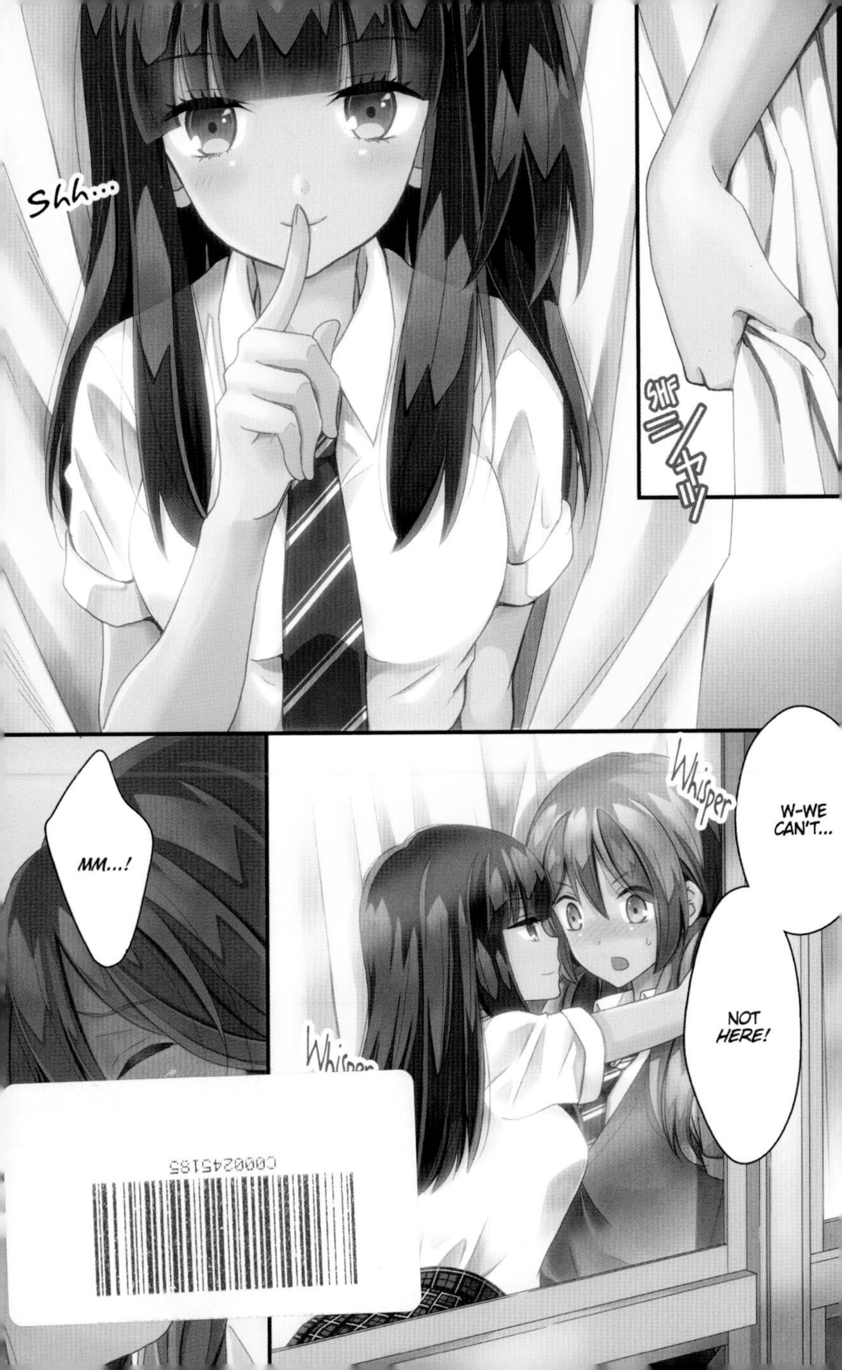
SHF
Shh...
Whisper
W-WE CAN'T...
NOT HERE!
MM...!

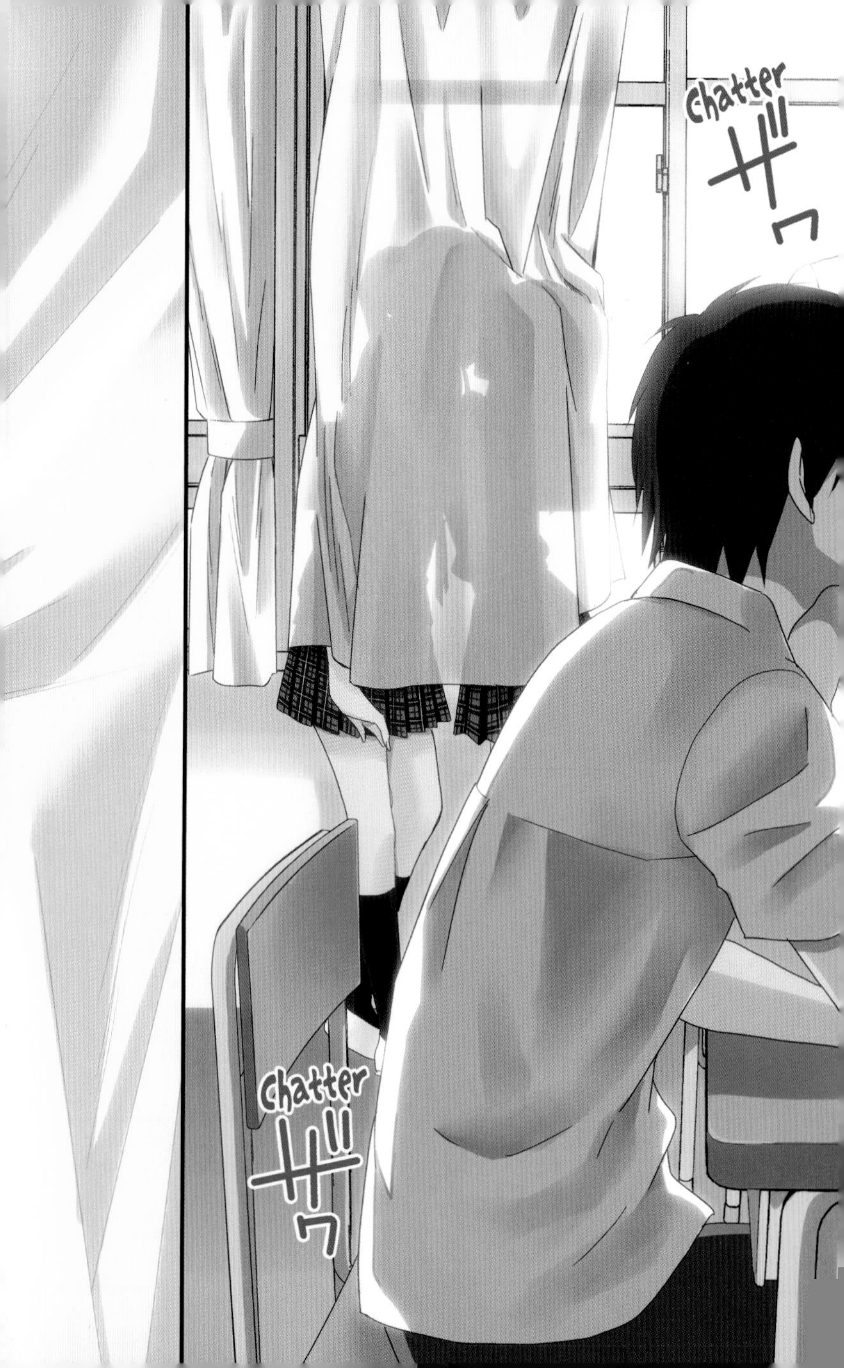
Chatter
ザワ
Chatter
ザワ

Afterword

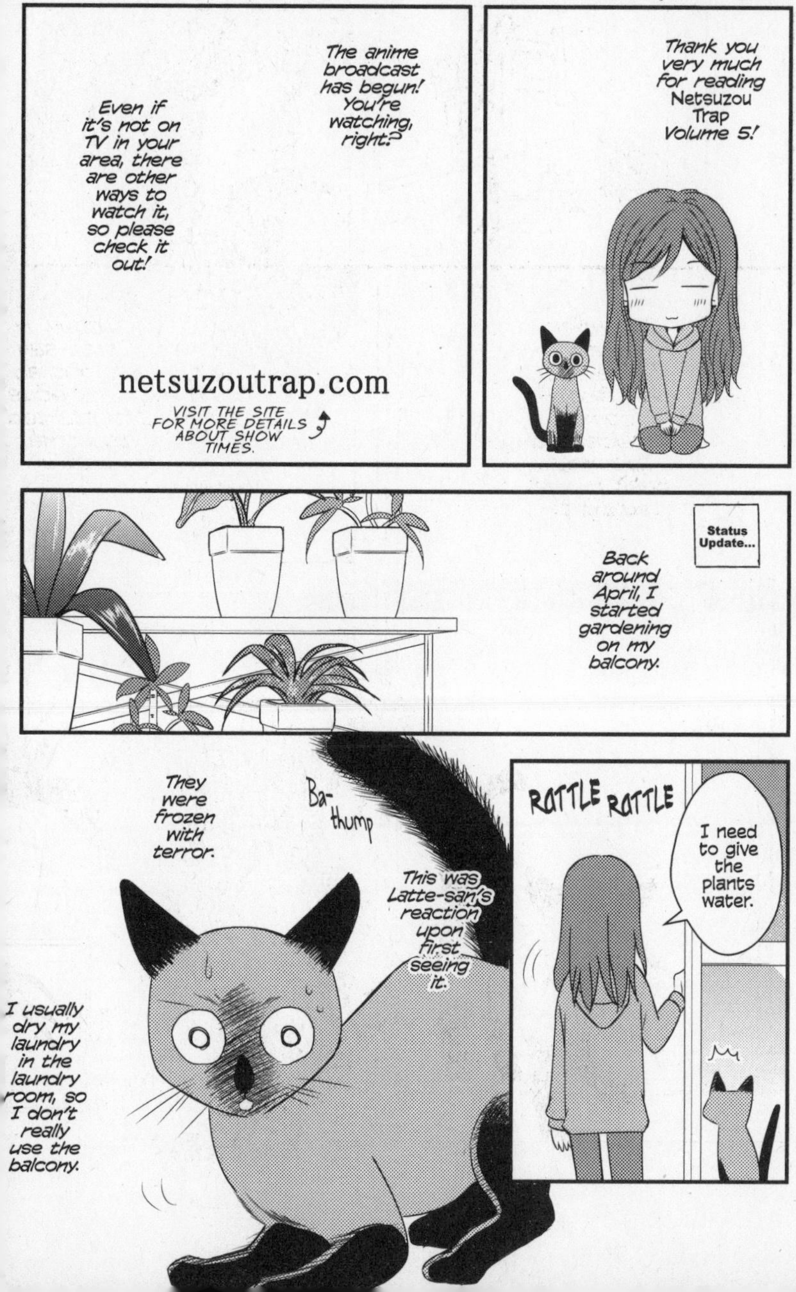
Thank you very much for reading Netsuzou Trap Volume 5!
The anime broadcast has begun! You're watching, right?
Even if it's not on TV in your area, there are other ways to watch it, so please check it out!
netsuzoutrap.com
VISIT THE SITE FOR MORE DETAILS ABOUT SHOW TIMES.
Status Update...
Back around April, I started gardening on my balcony.
RATTLE RATTLE
I need to give the plants water.
Ba-thump
They were frozen with terror.
This was Latte-san's reaction upon first seeing it.
I usually dry my laundry in the laundry room, so I don't really use the balcony.

Netsuzou TRap -NTR-

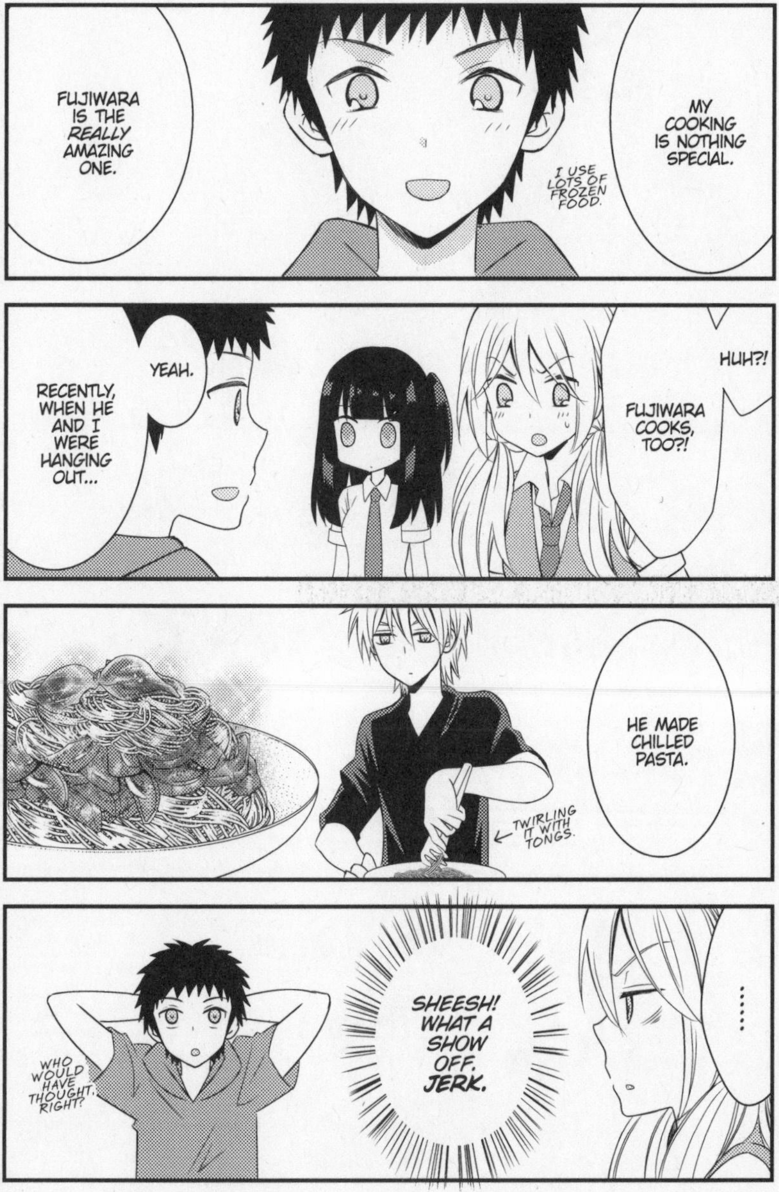
MY COOKING IS NOTHING SPECIAL.
I USE LOTS OF FROZEN FOOD.
FUJIWARA IS THE *REALLY* AMAZING ONE.
HUH?!
FUJIWARA COOKS, TOO?!
YEAH.
RECENTLY, WHEN HE AND I WERE HANGING OUT...
HE MADE CHILLED PASTA.
TWIRLING IT WITH TONGS.
......
SHEESH! WHAT A SHOW OFF. **JERK.**
WHO WOULD HAVE THOUGHT, RIGHT?

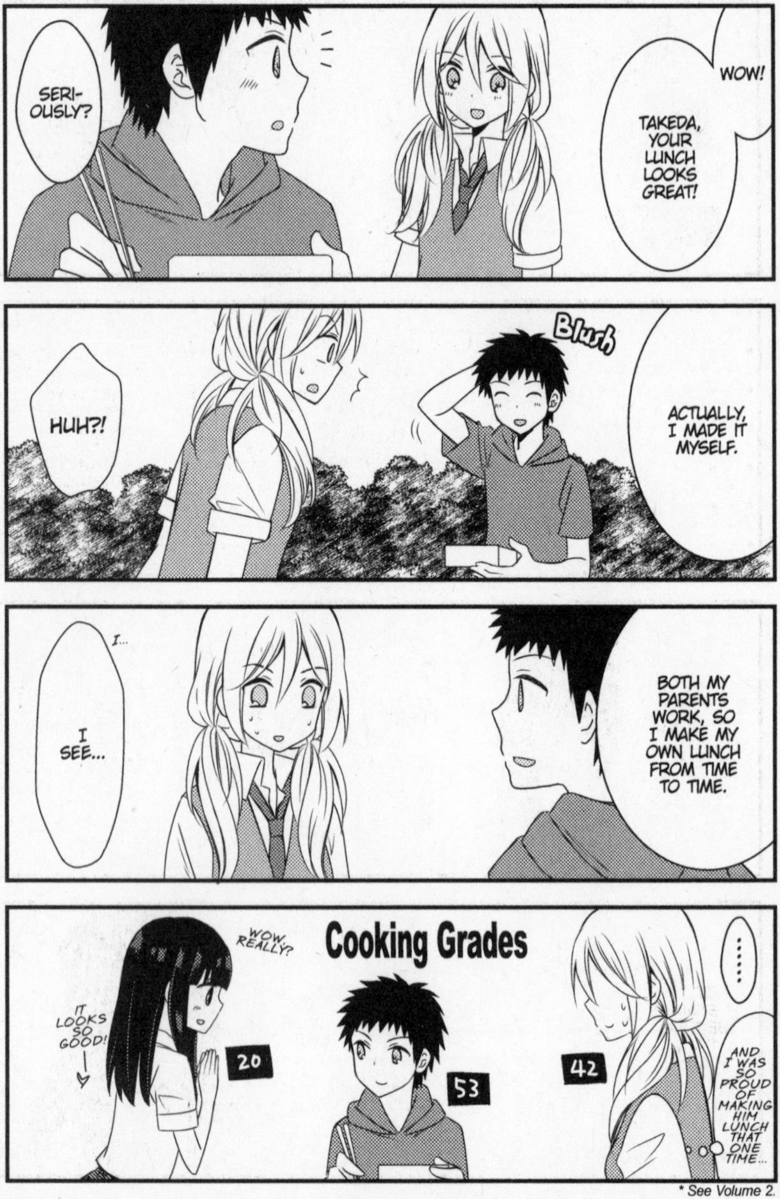
WOW!
TAKEDA, YOUR LUNCH LOOKS GREAT!
SERI-OUSLY?
ACTUALLY, I MADE IT MYSELF.
Blush
HUH?!
BOTH MY PARENTS WORK, SO I MAKE MY OWN LUNCH FROM TIME TO TIME.
I...
I SEE...
Cooking Grades
......
AND I WAS SO PROUD OF MAKING HIM LUNCH THAT ONE TIME...
42
53
WOW, REALLY?
20
IT LOOKS SO GOOD!

* See Volume 2.

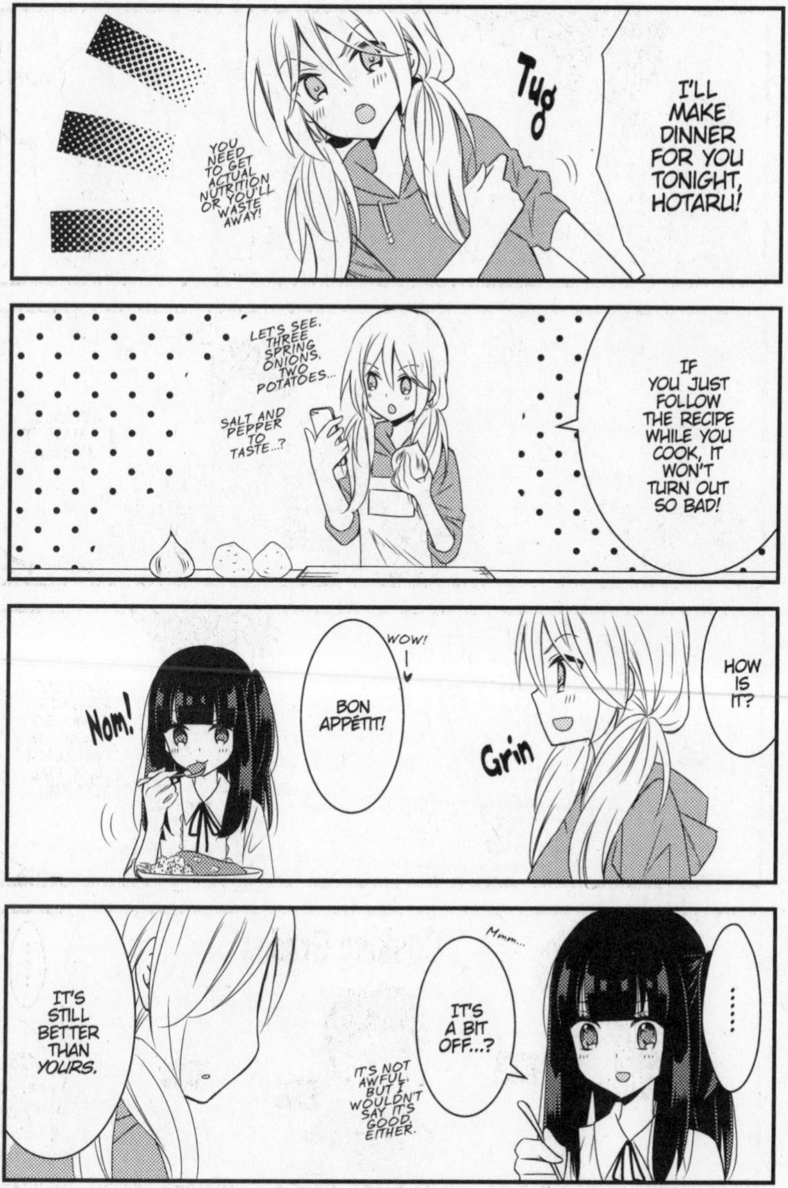
I'LL MAKE DINNER FOR YOU TONIGHT, HOTARU!
Tug
YOU NEED TO GET ACTUAL NUTRITION OR YOU'LL WASTE AWAY!
IF YOU JUST FOLLOW THE RECIPE WHILE YOU COOK, IT WON'T TURN OUT SO BAD!
LET'S SEE, THREE SPRING ONIONS, TWO POTATOES...
SALT AND PEPPER TO TASTE...?
HOW IS IT?
Grin
WOW!
BON APPÉTIT!
Nom!
......
Mmm...
IT'S A BIT OFF...?
IT'S NOT AWFUL, BUT I WOULDN'T SAY IT'S GOOD, EITHER.
IT'S STILL BETTER THAN *YOURS.*

NTR★C

Netsuzou Trap • Cooking

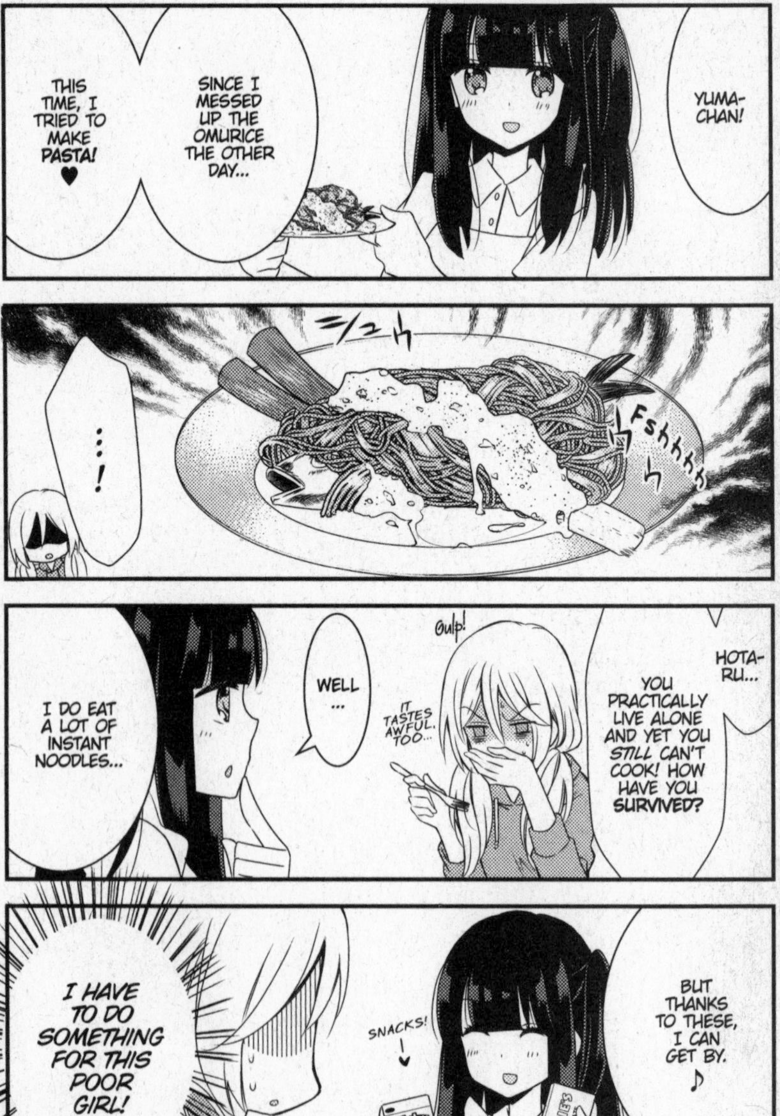
YUMA-CHAN!
SINCE I MESSED UP THE OMURICE THE OTHER DAY...
THIS TIME, I TRIED TO MAKE PASTA! ♥
Fshhhh
...!
HOTA-RU...
YOU PRACTICALLY LIVE ALONE AND YET YOU STILL CAN'T COOK! HOW HAVE YOU SURVIVED?
Gulp!
IT TASTES AWFUL, TOO...
WELL...
I DO EAT A LOT OF INSTANT NOODLES...
BUT THANKS TO THESE, I CAN GET BY. ♪
SNACKS!
I HAVE TO DO SOMETHING FOR THIS POOR GIRL!

Netsuzou TRap -NTR-

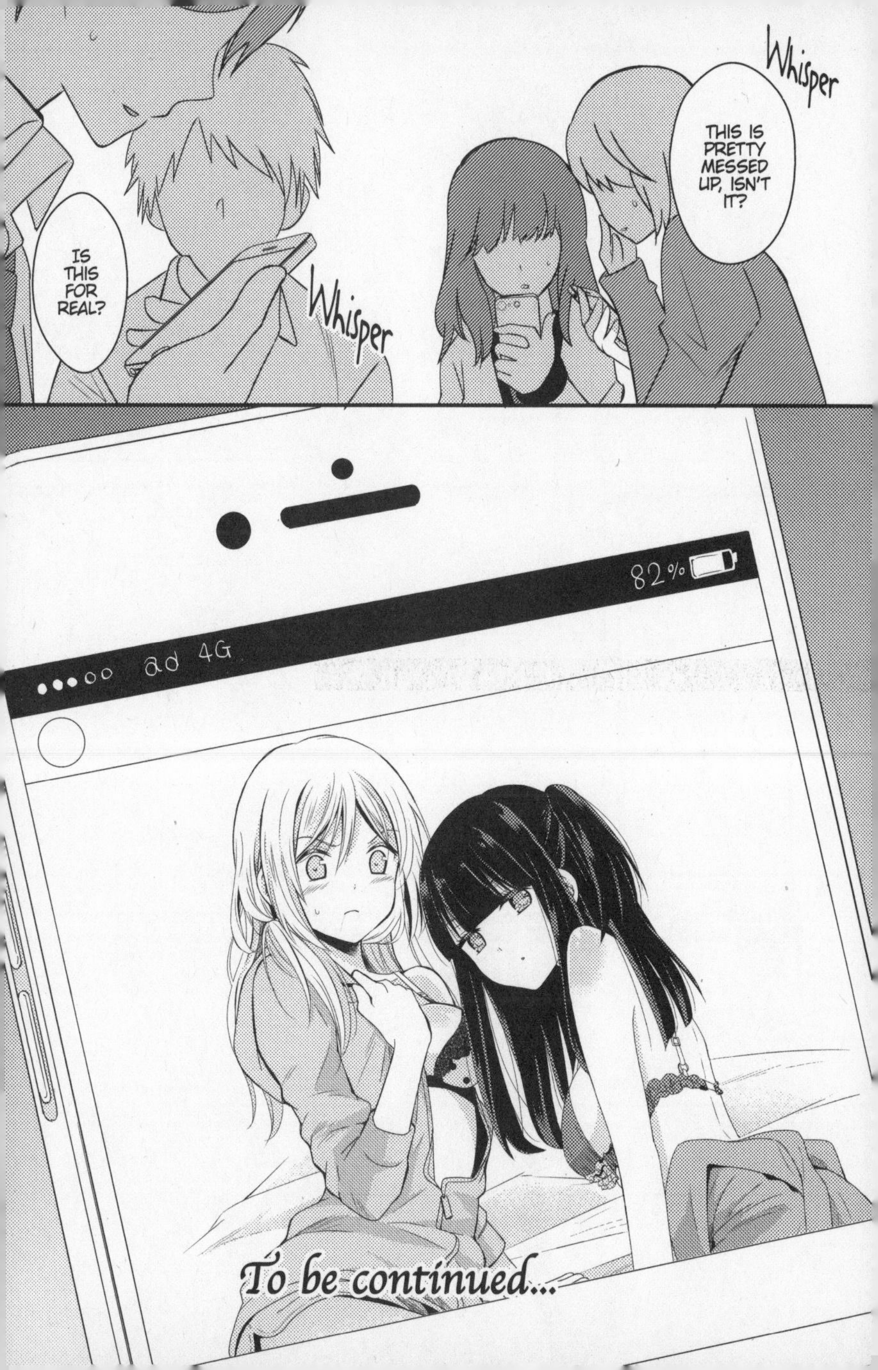
Whisper
THIS IS PRETTY MESSED UP, ISN'T IT?
Whisper
IS THIS FOR REAL?
82%
ad 4G
To be continued...

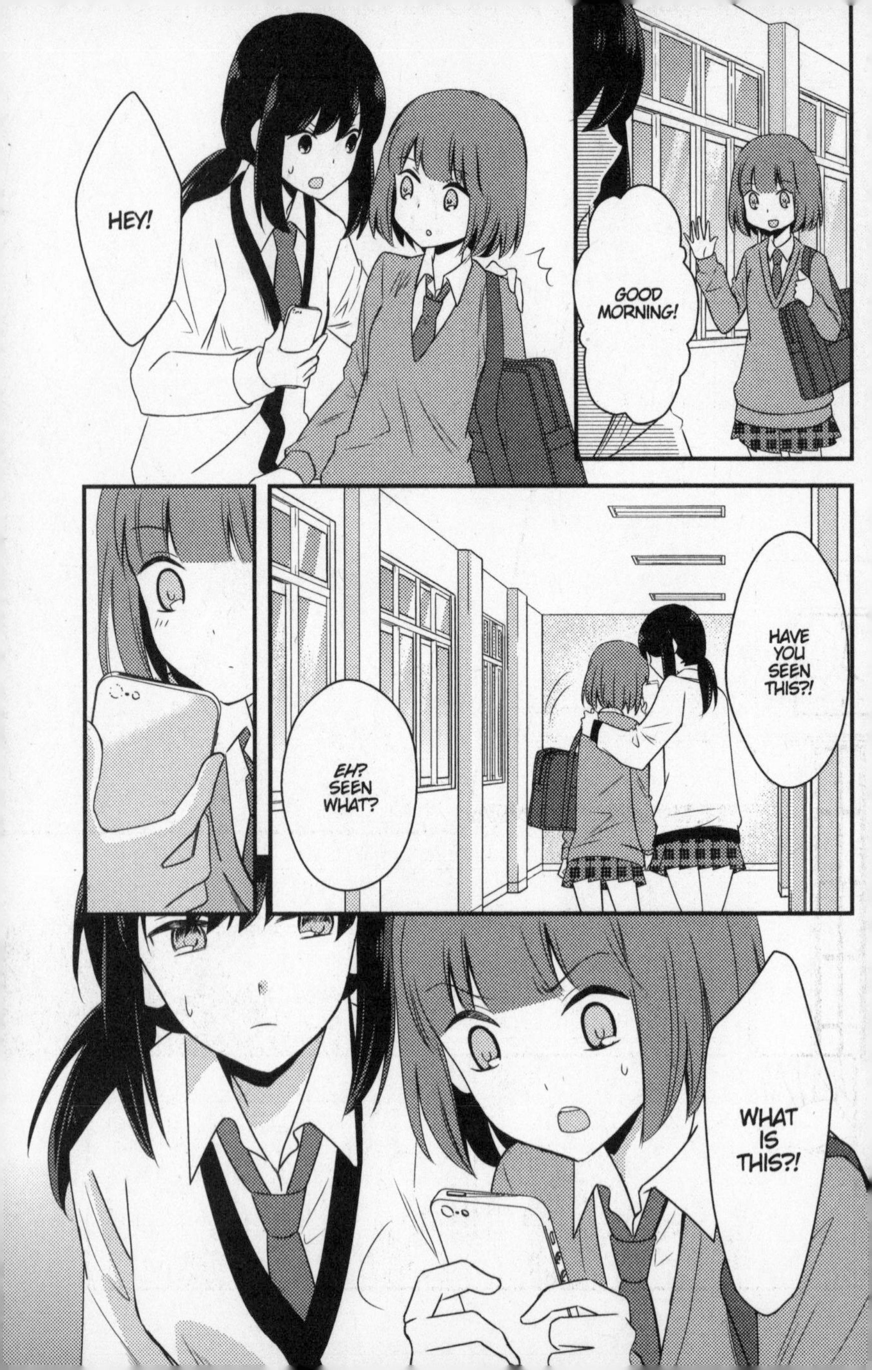
GOOD MORNING!
HEY!
HAVE YOU SEEN THIS?!
EH? SEEN WHAT?
WHAT IS THIS?!

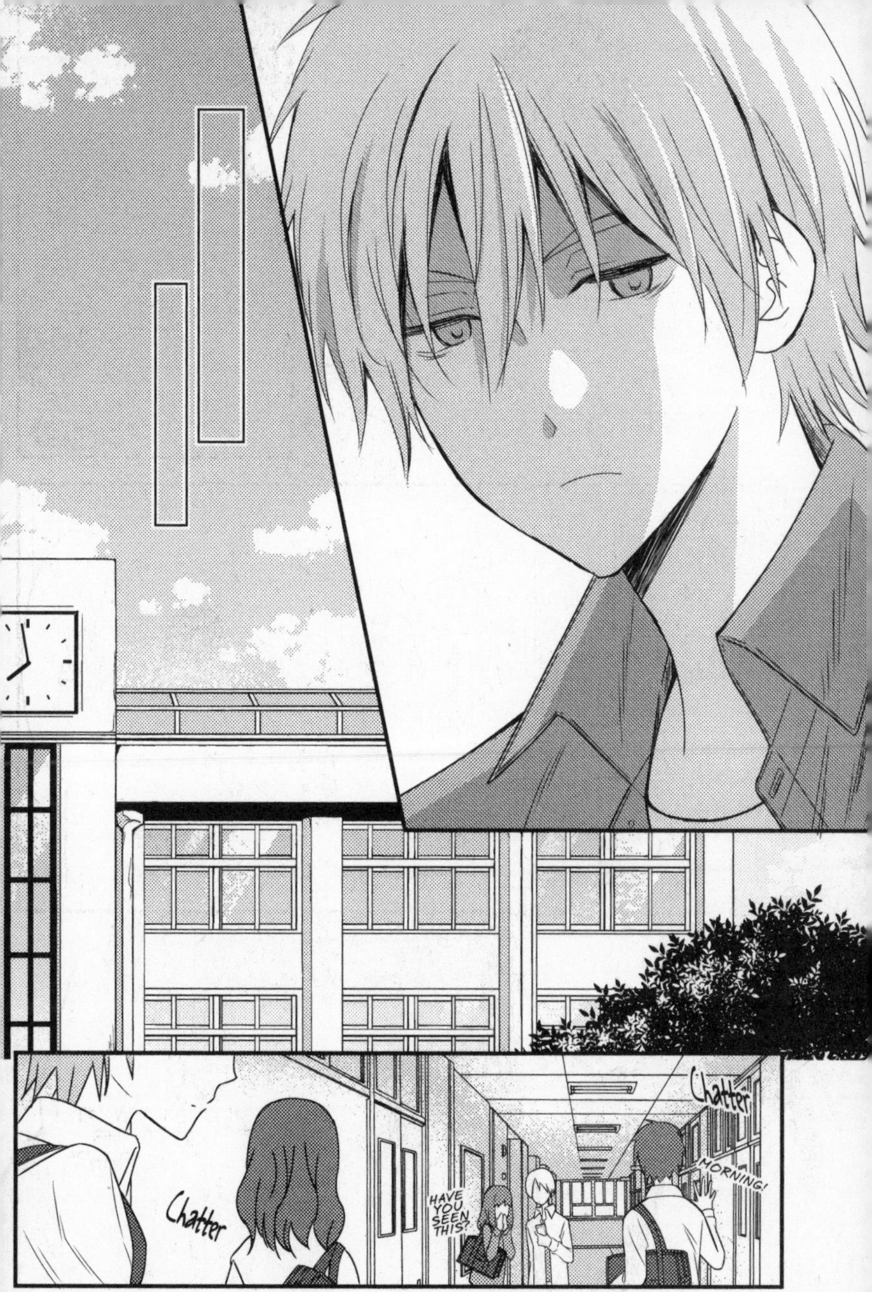
Chatter
MORNING!
HAVE YOU SEEN THIS?
Chatter

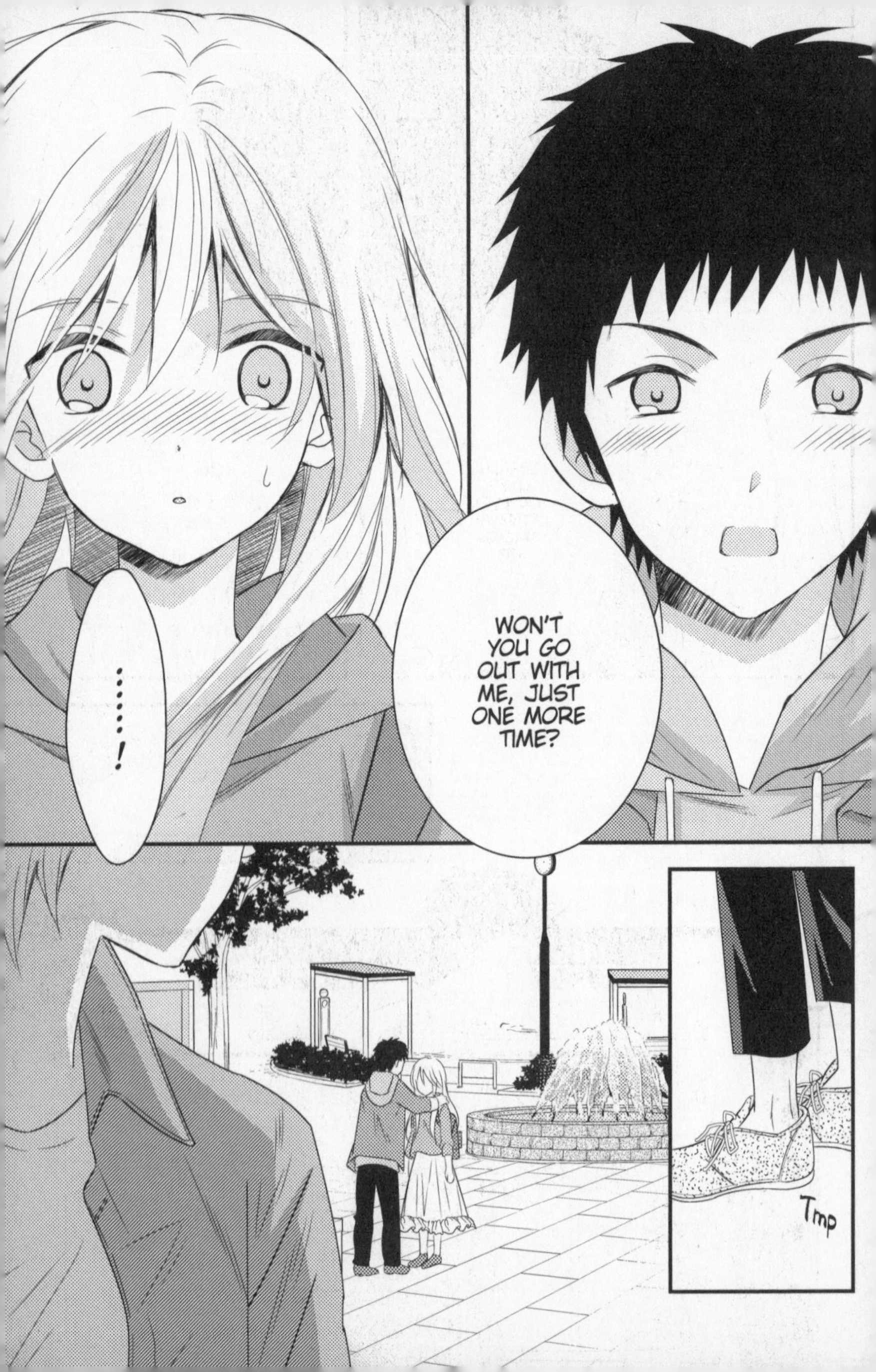

WON'T YOU GO OUT WITH ME, JUST ONE MORE TIME?
.....!
Tmp

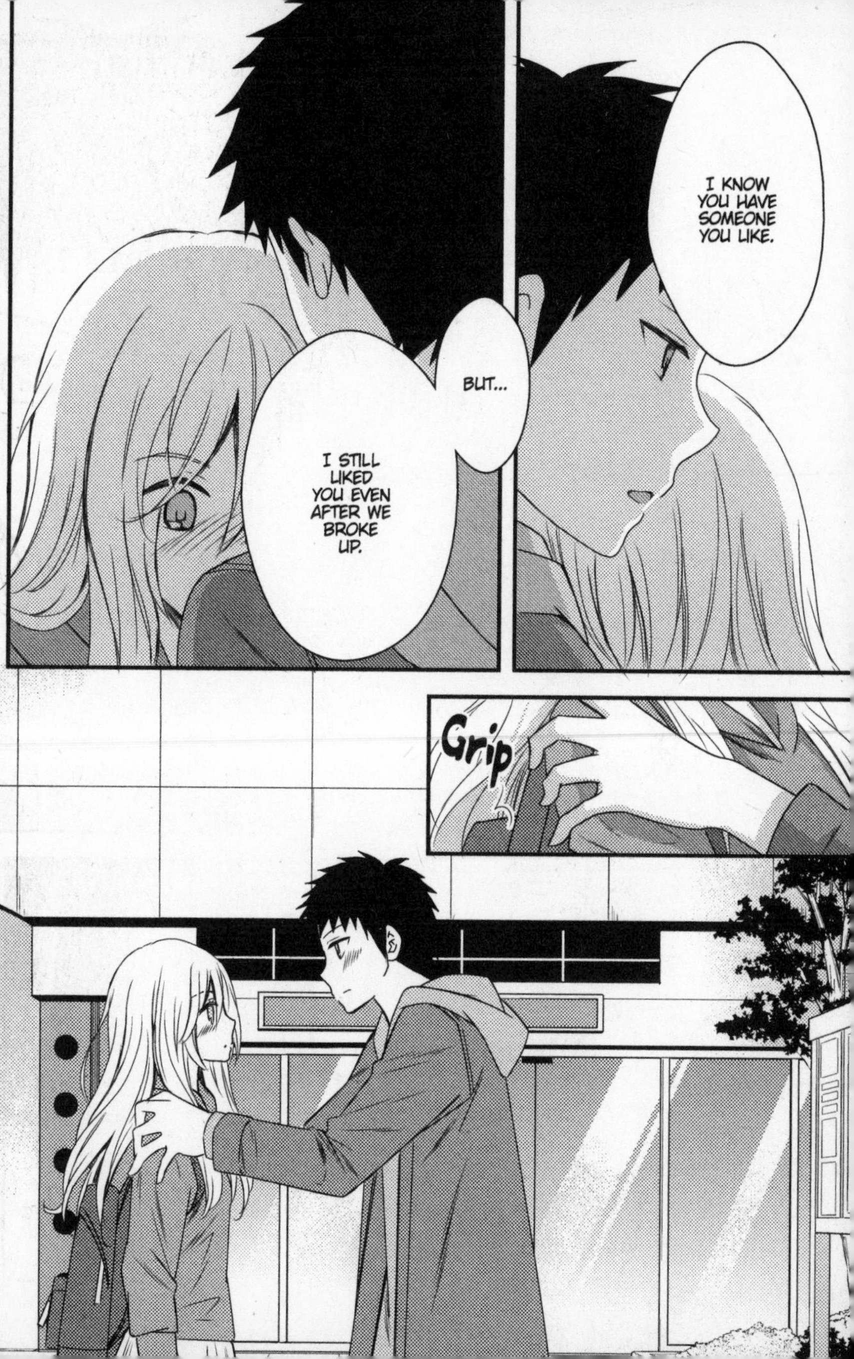
I KNOW YOU HAVE SOMEONE YOU LIKE.
BUT...
I STILL LIKED YOU EVEN AFTER WE BROKE UP.
Grip

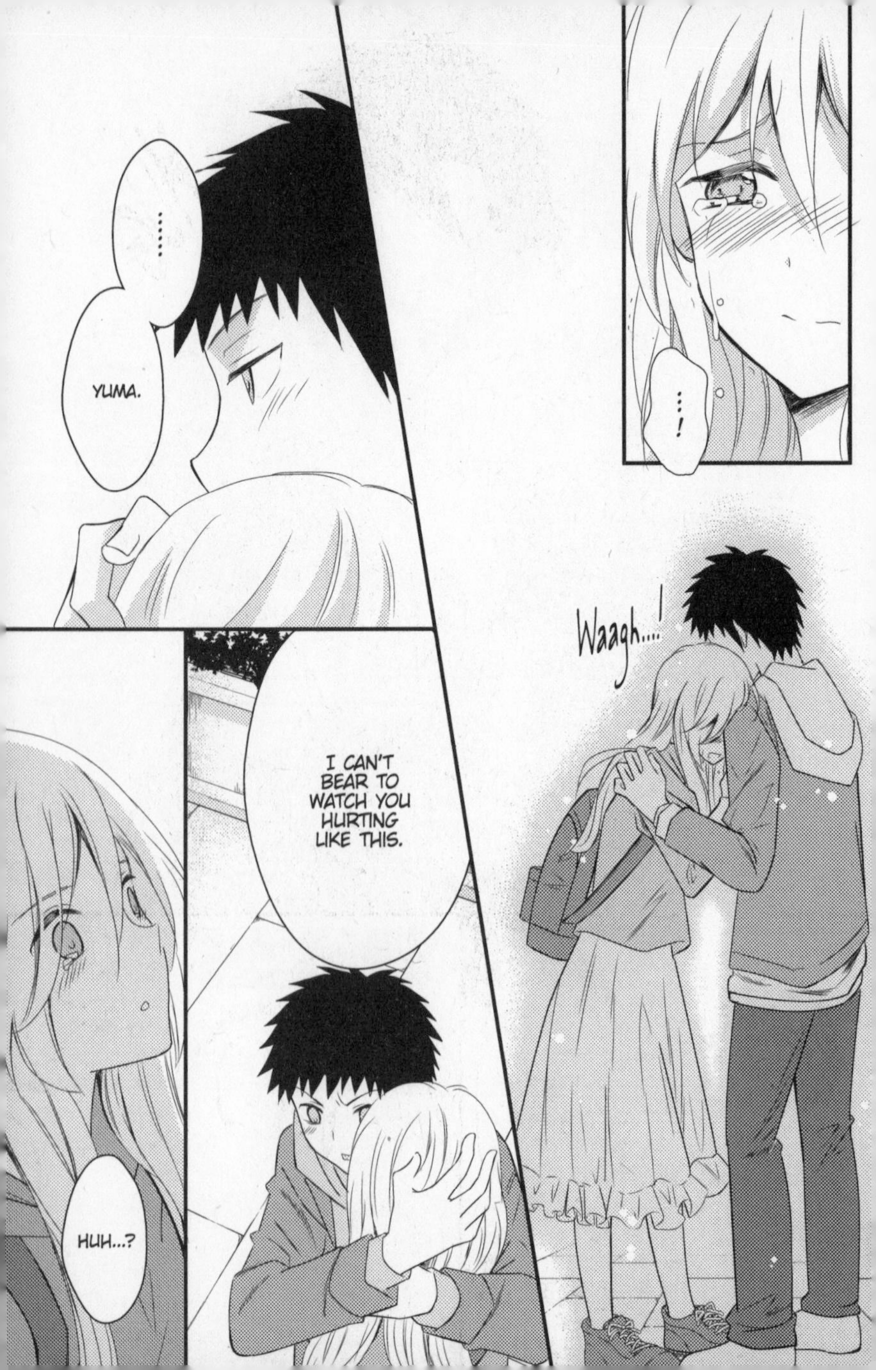
......
YUMA.
I CAN'T BEAR TO WATCH YOU HURTING LIKE THIS.
HUH...?
...!
Waagh....!

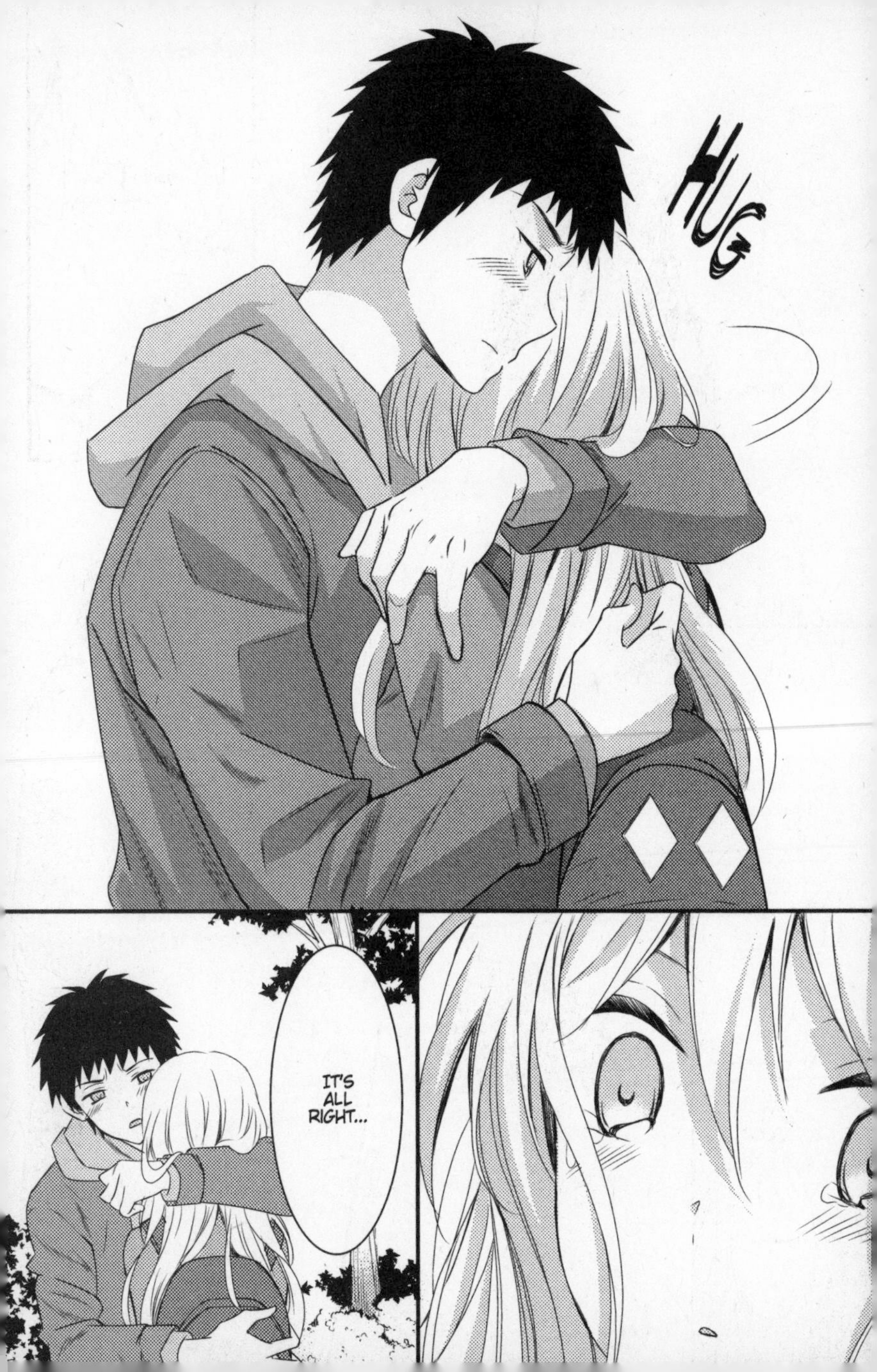
HUG
IT'S ALL RIGHT...

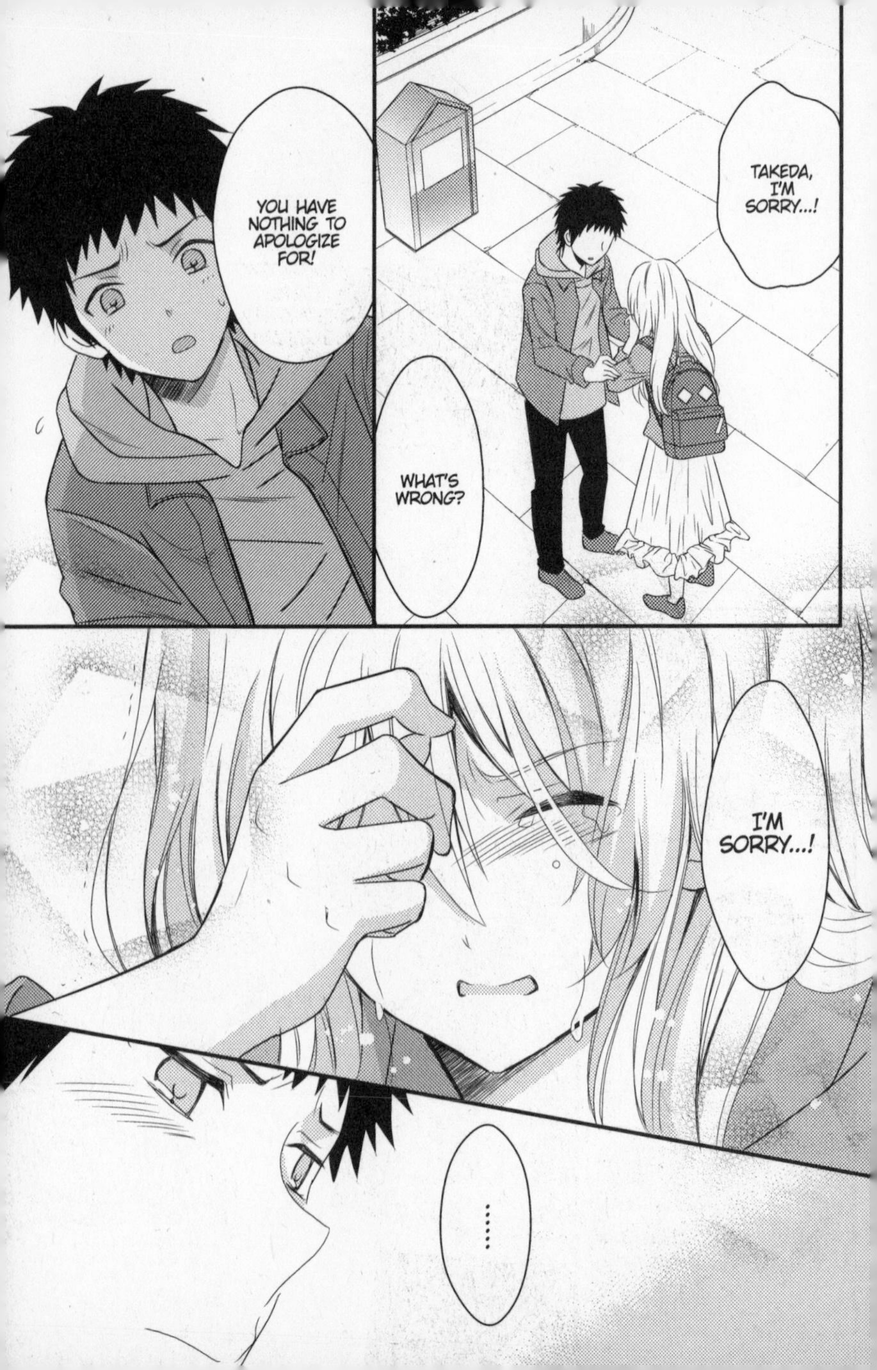
TAKEDA, I'M SORRY...!
WHAT'S WRONG?
YOU HAVE NOTHING TO APOLOGIZE FOR!
I'M SORRY...!
......

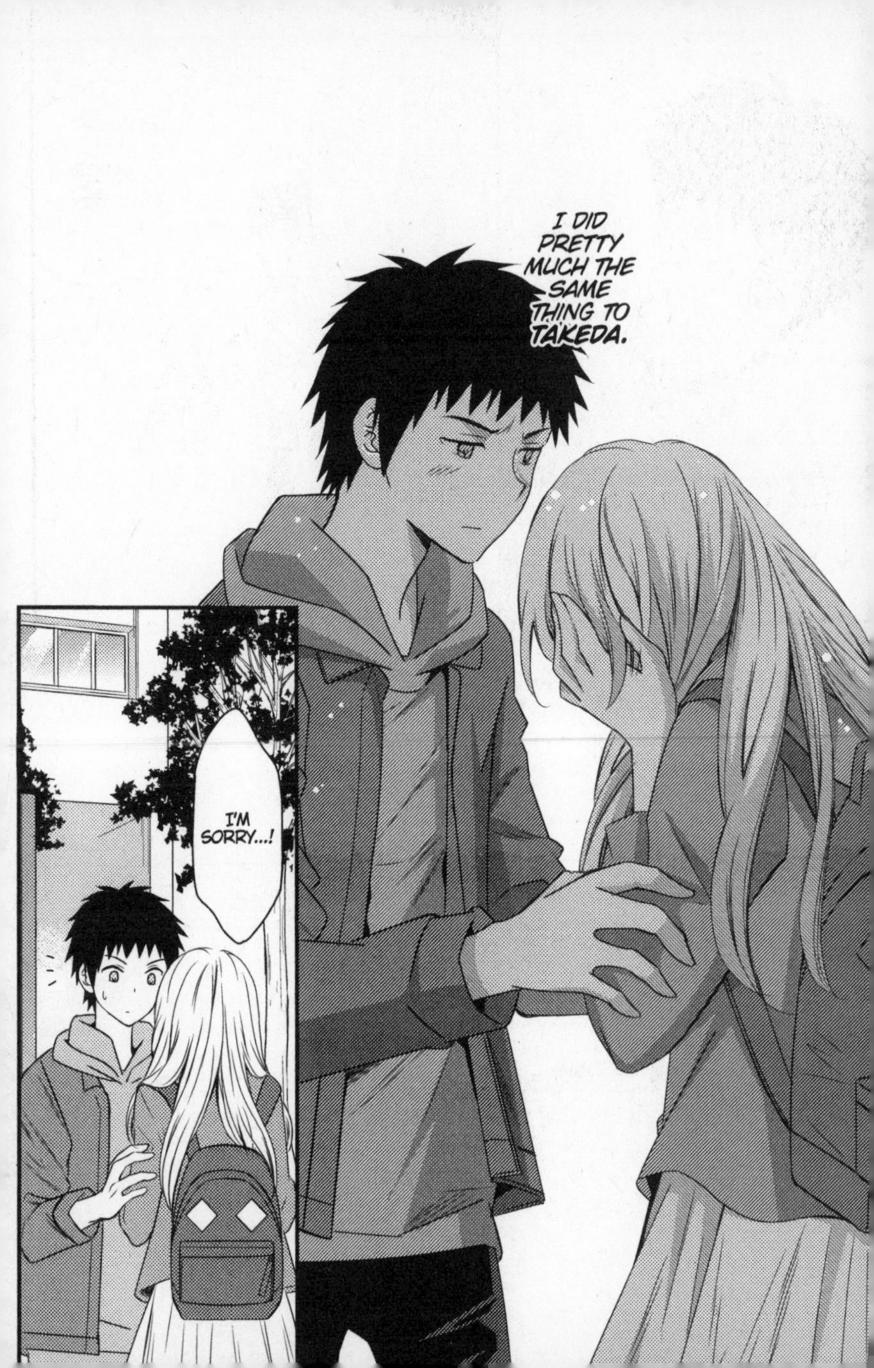
I DID PRETTY MUCH THE SAME THING TO TAKEDA.
I'M SORRY...!

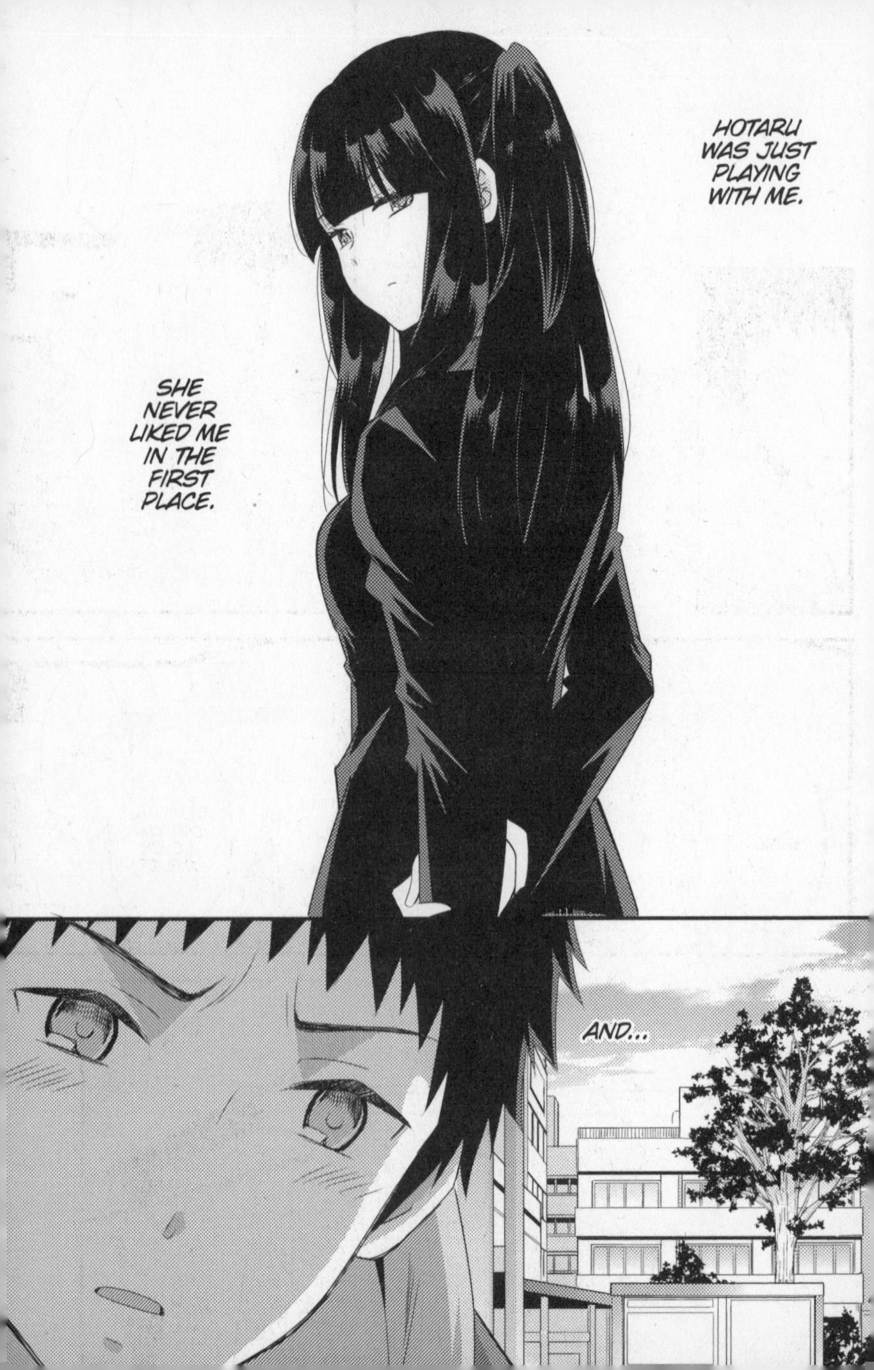
HOTARU WAS JUST PLAYING WITH ME.
SHE NEVER LIKED ME IN THE FIRST PLACE.
AND...

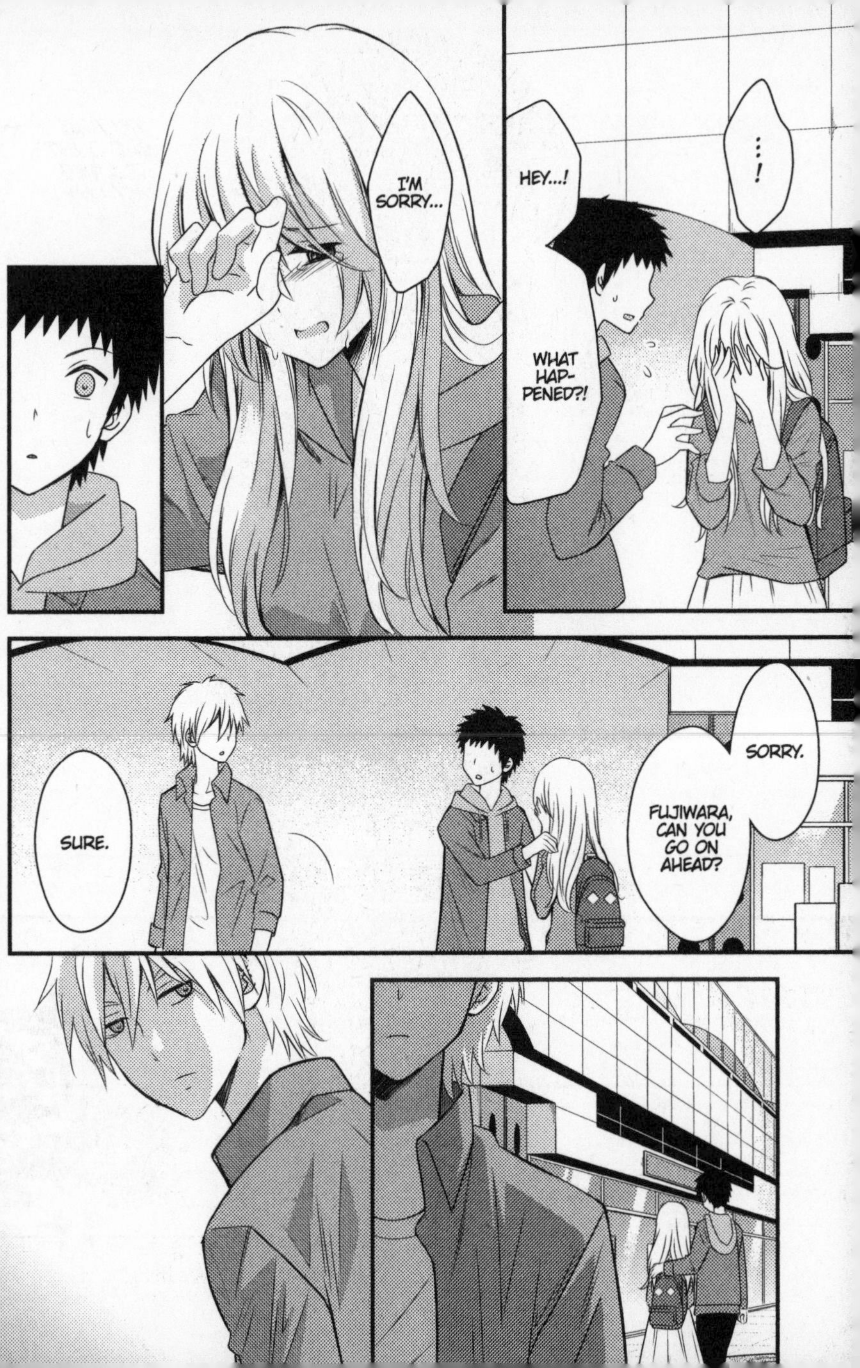
…!
HEY…!
WHAT HAP-PENED?!
I'M SORRY…
SORRY.
FUJIWARA, CAN YOU GO ON AHEAD?
SURE.

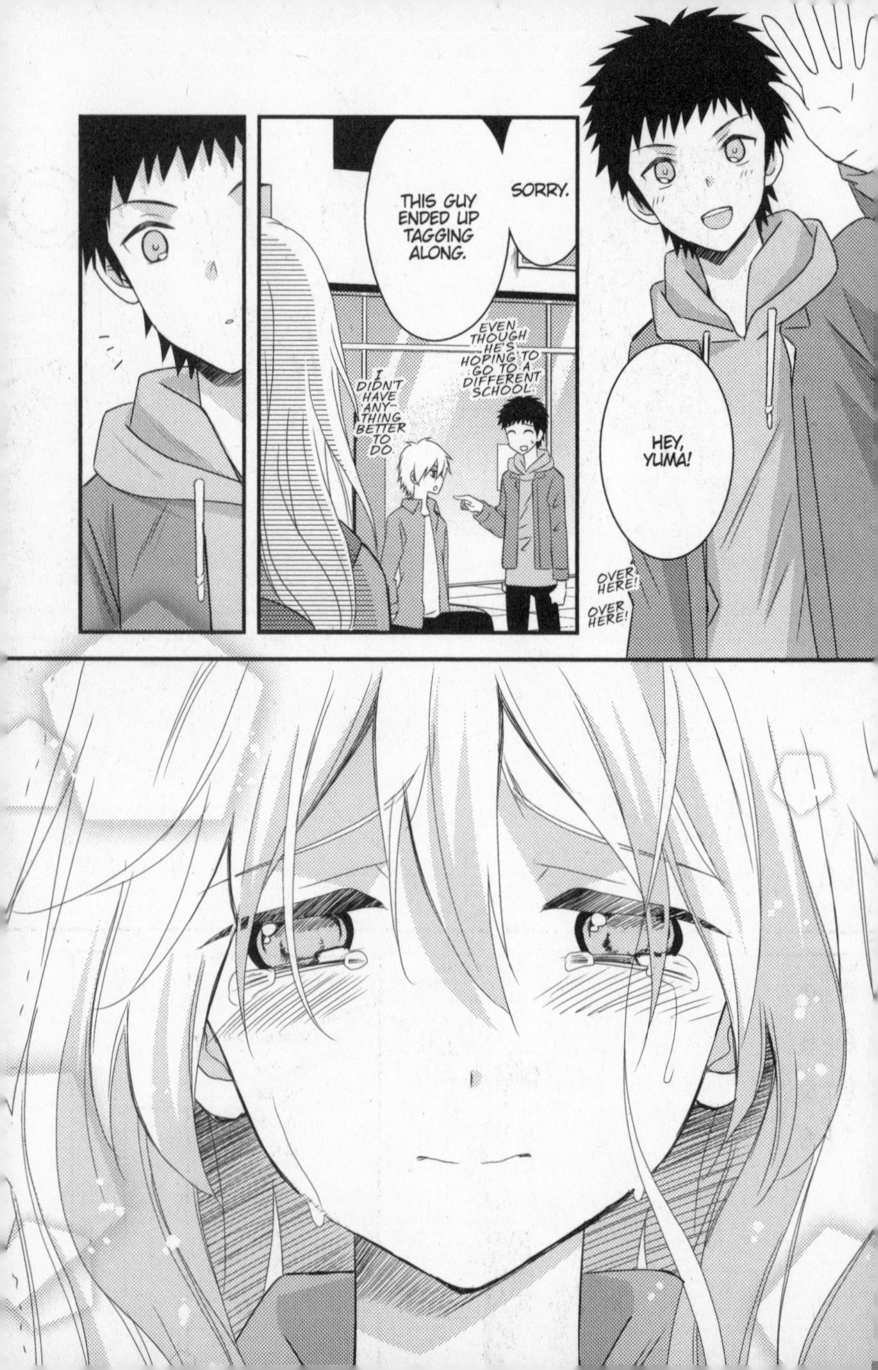
HEY, YUMA!
OVER HERE! OVER HERE!
SORRY.
THIS GUY ENDED UP TAGGING ALONG.
EVEN THOUGH HE'S HOPING TO GO TO A DIFFERENT SCHOOL.
I DIDN'T HAVE ANYTHING BETTER TO DO.

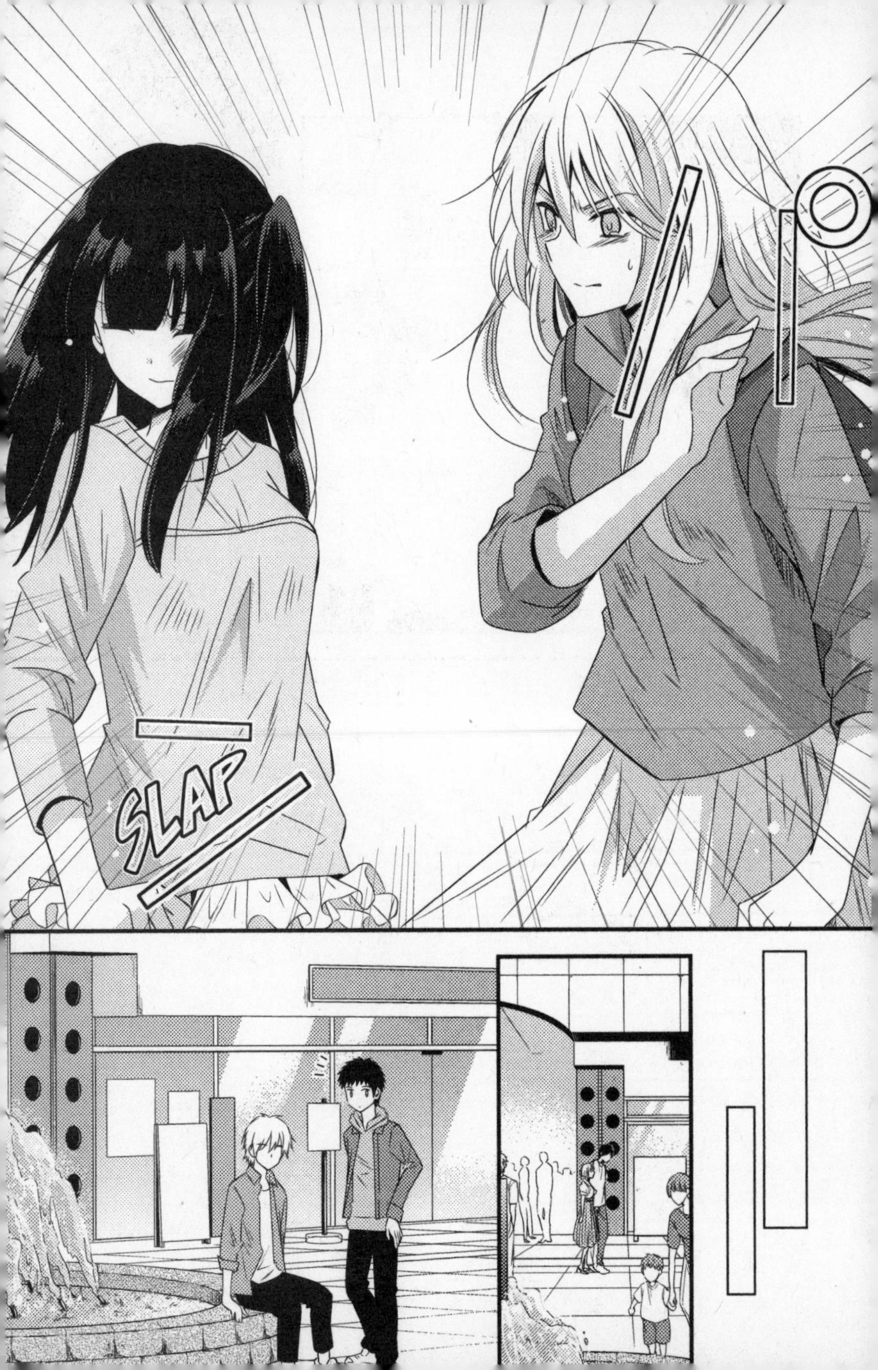
SLAP

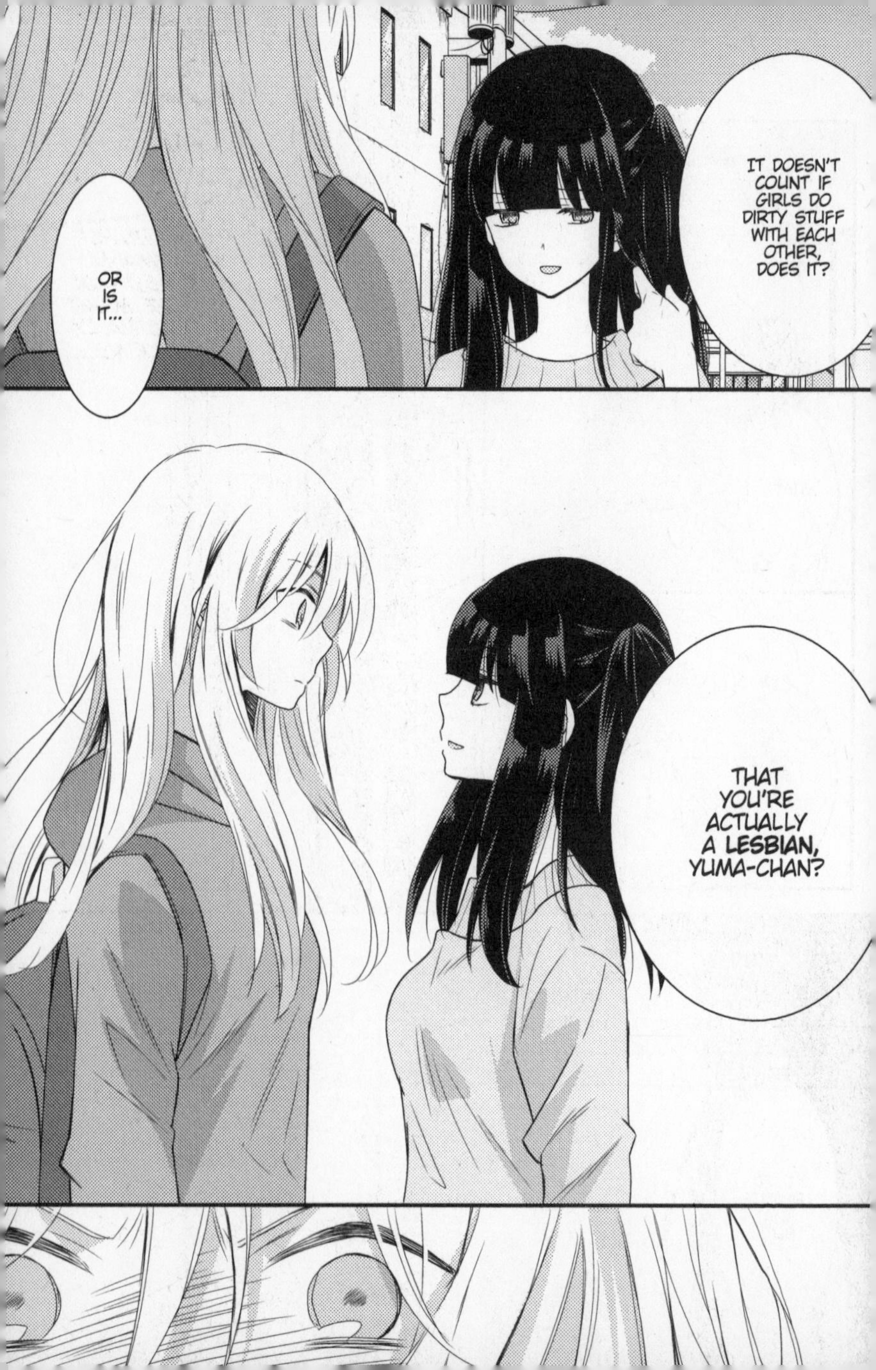
IT DOESN'T COUNT IF GIRLS DO DIRTY STUFF WITH EACH OTHER, DOES IT?
OR IS IT...
THAT YOU'RE ACTUALLY A LESBIAN, YUMA-CHAN?

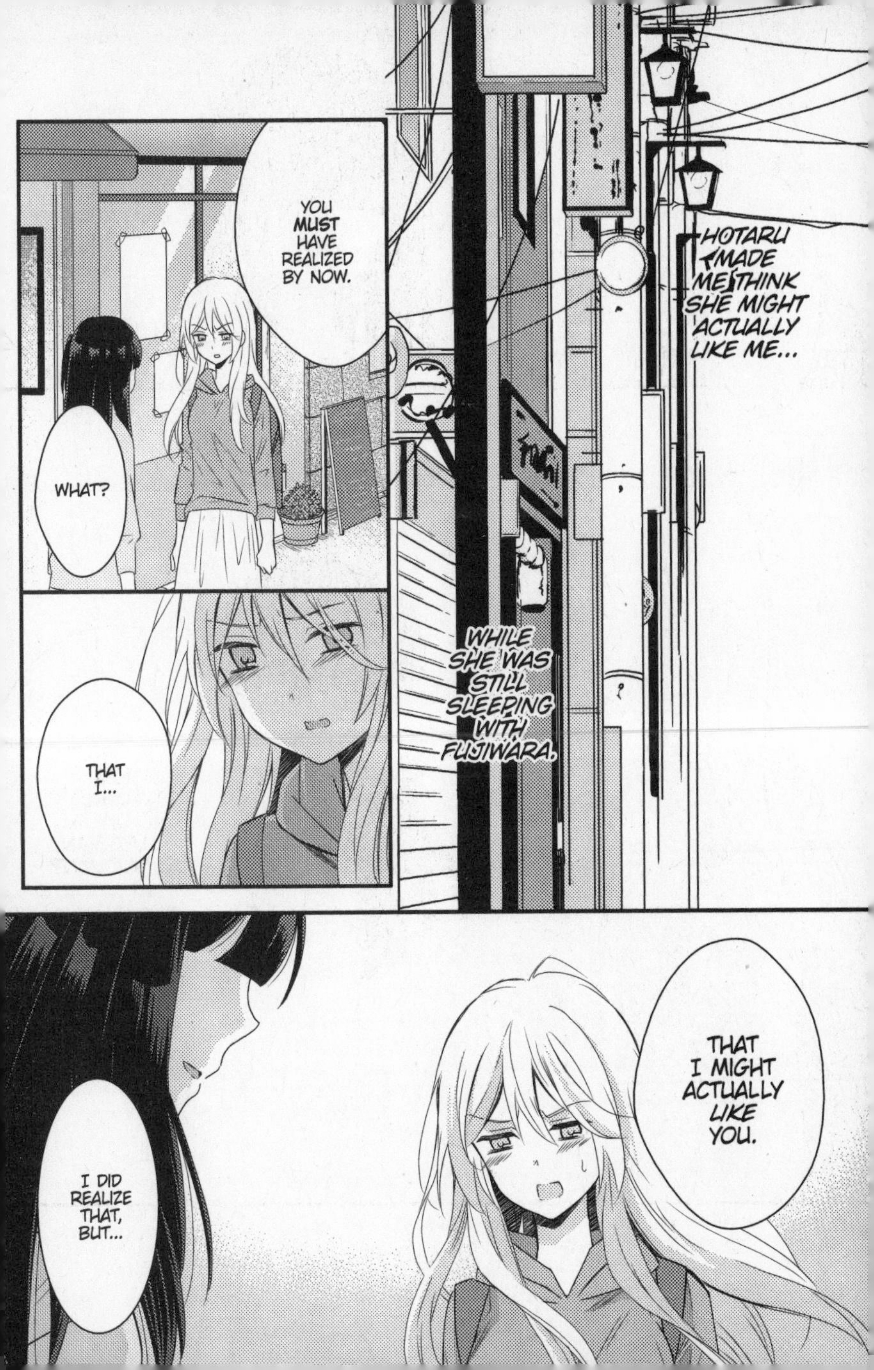
HOTARU MADE ME THINK SHE MIGHT ACTUALLY LIKE ME...
WHILE SHE WAS STILL SLEEPING WITH FUJIWARA.
YOU MUST HAVE REALIZED BY NOW.
WHAT?
THAT I...
THAT I MIGHT ACTUALLY LIKE YOU.
I DID REALIZE THAT, BUT...

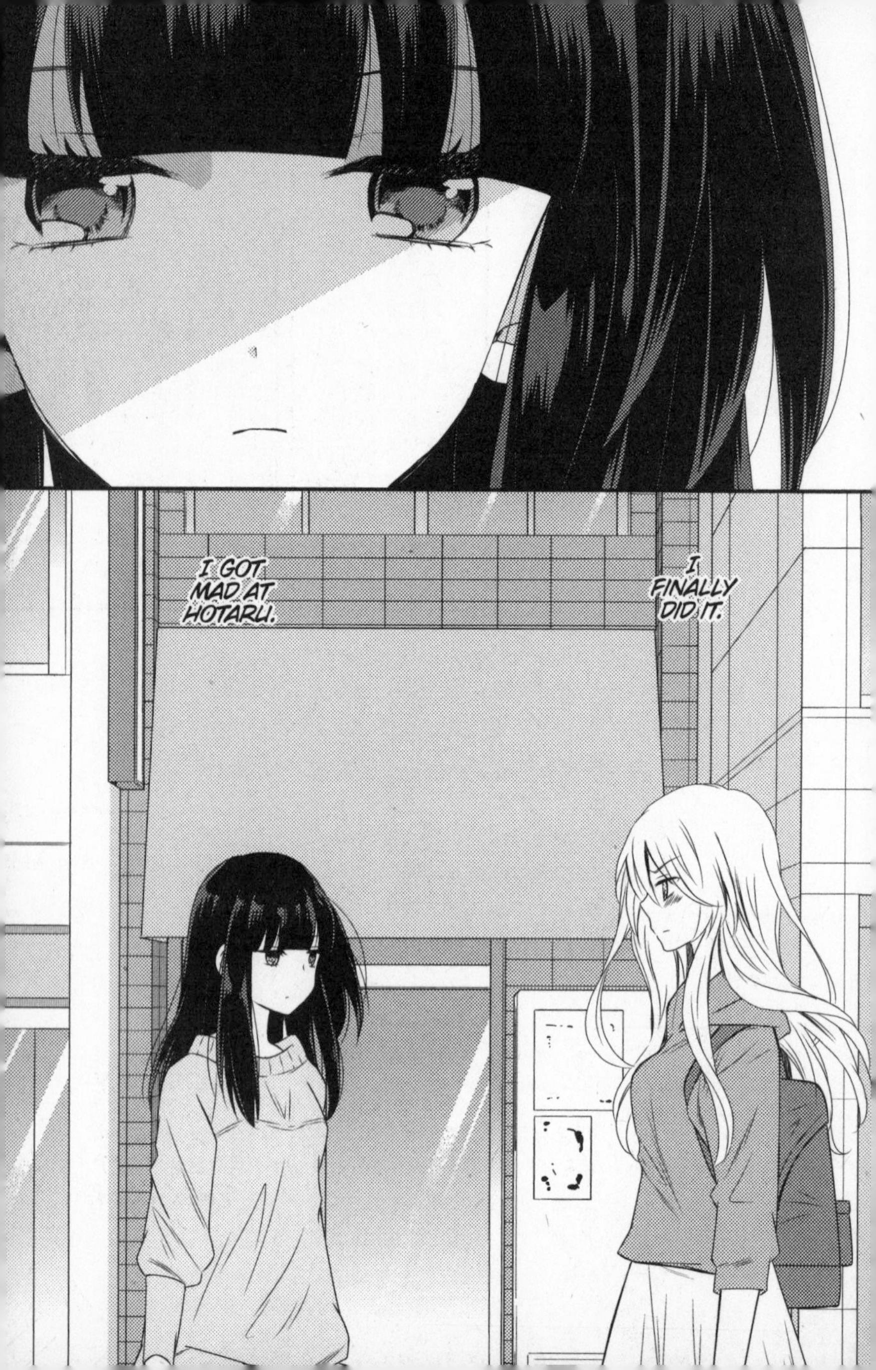
I FINALLY DID IT.
I GOT MAD AT HOTARU.

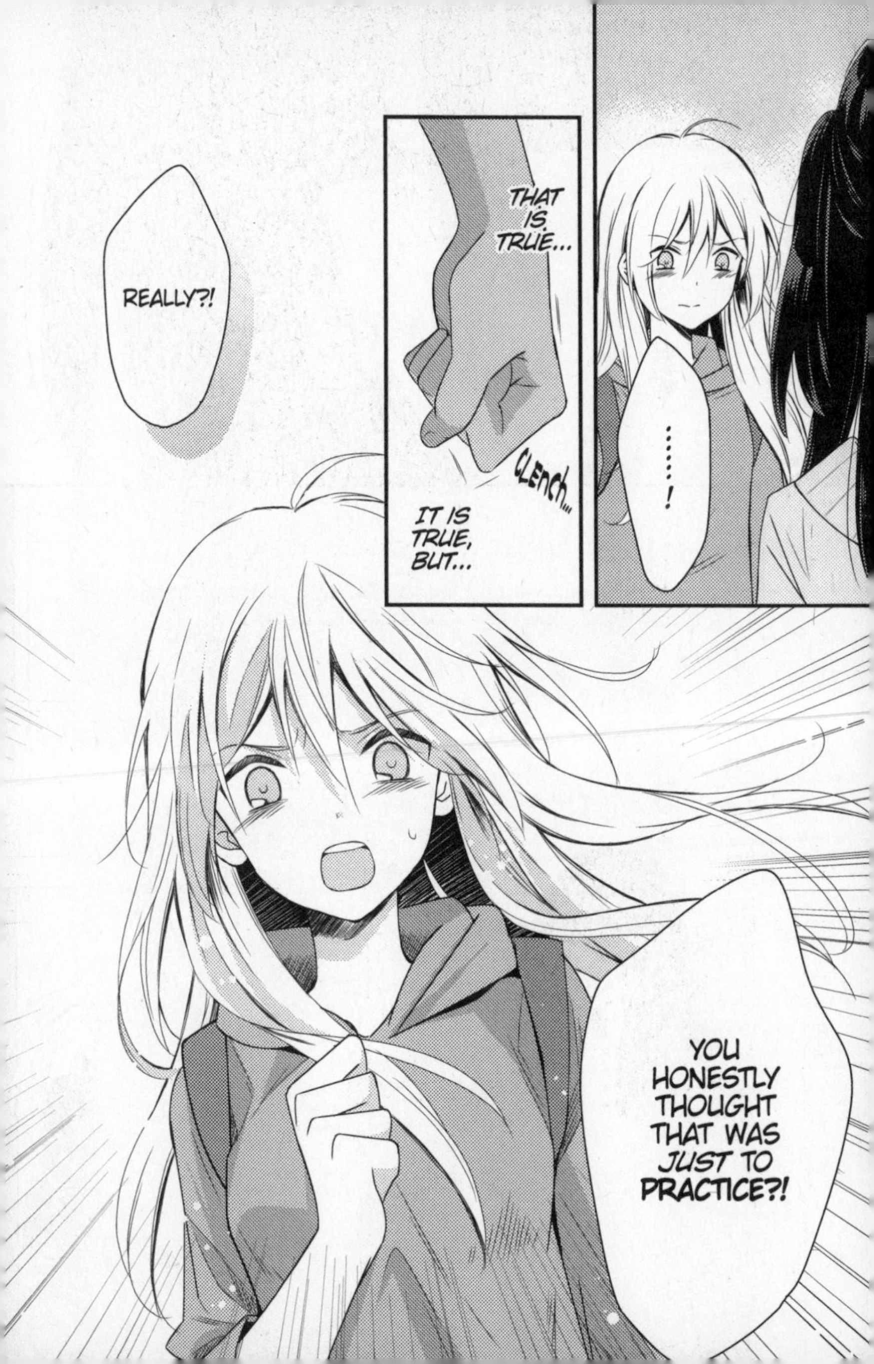
......!
THAT IS TRUE...
CLENCH...
IT IS TRUE, BUT...
REALLY?!
YOU HONESTLY THOUGHT THAT WAS JUST TO PRACTICE?!

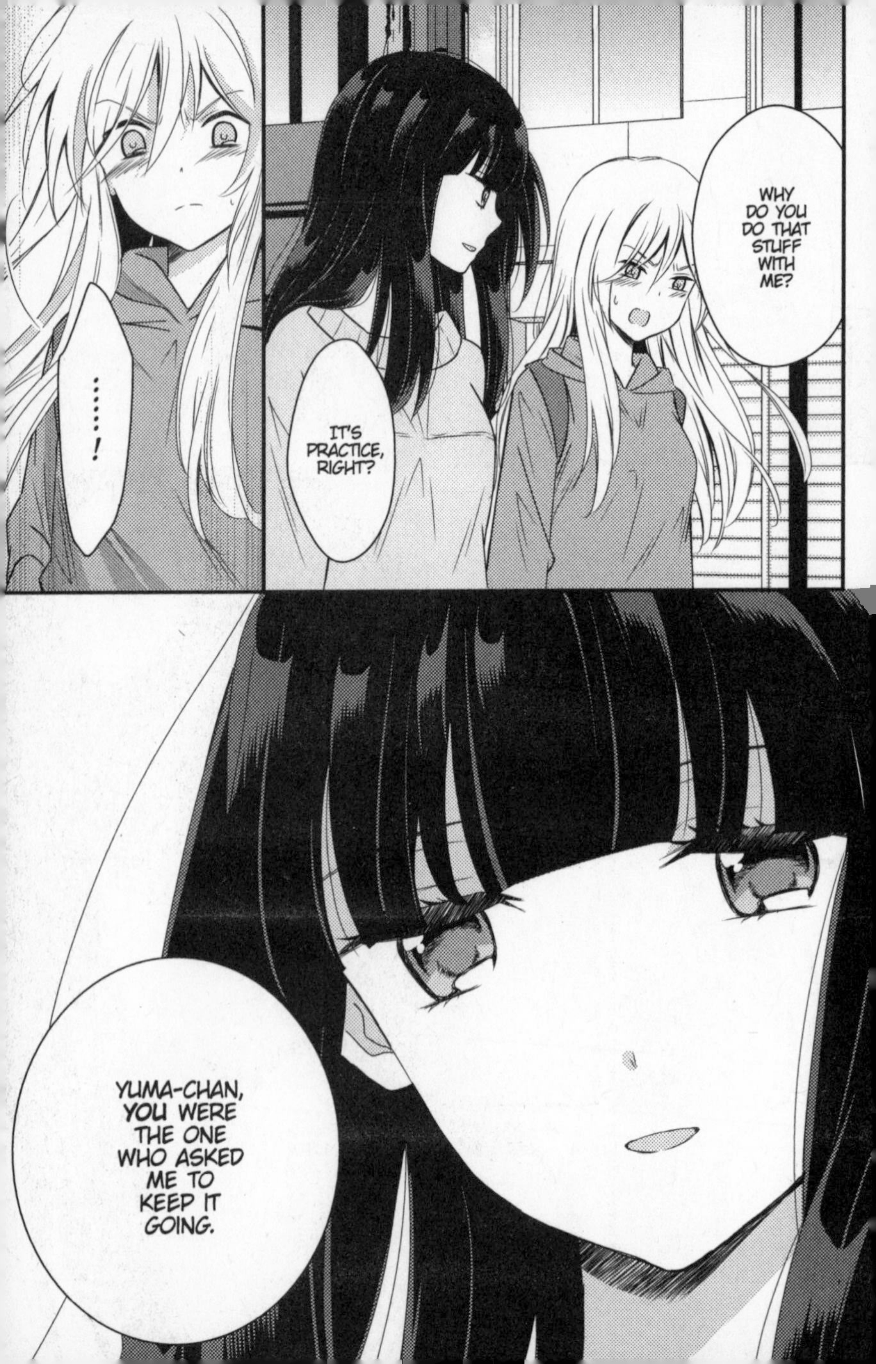
WHY DO YOU DO THAT STUFF WITH ME?
IT'S PRACTICE, RIGHT?
......!
YUMA-CHAN, YOU WERE THE ONE WHO ASKED ME TO KEEP IT GOING.

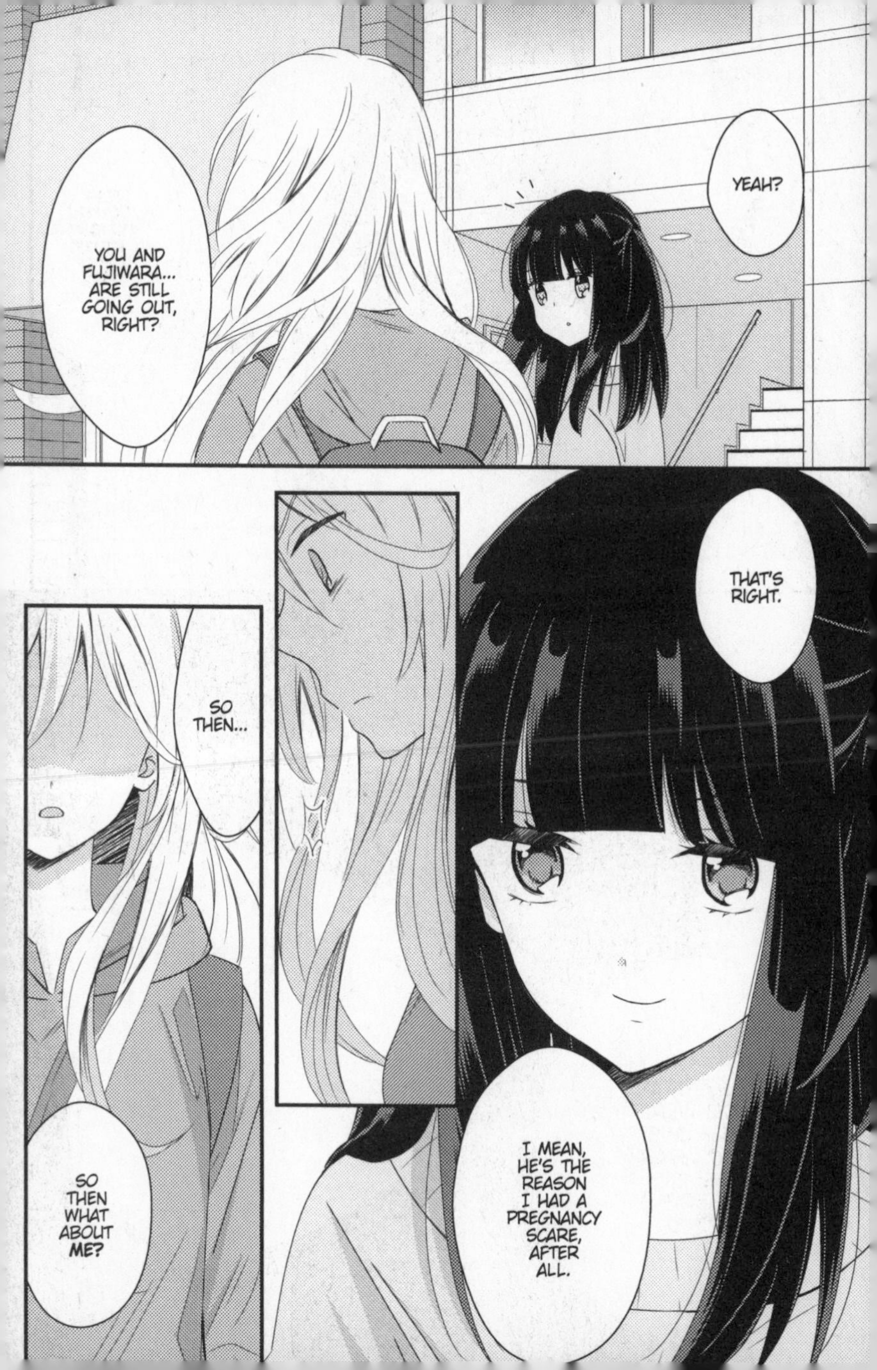
YEAH?
YOU AND FUJIWARA... ARE STILL GOING OUT, RIGHT?
THAT'S RIGHT.
I MEAN, HE'S THE REASON I HAD A PREGNANCY SCARE, AFTER ALL.
SO THEN...
SO THEN WHAT ABOUT ME?

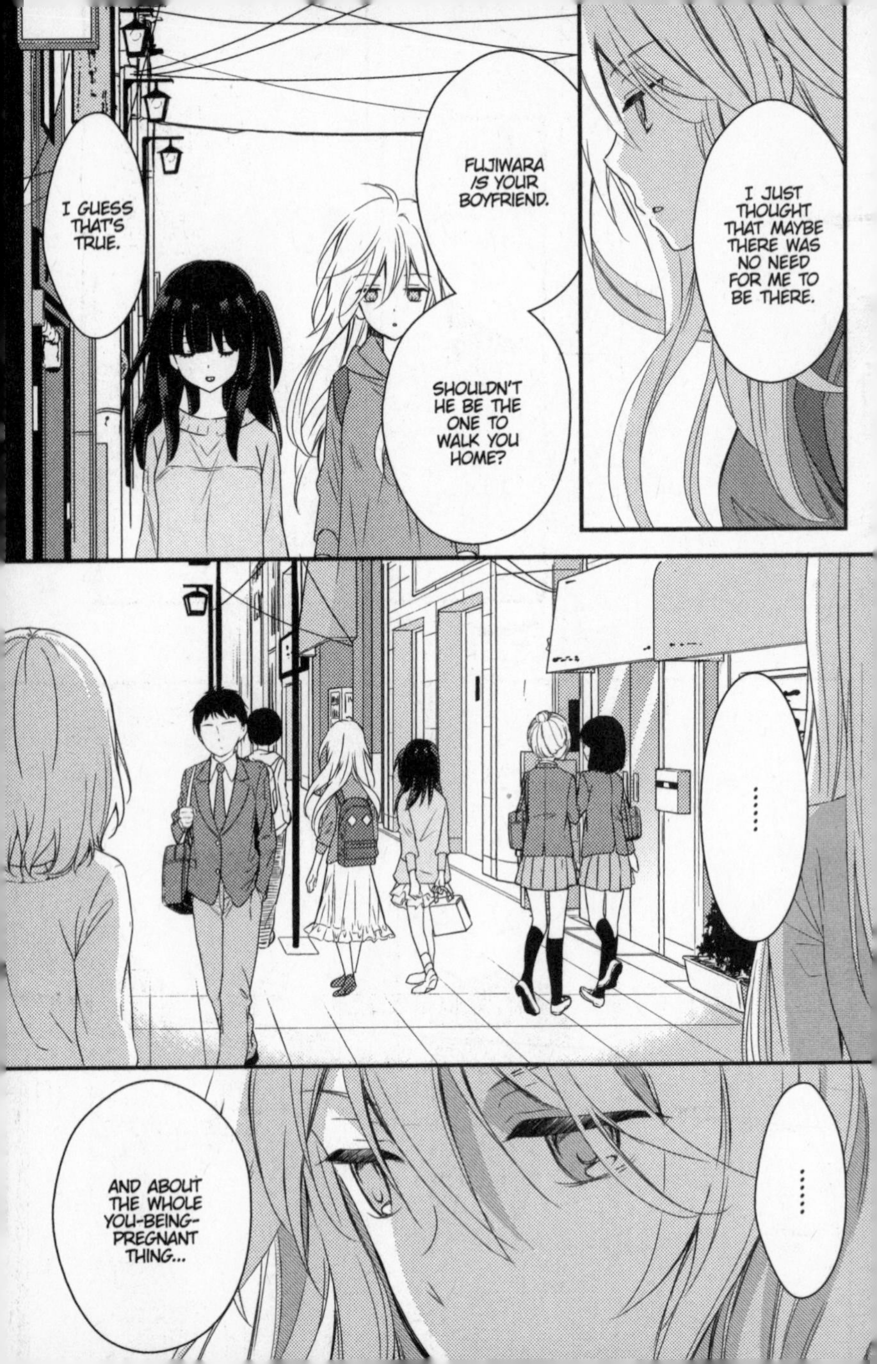
I JUST THOUGHT THAT MAYBE THERE WAS NO NEED FOR ME TO BE THERE.
FUJIWARA IS YOUR BOYFRIEND.
SHOULDN'T HE BE THE ONE TO WALK YOU HOME?
I GUESS THAT'S TRUE.
......
......
AND ABOUT THE WHOLE YOU-BEING-PREGNANT THING...

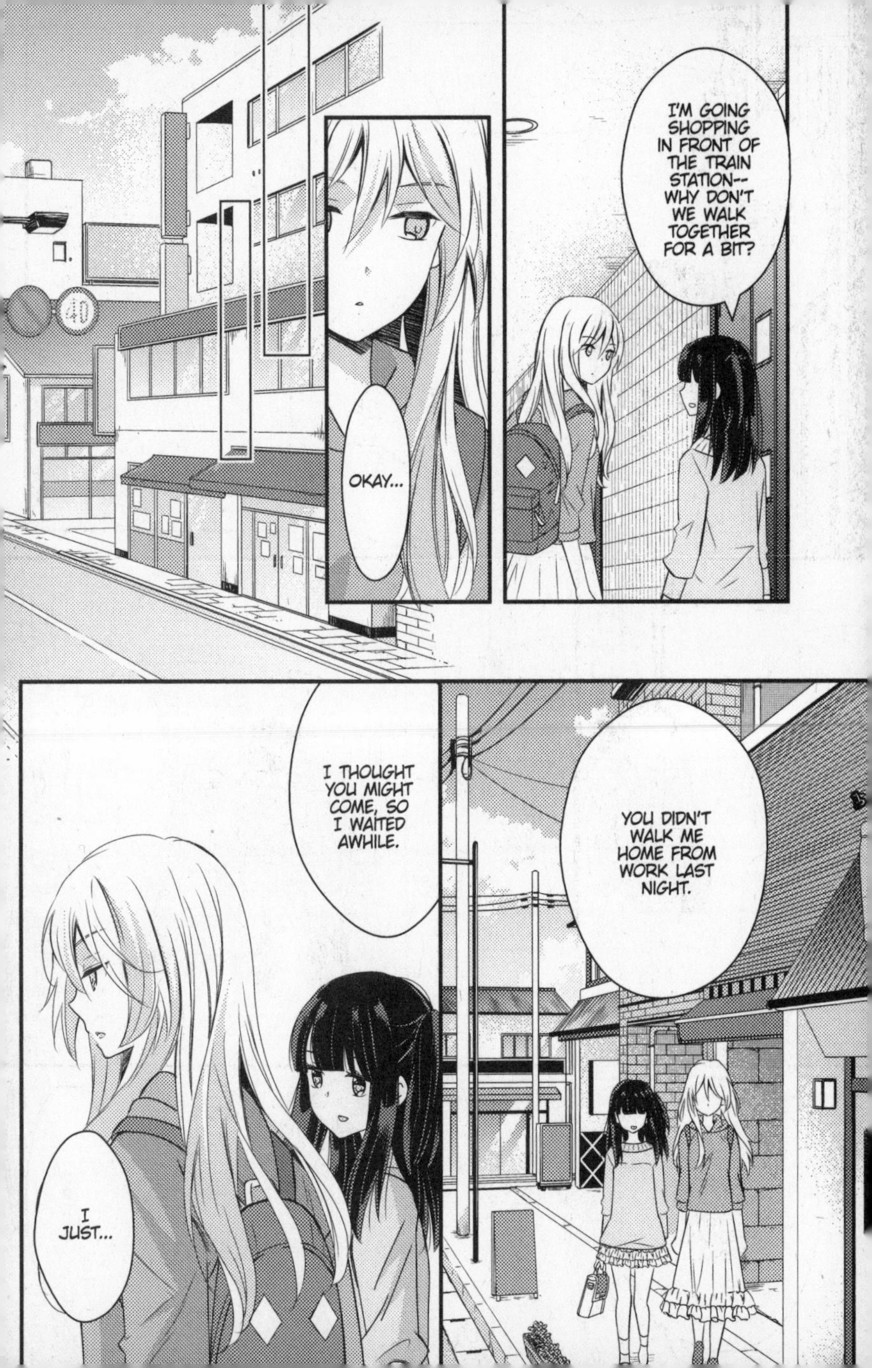
I'M GOING SHOPPING IN FRONT OF THE TRAIN STATION-- WHY DON'T WE WALK TOGETHER FOR A BIT?
OKAY...
YOU DIDN'T WALK ME HOME FROM WORK LAST NIGHT.
I THOUGHT YOU MIGHT COME, SO I WAITED AWHILE.
I JUST...

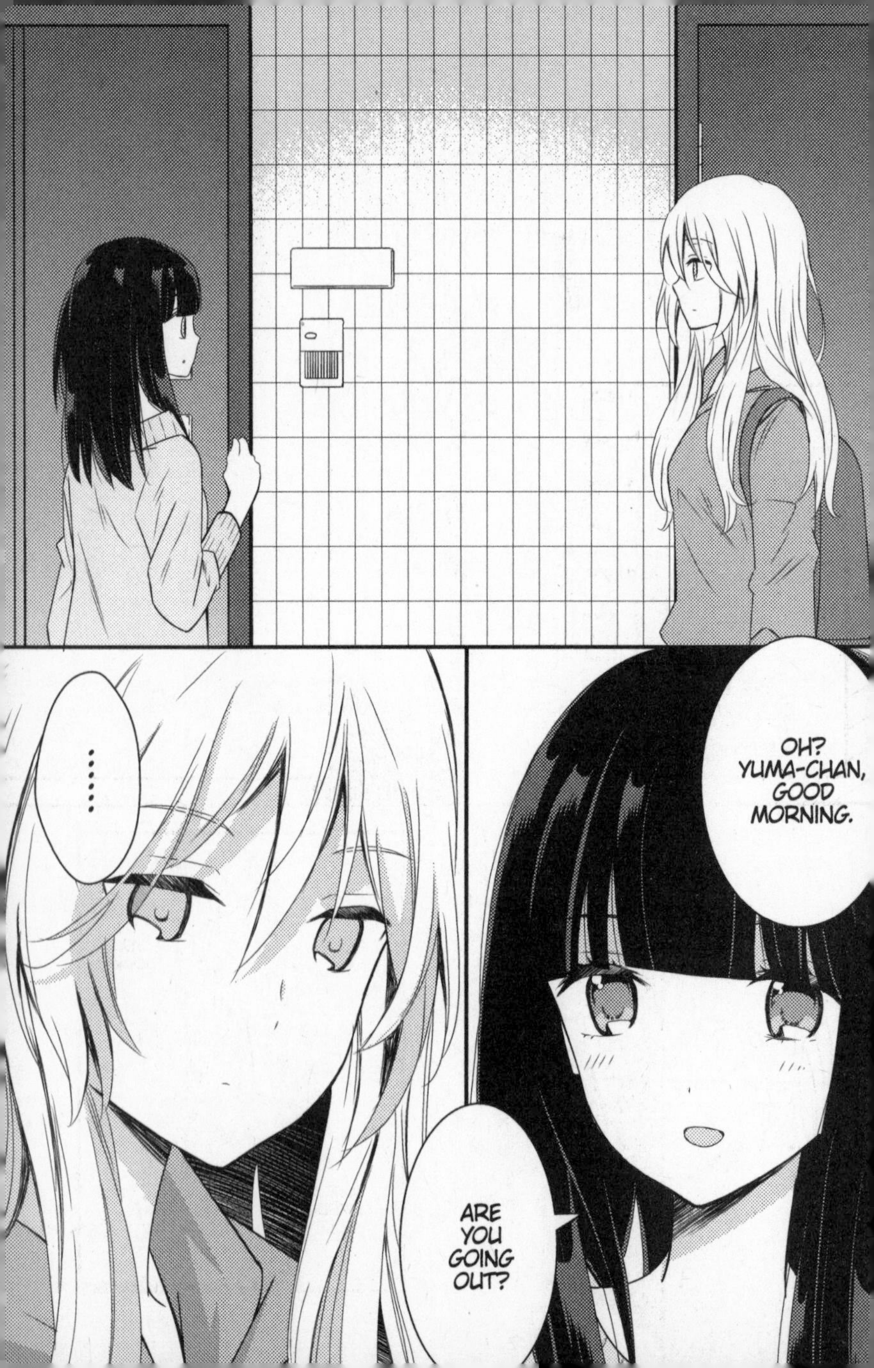
OH? YUMA-CHAN, GOOD MORNING.
ARE YOU GOING OUT?
......

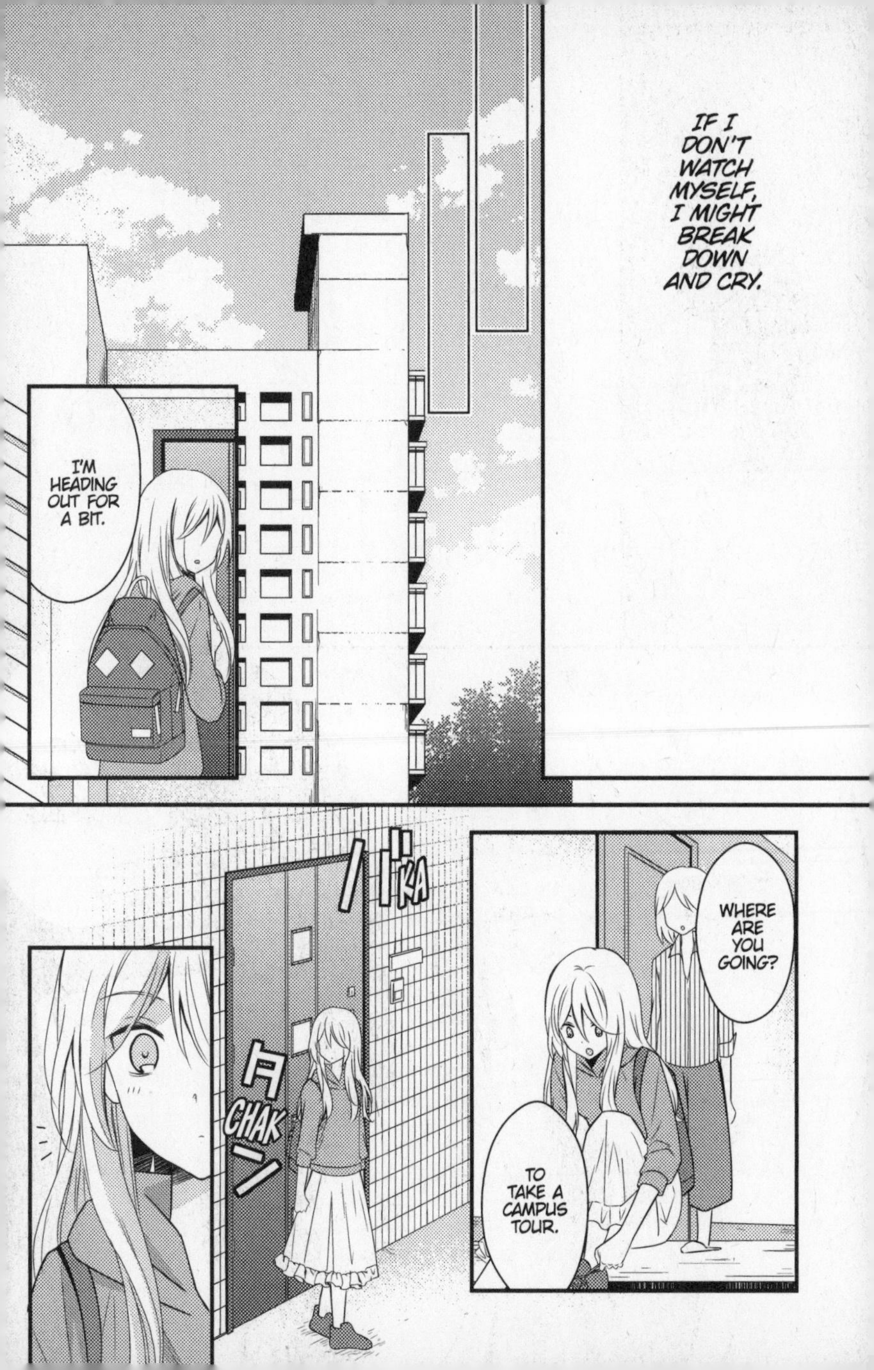
IF I DON'T WATCH MYSELF, I MIGHT BREAK DOWN AND CRY.
I'M HEADING OUT FOR A BIT.
WHERE ARE YOU GOING?
TO TAKE A CAMPUS TOUR.
KA
CHAK

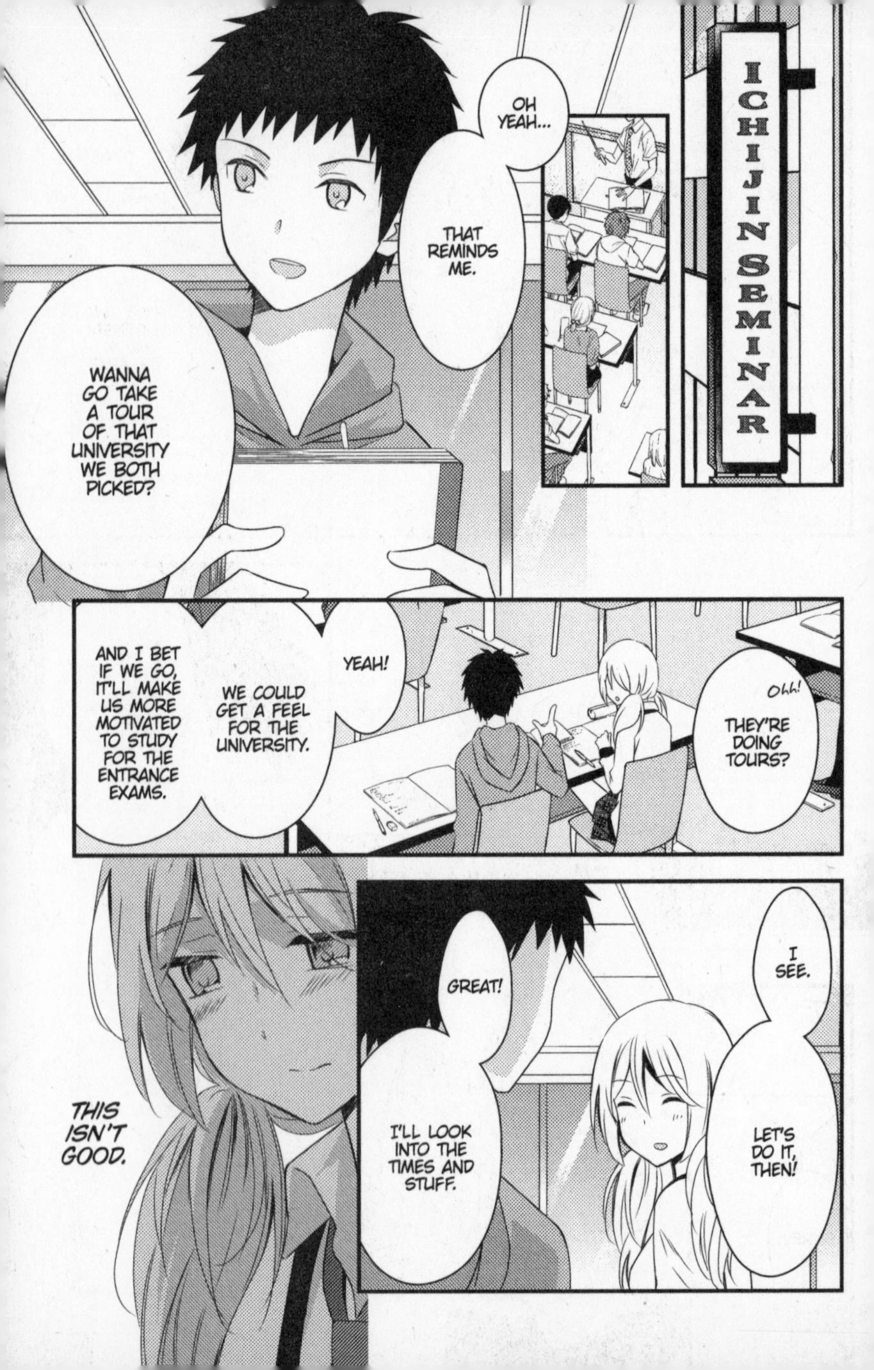
ICHIJIN SEMINAR
OH YEAH...
THAT REMINDS ME.
WANNA GO TAKE A TOUR OF THAT UNIVERSITY WE BOTH PICKED?
Ohh!
THEY'RE DOING TOURS?
YEAH!
WE COULD GET A FEEL FOR THE UNIVERSITY.
AND I BET IF WE GO, IT'LL MAKE US MORE MOTIVATED TO STUDY FOR THE ENTRANCE EXAMS.
I SEE.
LET'S DO IT, THEN!
GREAT!
I'LL LOOK INTO THE TIMES AND STUFF.
THIS ISN'T GOOD.

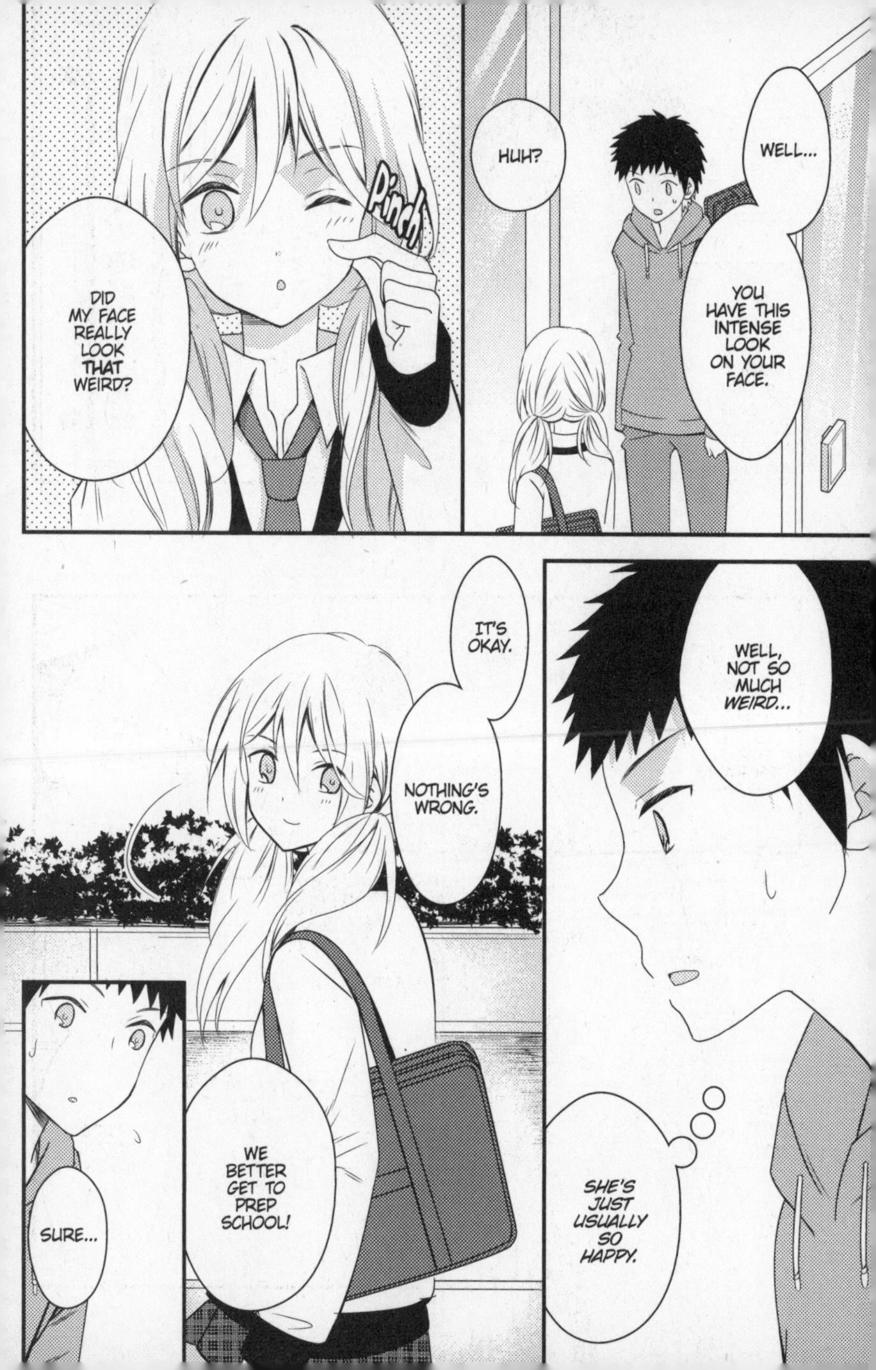
WELL...
HUH?
YOU HAVE THIS INTENSE LOOK ON YOUR FACE.
Pinch
DID MY FACE REALLY LOOK THAT WEIRD?
WELL, NOT SO MUCH WEIRD...
SHE'S JUST USUALLY SO HAPPY.
IT'S OKAY.
NOTHING'S WRONG.
WE BETTER GET TO PREP SCHOOL!
SURE...

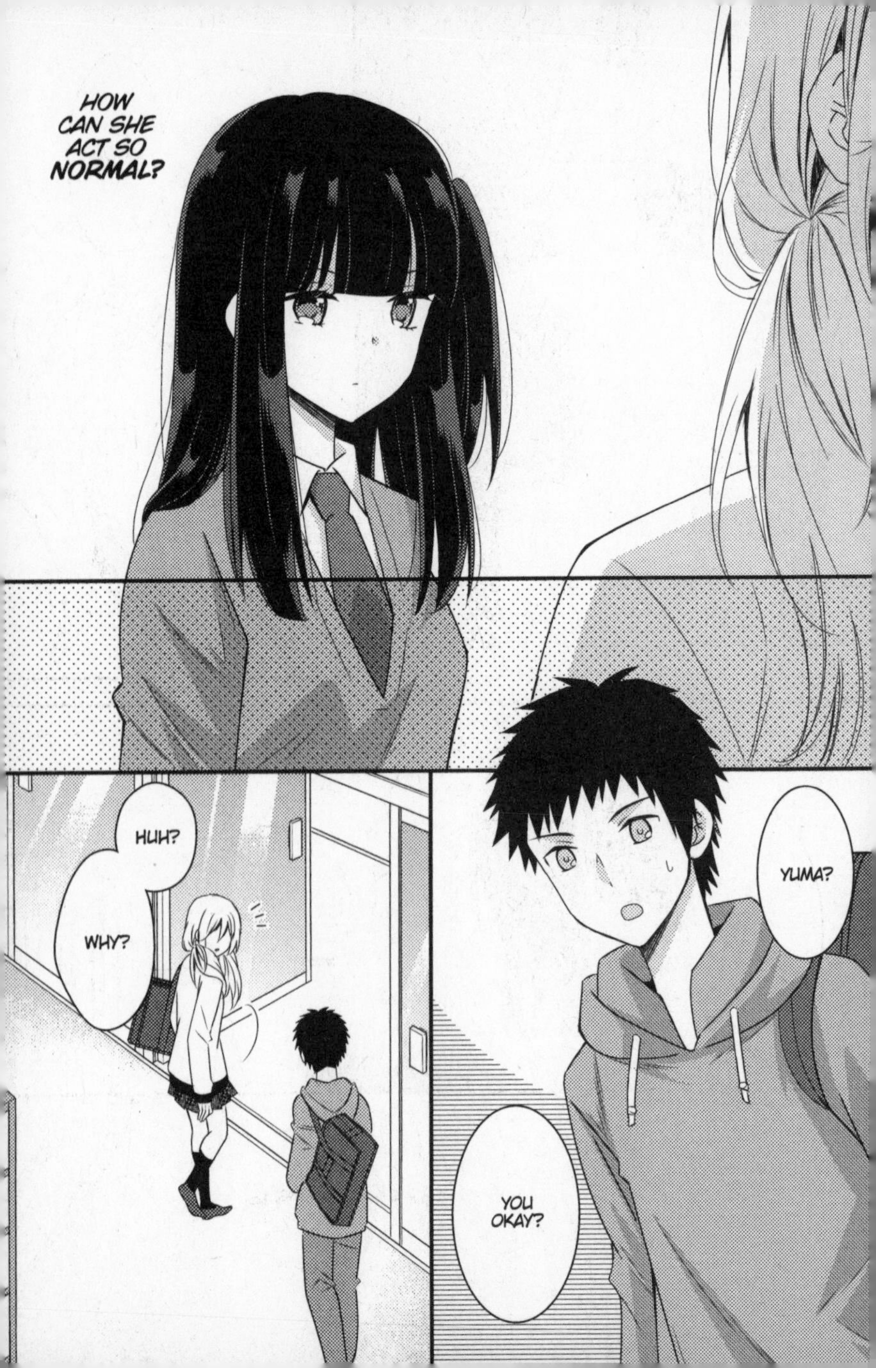
HOW CAN SHE ACT SO NORMAL?
YUMA?
YOU OKAY?
HUH?
WHY?

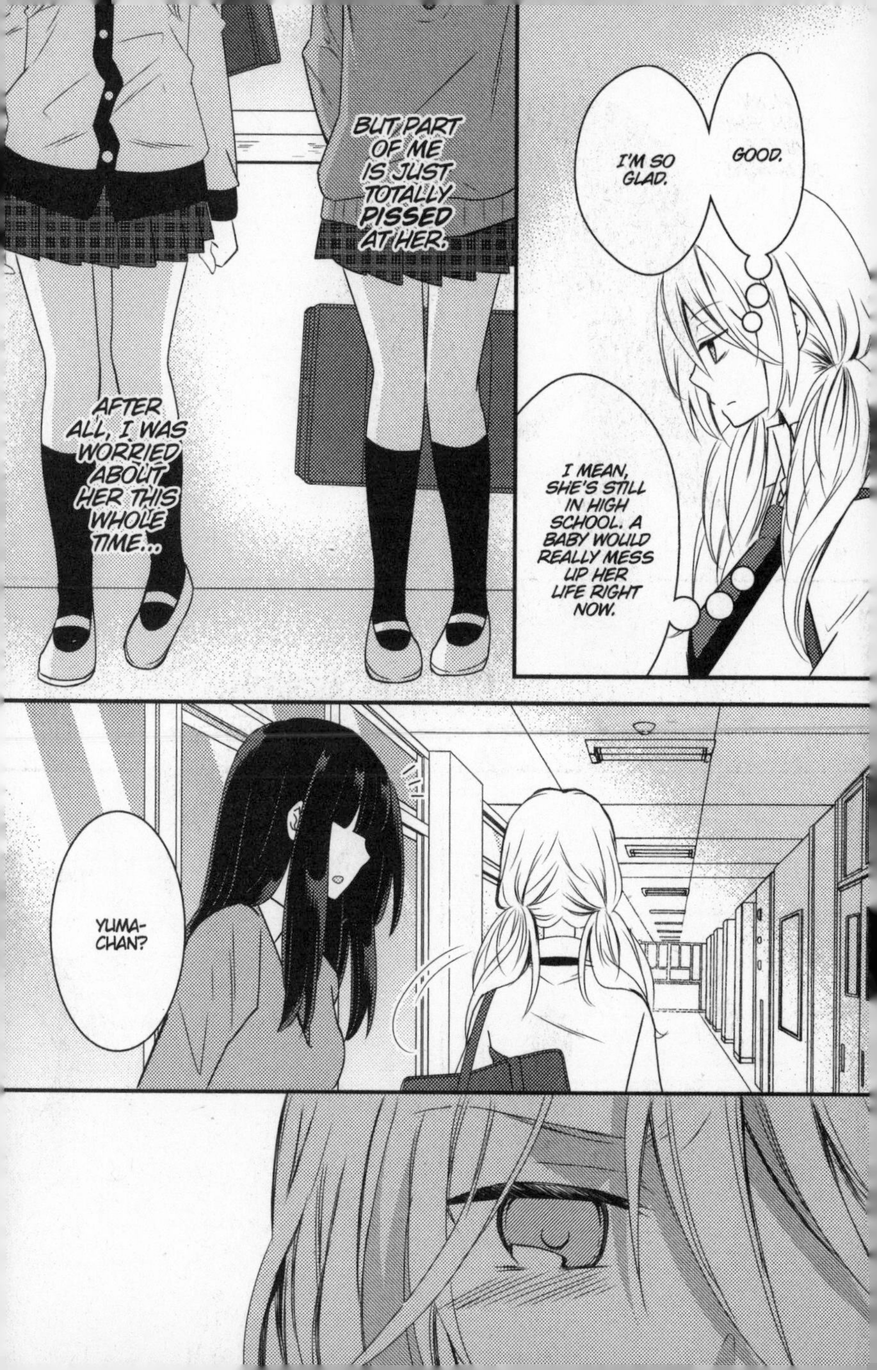
GOOD.
I'M SO GLAD.
I MEAN, SHE'S STILL IN HIGH SCHOOL. A BABY WOULD REALLY MESS UP HER LIFE RIGHT NOW.
BUT PART OF ME IS JUST TOTALLY PISSED AT HER.
AFTER ALL, I WAS WORRIED ABOUT HER THIS WHOLE TIME...
YUMA-CHAN?

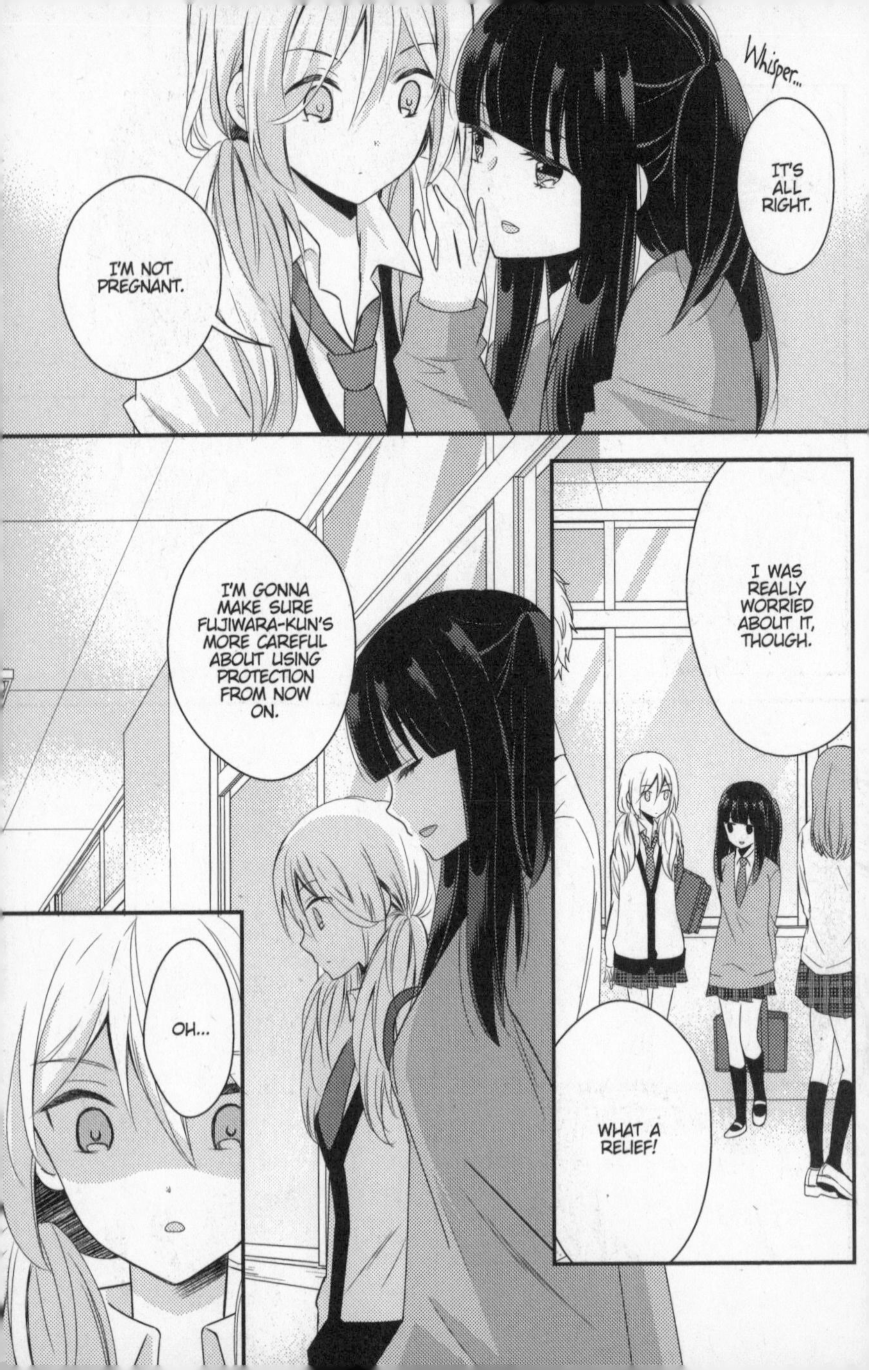
Whisper...
IT'S ALL RIGHT.
I'M NOT PREGNANT.
I WAS REALLY WORRIED ABOUT IT, THOUGH.
WHAT A RELIEF!
I'M GONNA MAKE SURE FUJIWARA-KUN'S MORE CAREFUL ABOUT USING PROTECTION FROM NOW ON.
OH...

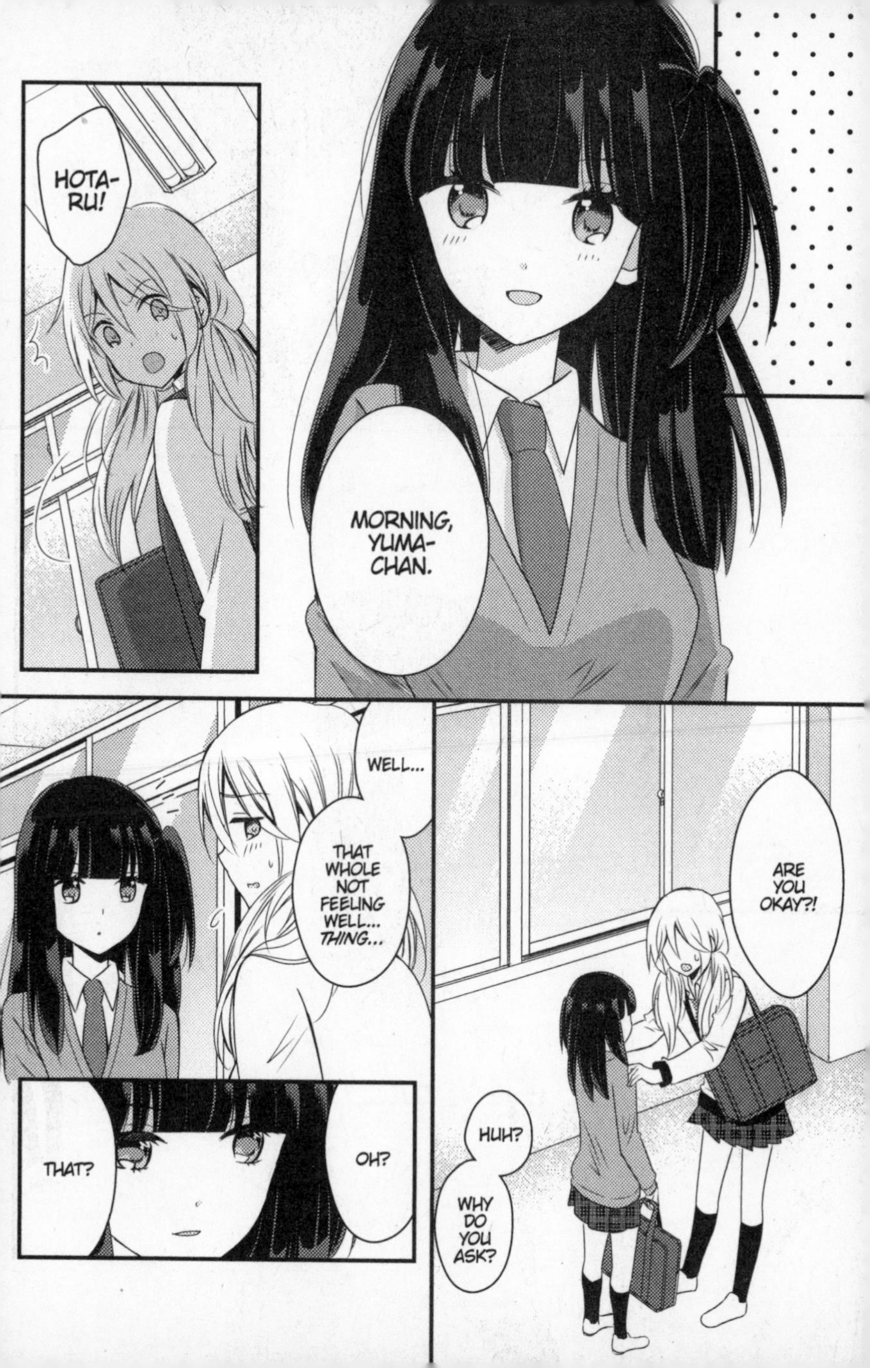
MORNING, YUMA-CHAN.
HOTA-RU!
ARE YOU OKAY?!
HUH?
WHY DO YOU ASK?
WELL...
THAT WHOLE NOT FEELING WELL... *THING*...
OH?
THAT?

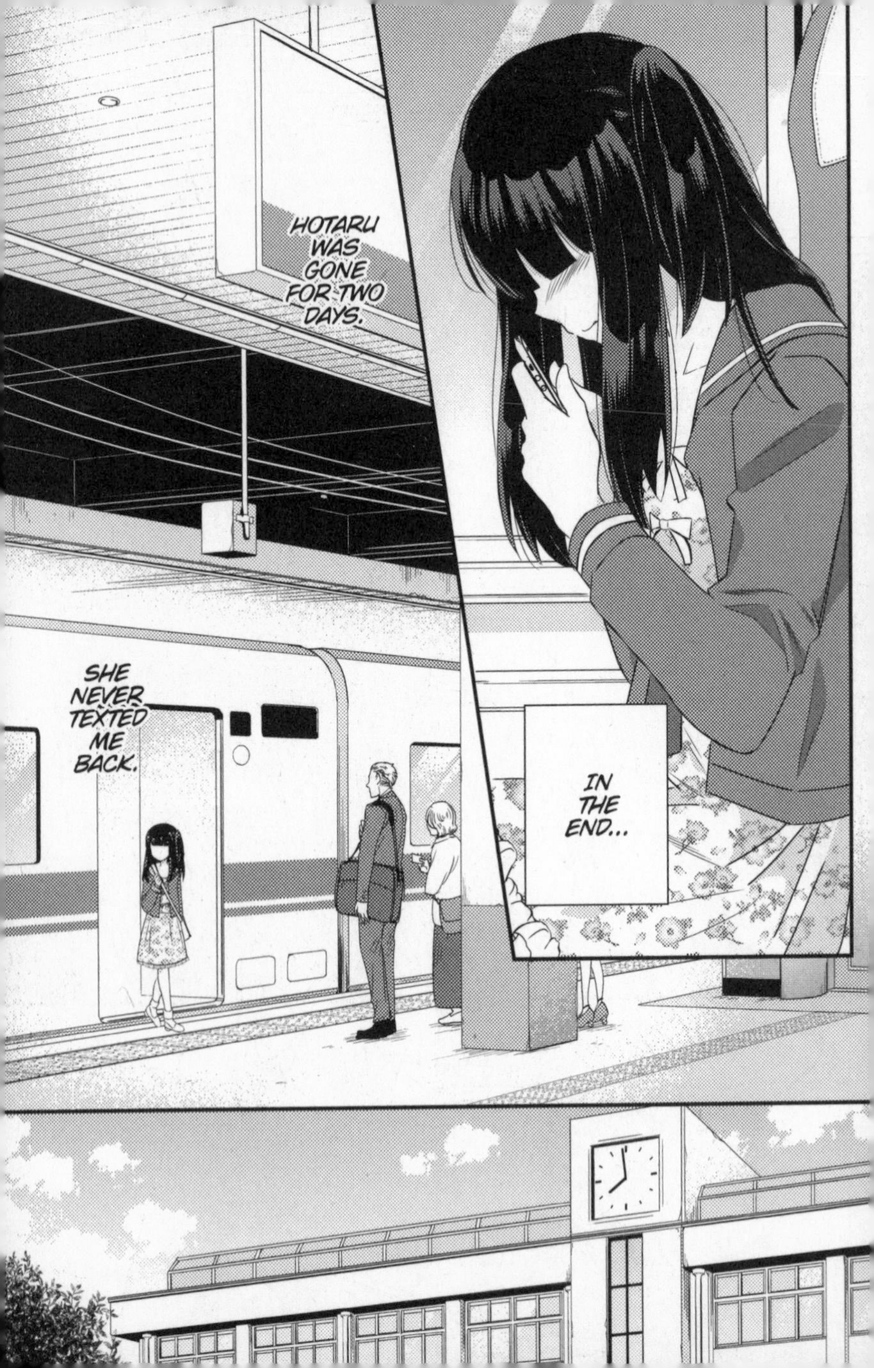
HOTARU WAS GONE FOR TWO DAYS.
SHE NEVER TEXTED ME BACK.
IN THE END...

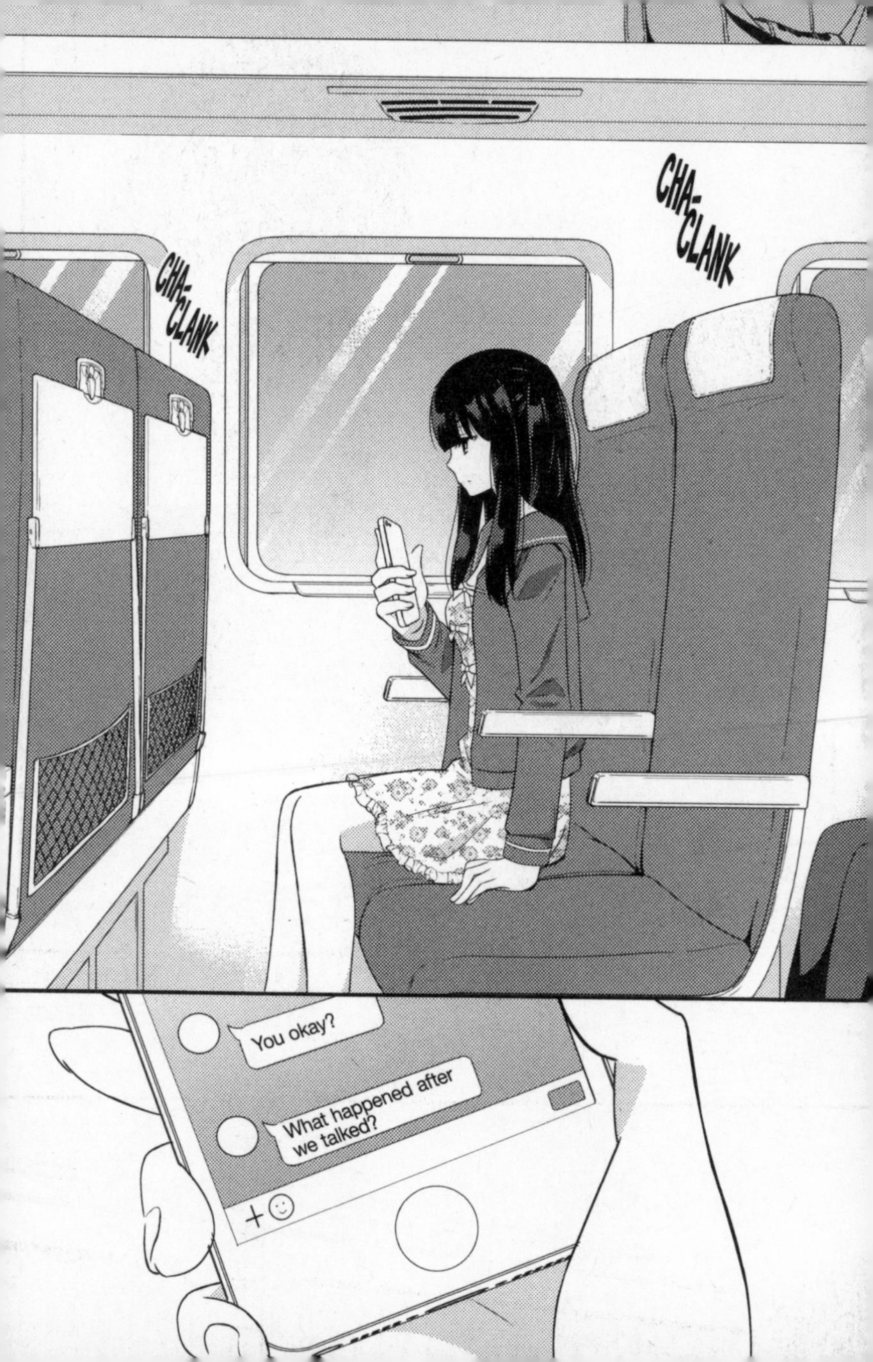
CHA-CLANK
CHA-CLANK
You okay?
What happened after we talked?

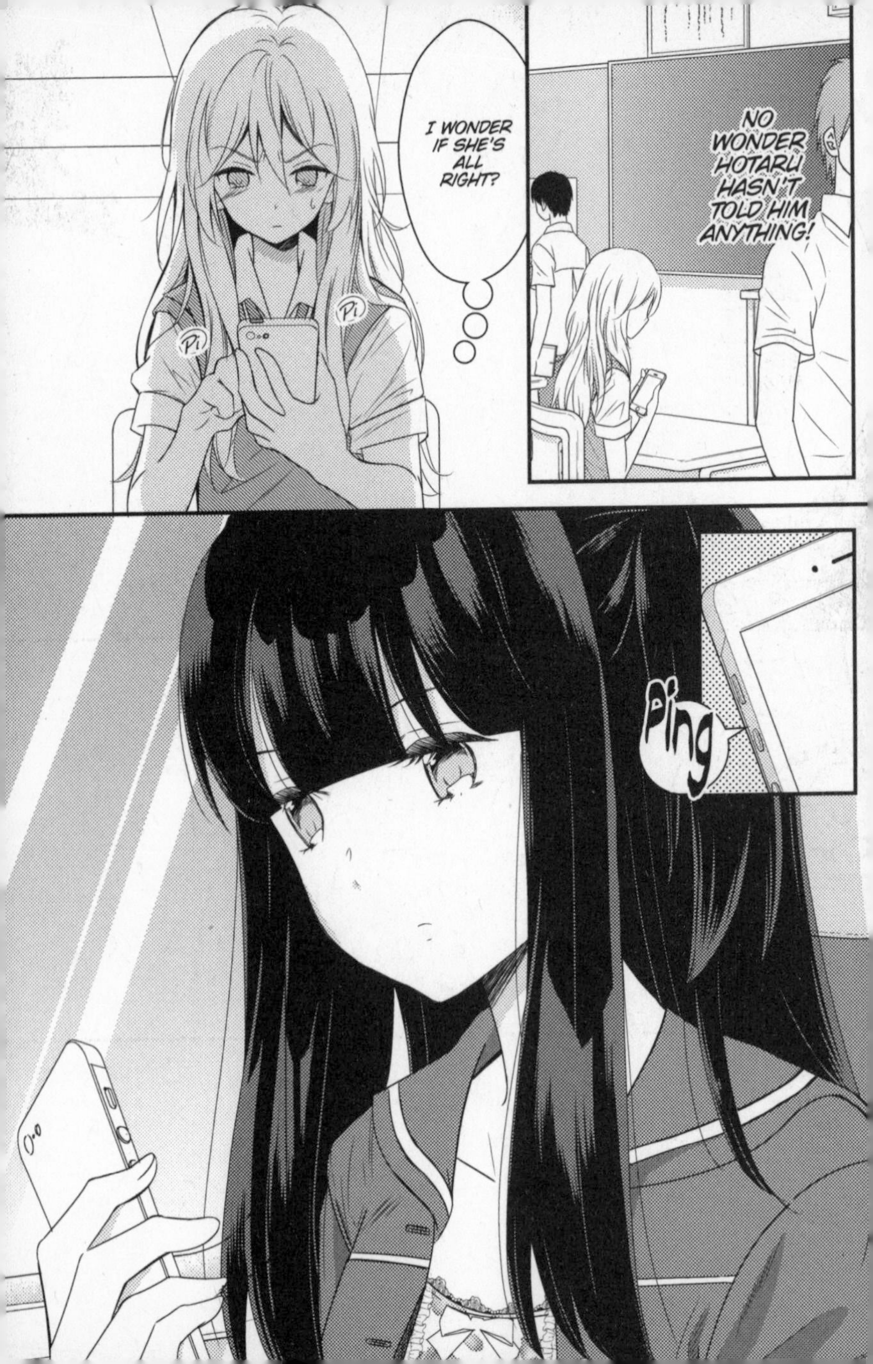
NO WONDER HOTARU HASN'T TOLD HIM ANYTHING!
I WONDER IF SHE'S ALL RIGHT?
Pi
Pi
Ping

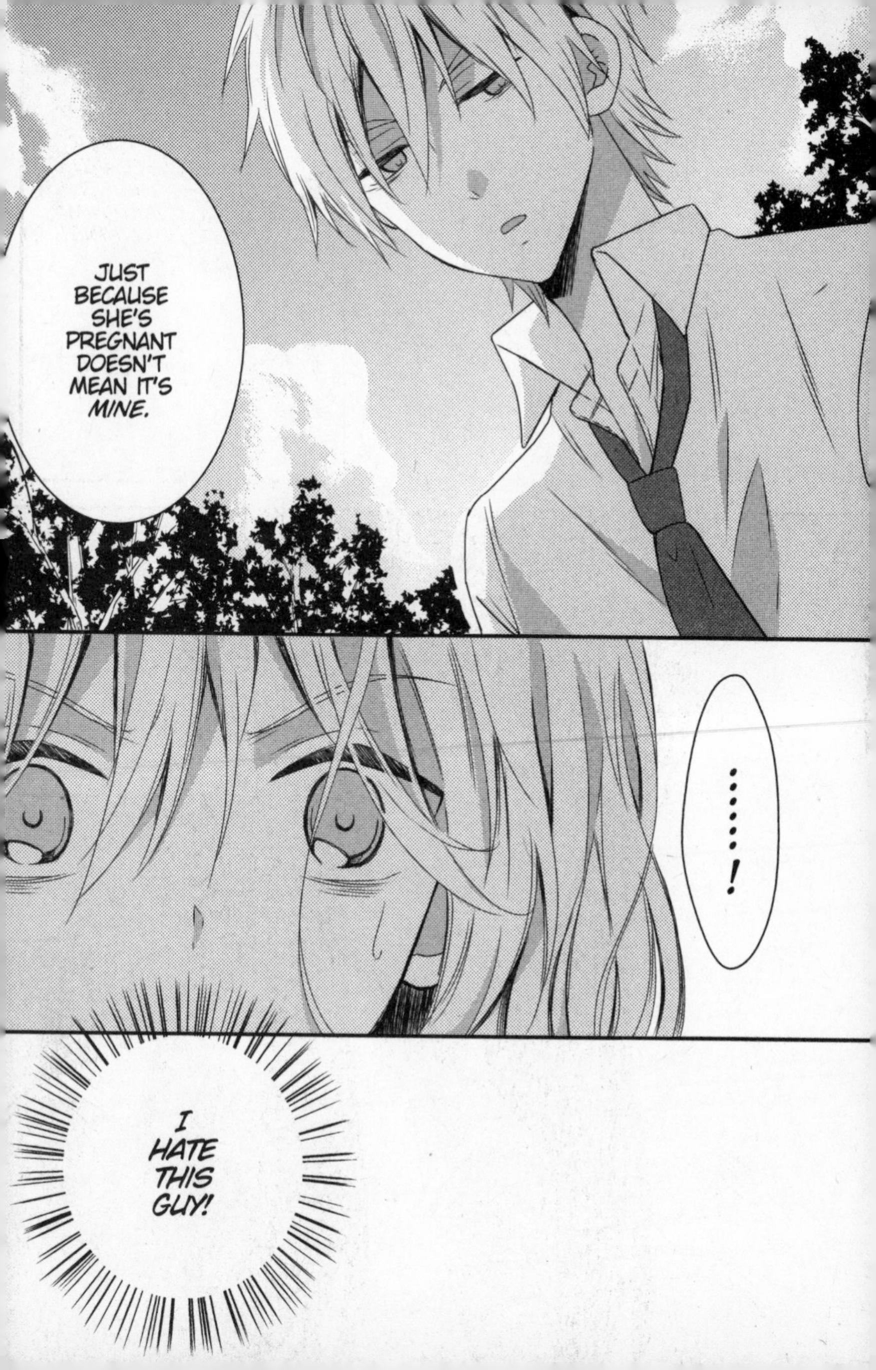
JUST BECAUSE SHE'S PREGNANT DOESN'T MEAN IT'S *MINE.*
......!
I HATE THIS GUY!

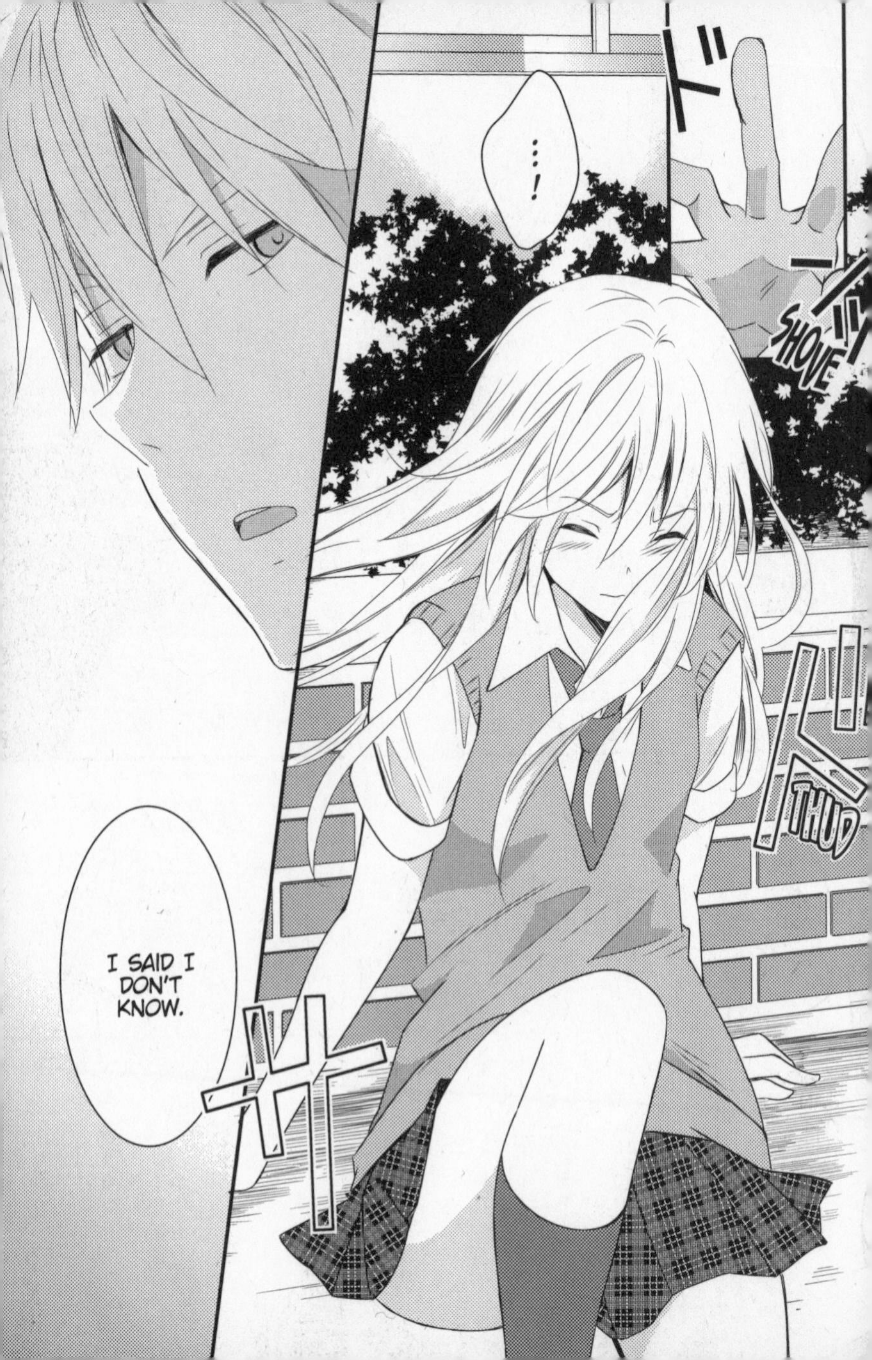
SHOVE
...!
THUD
I SAID I DON'T KNOW.

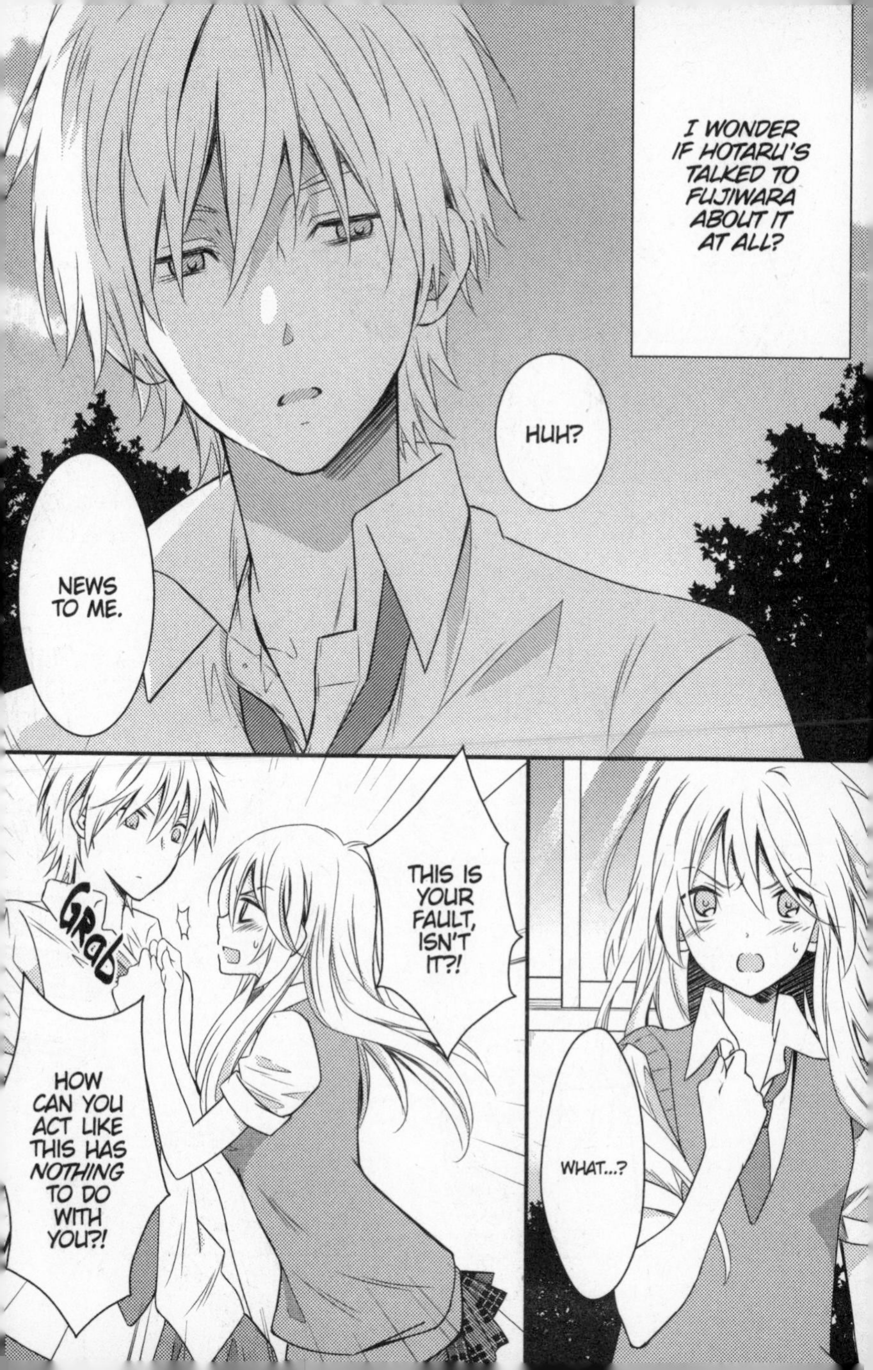
I WONDER IF HOTARU'S TALKED TO FUJIWARA ABOUT IT AT ALL?
HUH?
NEWS TO ME.
WHAT...?
THIS IS YOUR FAULT, ISN'T IT?!
GRAB
HOW CAN YOU ACT LIKE THIS HAS *NOTHING* TO DO WITH YOU?!

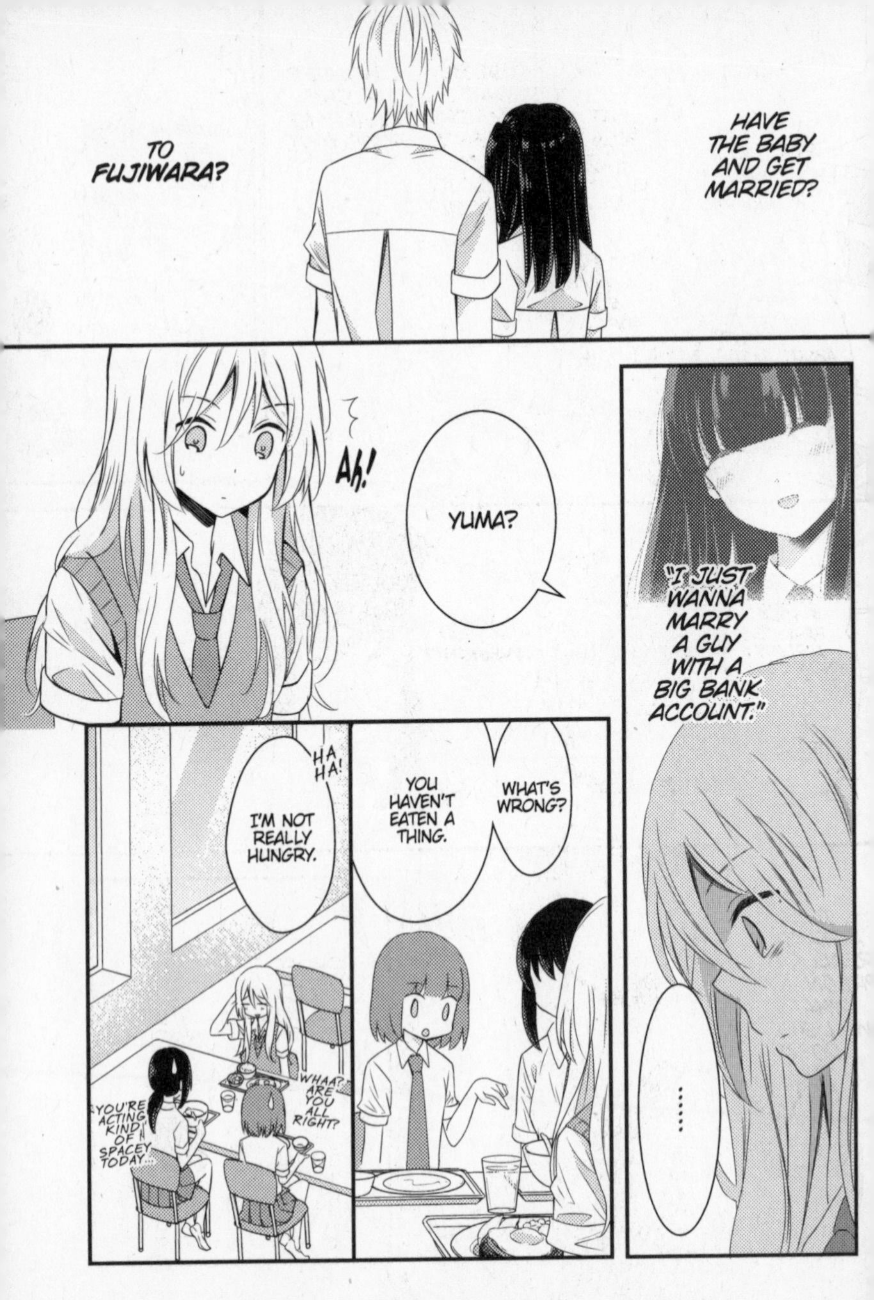

HAVE THE BABY AND GET MARRIED?
TO FUJIWARA?
"I JUST WANNA MARRY A GUY WITH A BIG BANK ACCOUNT."
......
YUMA?
Ah!
WHAT'S WRONG?
YOU HAVEN'T EATEN A THING.
HA HA!
I'M NOT REALLY HUNGRY.
WHAA? ARE YOU ALL RIGHT?
YOU'RE ACTING KIND OF SPACEY TODAY...

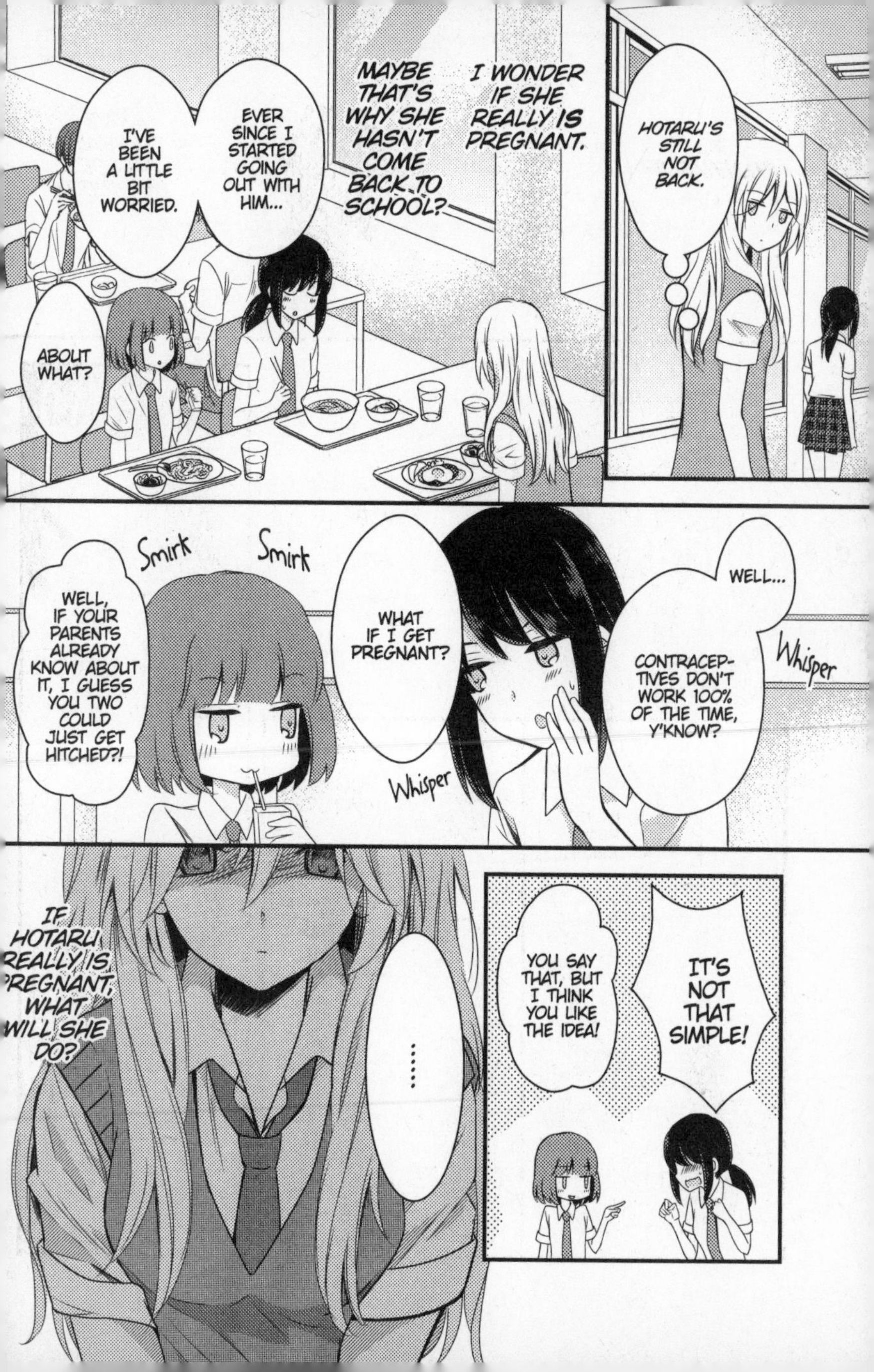
HOTARU'S STILL NOT BACK.
I WONDER IF SHE REALLY IS PREGNANT.
MAYBE THAT'S WHY SHE HASN'T COME BACK TO SCHOOL?
EVER SINCE I STARTED GOING OUT WITH HIM...
I'VE BEEN A LITTLE BIT WORRIED.
ABOUT WHAT?
WELL...
CONTRACEPTIVES DON'T WORK 100% OF THE TIME, Y'KNOW?
Whisper
WHAT IF I GET PREGNANT?
Whisper
Smirk
Smirk
WELL, IF YOUR PARENTS ALREADY KNOW ABOUT IT, I GUESS YOU TWO COULD JUST GET HITCHED?!
IT'S NOT THAT SIMPLE!
YOU SAY THAT, BUT I THINK YOU LIKE THE IDEA!
......
IF HOTARU REALLY IS PREGNANT, WHAT WILL SHE DO?

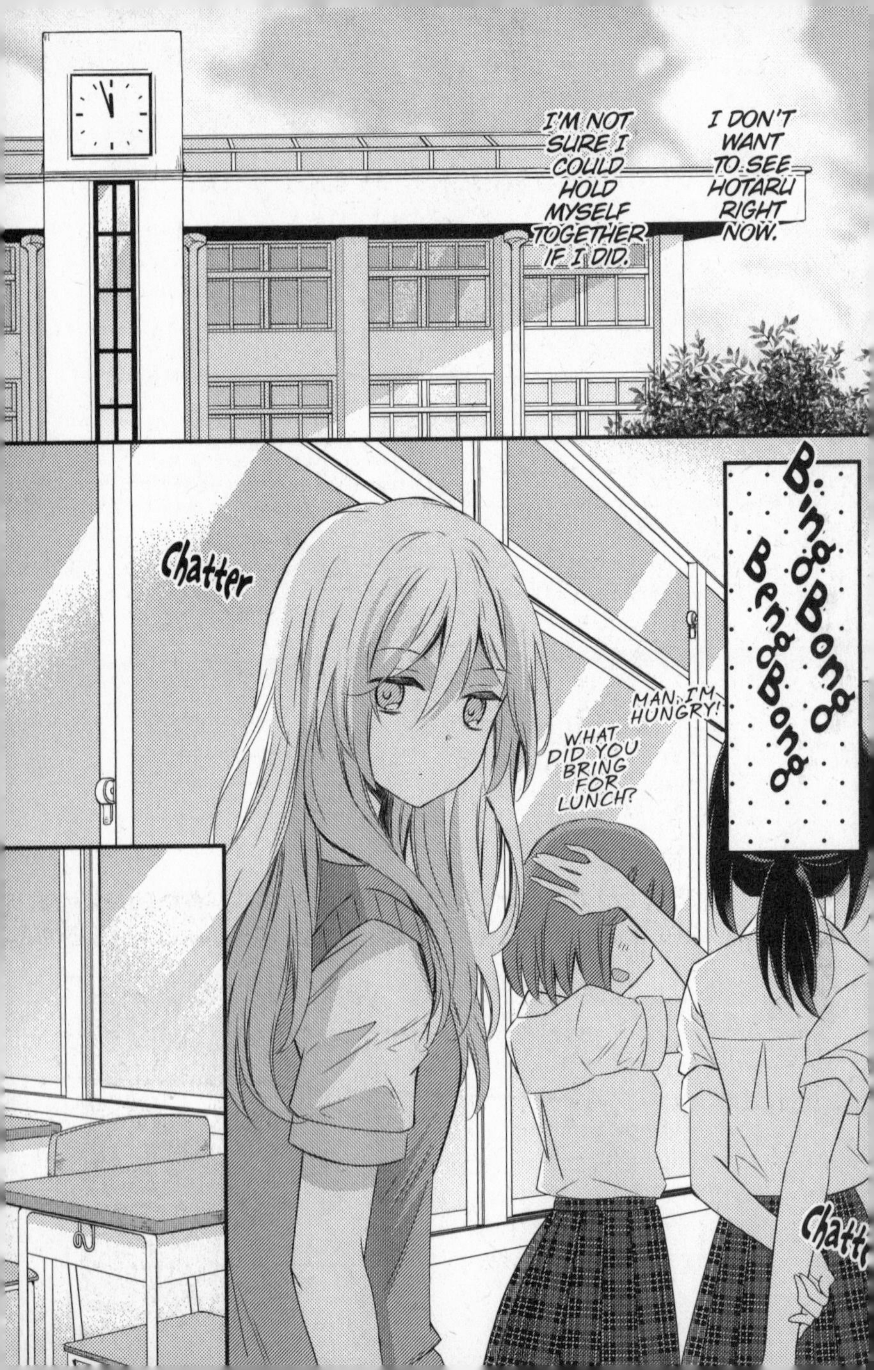
I DON'T WANT TO SEE HOTARU RIGHT NOW.
I'M NOT SURE I COULD HOLD MYSELF TOGETHER IF I DID.
Bing Bong Beng Bong
MAN, I'M HUNGRY!
WHAT DID YOU BRING FOR LUNCH?
Chatte
Chatter

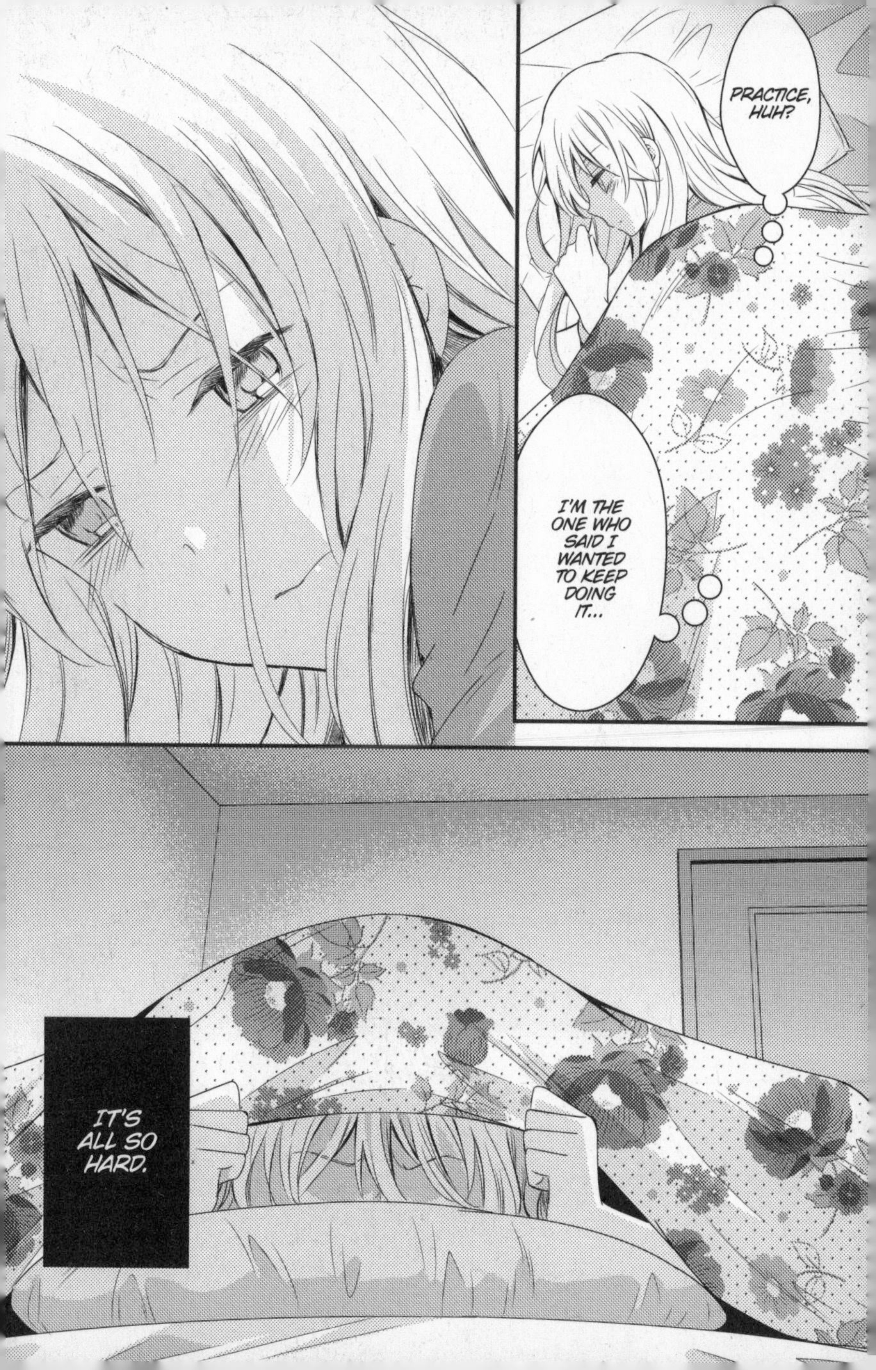
PRACTICE, HUH?
I'M THE ONE WHO SAID I WANTED TO KEEP DOING IT...
IT'S ALL SO HARD.

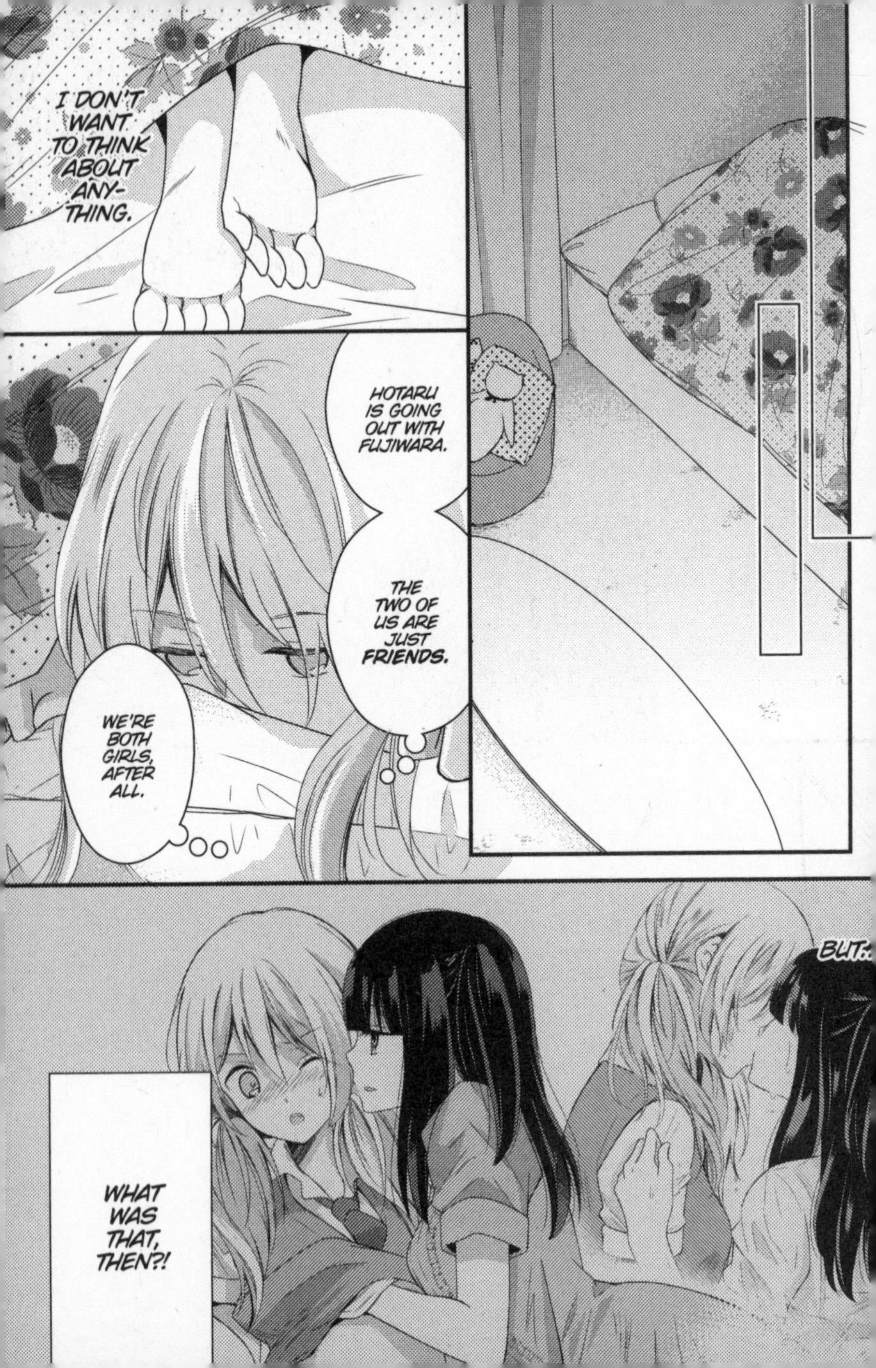
I DON'T WANT TO THINK ABOUT ANY-THING.
HOTARU IS GOING OUT WITH FUJIWARA.
THE TWO OF US ARE JUST FRIENDS.
WE'RE BOTH GIRLS, AFTER ALL.
BUT...
WHAT WAS THAT, THEN?!

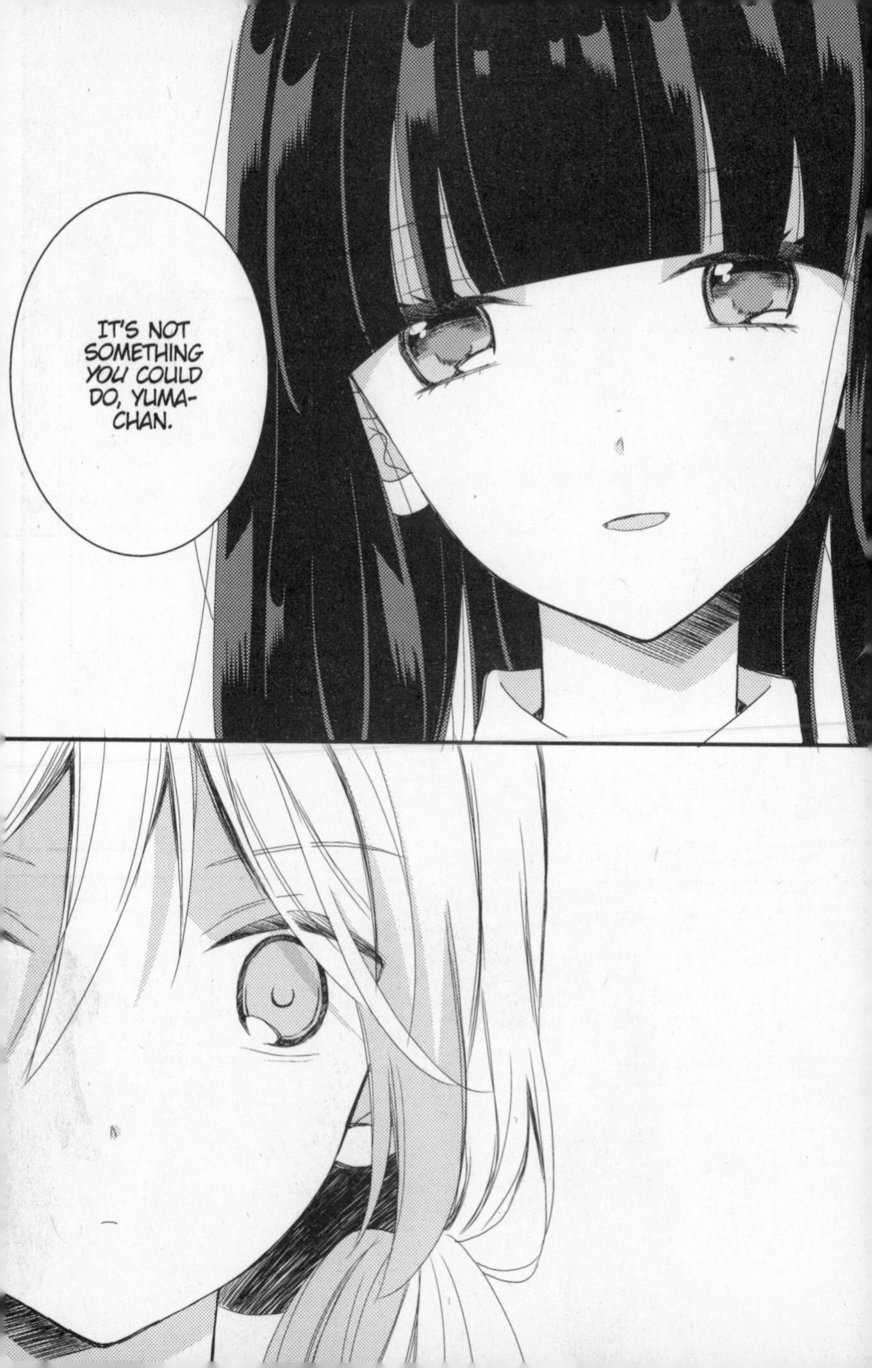
IT'S NOT SOMETHING YOU COULD DO, YUMA-CHAN.

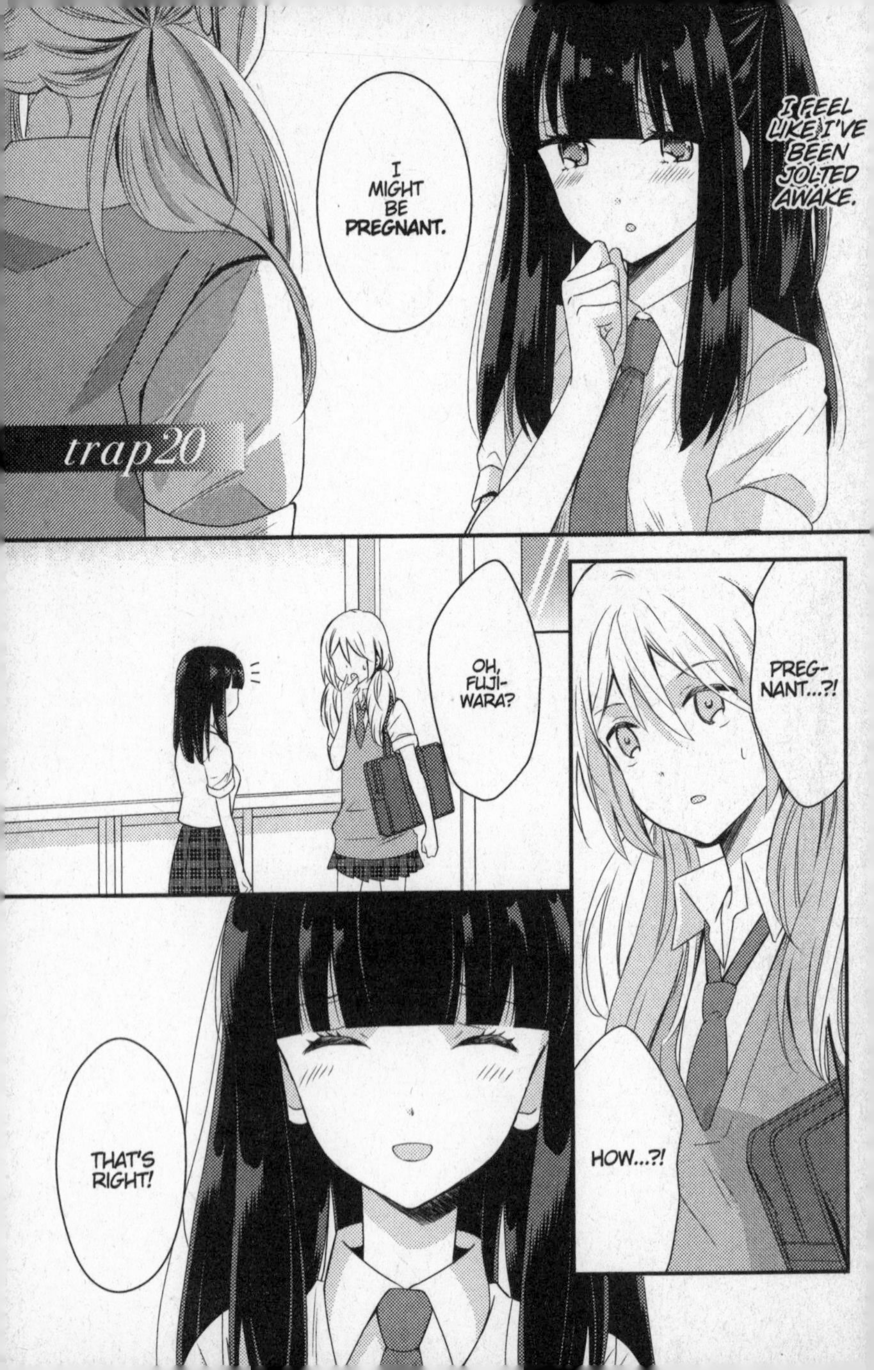
I FEEL LIKE I'VE BEEN JOLTED AWAKE.
I MIGHT BE PREGNANT.
trap20
PREG-NANT...?!
HOW...?!
OH, FUJI-WARA?
THAT'S RIGHT!

Netsuzou TRap -NTR-

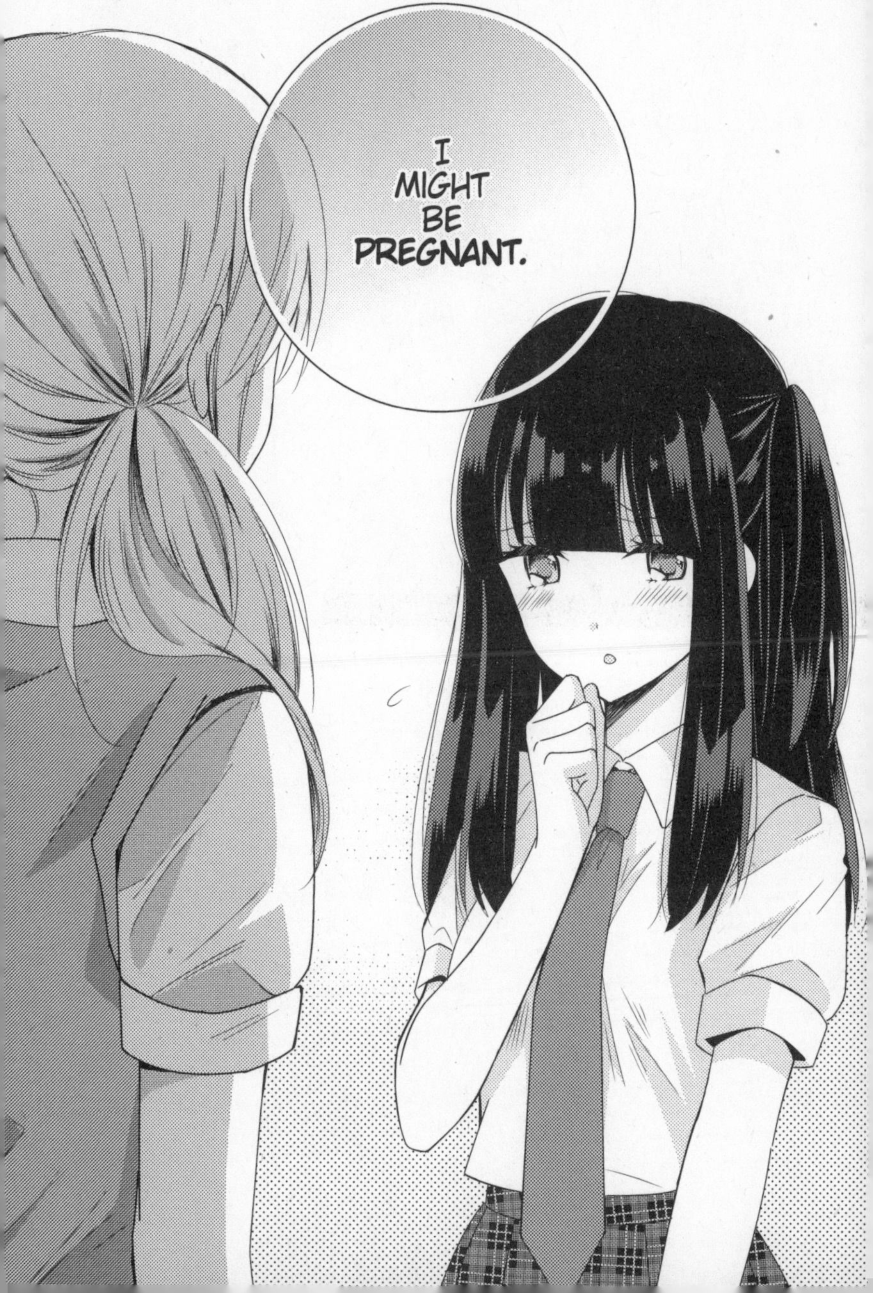
I MIGHT BE PREGNANT.

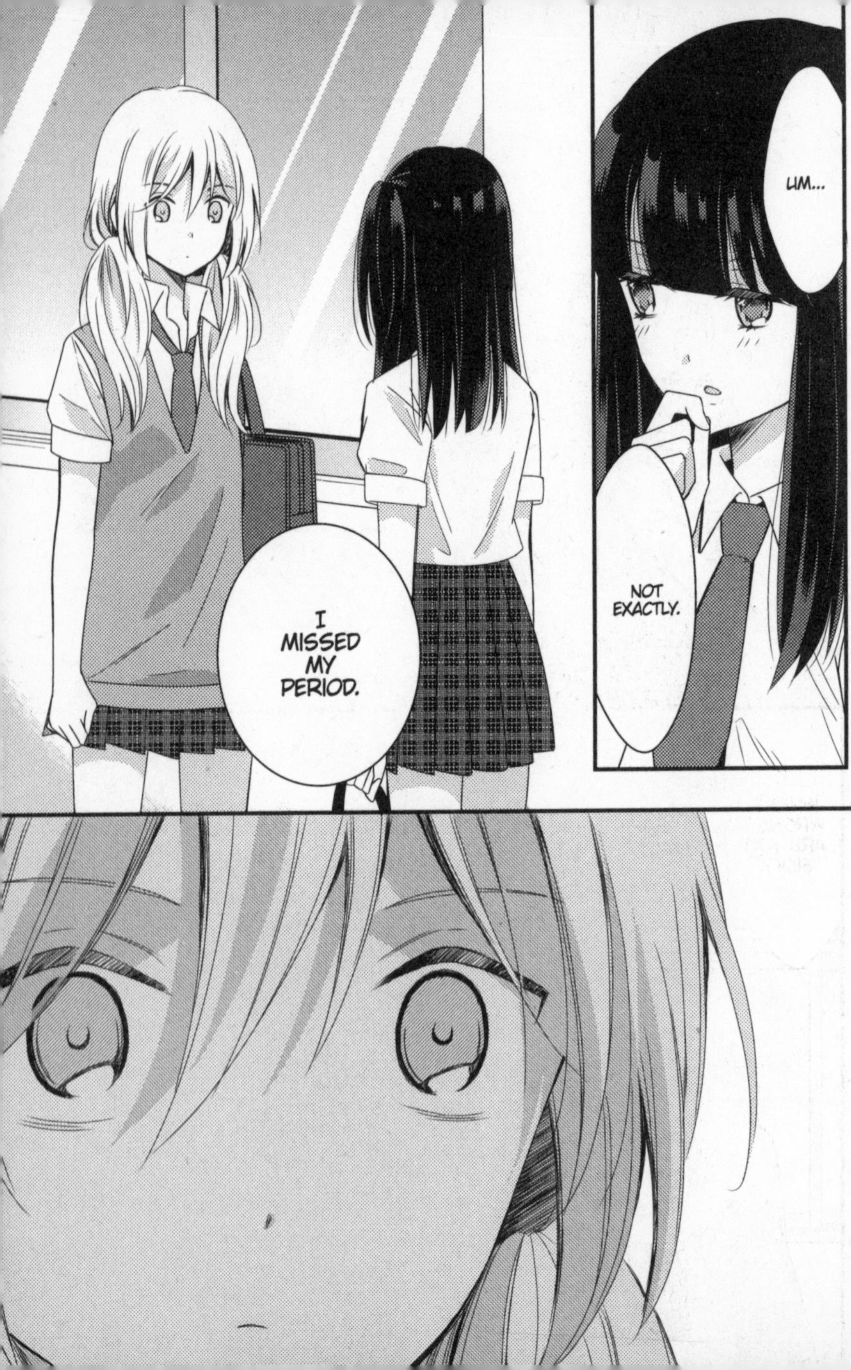
UM...
NOT EXACTLY.
I MISSED MY PERIOD.

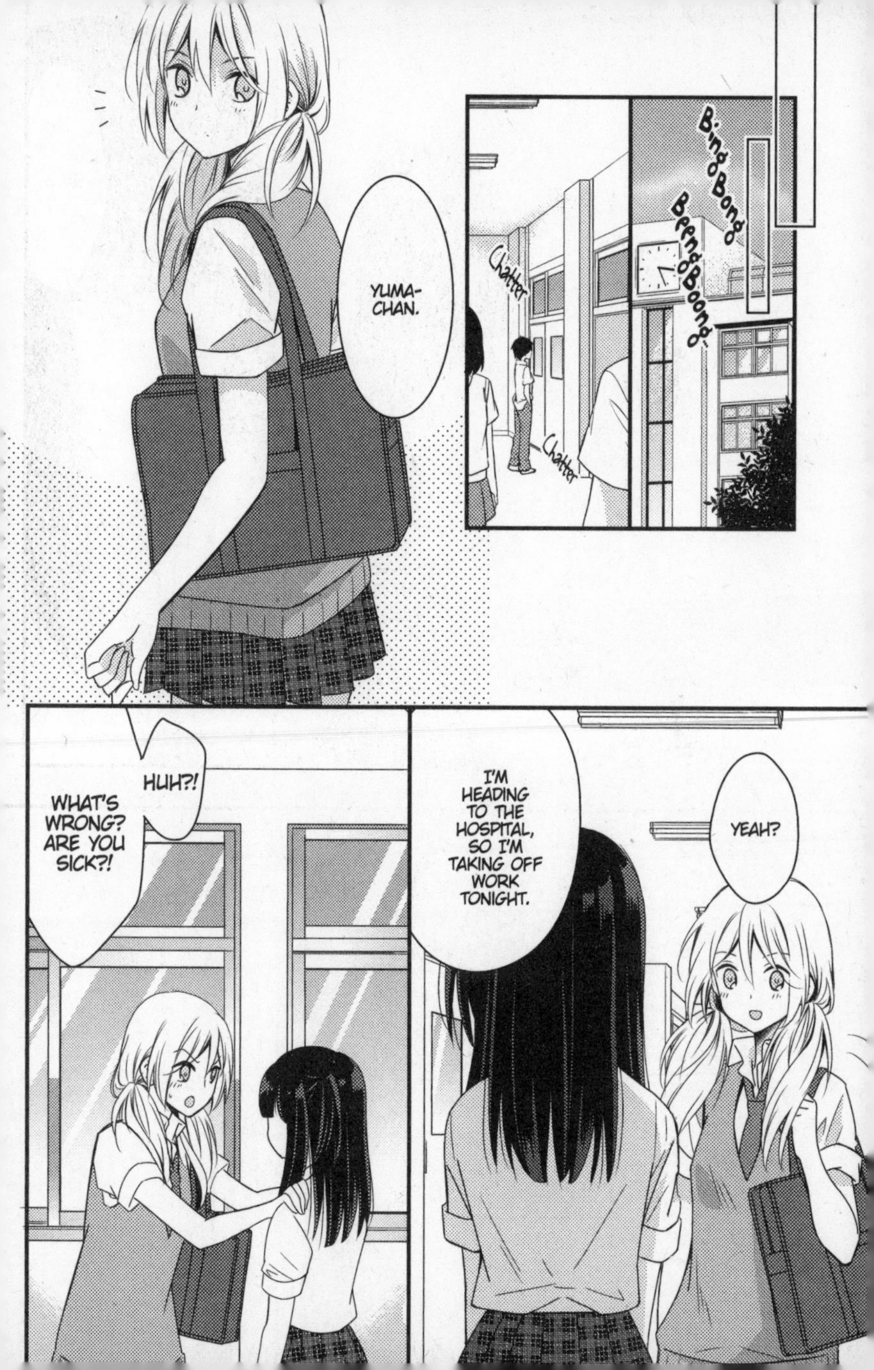
Bing Bong
Beeng Boong...
Chatter
Chatter
YUMA-CHAN.
YEAH?
I'M HEADING TO THE HOSPITAL, SO I'M TAKING OFF WORK TONIGHT.
HUH?!
WHAT'S WRONG? ARE YOU SICK?!

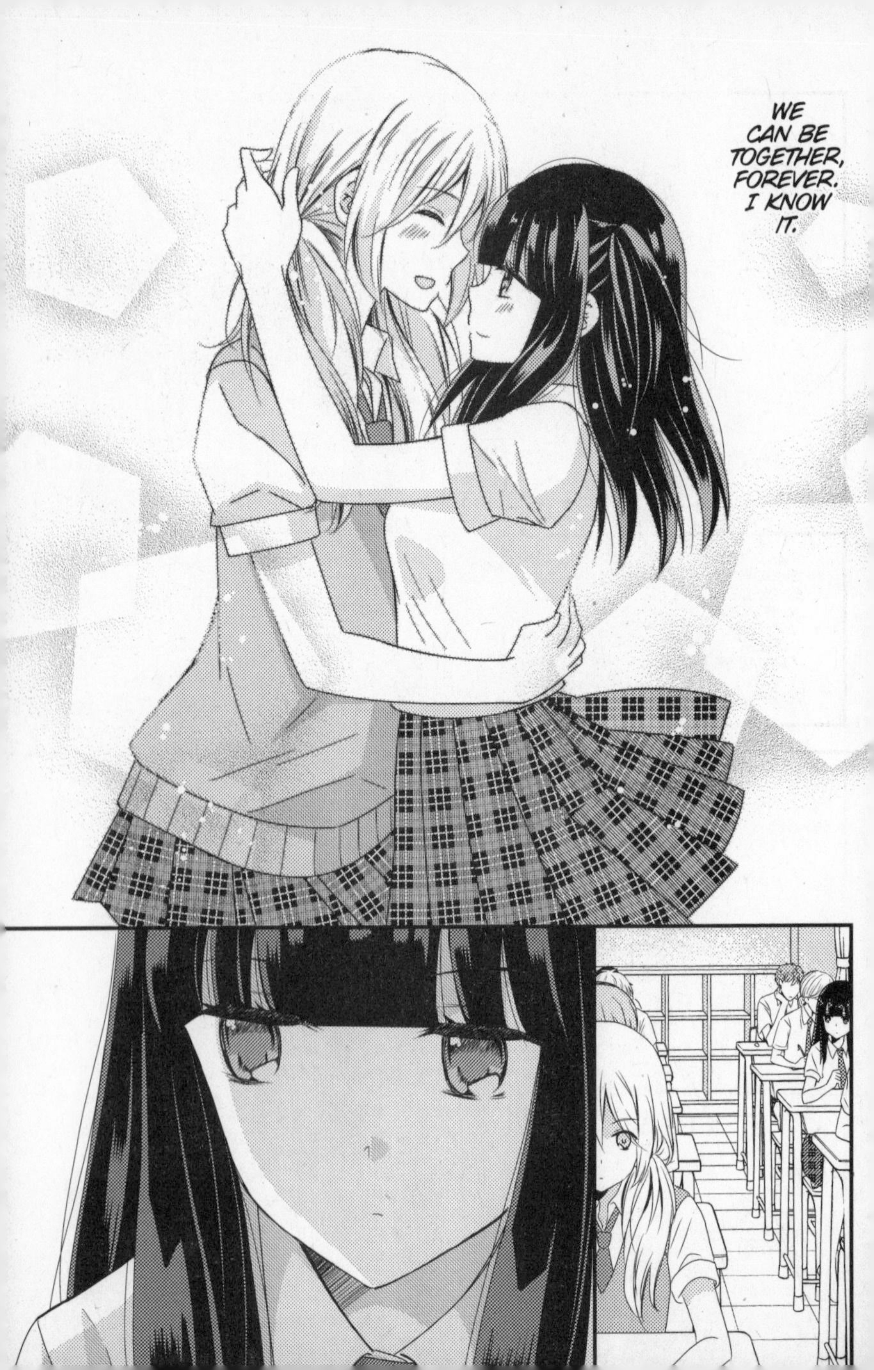
WE CAN BE TOGETHER, FOREVER. I KNOW IT.

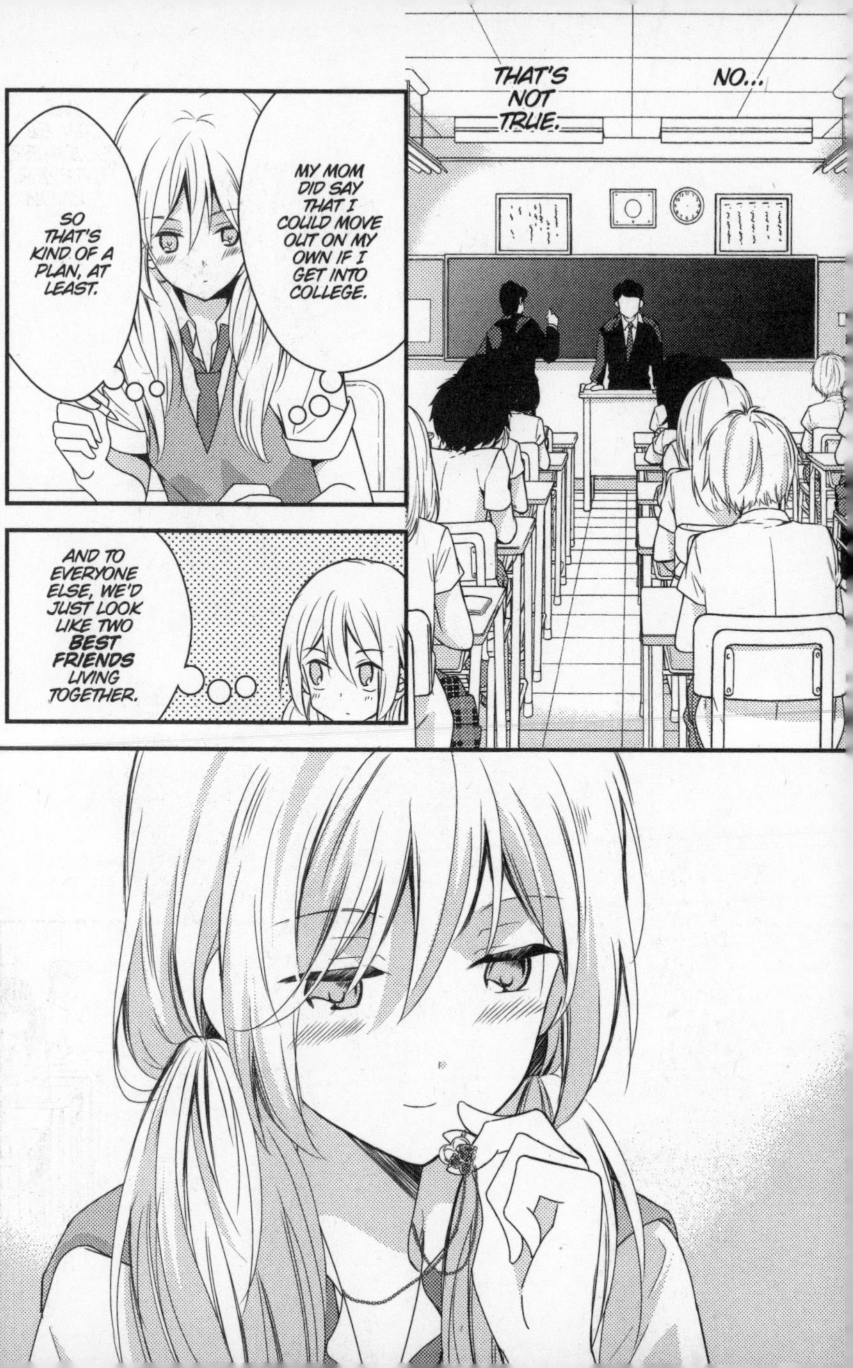
NO...
THAT'S NOT TRUE.
MY MOM DID SAY THAT I COULD MOVE OUT ON MY OWN IF I GET INTO COLLEGE.
SO THAT'S KIND OF A PLAN, AT LEAST.
AND TO EVERYONE ELSE, WE'D JUST LOOK LIKE TWO BEST FRIENDS LIVING TOGETHER.

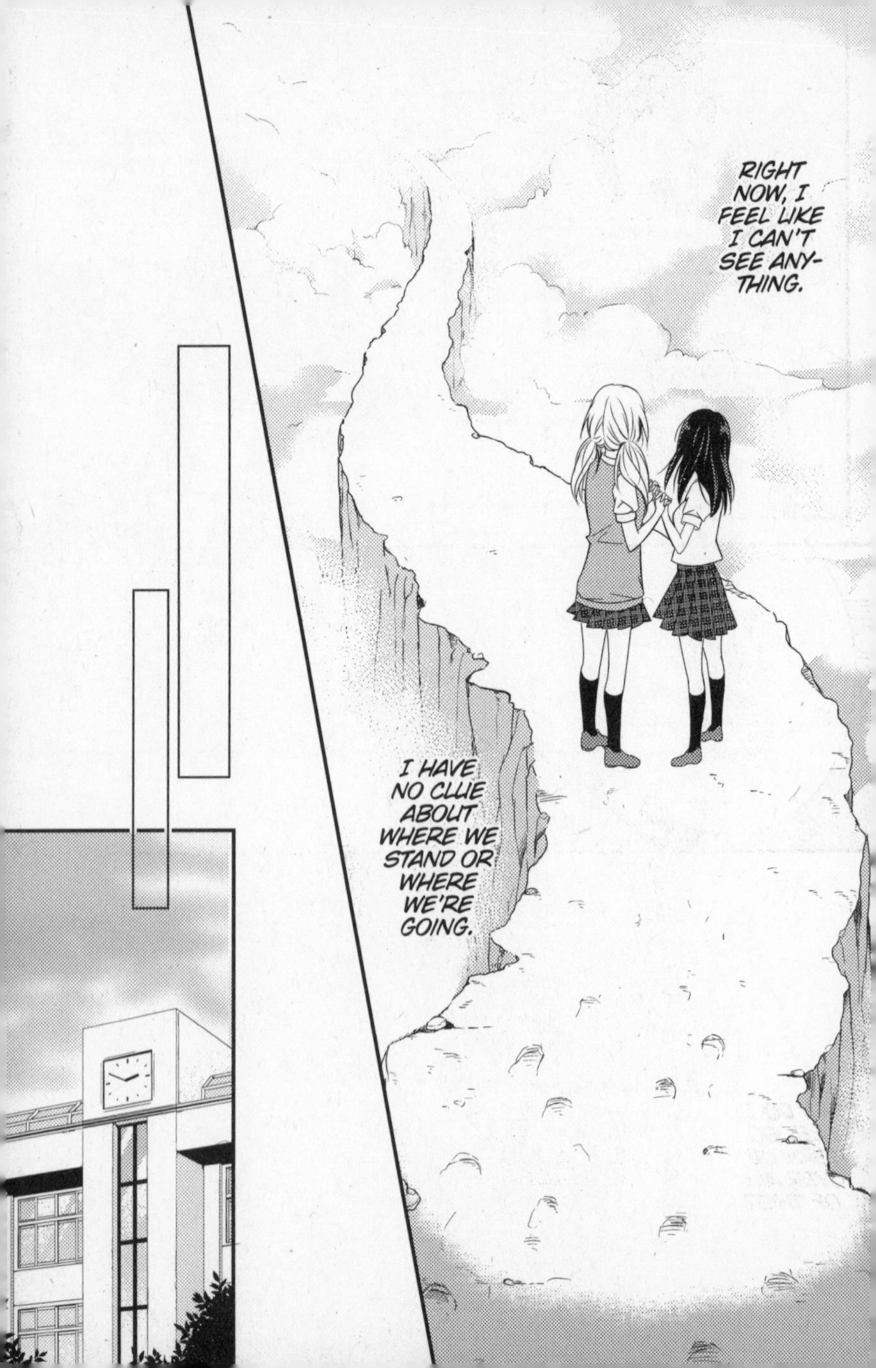
RIGHT NOW, I FEEL LIKE I CAN'T SEE ANY-THING.
I HAVE NO CLUE ABOUT WHERE WE STAND OR WHERE WE'RE GOING.

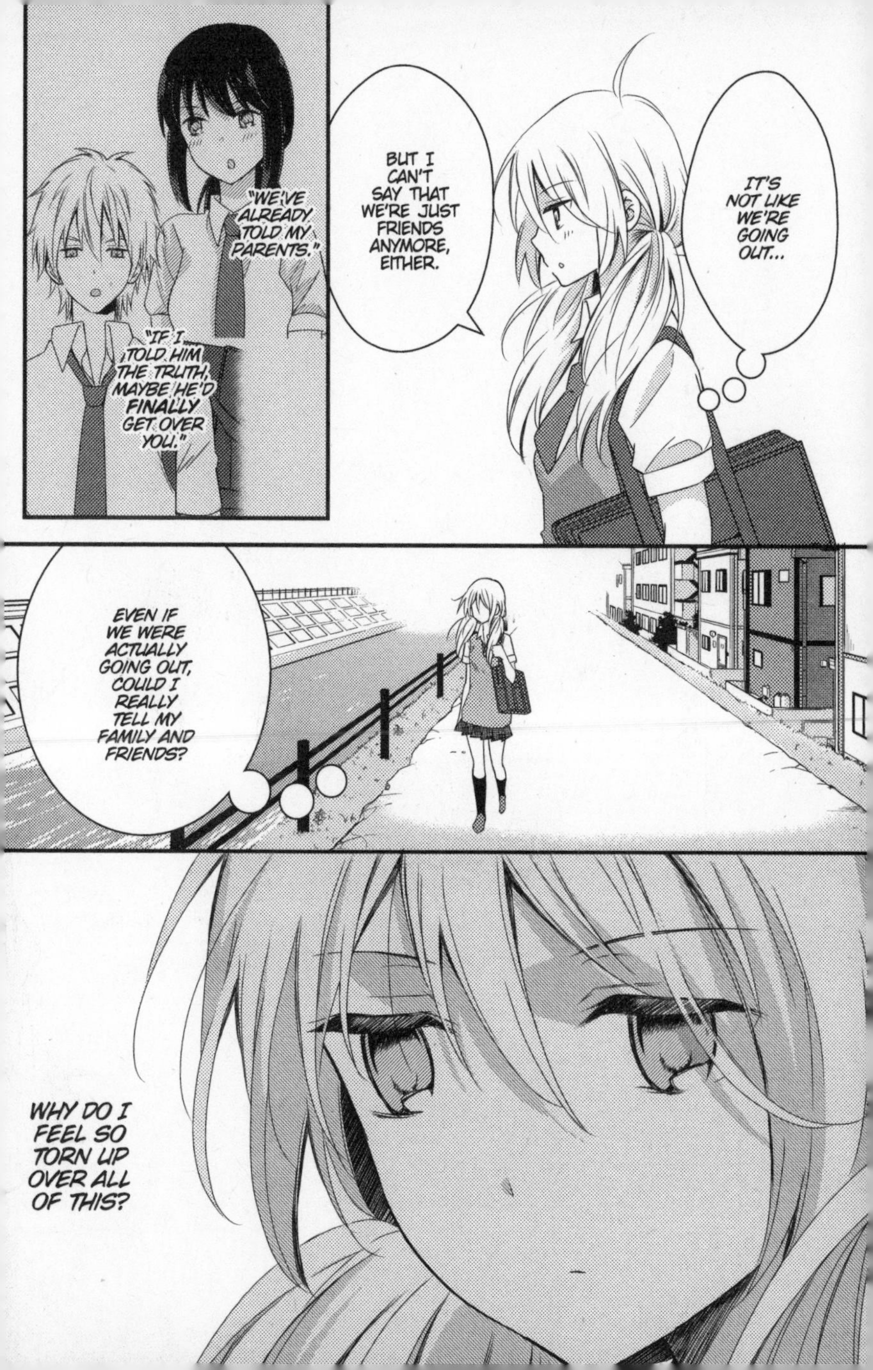
IT'S NOT LIKE WE'RE GOING OUT...
BUT I CAN'T SAY THAT WE'RE JUST FRIENDS ANYMORE, EITHER.
"WE'VE ALREADY TOLD MY PARENTS."
"IF I TOLD HIM THE TRUTH, MAYBE HE'D FINALLY GET OVER YOU."
EVEN IF WE WERE ACTUALLY GOING OUT, COULD I REALLY TELL MY FAMILY AND FRIENDS?
WHY DO I FEEL SO TORN UP OVER ALL OF THIS?

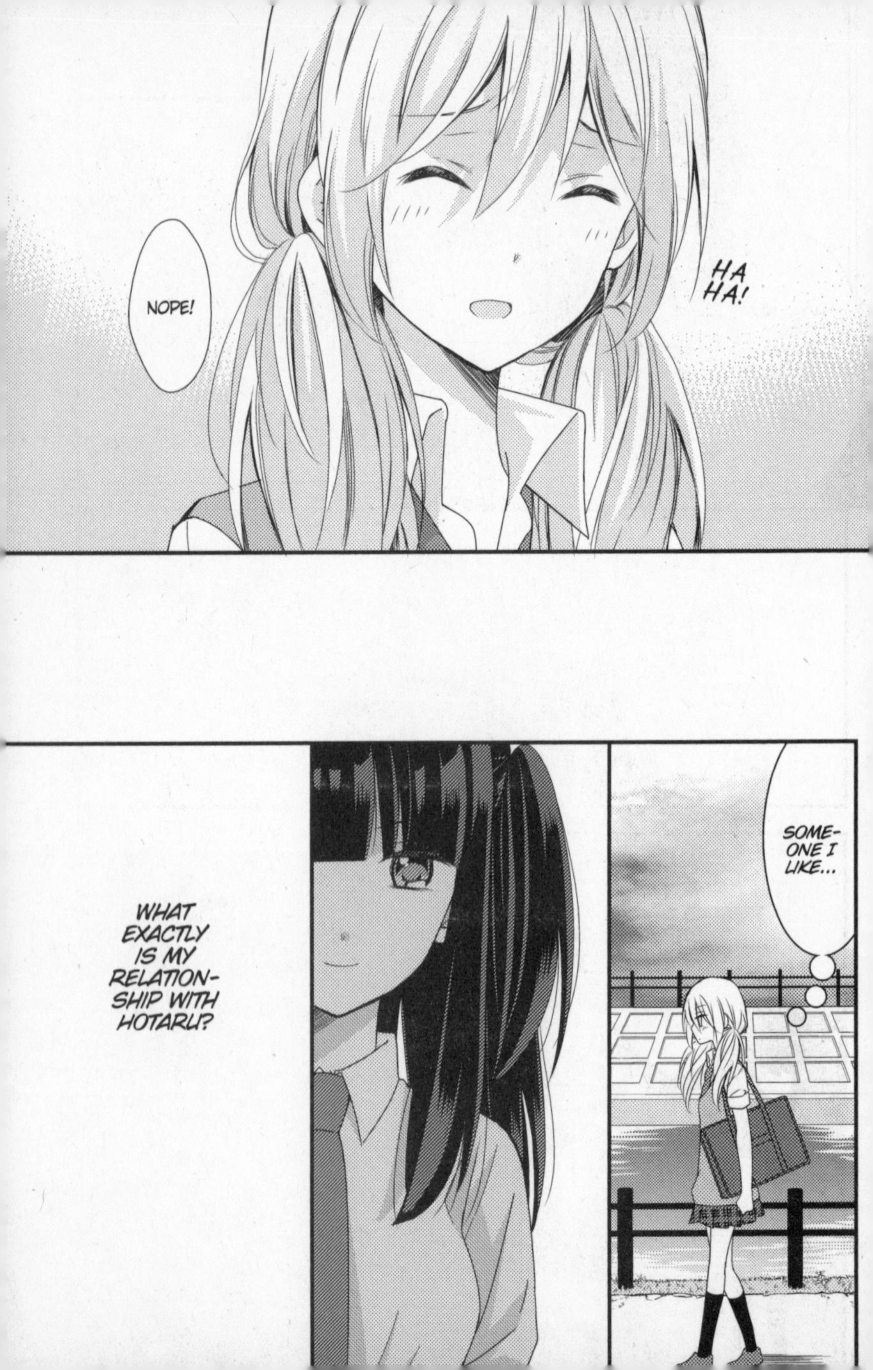
HA HA!
NOPE!
SOME-ONE I LIKE...
WHAT EXACTLY IS MY RELATION-SHIP WITH HOTARU?

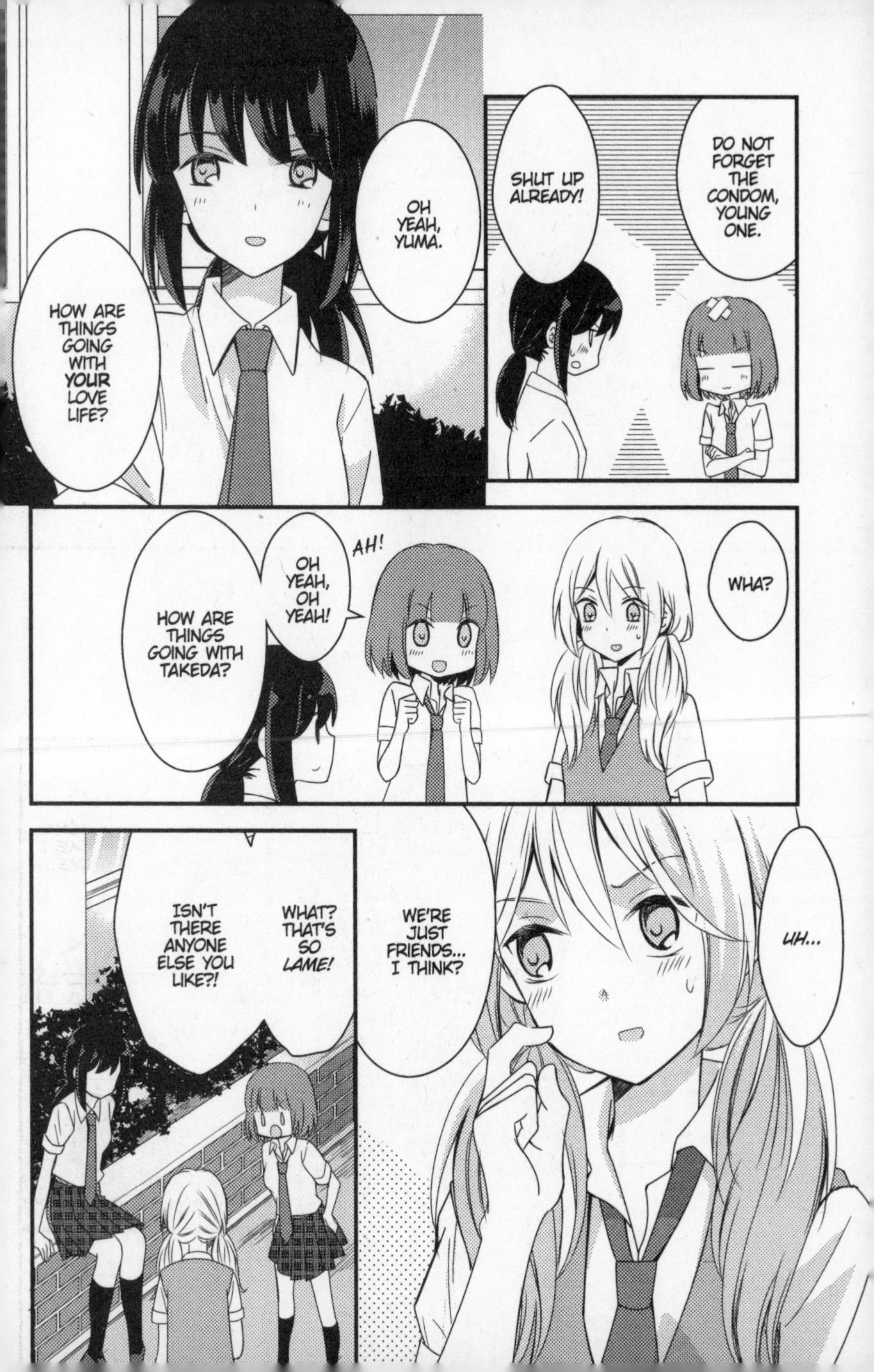

DO NOT FORGET THE CONDOM, YOUNG ONE.
SHUT UP ALREADY!
OH YEAH, YUMA.
HOW ARE THINGS GOING WITH YOUR LOVE LIFE?
WHA?
AH!
OH YEAH, OH YEAH!
HOW ARE THINGS GOING WITH TAKEDA?
UH...
WE'RE JUST FRIENDS... I THINK?
WHAT? THAT'S SO LAME!
ISN'T THERE ANYONE ELSE YOU LIKE?!

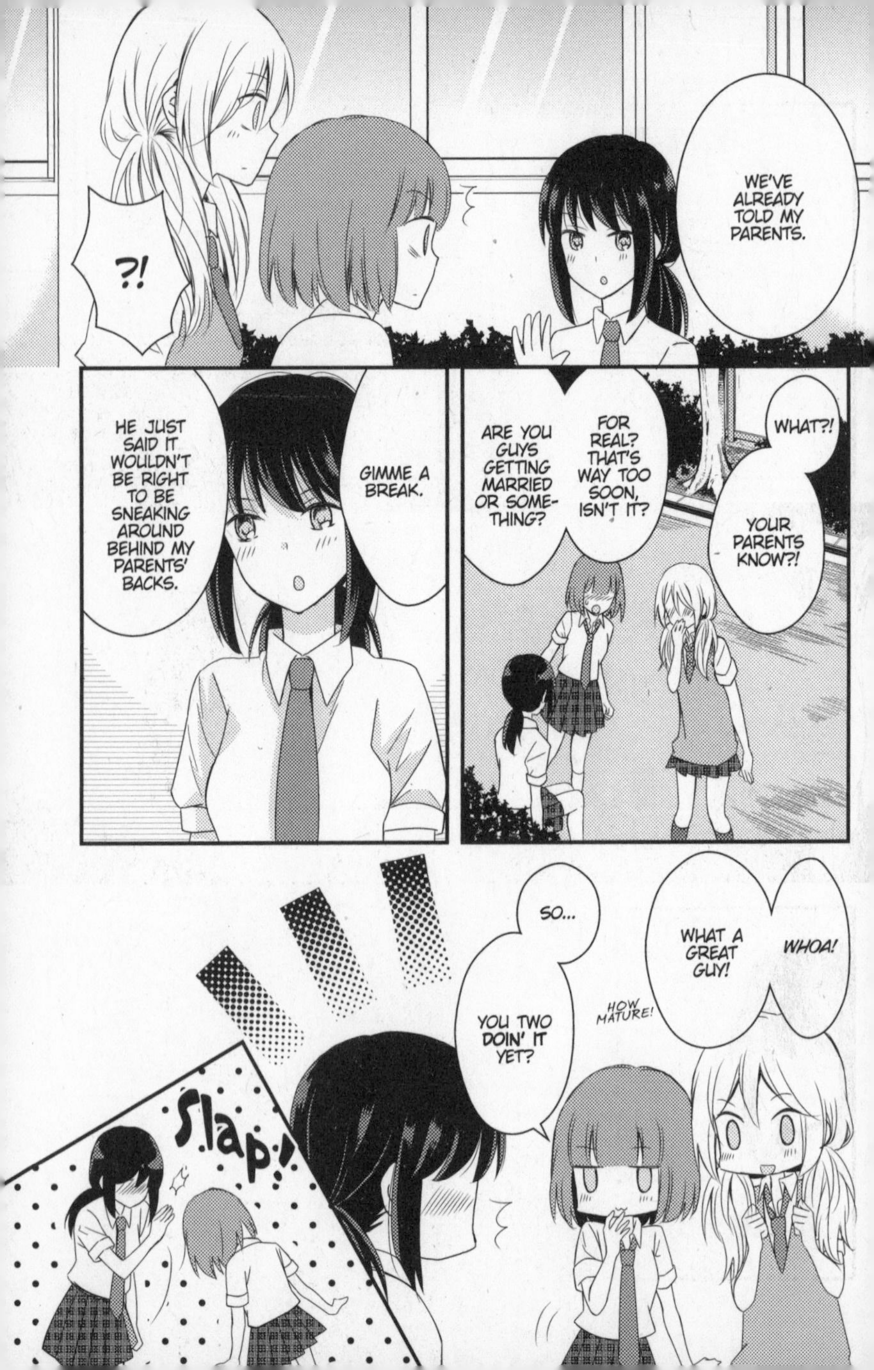
WE'VE ALREADY TOLD MY PARENTS.
?!
WHAT?!
YOUR PARENTS KNOW?!
FOR REAL? THAT'S WAY TOO SOON, ISN'T IT?
ARE YOU GUYS GETTING MARRIED OR SOME-THING?
GIMME A BREAK.
HE JUST SAID IT WOULDN'T BE RIGHT TO BE SNEAKING AROUND BEHIND MY PARENTS' BACKS.
WHOA!
WHAT A GREAT GUY!
HOW MATURE!
SO...
YOU TWO DOIN' IT YET?
Slap!

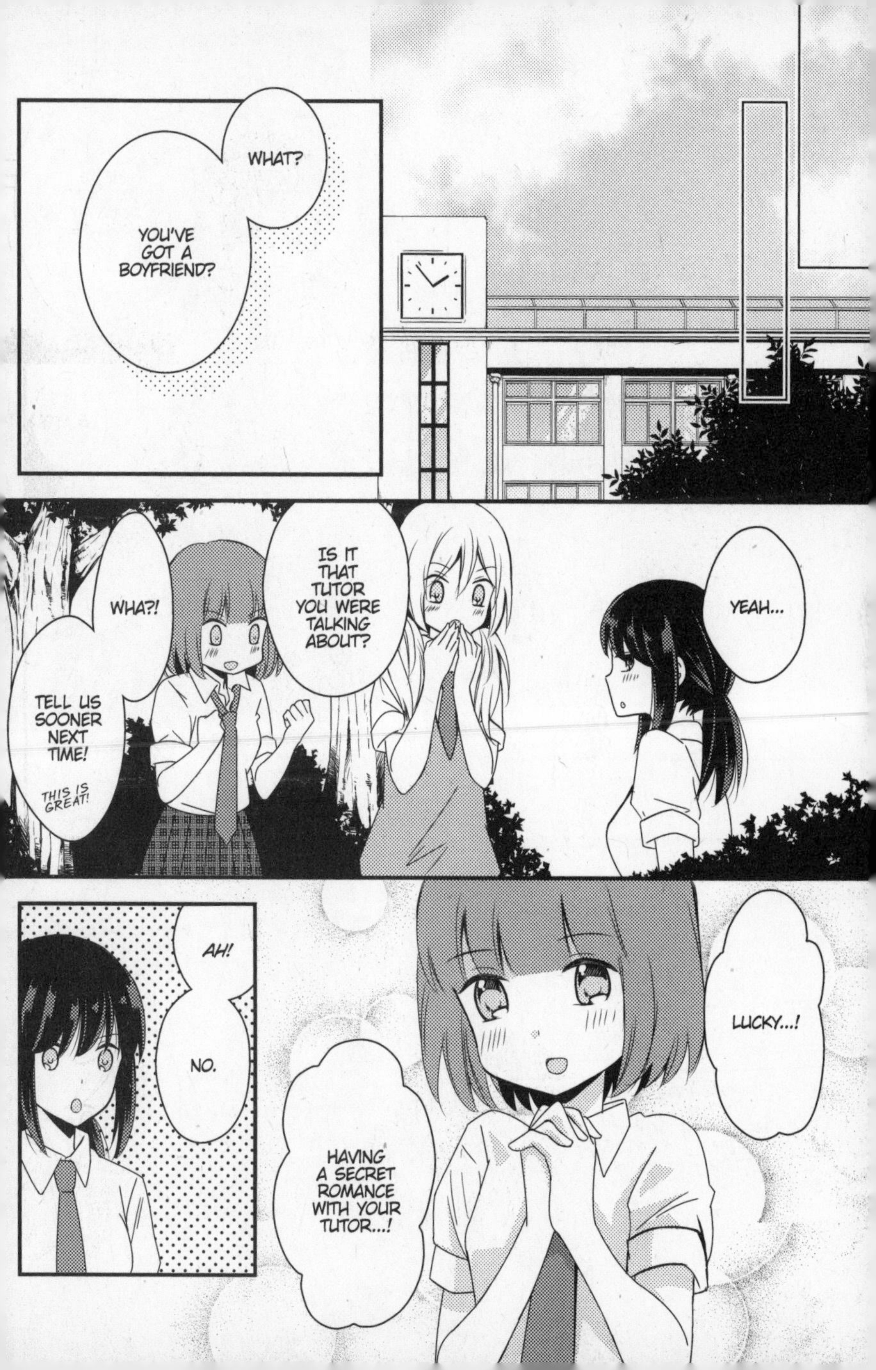
WHAT?
YOU'VE GOT A BOYFRIEND?
YEAH...
IS IT THAT TUTOR YOU WERE TALKING ABOUT?
WHA?!
TELL US SOONER NEXT TIME!
THIS IS GREAT!
LUCKY...!
HAVING A SECRET ROMANCE WITH YOUR TUTOR...!
AH!
NO.

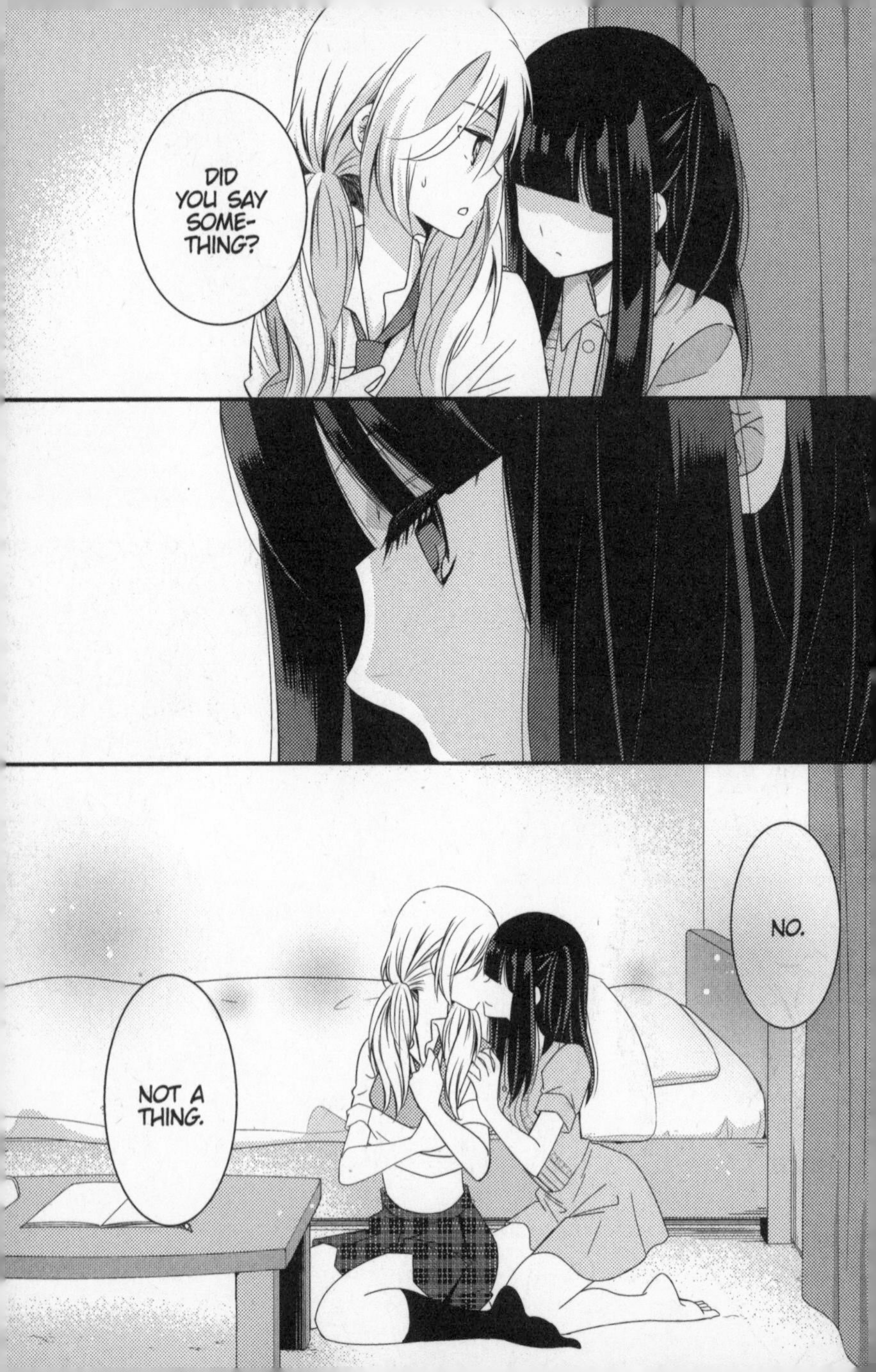
DID YOU SAY SOME-THING?
NO.
NOT A THING.

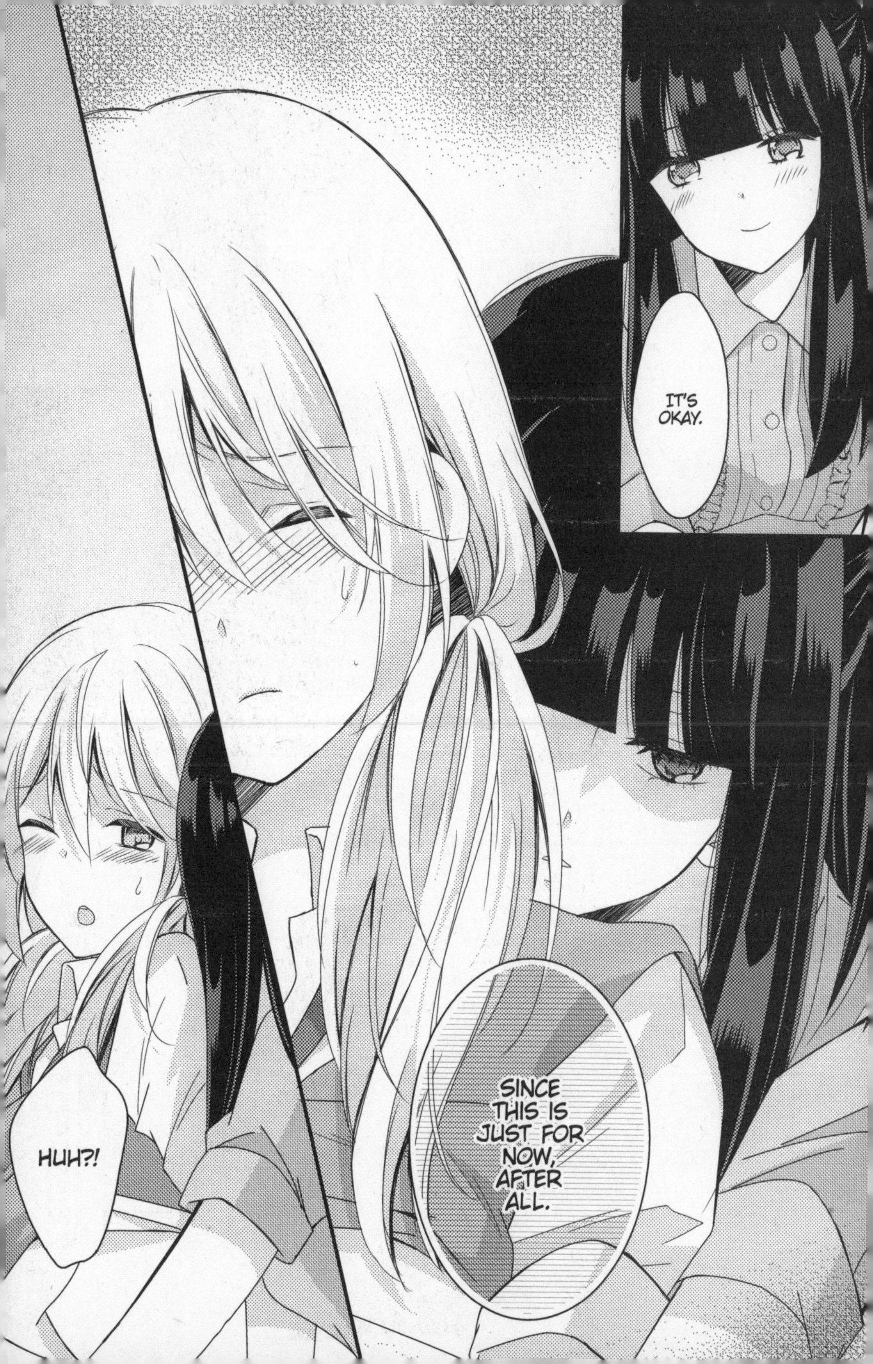
IT'S OKAY.
SINCE THIS IS JUST FOR NOW, AFTER ALL.
HUH?!

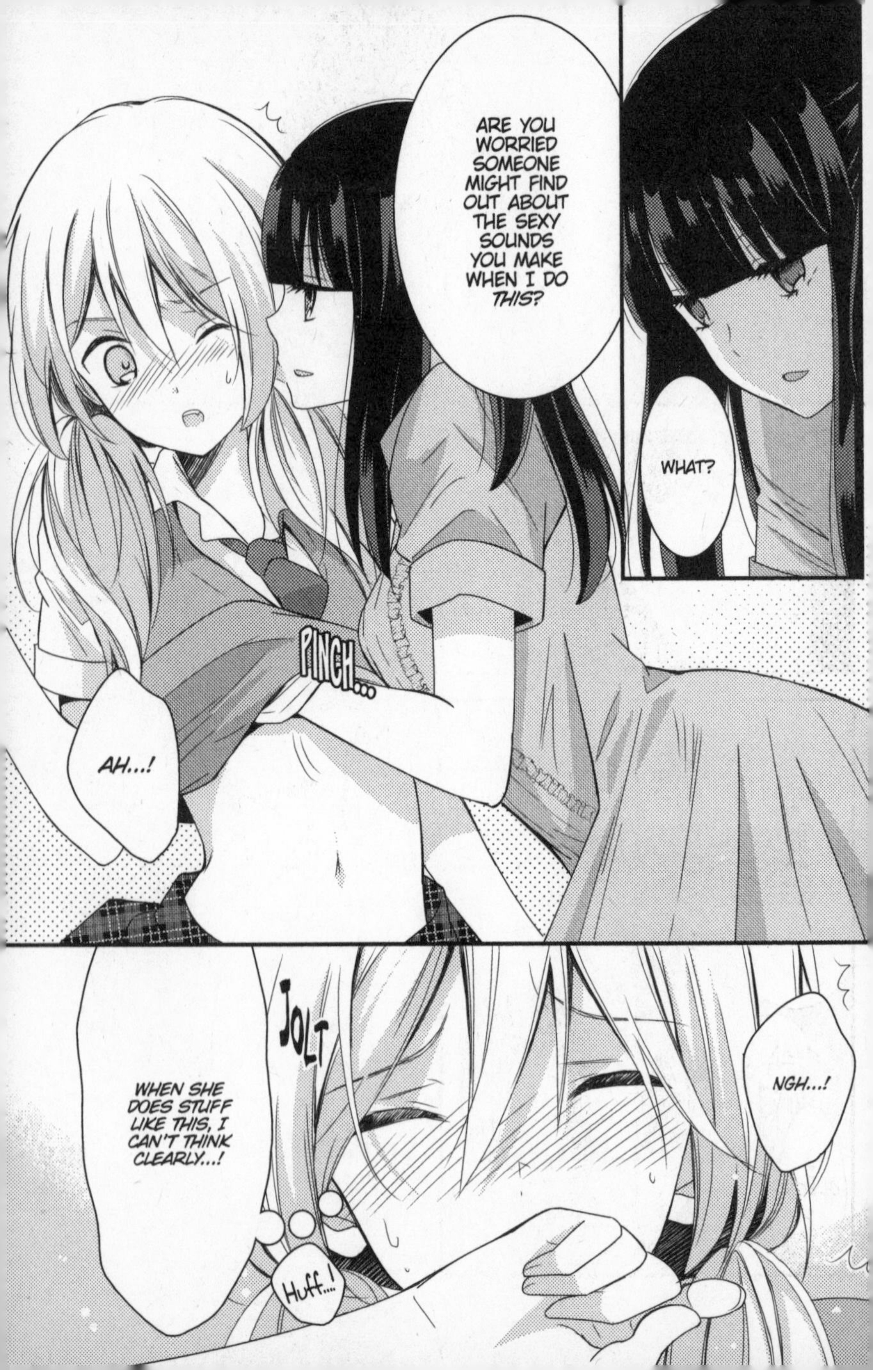
WHAT?
ARE YOU WORRIED SOMEONE MIGHT FIND OUT ABOUT THE SEXY SOUNDS YOU MAKE WHEN I DO *THIS?*
PINCH...
AH...!
NGH...!
JOLT
WHEN SHE DOES STUFF LIKE THIS, I CAN'T THINK CLEARLY...!
Huff...!

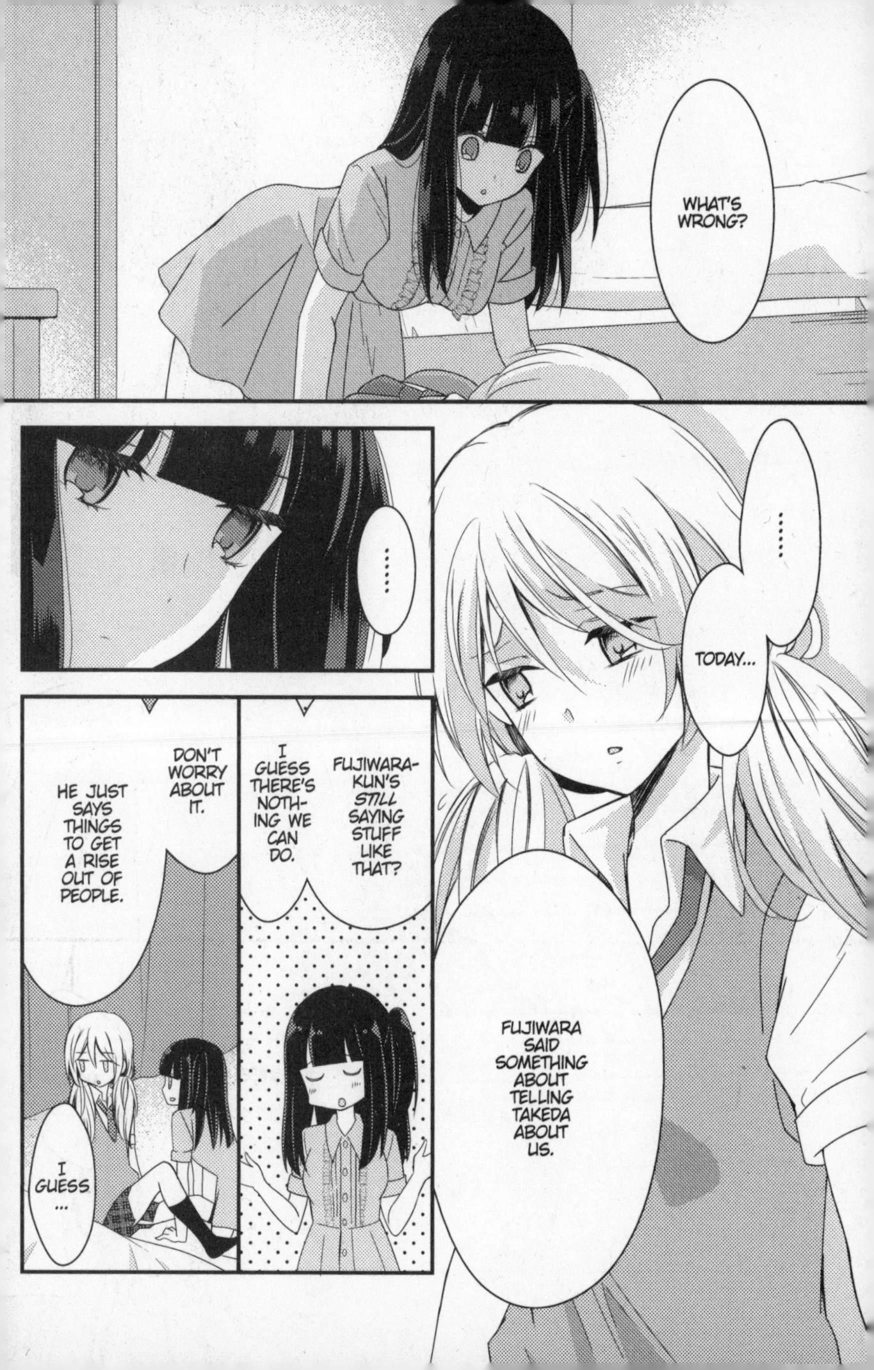
WHAT'S WRONG?
......
TODAY...
FUJIWARA SAID SOMETHING ABOUT TELLING TAKEDA ABOUT US.
......
FUJIWARA-KUN'S *STILL* SAYING STUFF LIKE THAT?
I GUESS THERE'S NOTHING WE CAN DO.
DON'T WORRY ABOUT IT.
HE JUST SAYS THINGS TO GET A RISE OUT OF PEOPLE.
I GUESS...

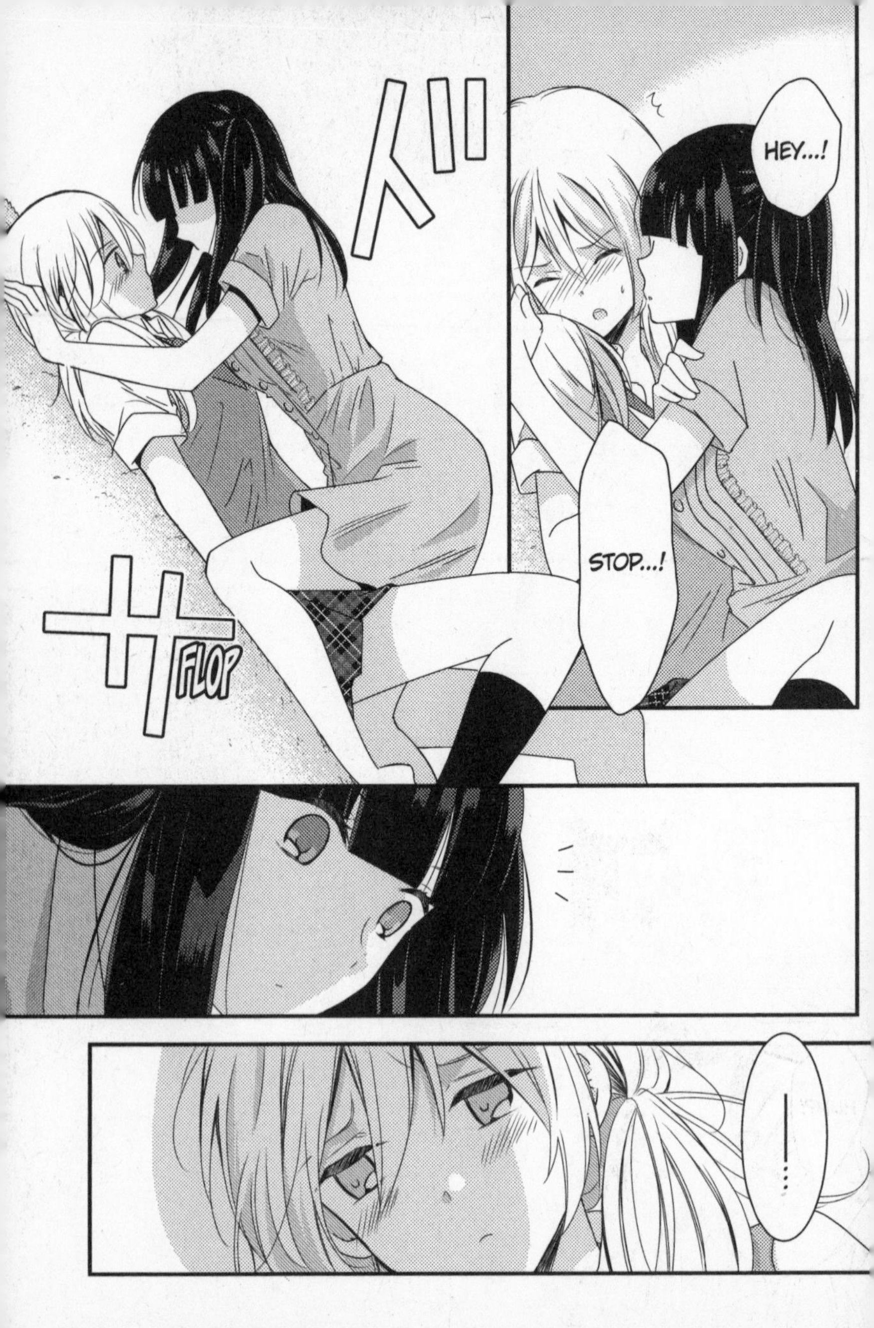
HEY...!
STOP...!
FLOP

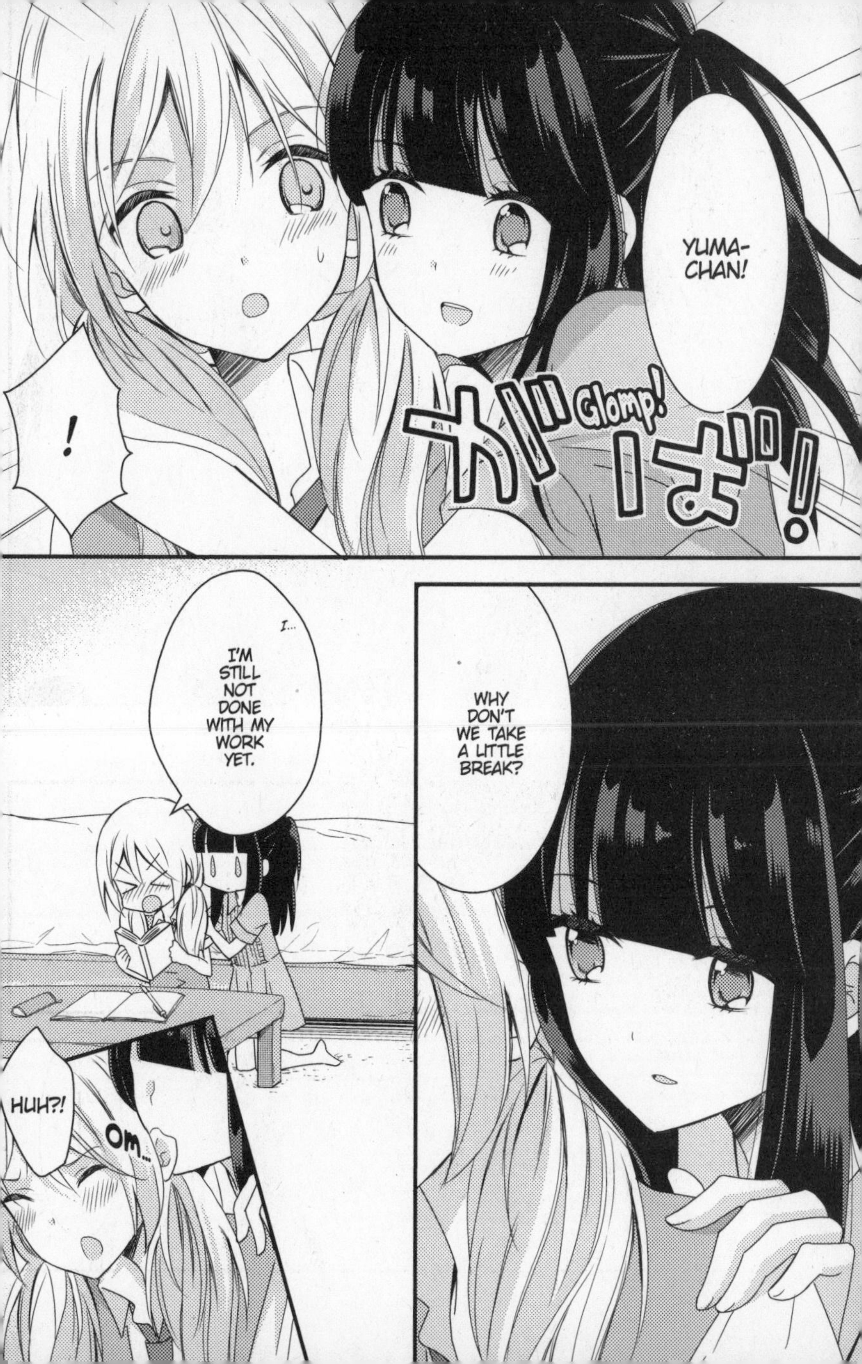

YUMA-CHAN!
Glomp!
!
WHY DON'T WE TAKE A LITTLE BREAK?
I...
I'M STILL NOT DONE WITH MY WORK YET.
HUH?!
Om...

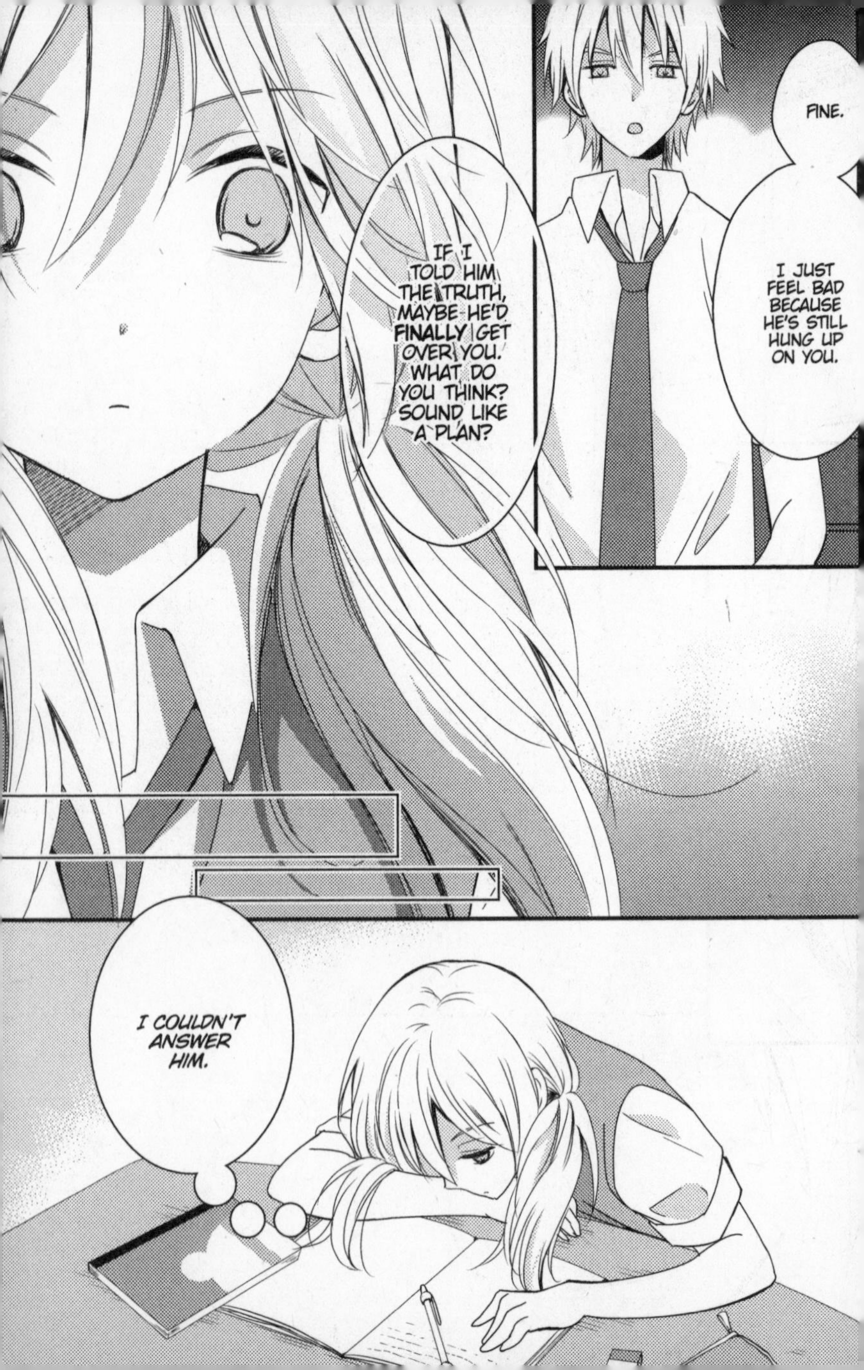
FINE.
I JUST FEEL BAD BECAUSE HE'S STILL HUNG UP ON YOU.
IF I TOLD HIM THE TRUTH, MAYBE HE'D FINALLY GET OVER YOU. WHAT DO YOU THINK? SOUND LIKE A PLAN?
I COULDN'T ANSWER HIM.

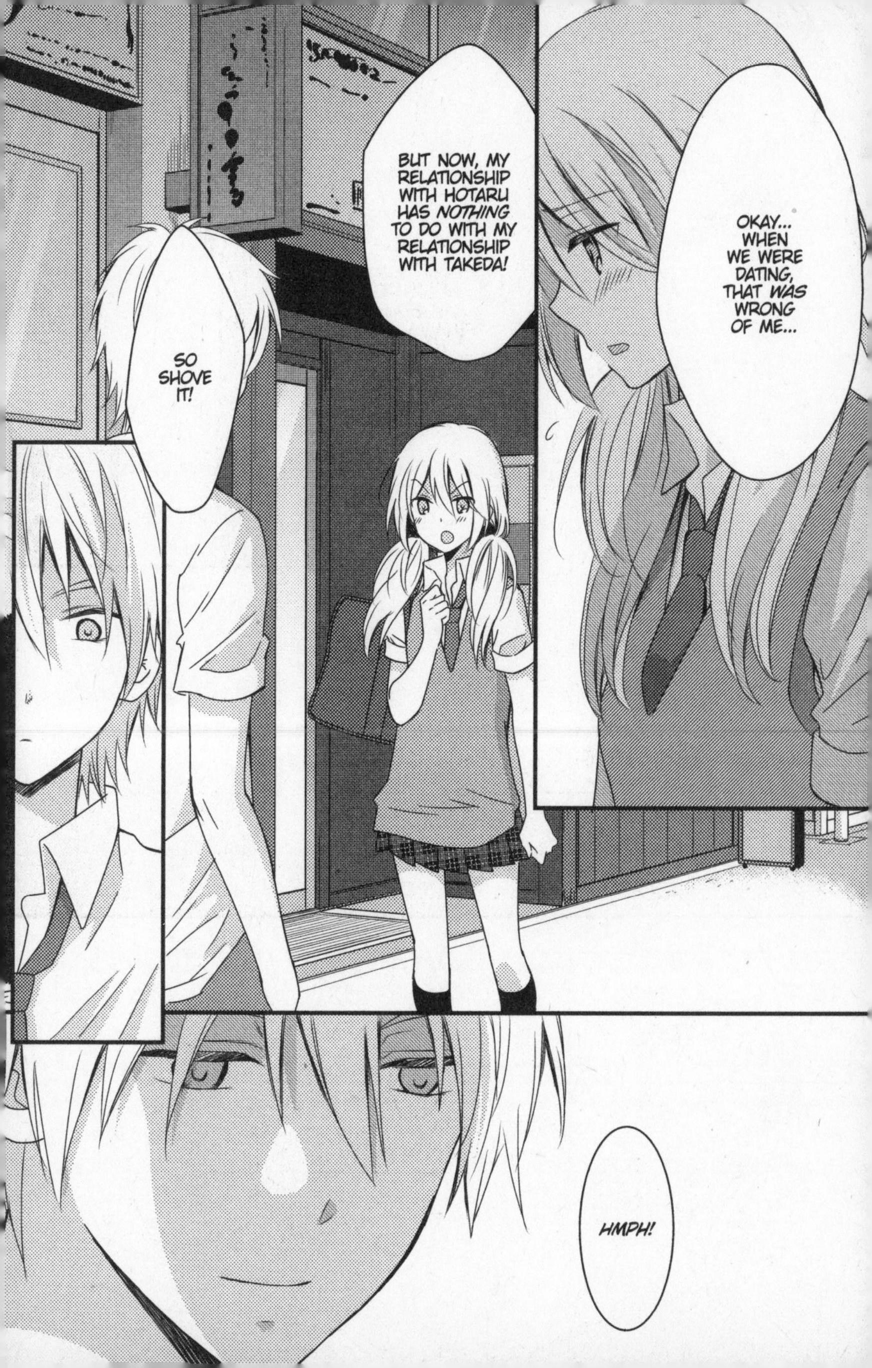
OKAY... WHEN WE WERE DATING, THAT *WAS* WRONG OF ME...
BUT NOW, MY RELATIONSHIP WITH HOTARU HAS *NOTHING* TO DO WITH MY RELATIONSHIP WITH TAKEDA!
SO SHOVE IT!
HMPH!

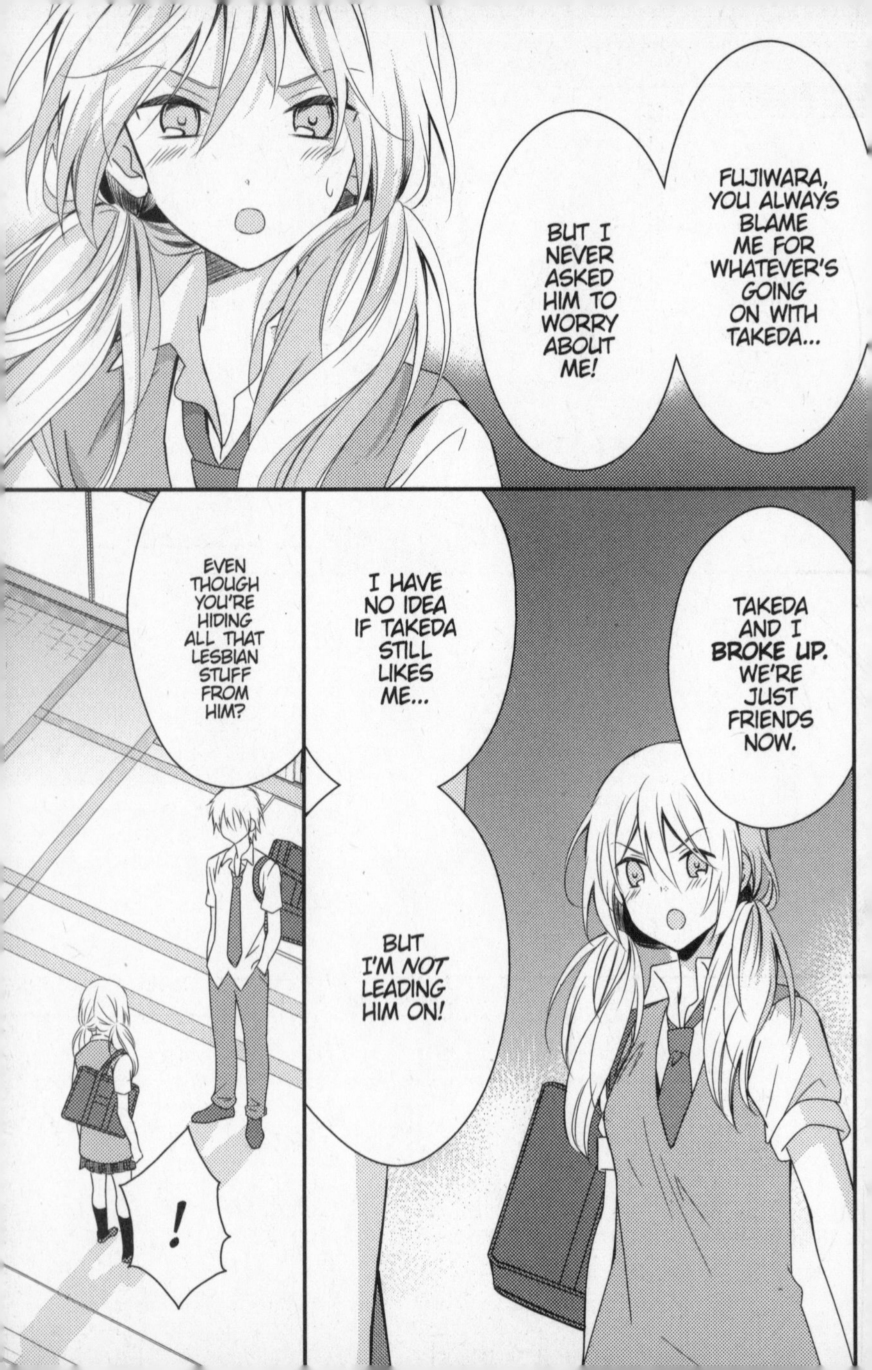
FUJIWARA, YOU ALWAYS BLAME ME FOR WHATEVER'S GOING ON WITH TAKEDA...
BUT I NEVER ASKED HIM TO WORRY ABOUT ME!
TAKEDA AND I BROKE UP. WE'RE JUST FRIENDS NOW.
I HAVE NO IDEA IF TAKEDA STILL LIKES ME...
BUT I'M *NOT* LEADING HIM ON!
EVEN THOUGH YOU'RE HIDING ALL THAT LESBIAN STUFF FROM HIM?
!

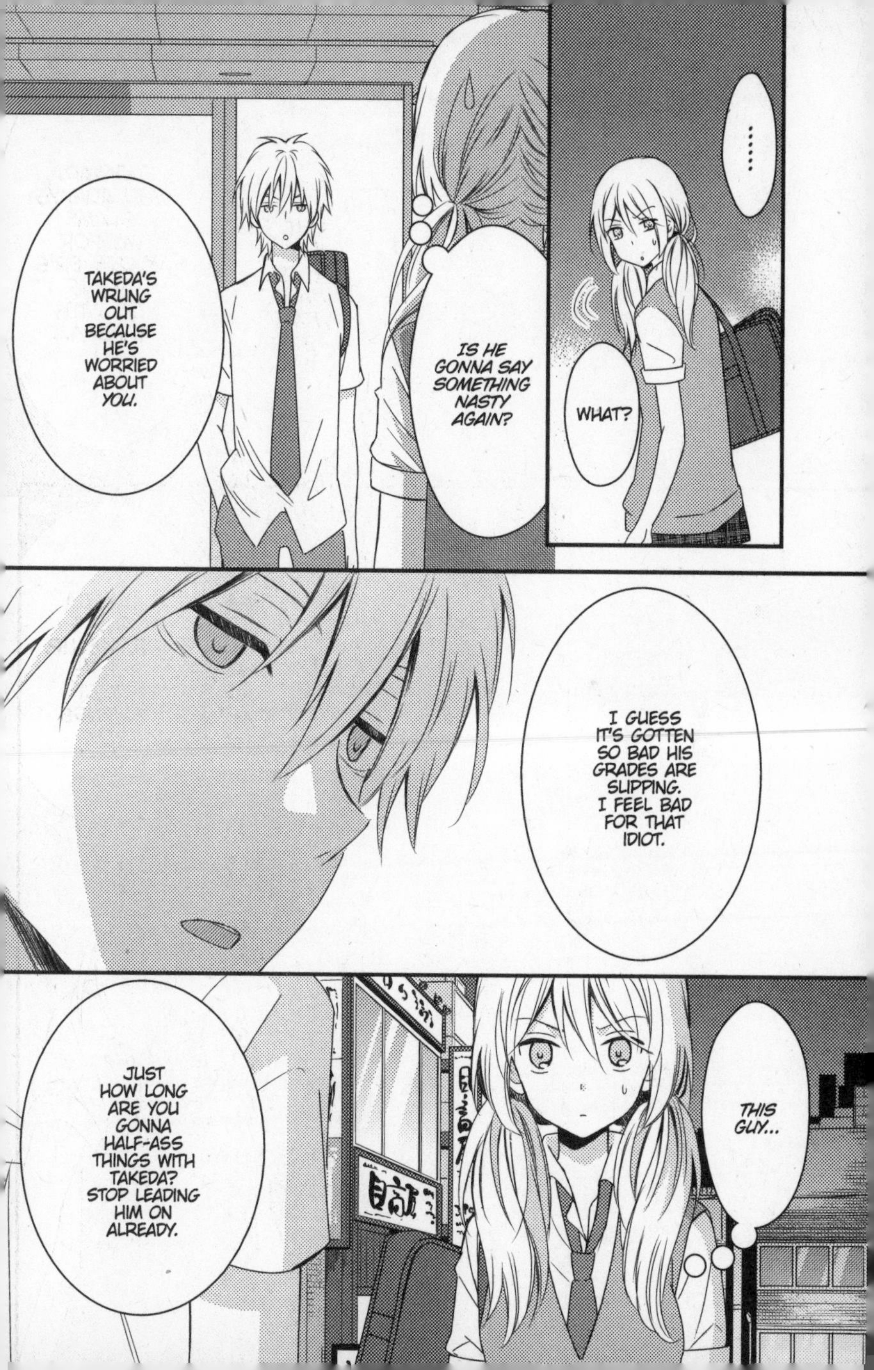
......
WHAT?
IS HE GONNA SAY SOMETHING NASTY AGAIN?
TAKEDA'S WRUNG OUT BECAUSE HE'S WORRIED ABOUT YOU.
I GUESS IT'S GOTTEN SO BAD HIS GRADES ARE SLIPPING. I FEEL BAD FOR THAT IDIOT.
THIS GUY...
JUST HOW LONG ARE YOU GONNA HALF-ASS THINGS WITH TAKEDA? STOP LEADING HIM ON ALREADY.

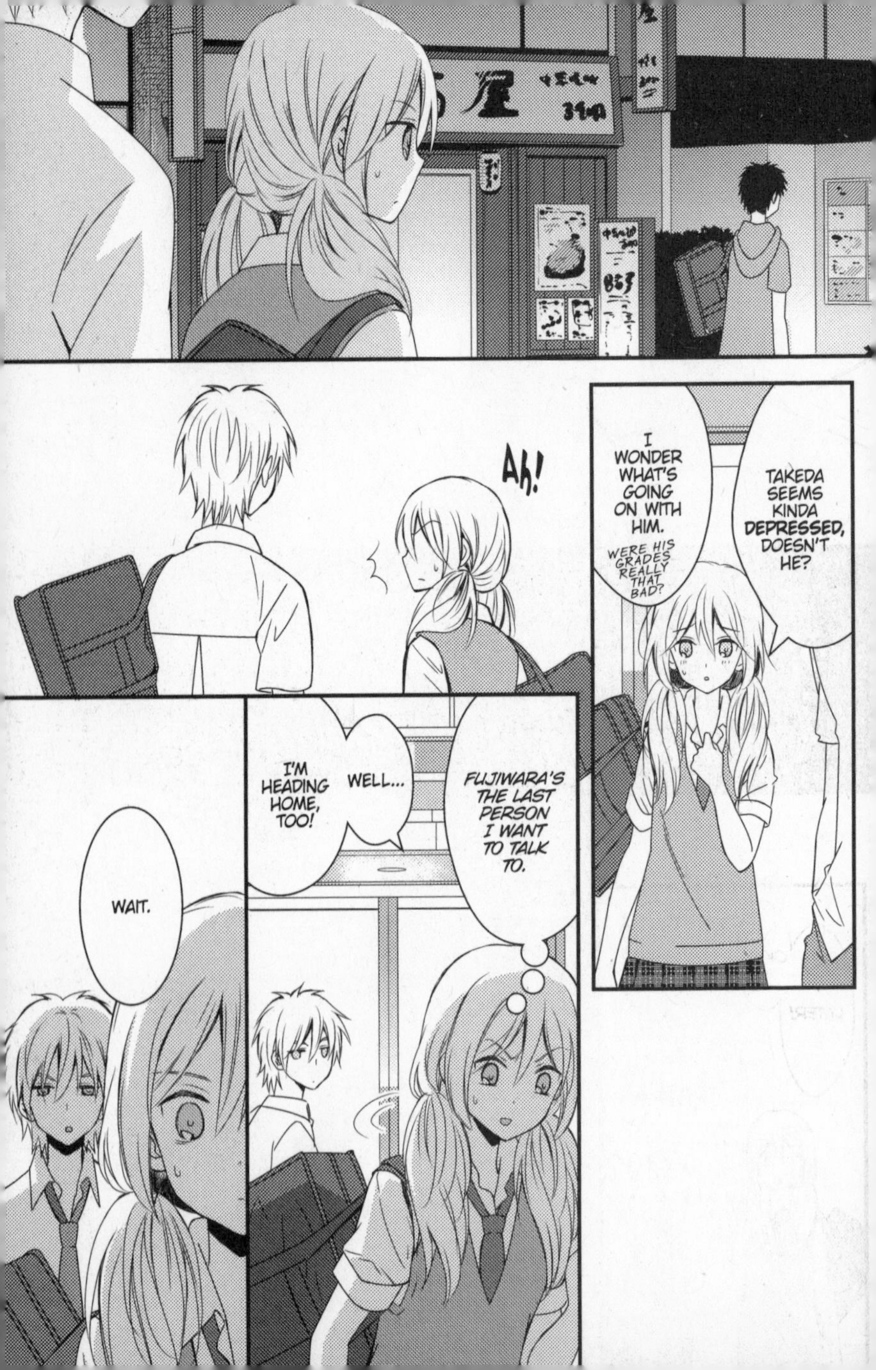
TAKEDA SEEMS KINDA DEPRESSED, DOESN'T HE?
I WONDER WHAT'S GOING ON WITH HIM.
WERE HIS GRADES REALLY THAT BAD?
Ah!
FUJIWARA'S THE LAST PERSON I WANT TO TALK TO.
WELL...
I'M HEADING HOME, TOO!
WAIT.

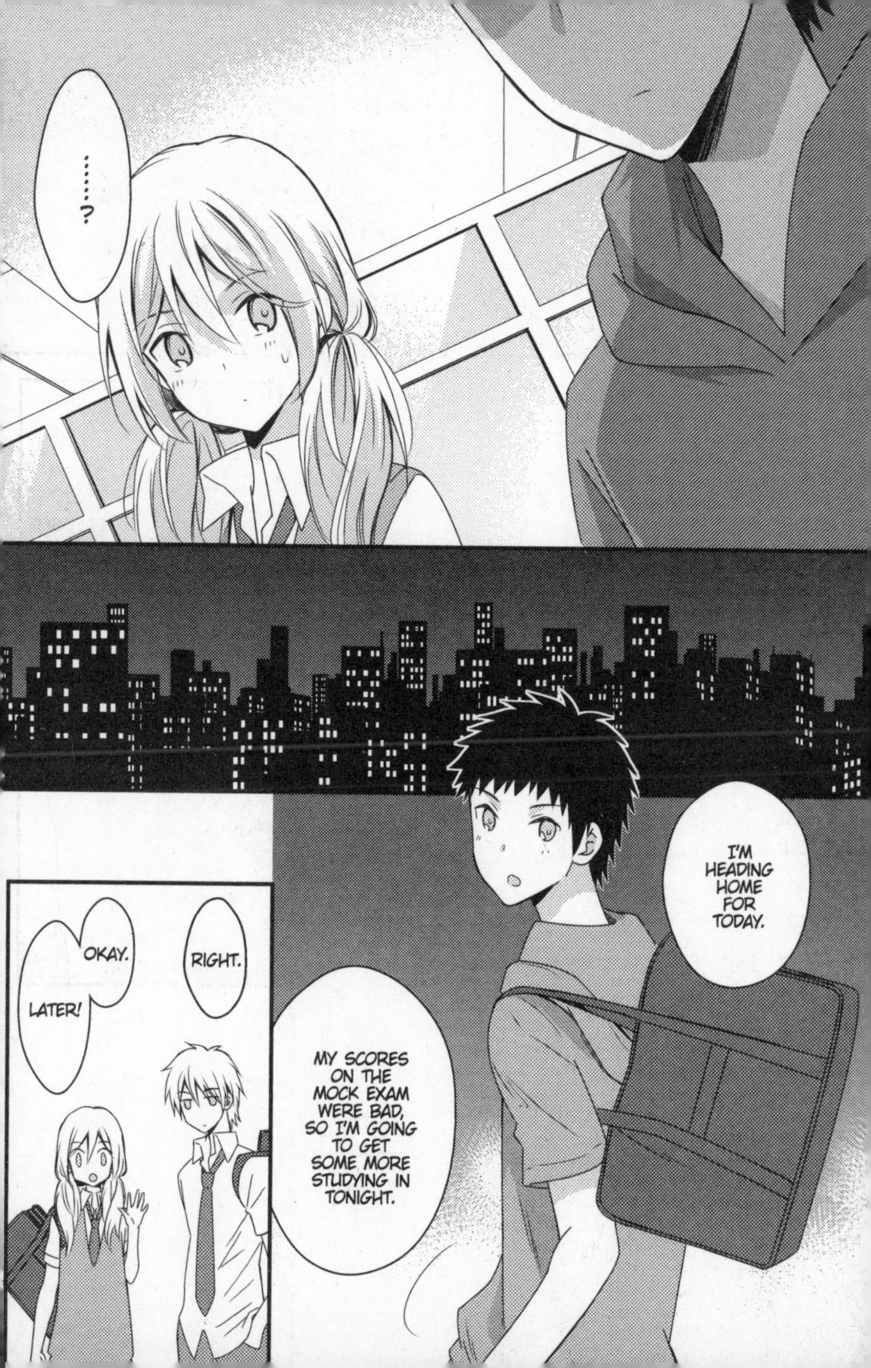
......?
I'M HEADING HOME FOR TODAY.
MY SCORES ON THE MOCK EXAM WERE BAD, SO I'M GOING TO GET SOME MORE STUDYING IN TONIGHT.
RIGHT.
OKAY.
LATER!

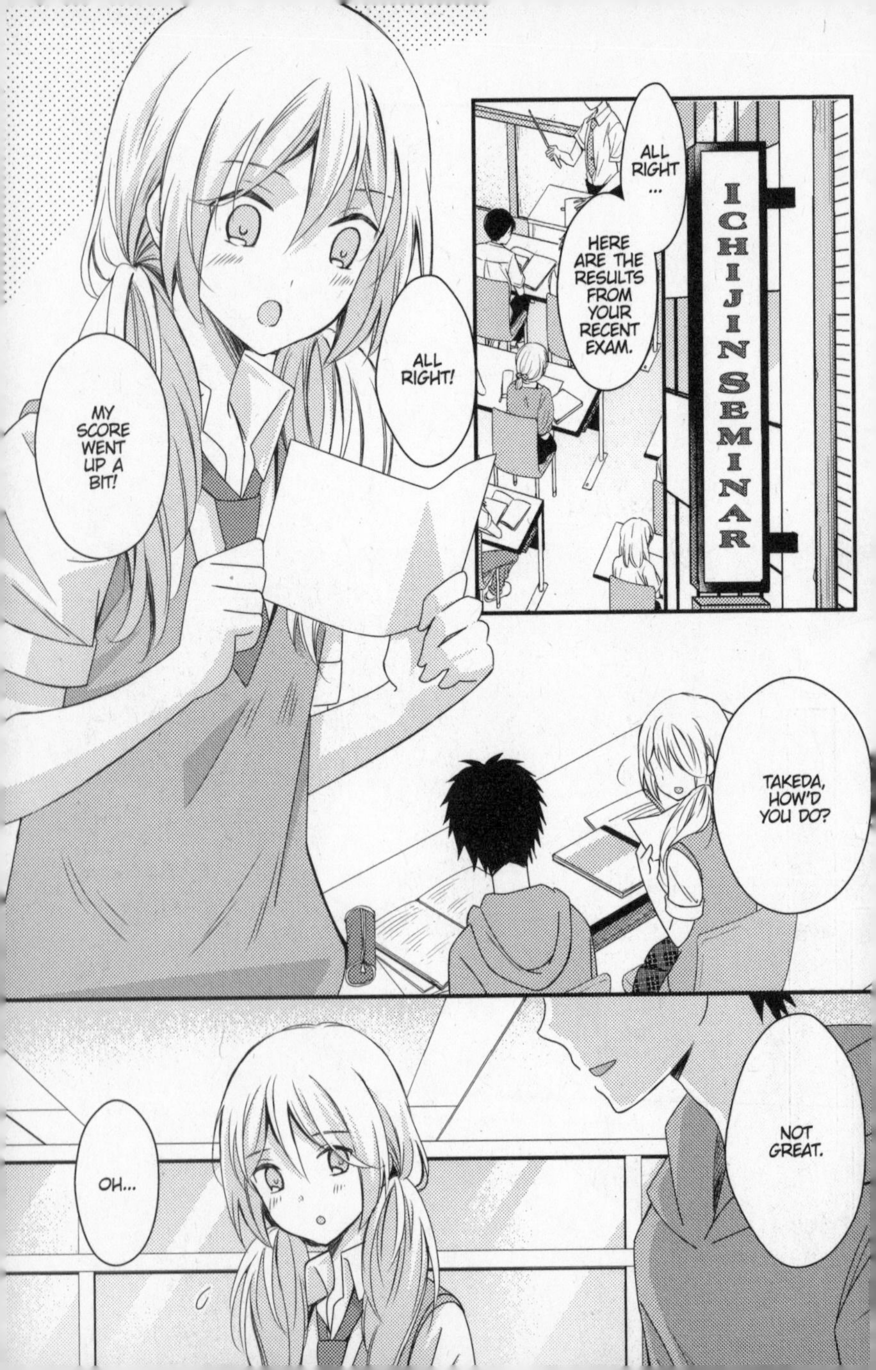
ICHIJIN SEMINAR
ALL RIGHT ...
HERE ARE THE RESULTS FROM YOUR RECENT EXAM.
ALL RIGHT!
MY SCORE WENT UP A BIT!
TAKEDA, HOW'D YOU DO?
NOT GREAT.
OH...

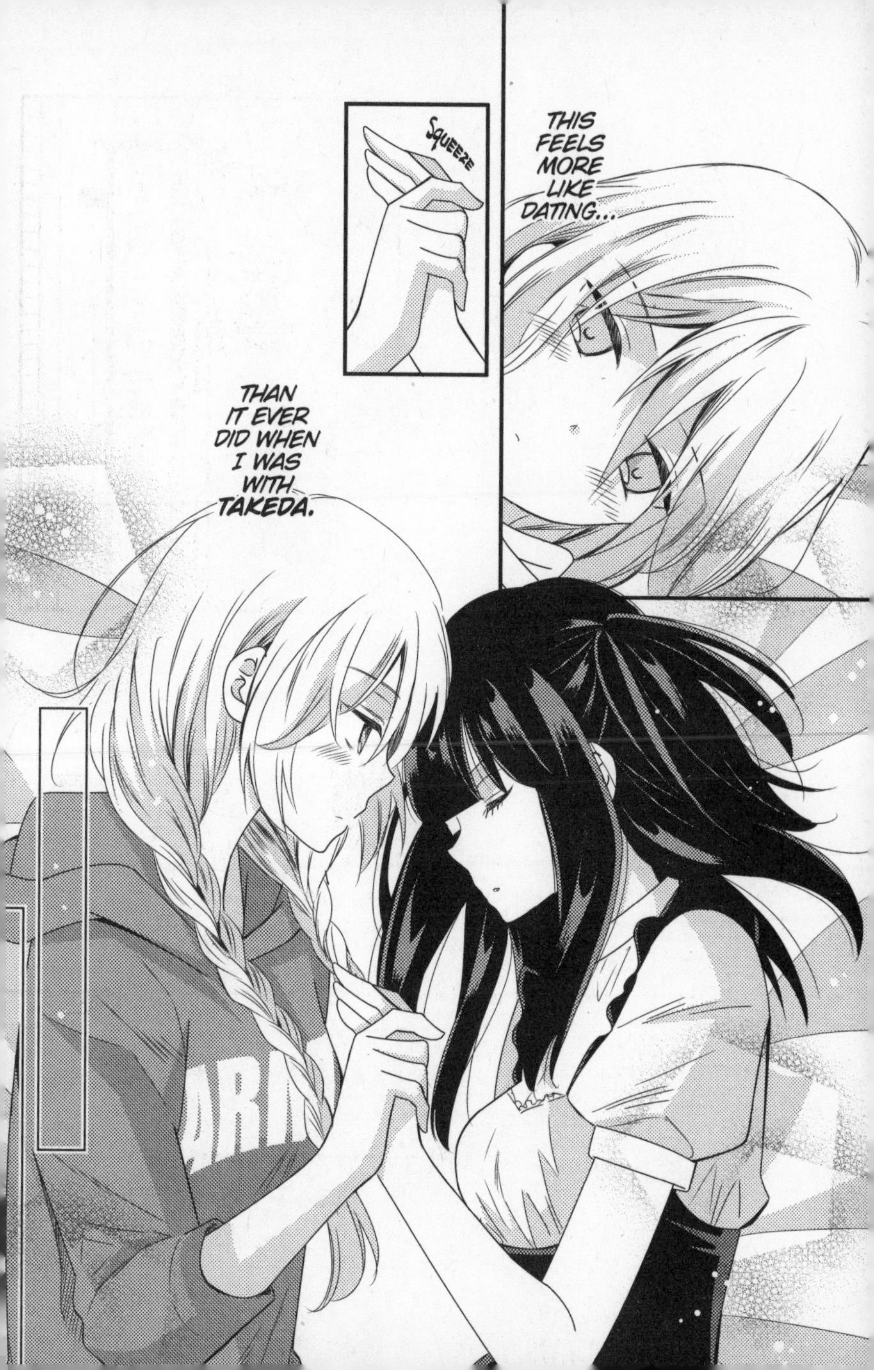
THIS FEELS MORE LIKE DATING...
Squeeze
THAN IT EVER DID WHEN I WAS WITH TAKEDA.

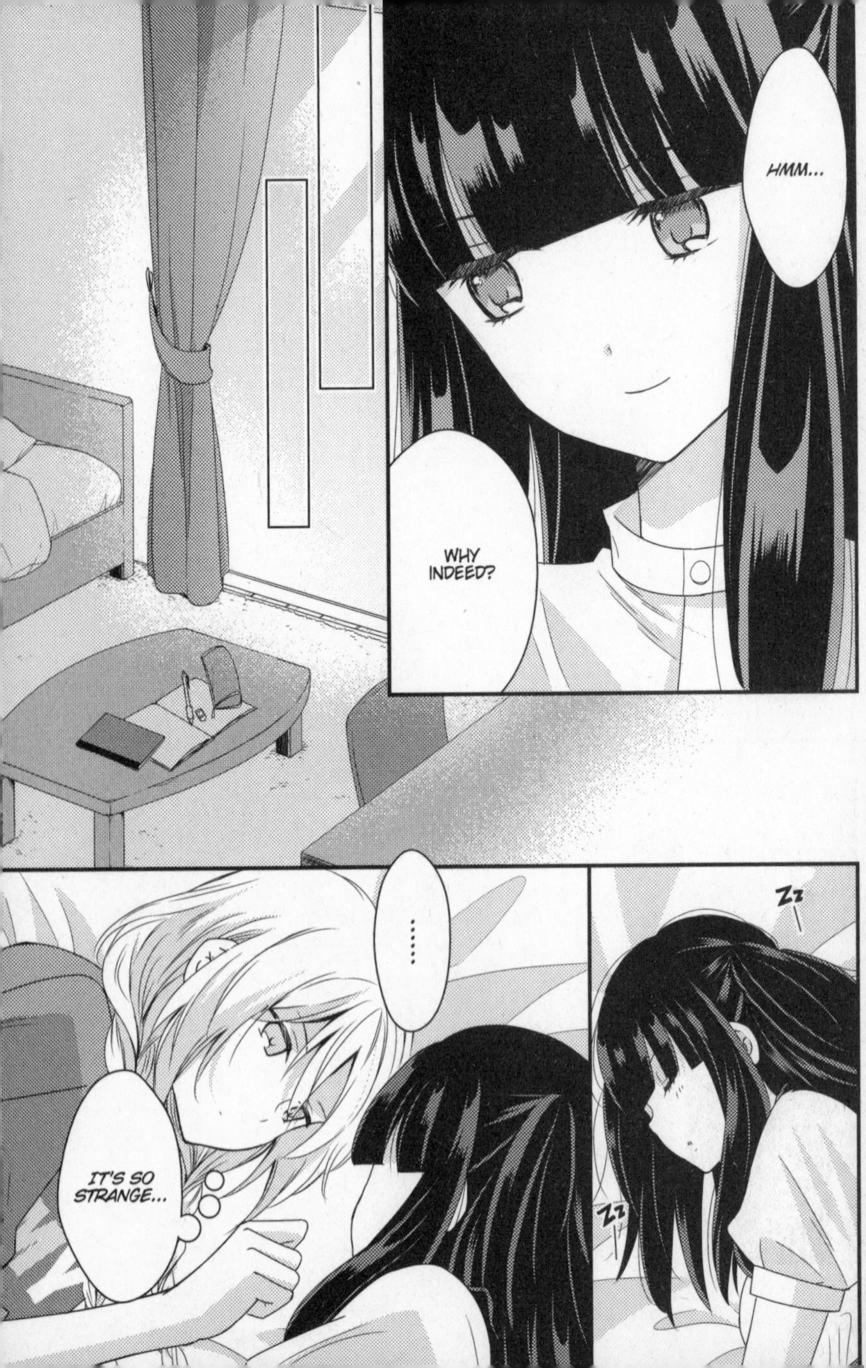
HMM...
WHY INDEED?
ZZ
ZZ
......
IT'S SO STRANGE...

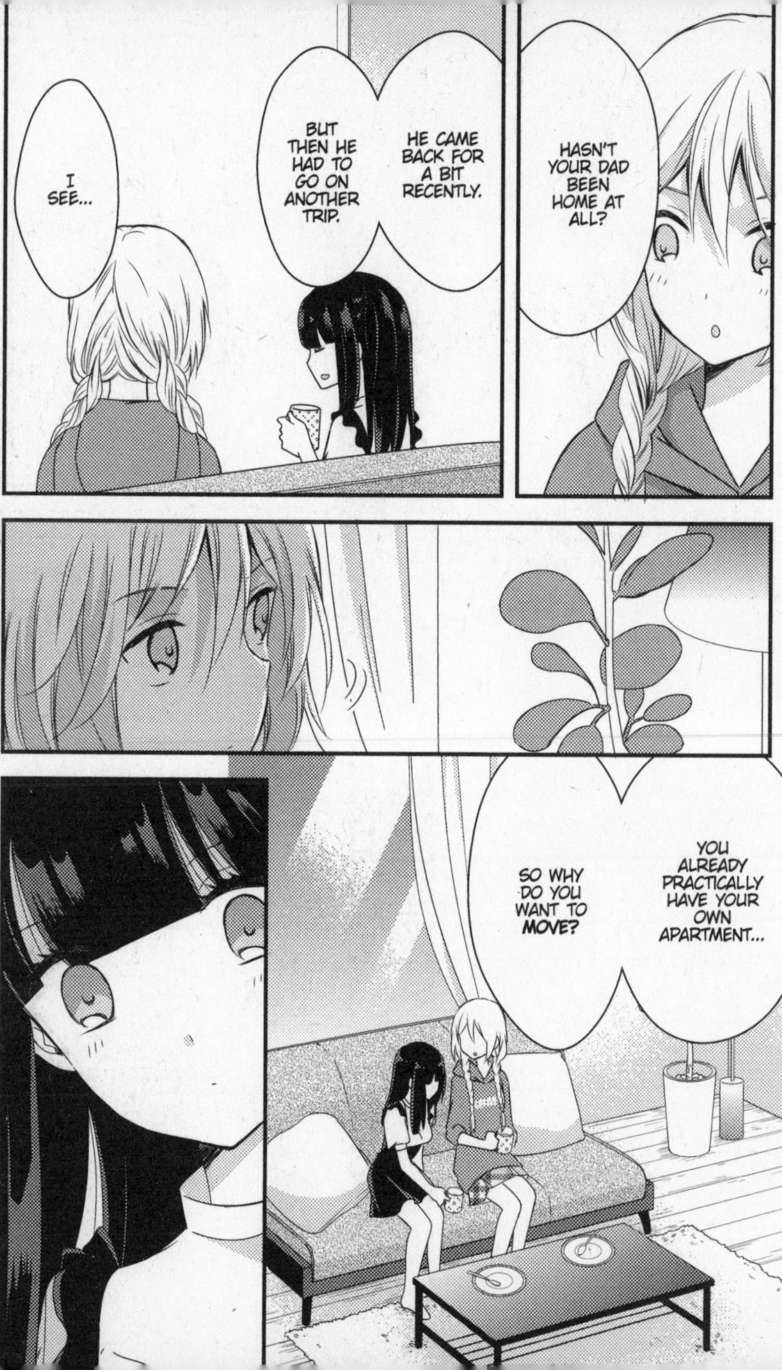
HASN'T YOUR DAD BEEN HOME AT ALL?
HE CAME BACK FOR A BIT RECENTLY.
BUT THEN HE HAD TO GO ON ANOTHER TRIP.
I SEE...
YOU ALREADY PRACTICALLY HAVE YOUR OWN APARTMENT...
SO WHY DO YOU WANT TO **MOVE?**

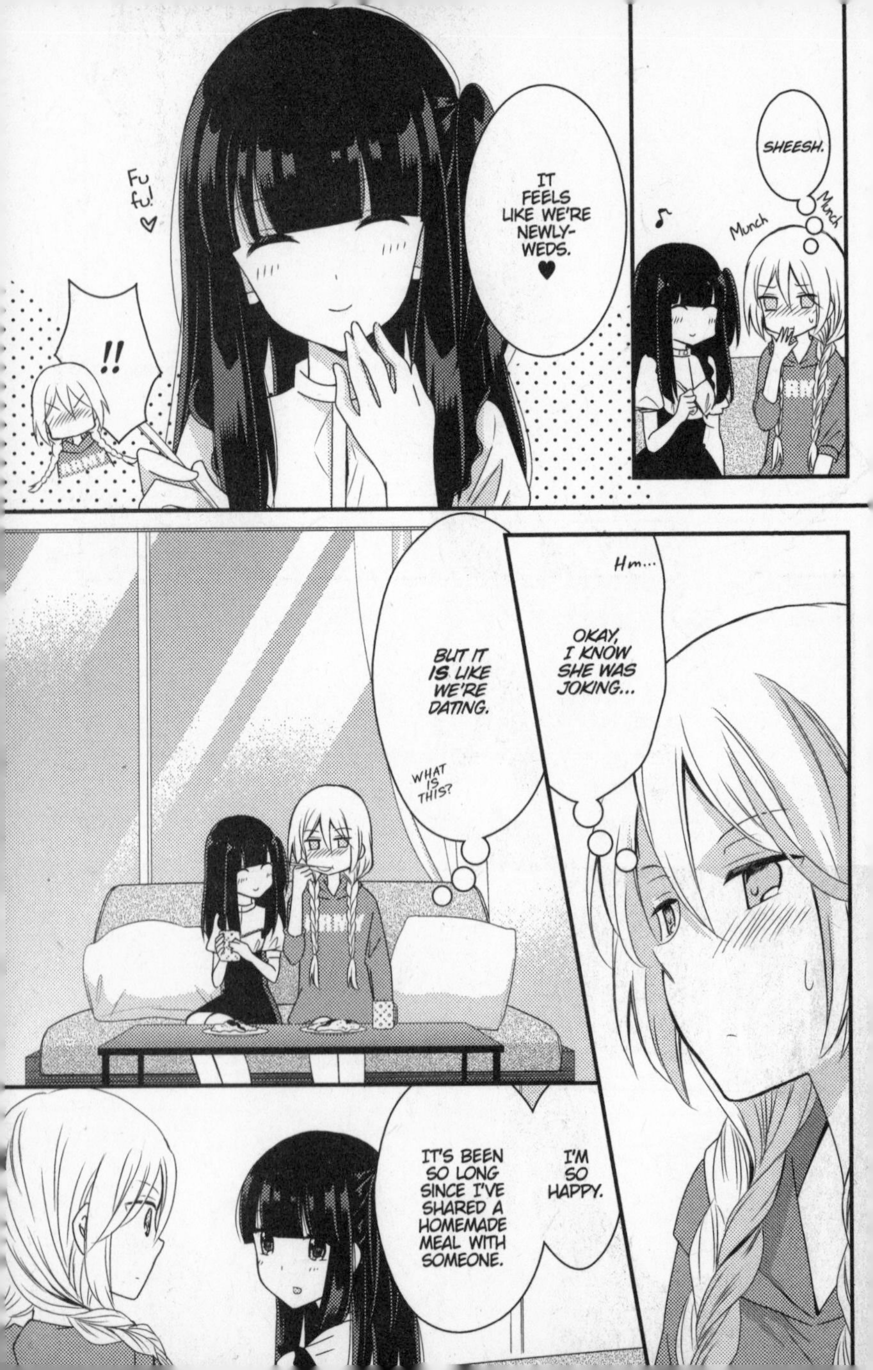
SHEESH.
Munch
Munch
♪
IT FEELS LIKE WE'RE NEWLY-WEDS. ♥
Fu fu! ♥
!!
Hm...
OKAY, I KNOW SHE WAS JOKING...
BUT IT IS LIKE WE'RE DATING.
WHAT IS THIS?
I'M SO HAPPY.
IT'S BEEN SO LONG SINCE I'VE SHARED A HOMEMADE MEAL WITH SOMEONE.

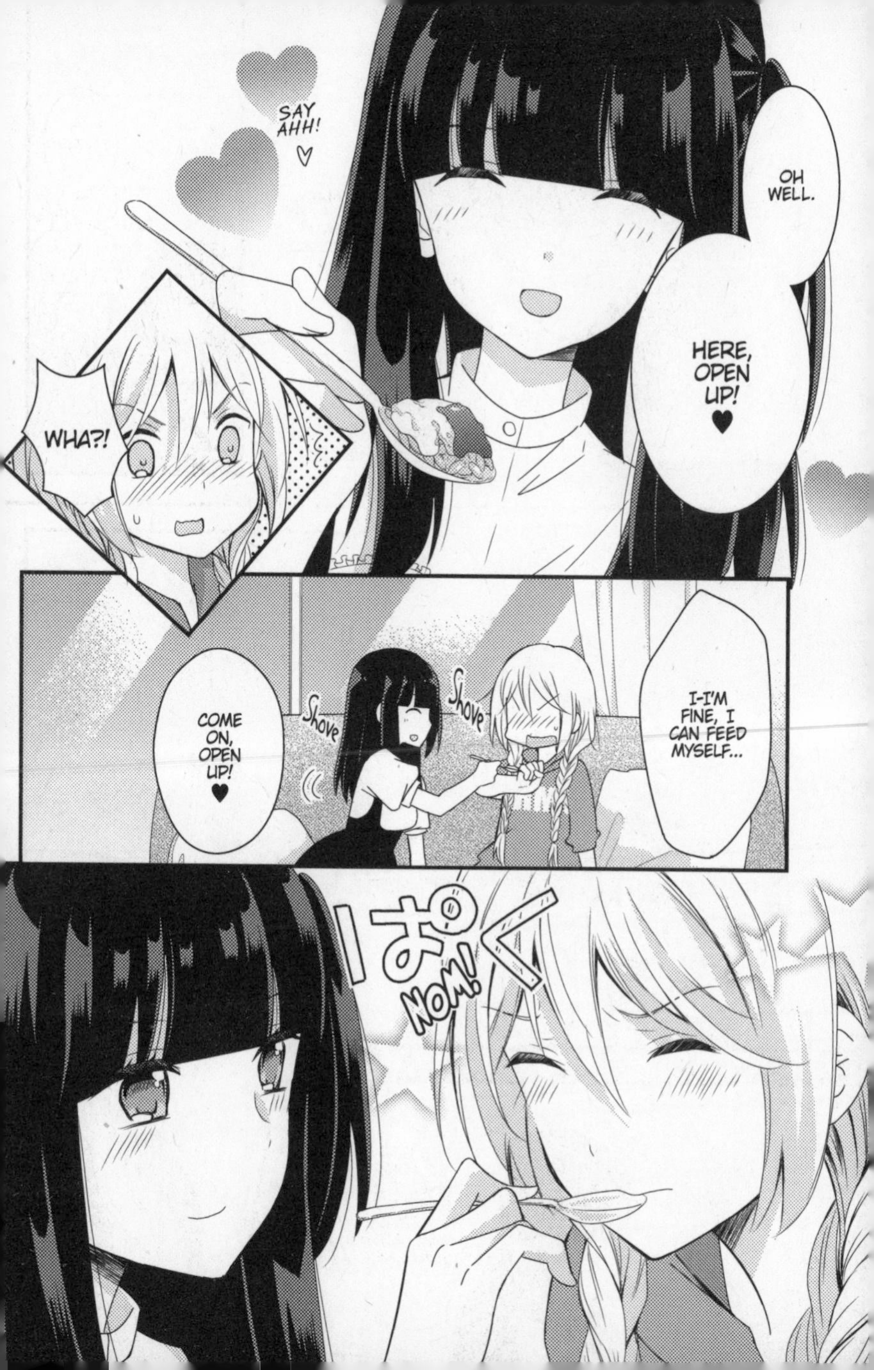
OH WELL.
HERE, OPEN UP! ♥
SAY AHH! ♡
WHA?!
I-I'M FINE, I CAN FEED MYSELF...
Shove
Shove
COME ON, OPEN UP! ♥
ぱく
NOM!

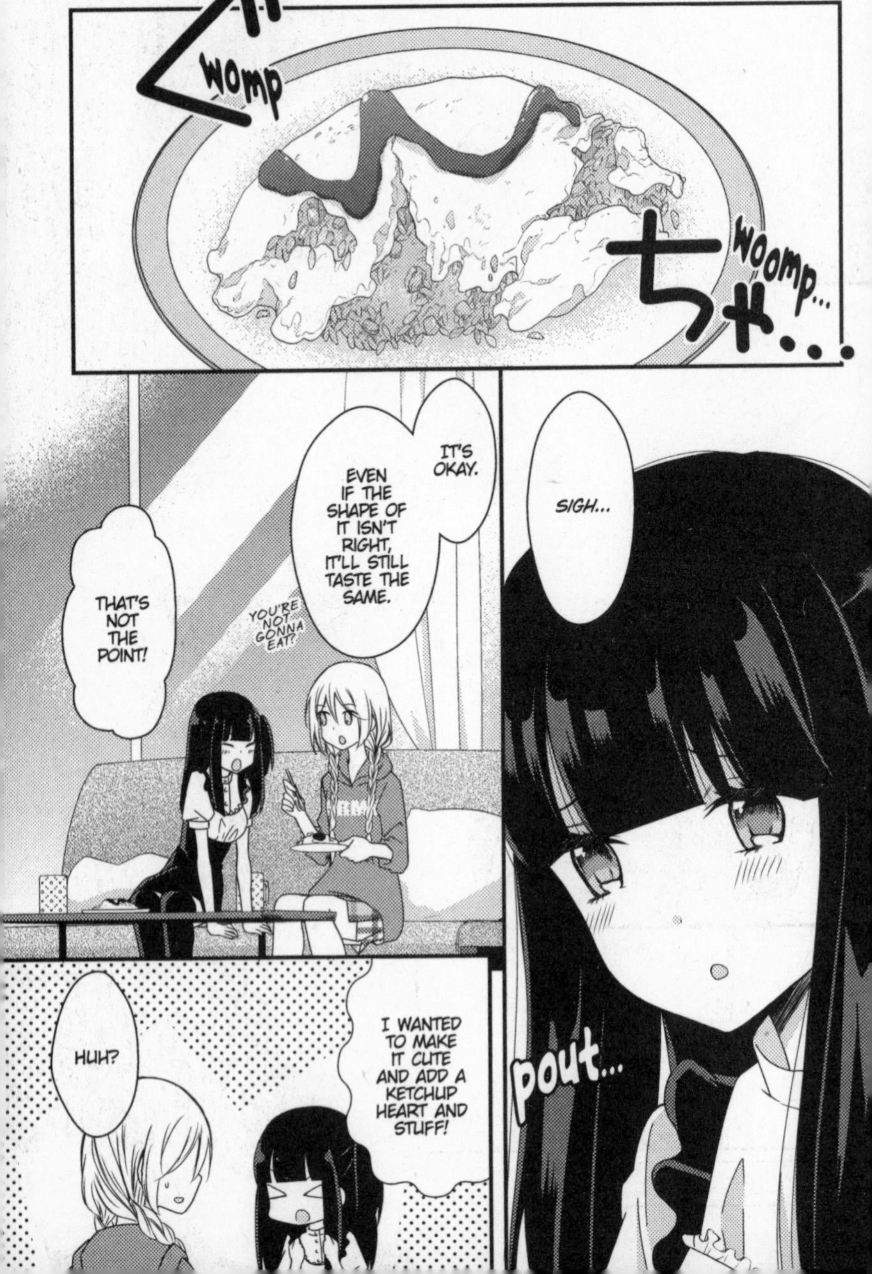
woomp...
womp
SIGH...
pout...
IT'S OKAY.
EVEN IF THE SHAPE OF IT ISN'T RIGHT, IT'LL STILL TASTE THE SAME.
YOU'RE NOT GONNA EAT?
THAT'S NOT THE POINT!
I WANTED TO MAKE IT CUTE AND ADD A KETCHUP HEART AND STUFF!
HUH?

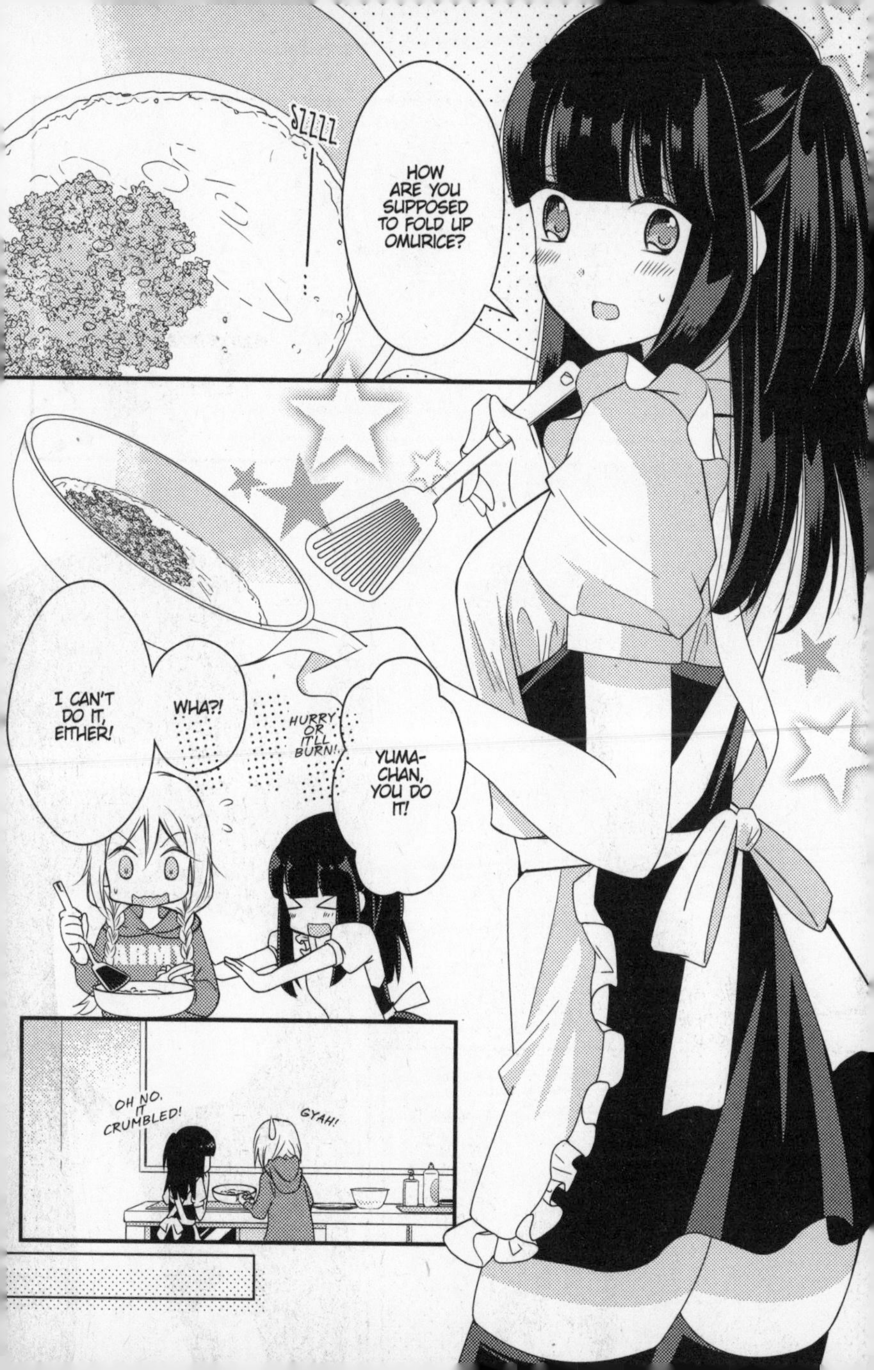
HOW ARE YOU SUPPOSED TO FOLD UP OMURICE?
SZZZZ
YUMA-CHAN, YOU DO IT!
HURRY OR IT'LL BURN!
WHA?!
I CAN'T DO IT, EITHER!
GYAH!
OH NO, IT CRUMBLED!

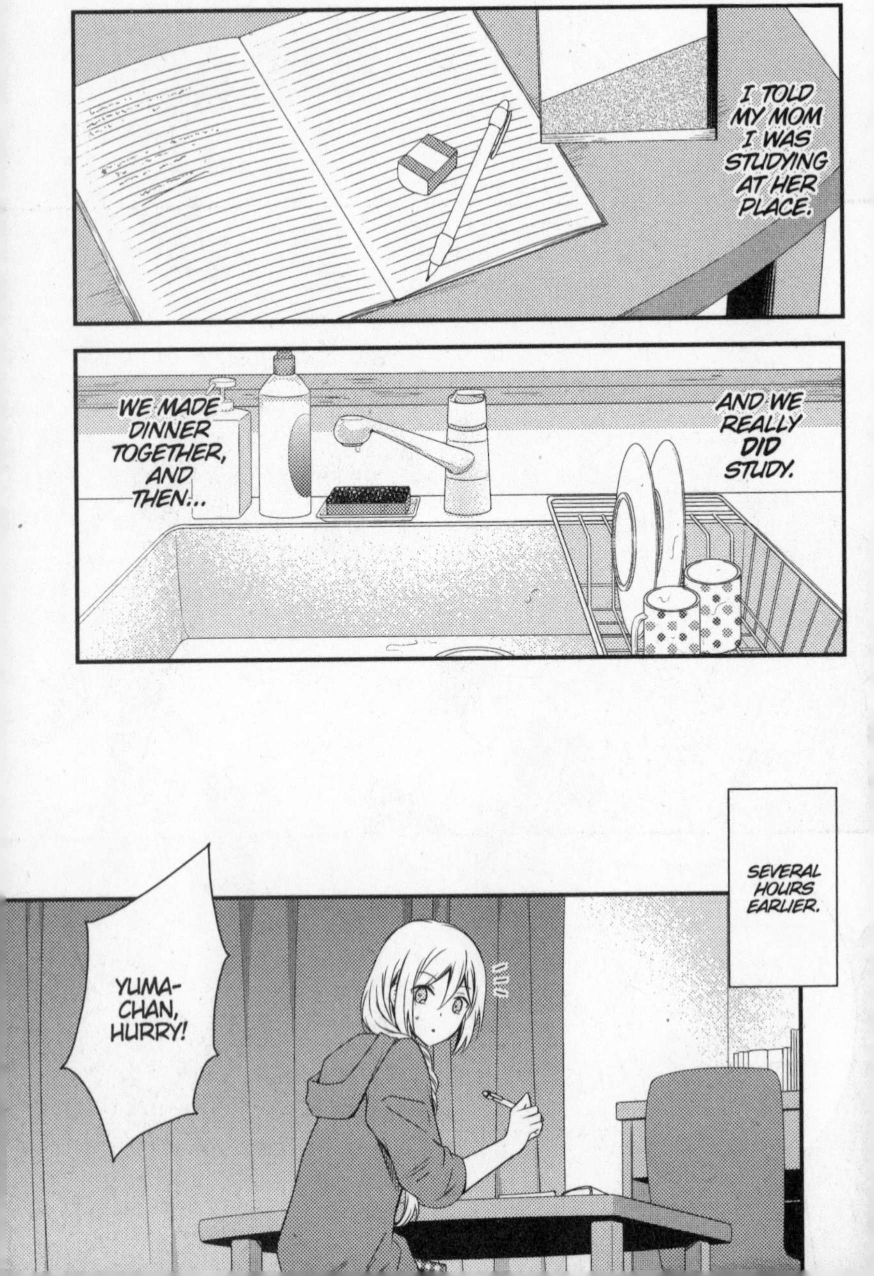
I TOLD MY MOM I WAS STUDYING AT HER PLACE.
AND WE REALLY DID STUDY.
WE MADE DINNER TOGETHER, AND THEN...
SEVERAL HOURS EARLIER.
YUMA-CHAN, HURRY!

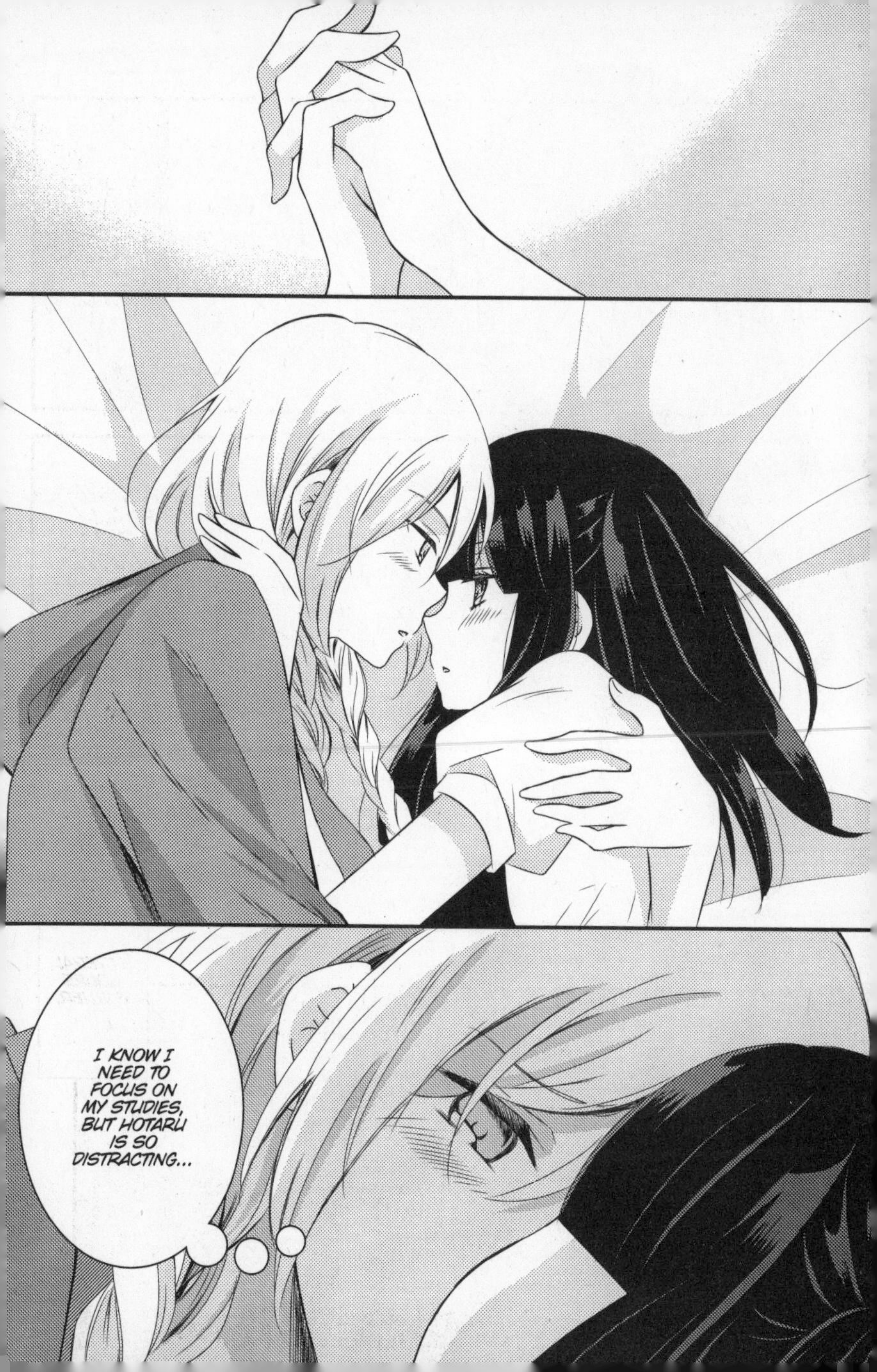
I KNOW I NEED TO FOCUS ON MY STUDIES, BUT HOTARU IS SO DISTRACTING...

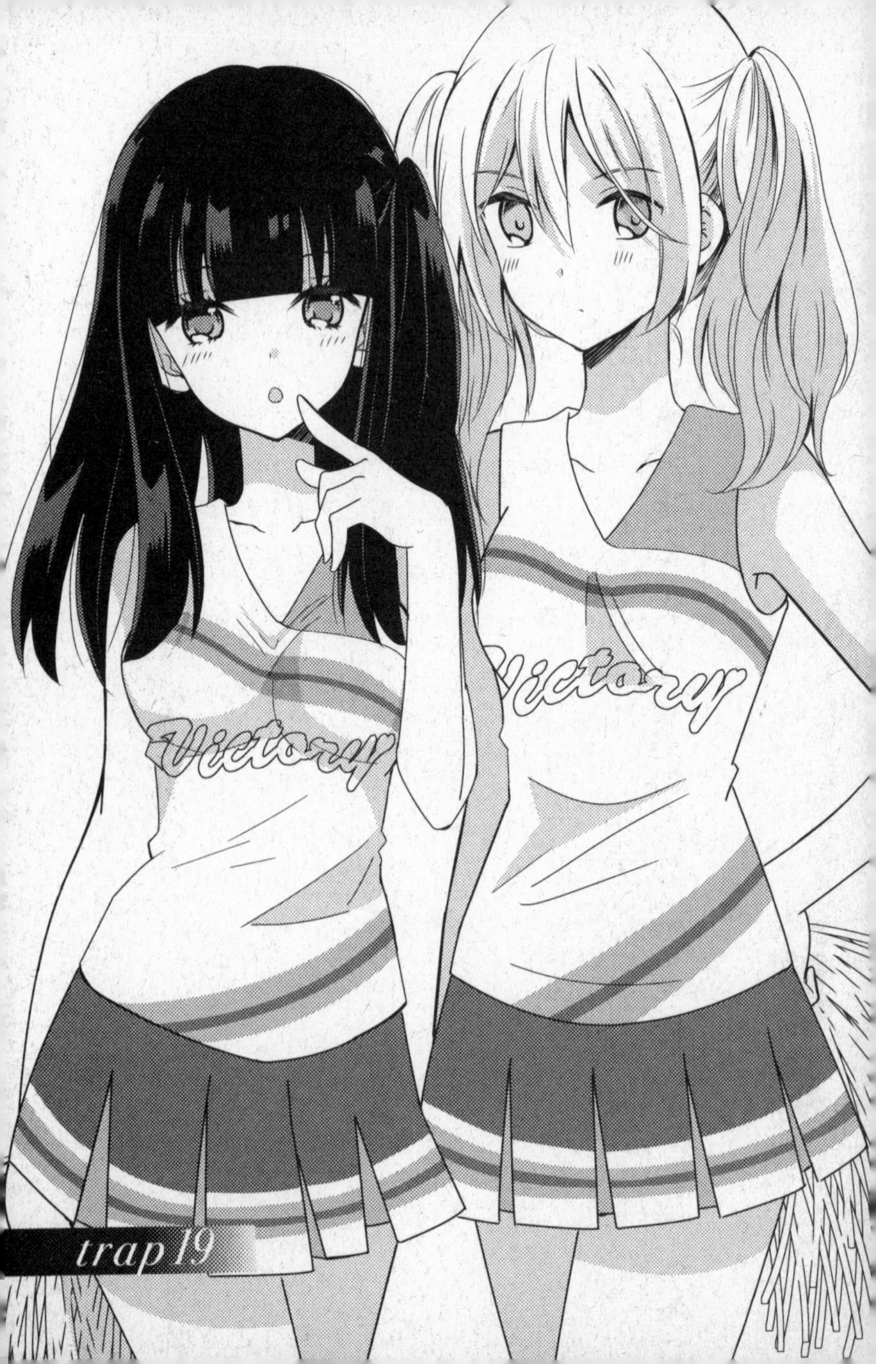
Victory
Victory
trap 19

Netsuzou TRap -NTR-

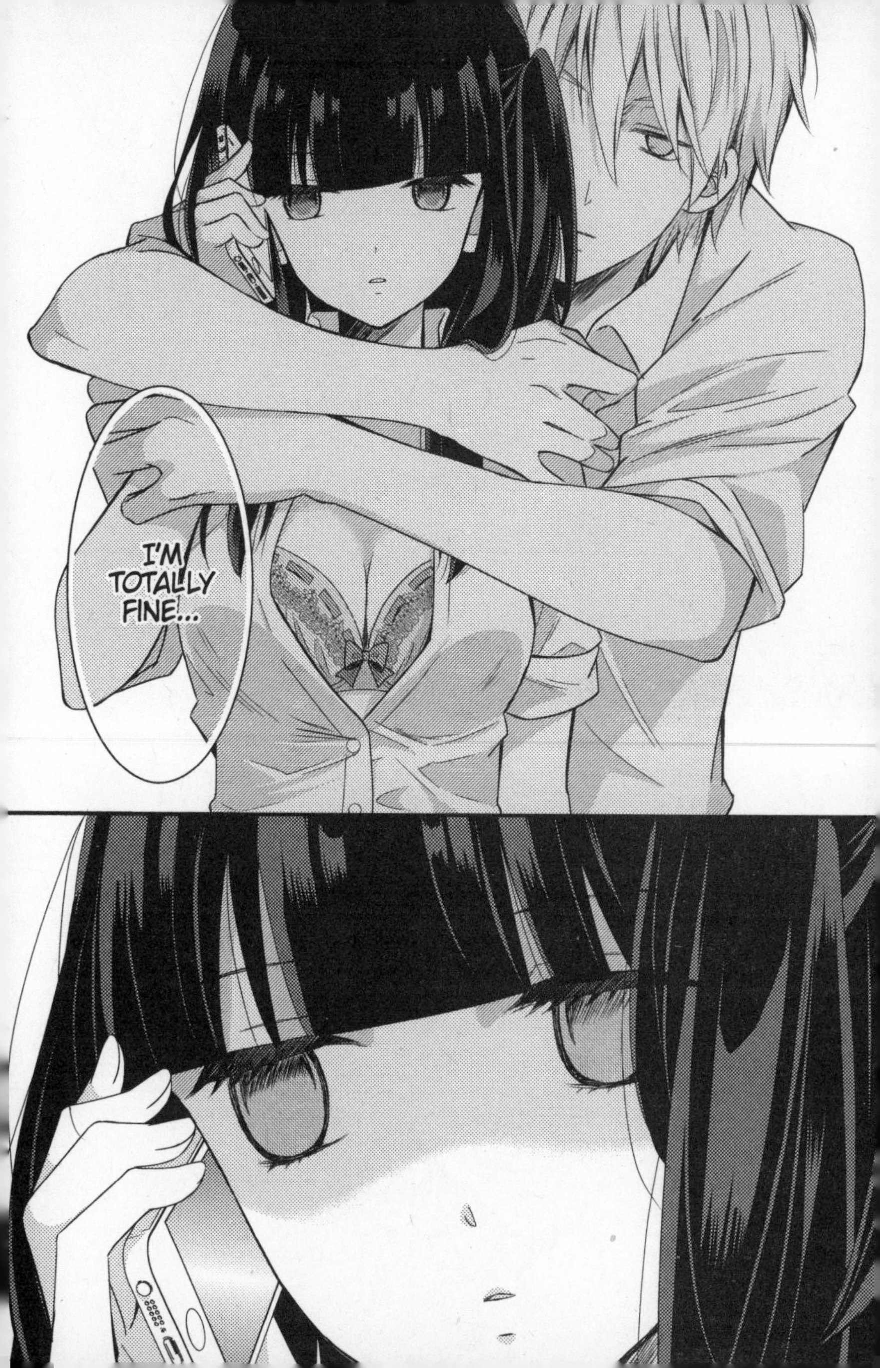
I'M TOTALLY FINE...

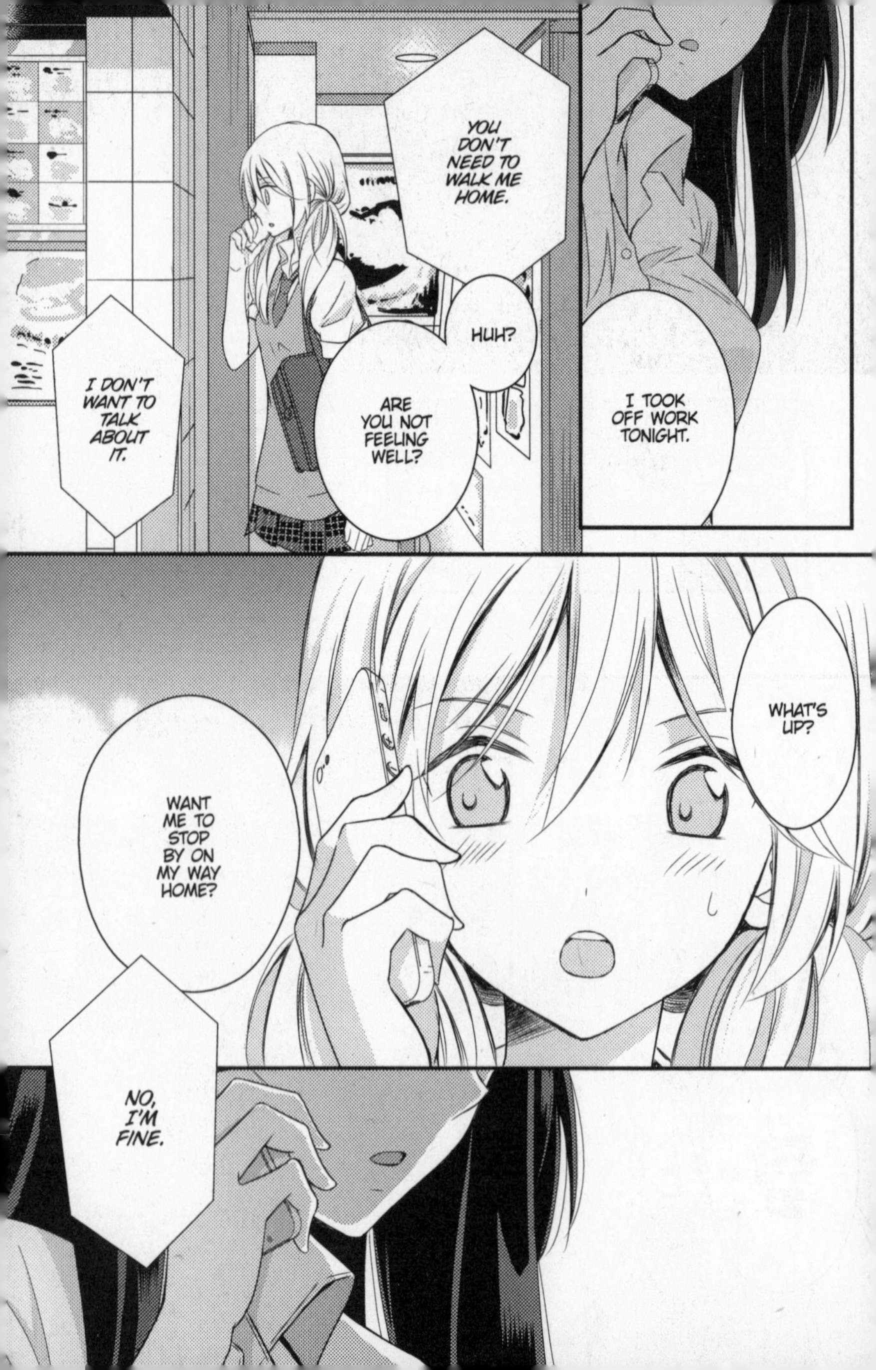
I TOOK OFF WORK TONIGHT.
YOU DON'T NEED TO WALK ME HOME.
HUH?
ARE YOU NOT FEELING WELL?
I DON'T WANT TO TALK ABOUT IT.
WHAT'S UP?
WANT ME TO STOP BY ON MY WAY HOME?
NO, I'M FINE.

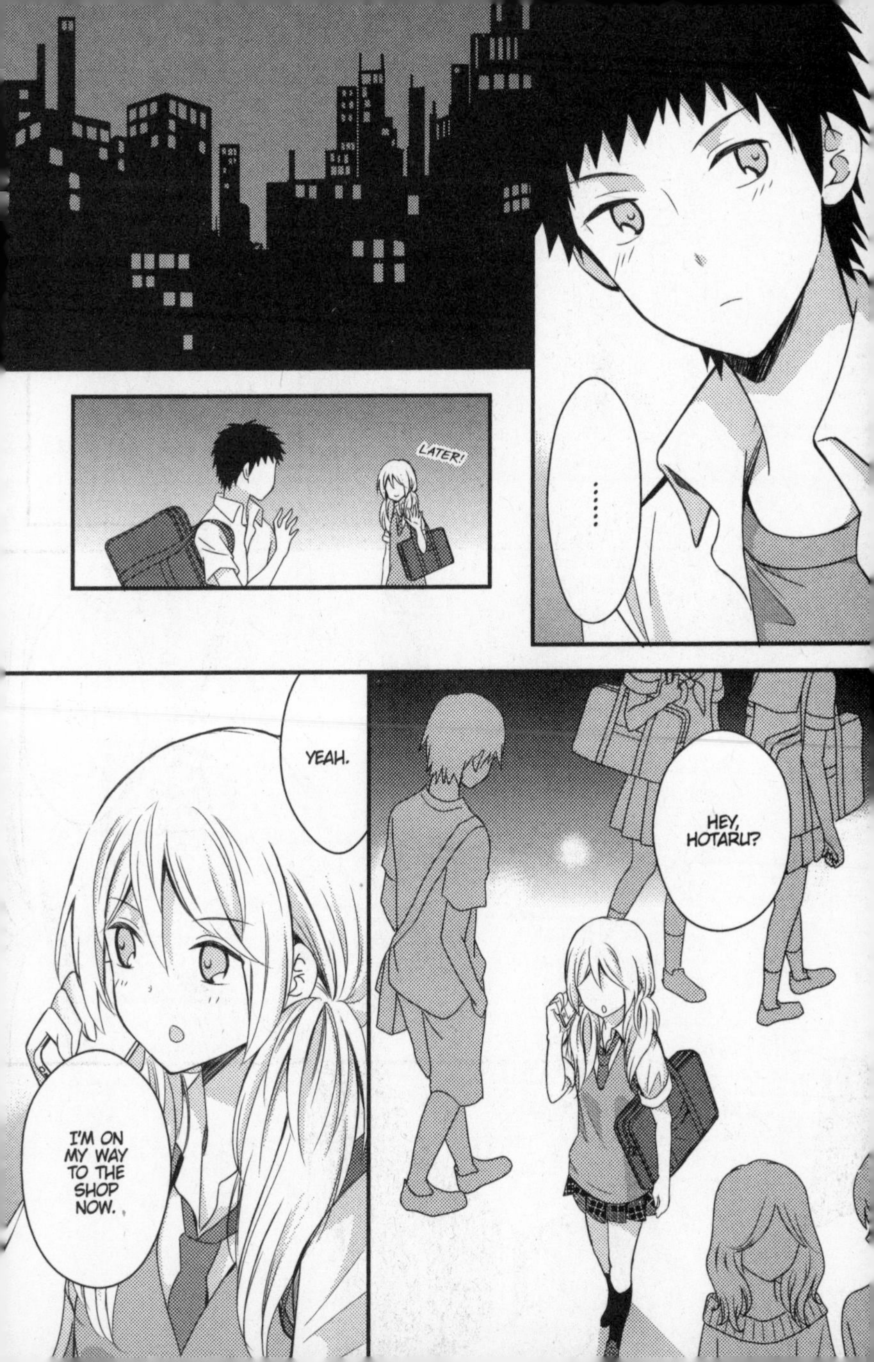
......
LATER!
HEY, HOTARU?
YEAH.
I'M ON MY WAY TO THE SHOP NOW.

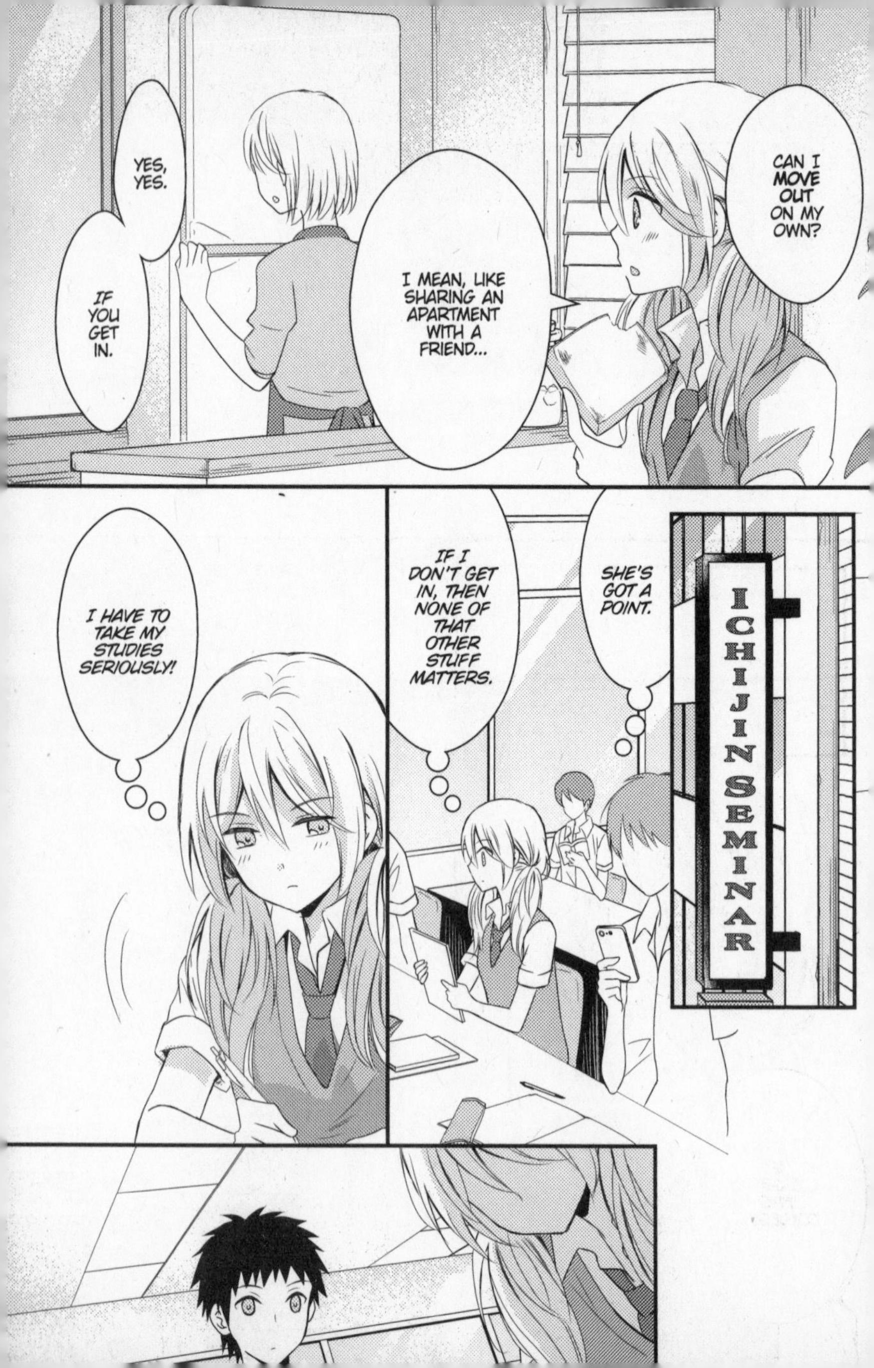
CAN I MOVE OUT ON MY OWN?
I MEAN, LIKE SHARING AN APARTMENT WITH A FRIEND...
YES, YES.
IF YOU GET IN.
ICHIJIN SEMINAR
SHE'S GOT A POINT.
IF I DON'T GET IN, THEN NONE OF THAT OTHER STUFF MATTERS.
I HAVE TO TAKE MY STUDIES SERIOUSLY!

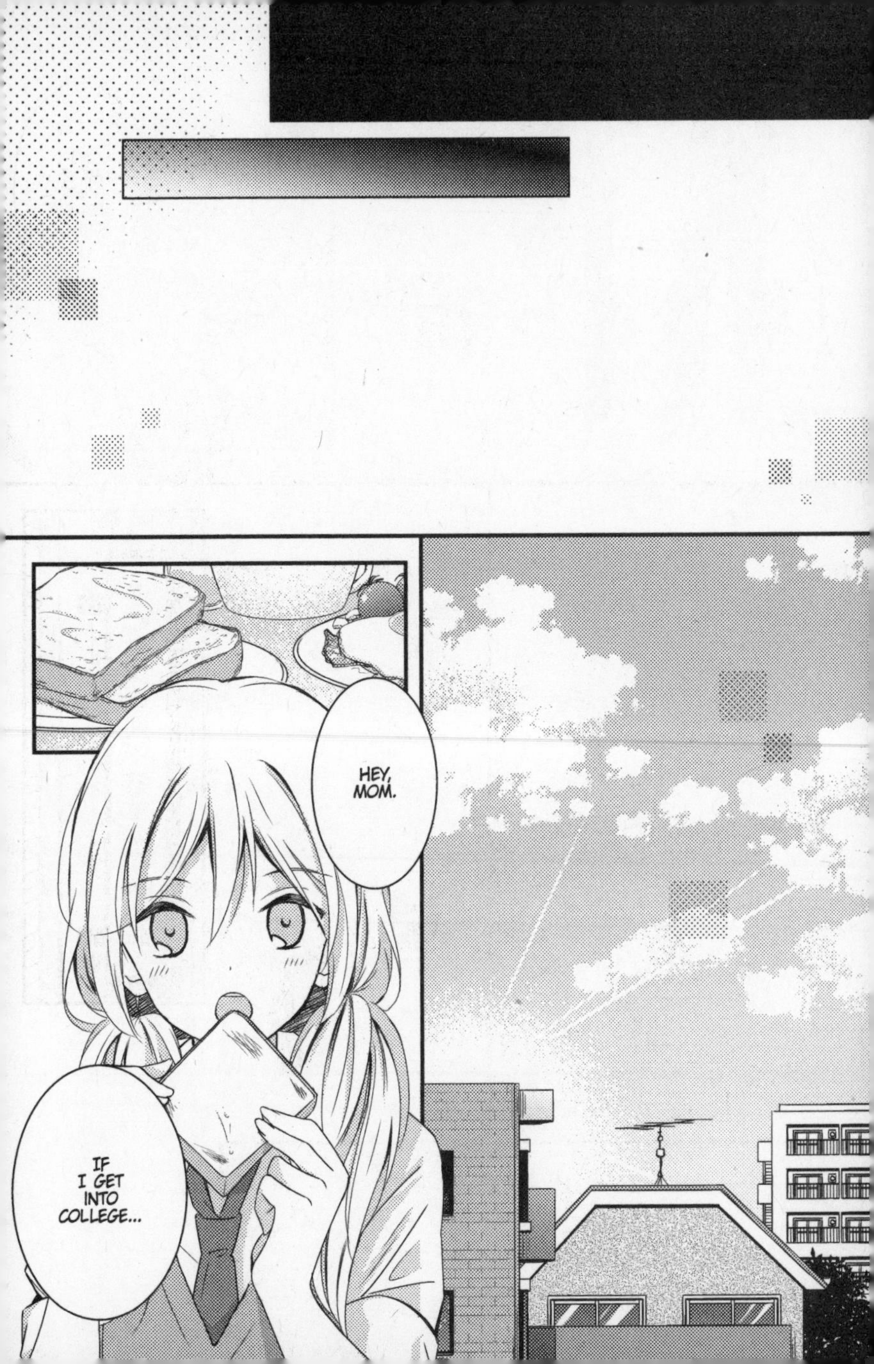
HEY, MOM.
IF I GET INTO COLLEGE...

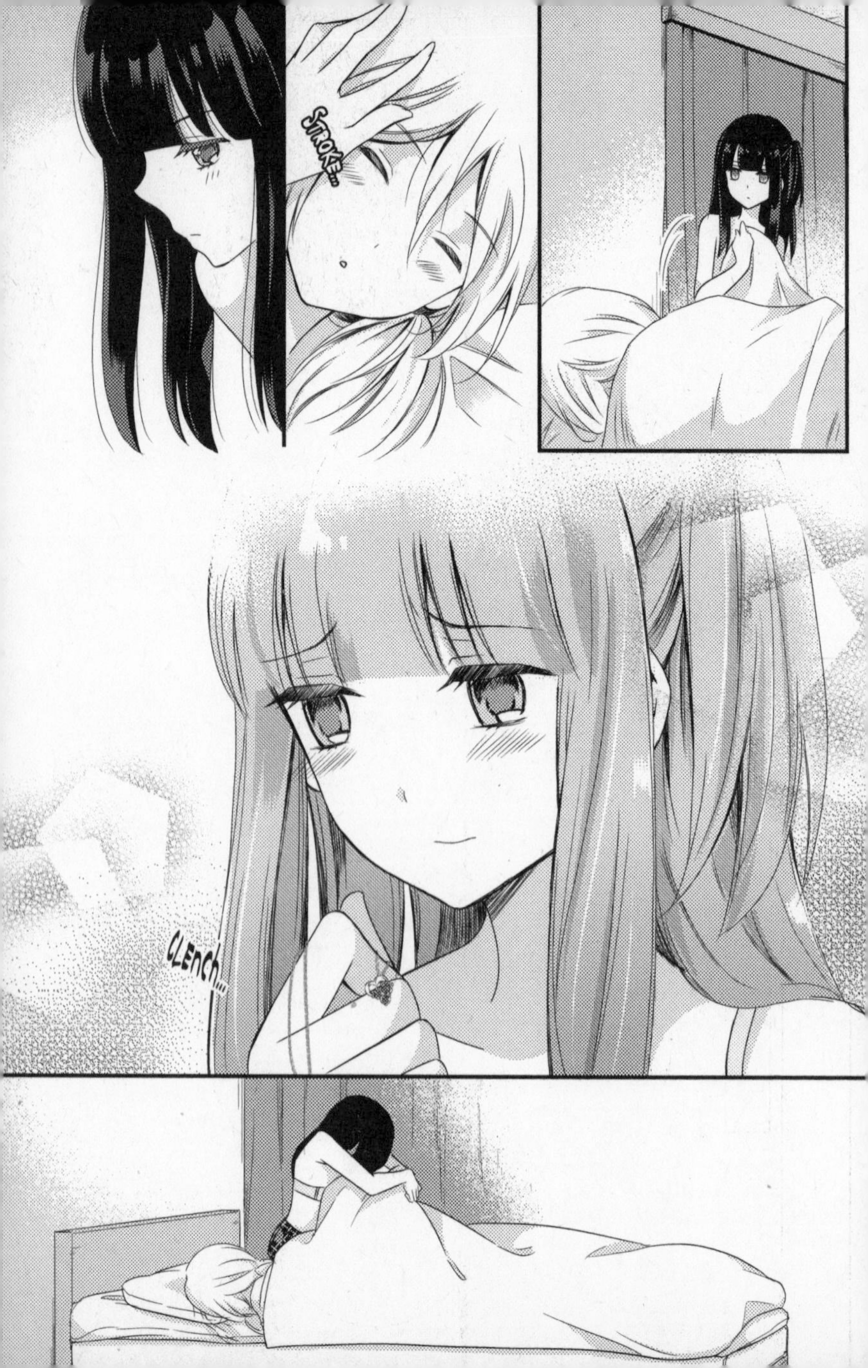
STROKE...
CLENCH...

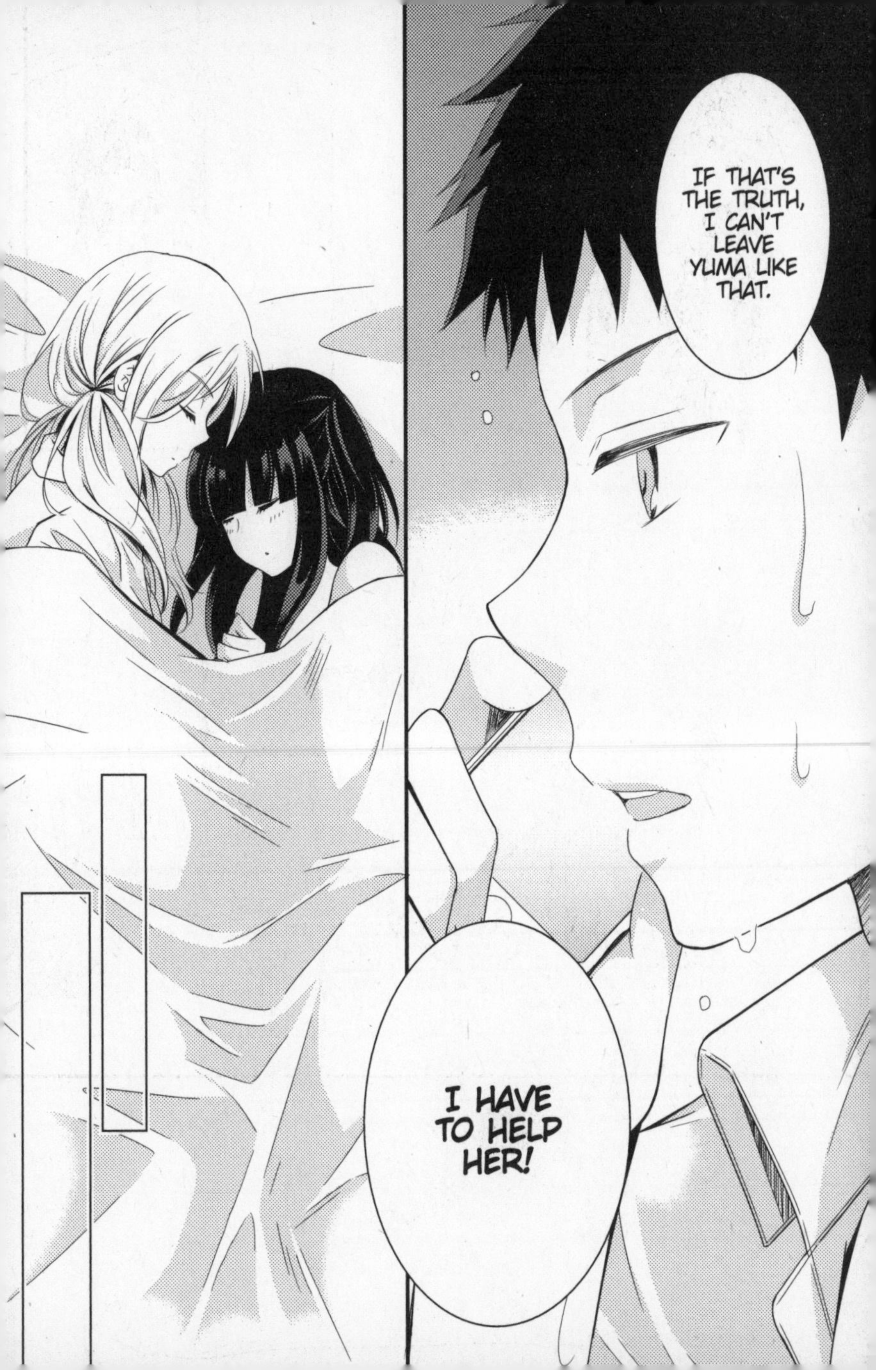
IF THAT'S THE TRUTH, I CAN'T LEAVE YUMA LIKE THAT.
I HAVE TO HELP HER!

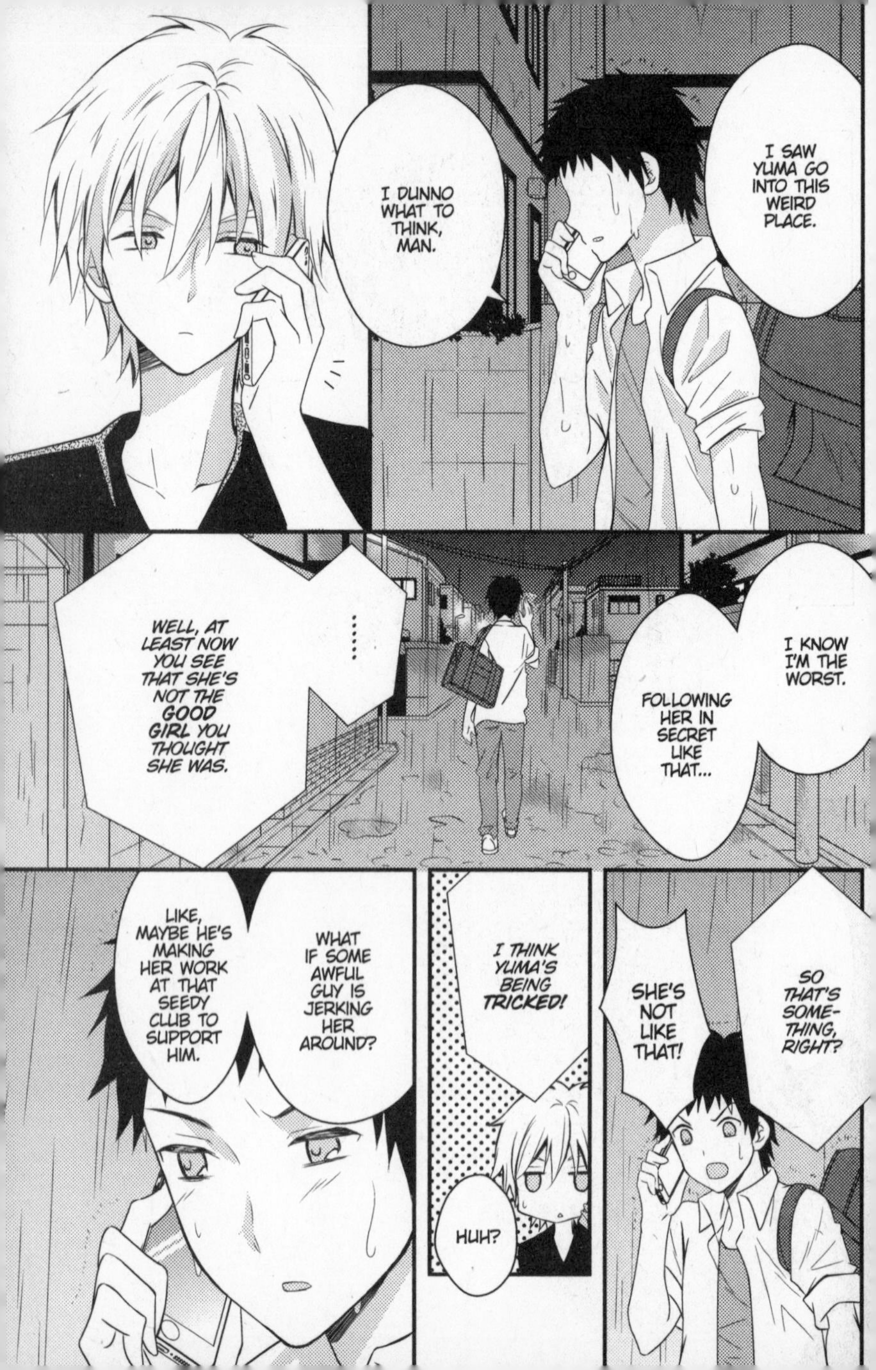
I SAW YUMA GO INTO THIS WEIRD PLACE.
I DUNNO WHAT TO THINK, MAN.
I KNOW I'M THE WORST.
FOLLOWING HER IN SECRET LIKE THAT...
......
WELL, AT LEAST NOW YOU SEE THAT SHE'S NOT THE **GOOD GIRL** YOU THOUGHT SHE WAS.
SO THAT'S SOME-THING, RIGHT?
SHE'S NOT LIKE THAT!
I THINK YUMA'S BEING **TRICKED!**
HUH?
WHAT IF SOME AWFUL GUY IS JERKING HER AROUND?
LIKE, MAYBE HE'S MAKING HER WORK AT THAT SEEDY CLUB TO SUPPORT HIM.

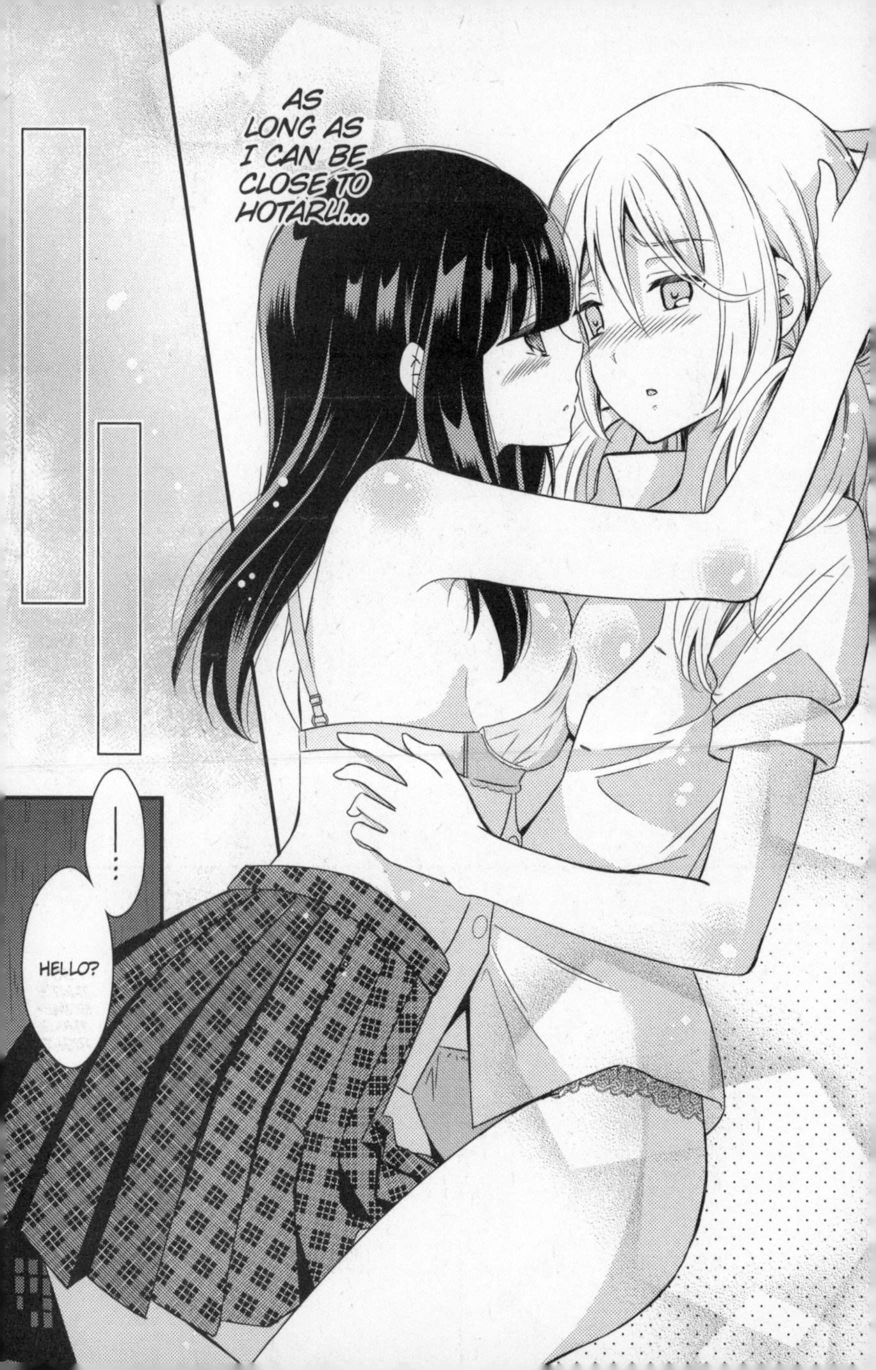
AS LONG AS I CAN BE CLOSE TO HOTARU...
—...
HELLO?

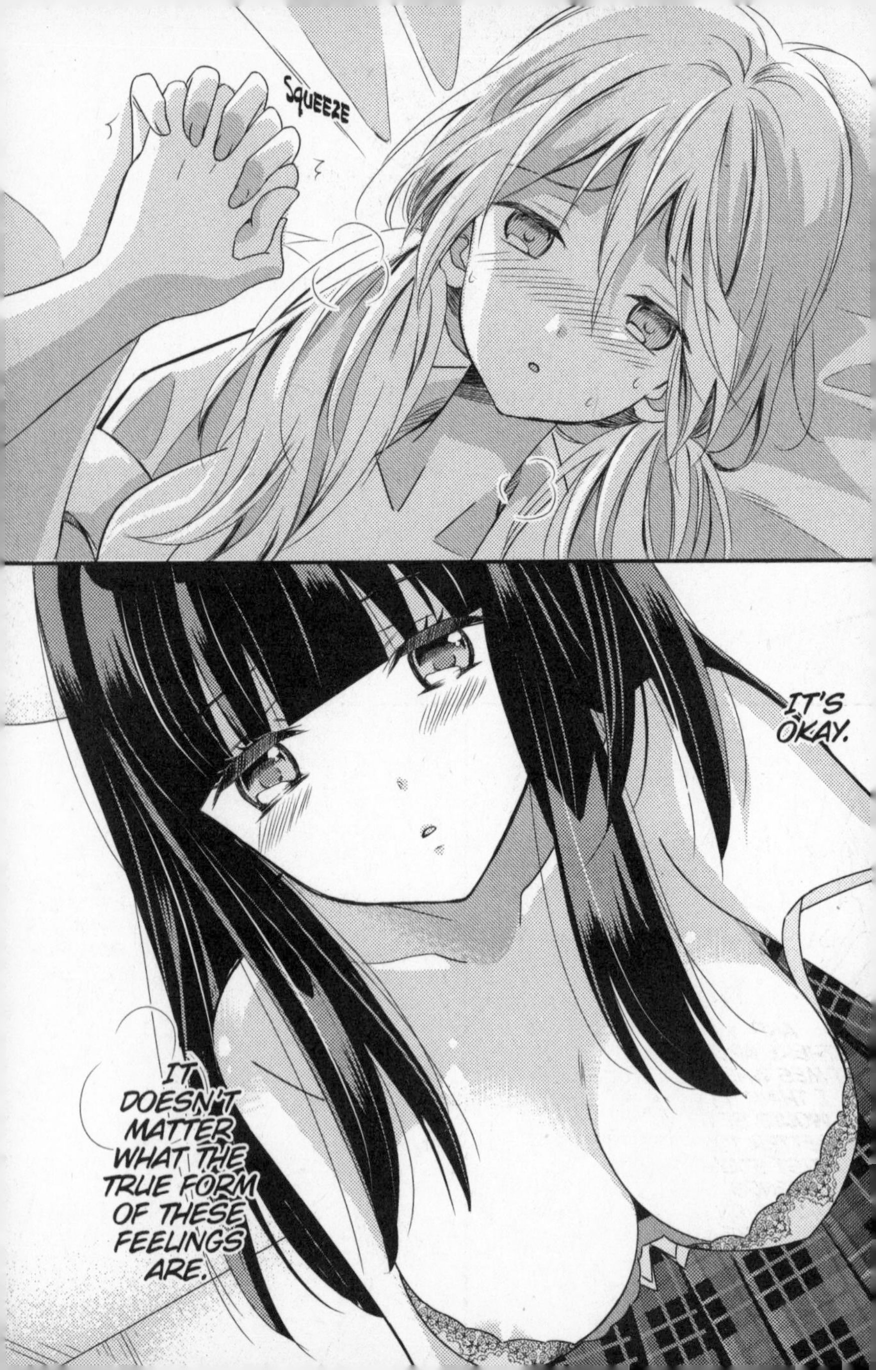
SQUEEZE
IT'S OKAY.
IT DOESN'T MATTER WHAT THE TRUE FORM OF THESE FEELINGS ARE.

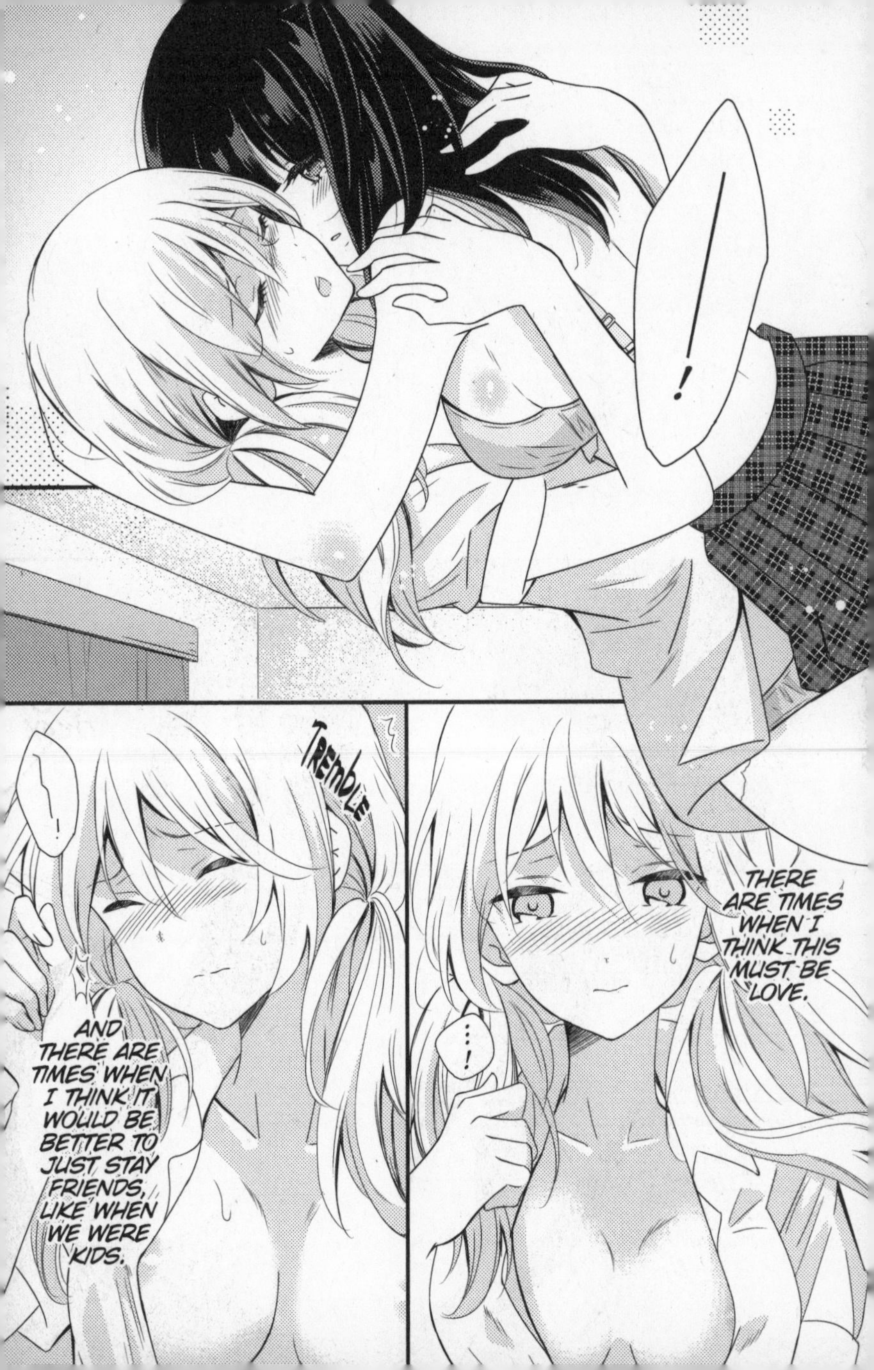
!
THERE ARE TIMES WHEN I THINK THIS MUST BE LOVE.
...!
TREMBLE
!
AND THERE ARE TIMES WHEN I THINK IT WOULD BE BETTER TO JUST STAY FRIENDS, LIKE WHEN WE WERE KIDS.

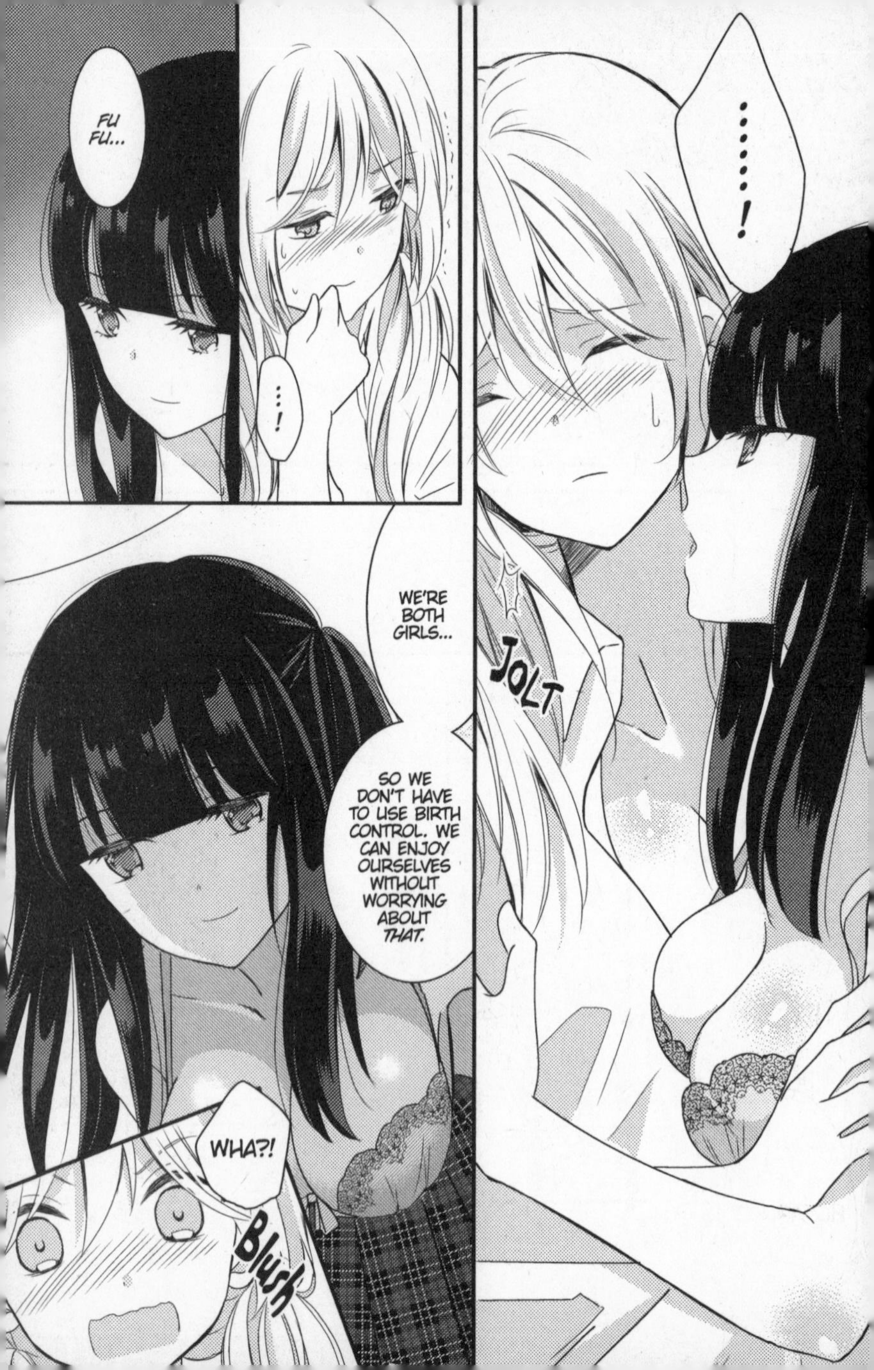
......!
JOLT
...!
FU FU...
WE'RE BOTH GIRLS...
SO WE DON'T HAVE TO USE BIRTH CONTROL. WE CAN ENJOY OURSELVES WITHOUT WORRYING ABOUT *THAT*.
WHA?!
Blush

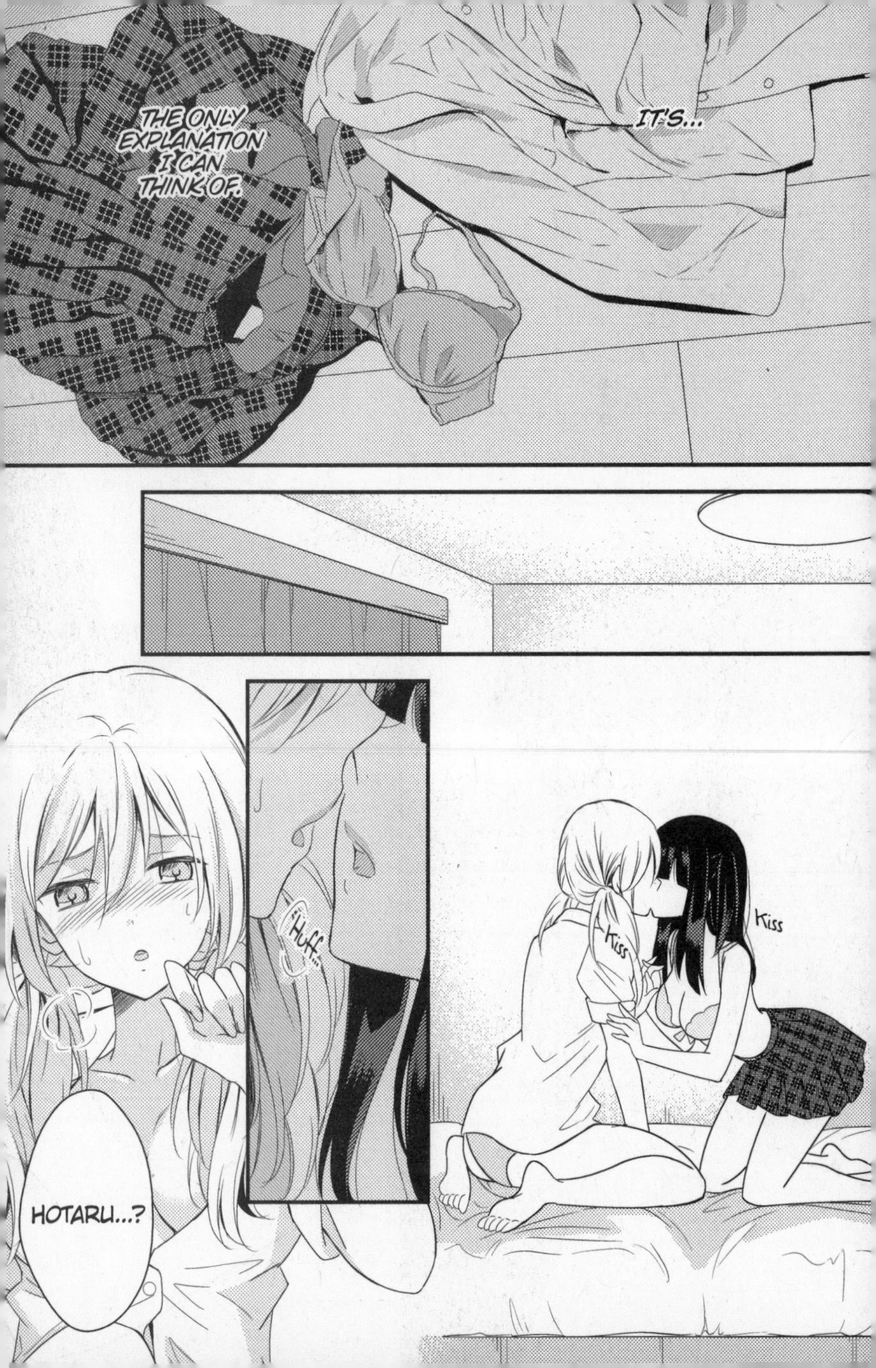
IT'S...
THE ONLY EXPLANATION I CAN THINK OF.
Kiss
Kiss
Huff...
HOTARU...?

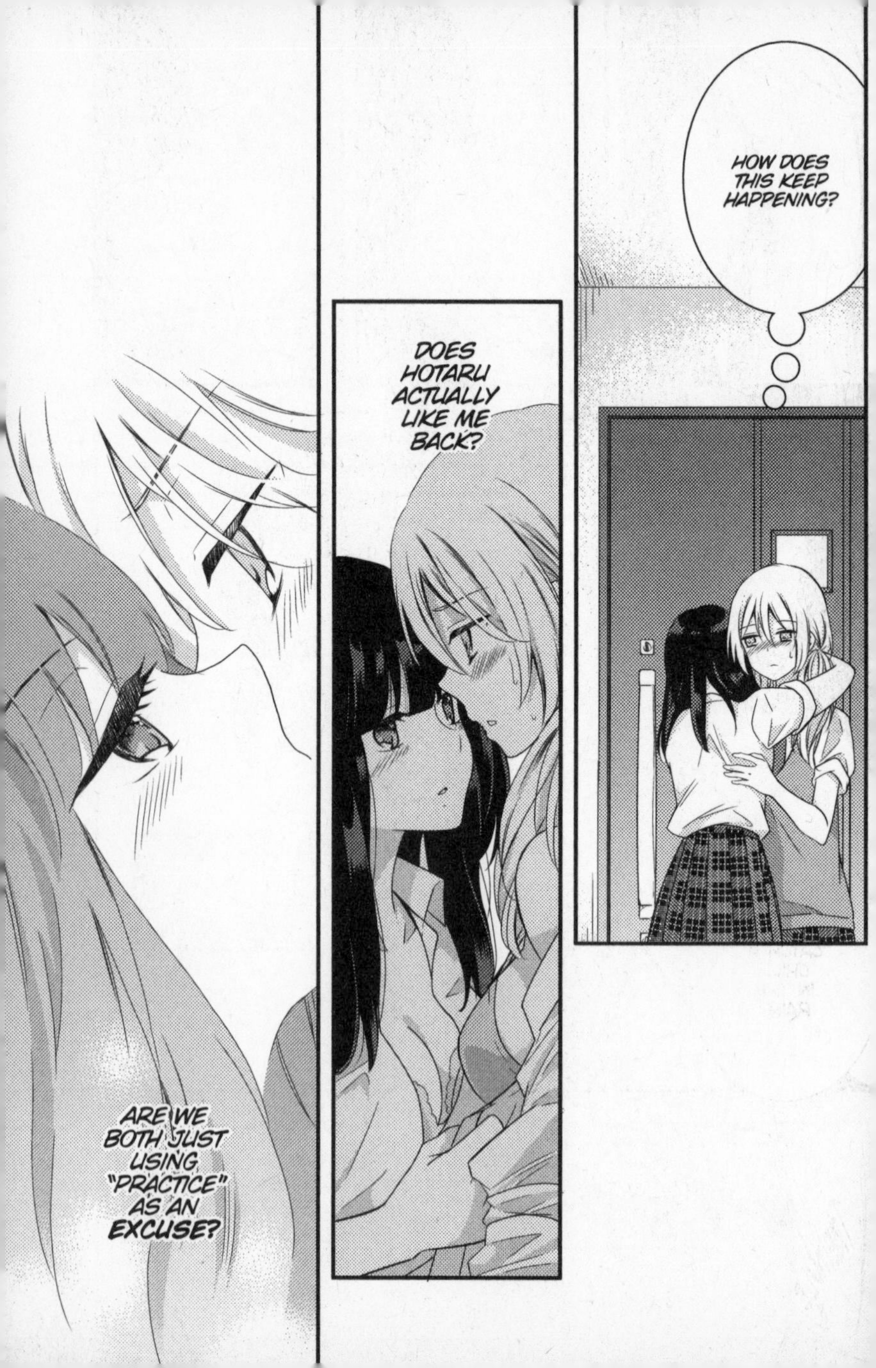
HOW DOES THIS KEEP HAPPENING?
DOES HOTARU ACTUALLY LIKE ME BACK?
ARE WE BOTH JUST USING "PRACTICE" AS AN EXCUSE?

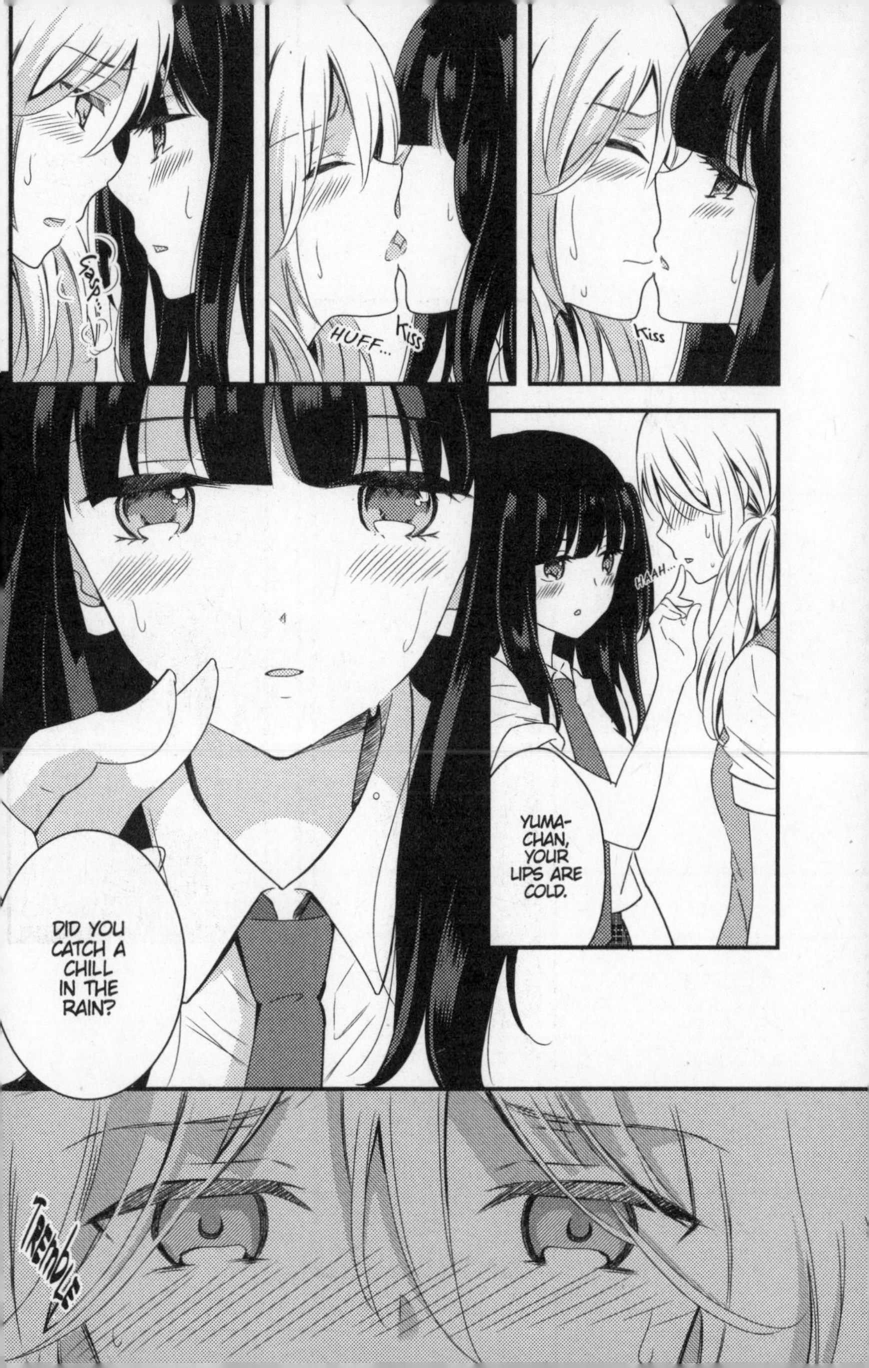
Kiss
Kiss
HUFF...
Gasp...
HAAH...
YUMA-CHAN, YOUR LIPS ARE COLD.
DID YOU CATCH A CHILL IN THE RAIN?
TREMBLE

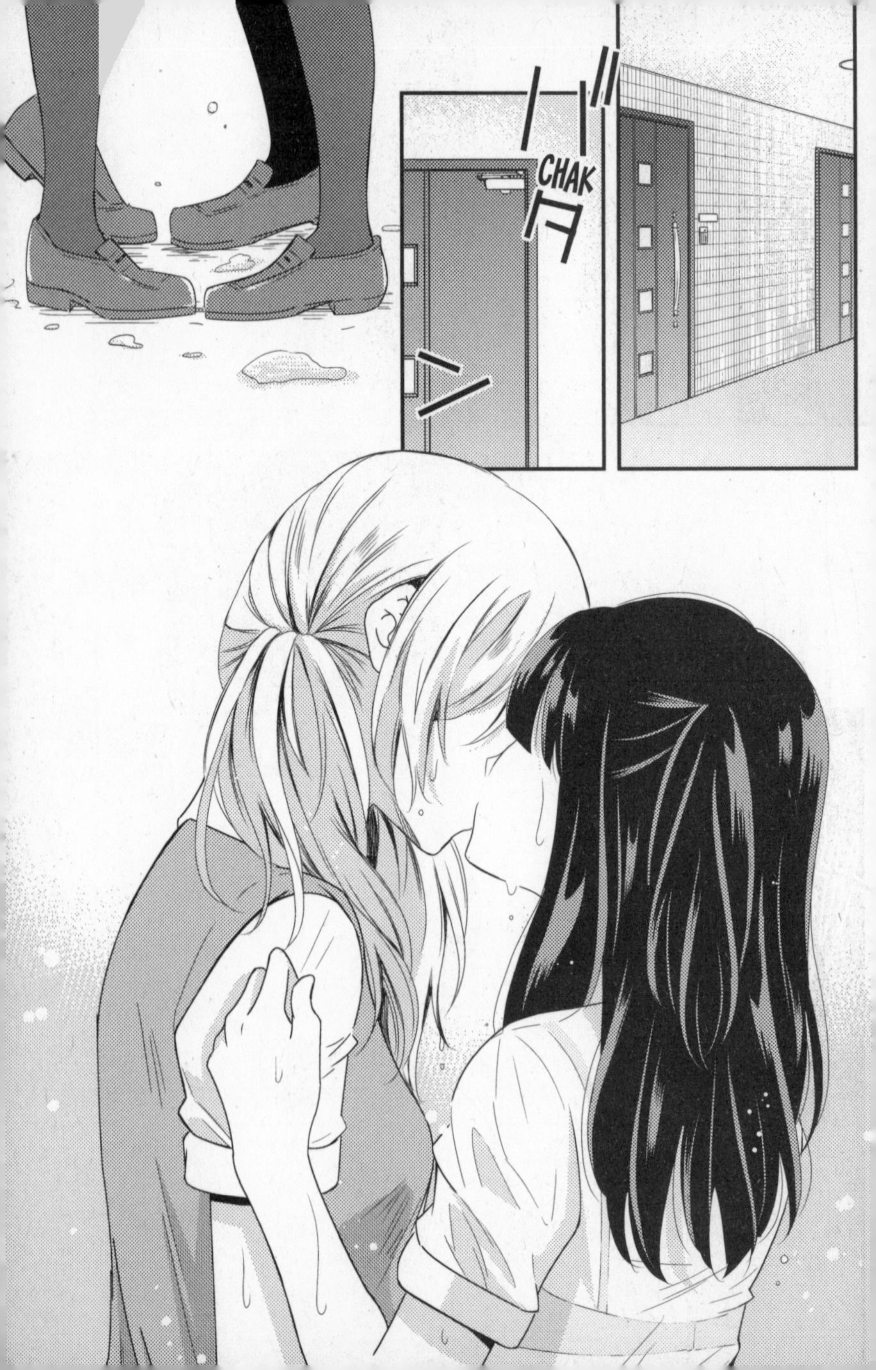
CHAK

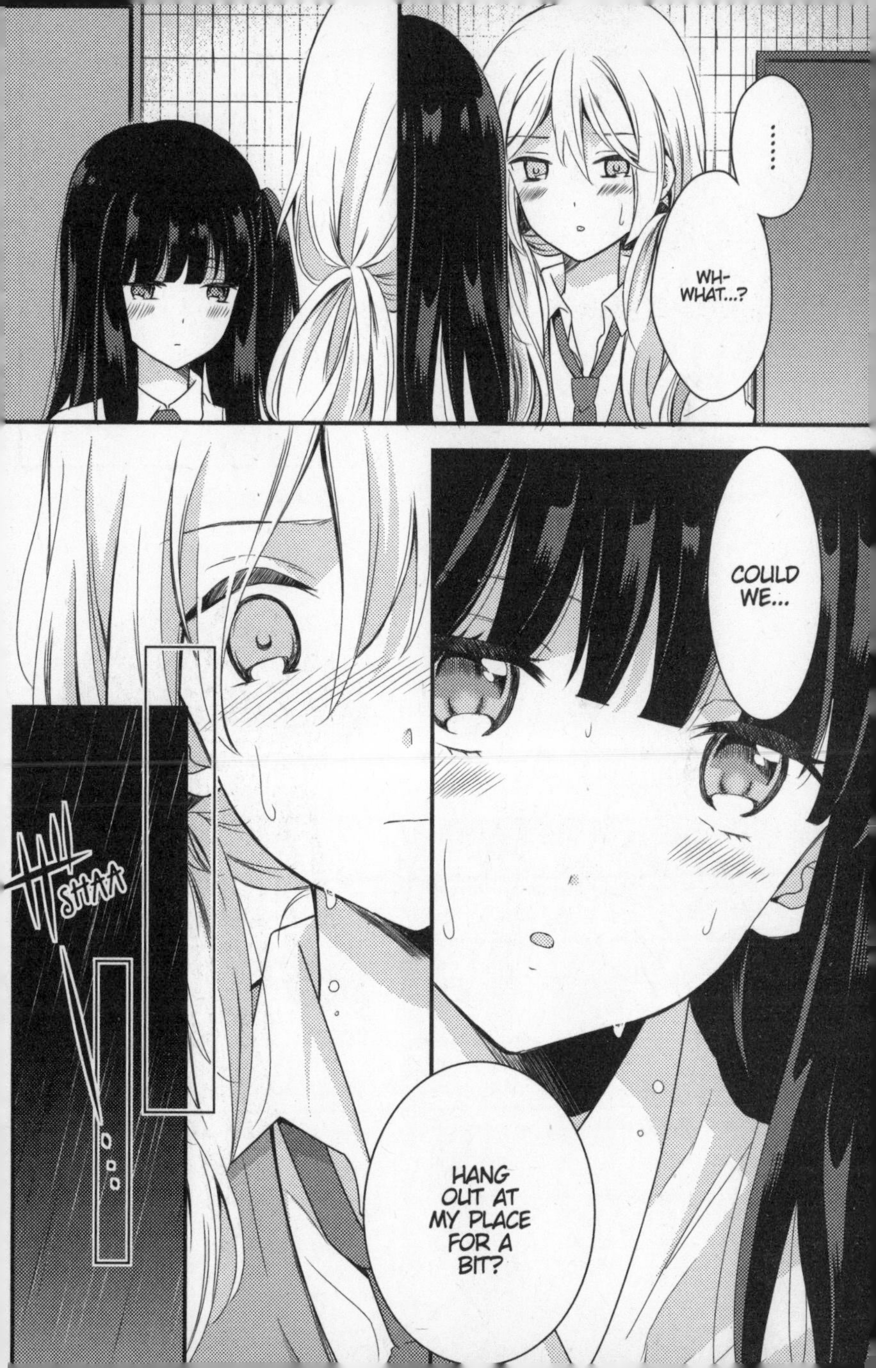
......
WH- WHAT...?
COULD WE...
HANG OUT AT MY PLACE FOR A BIT?
SHAA

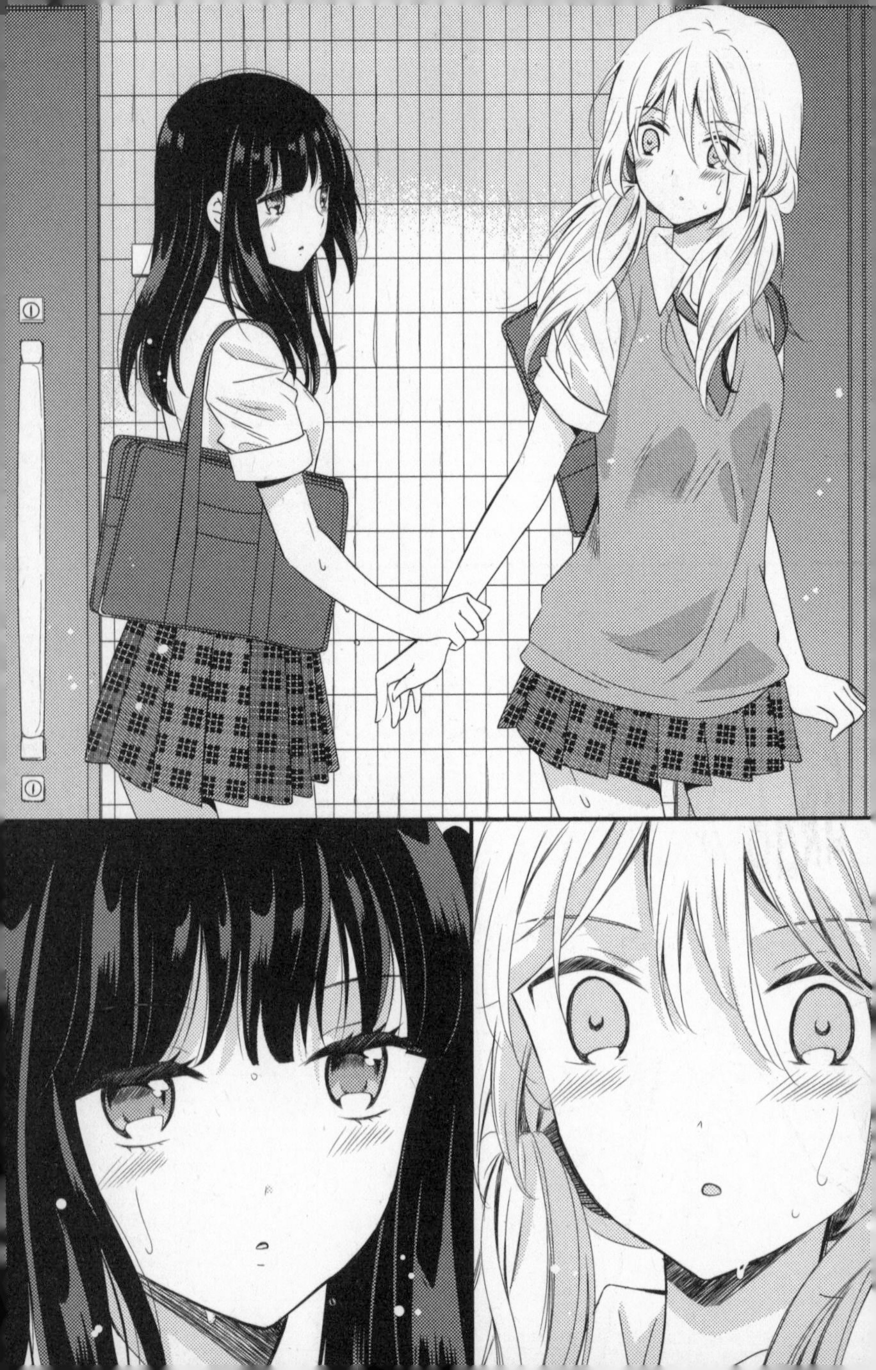

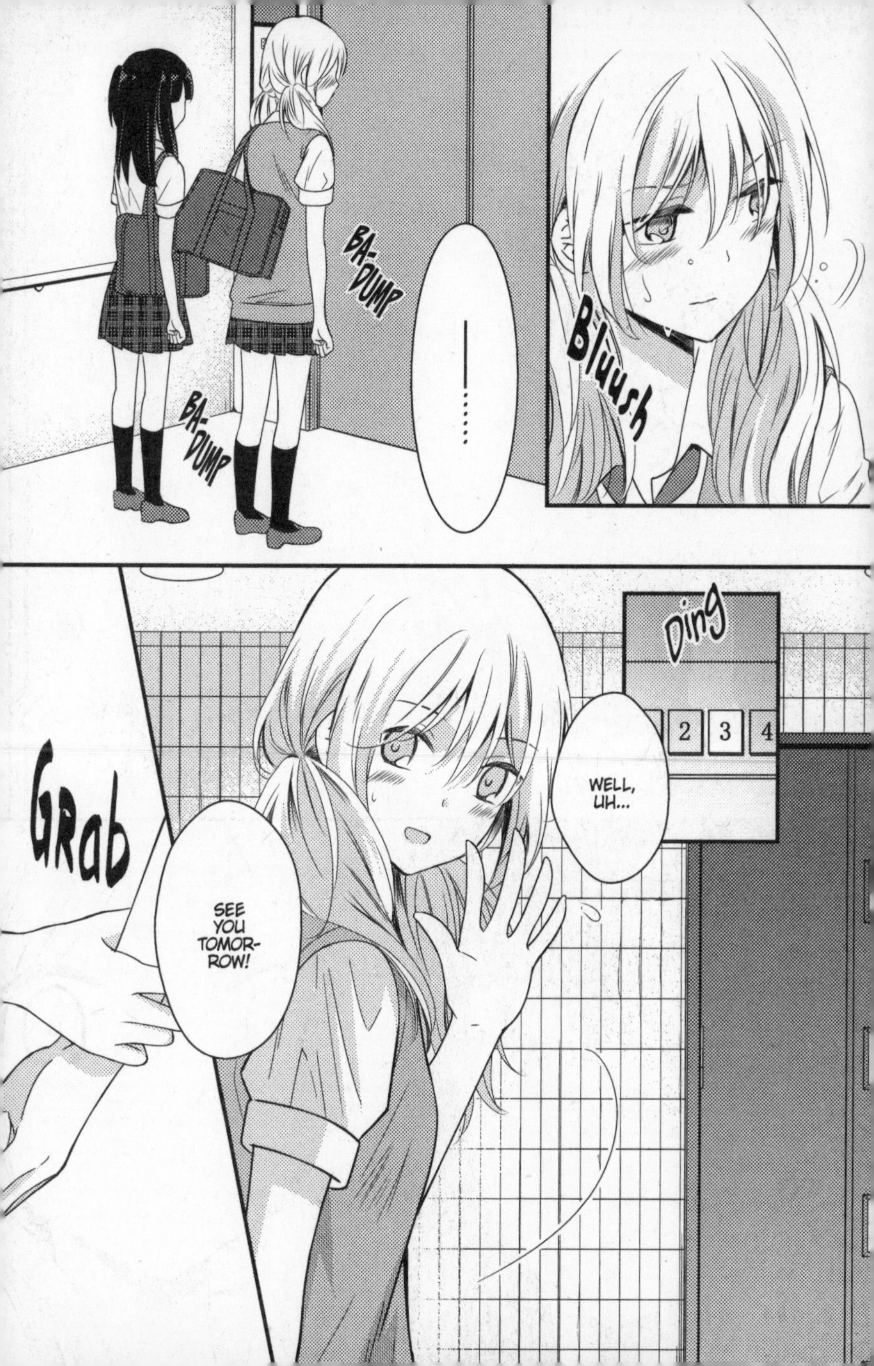
Bluush
—......
BA-DUMP
BA-DUMP
Ding
WELL, UH...
SEE YOU TOMOR-ROW!
Grab

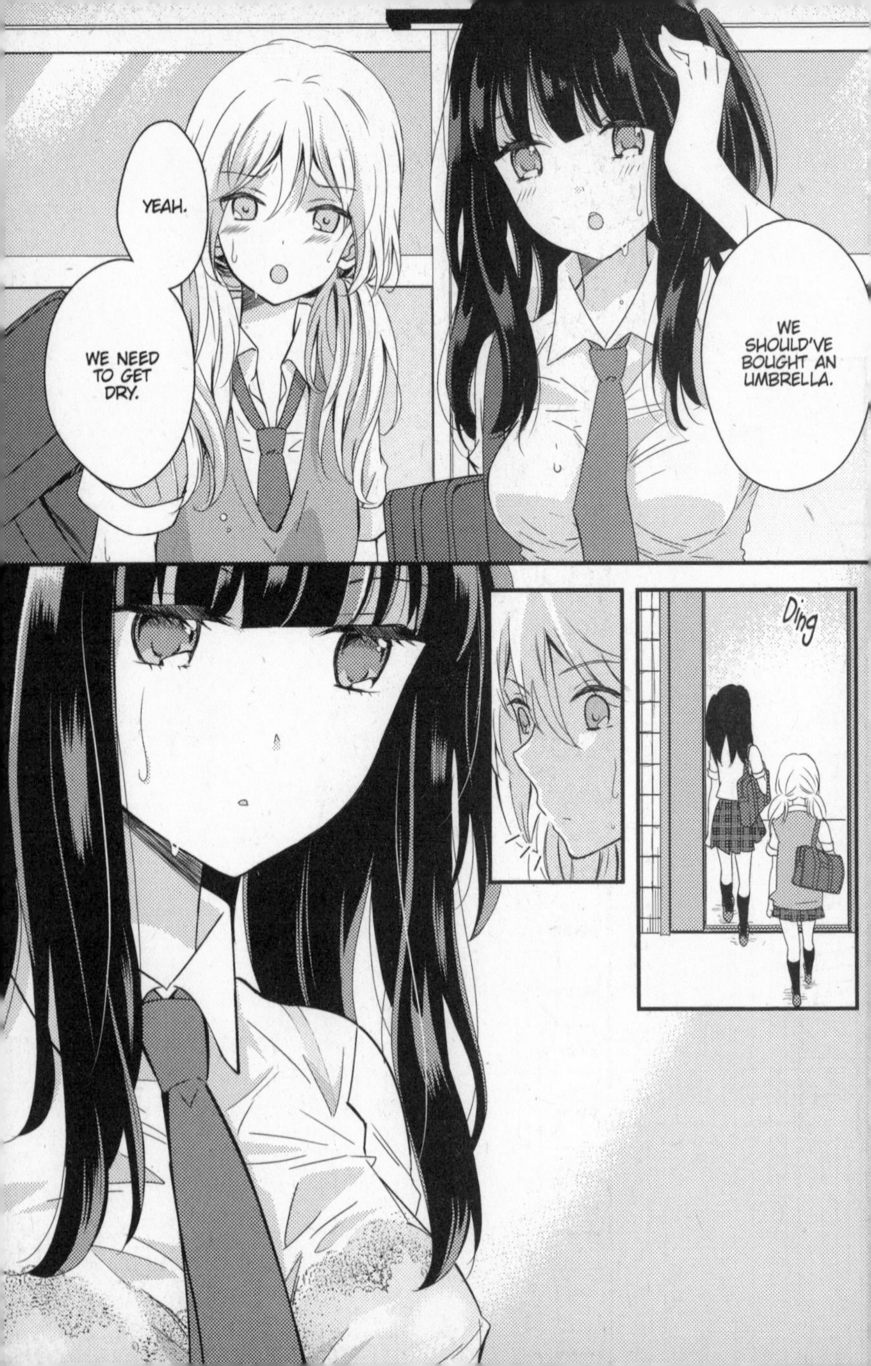
WE SHOULD'VE BOUGHT AN UMBRELLA.
YEAH.
WE NEED TO GET DRY.
Ding

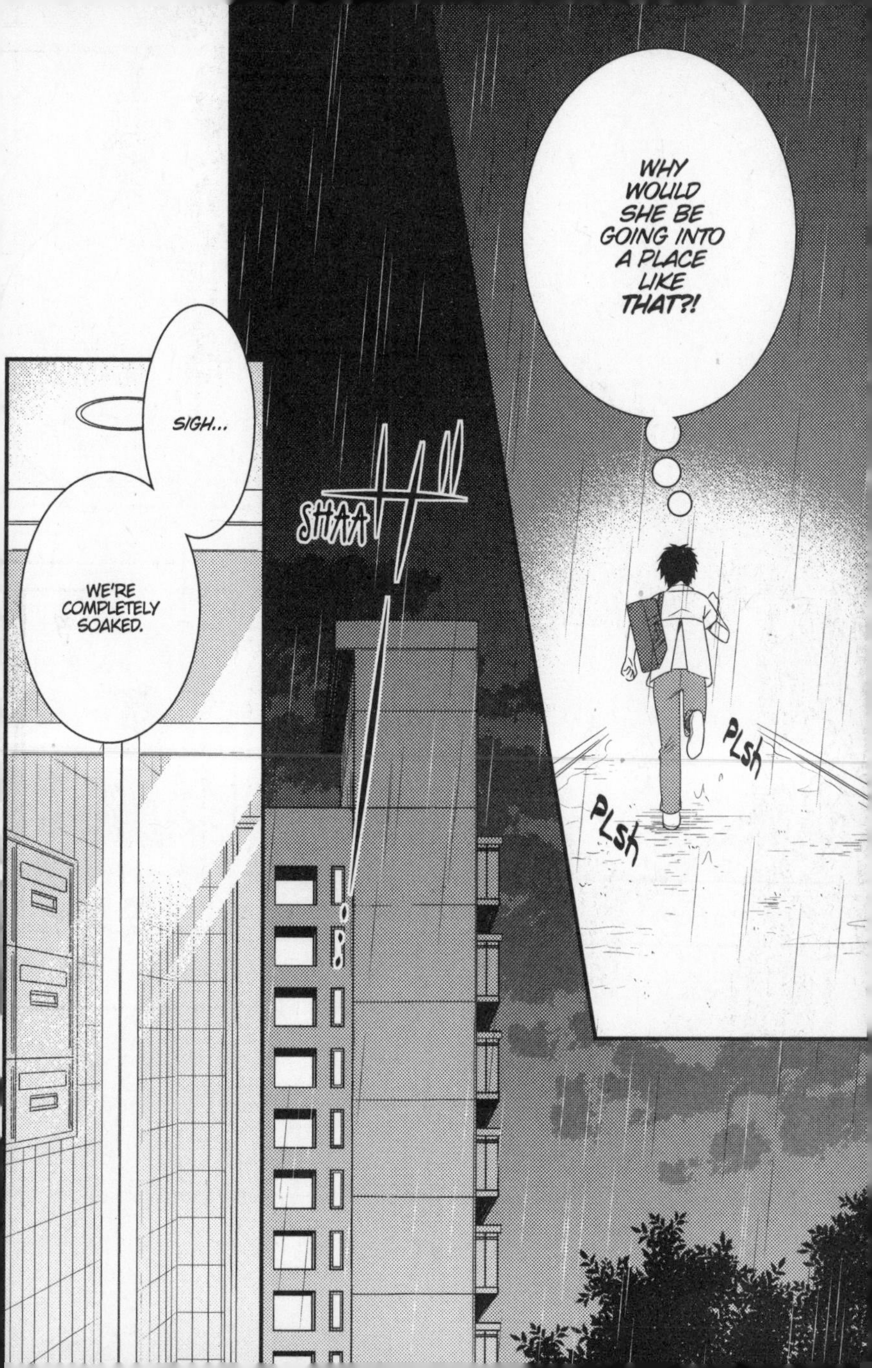
WHY WOULD SHE BE GOING INTO A PLACE LIKE THAT?!
PLsh
PLsh
SHAAA
SIGH...
WE'RE COMPLETELY SOAKED.

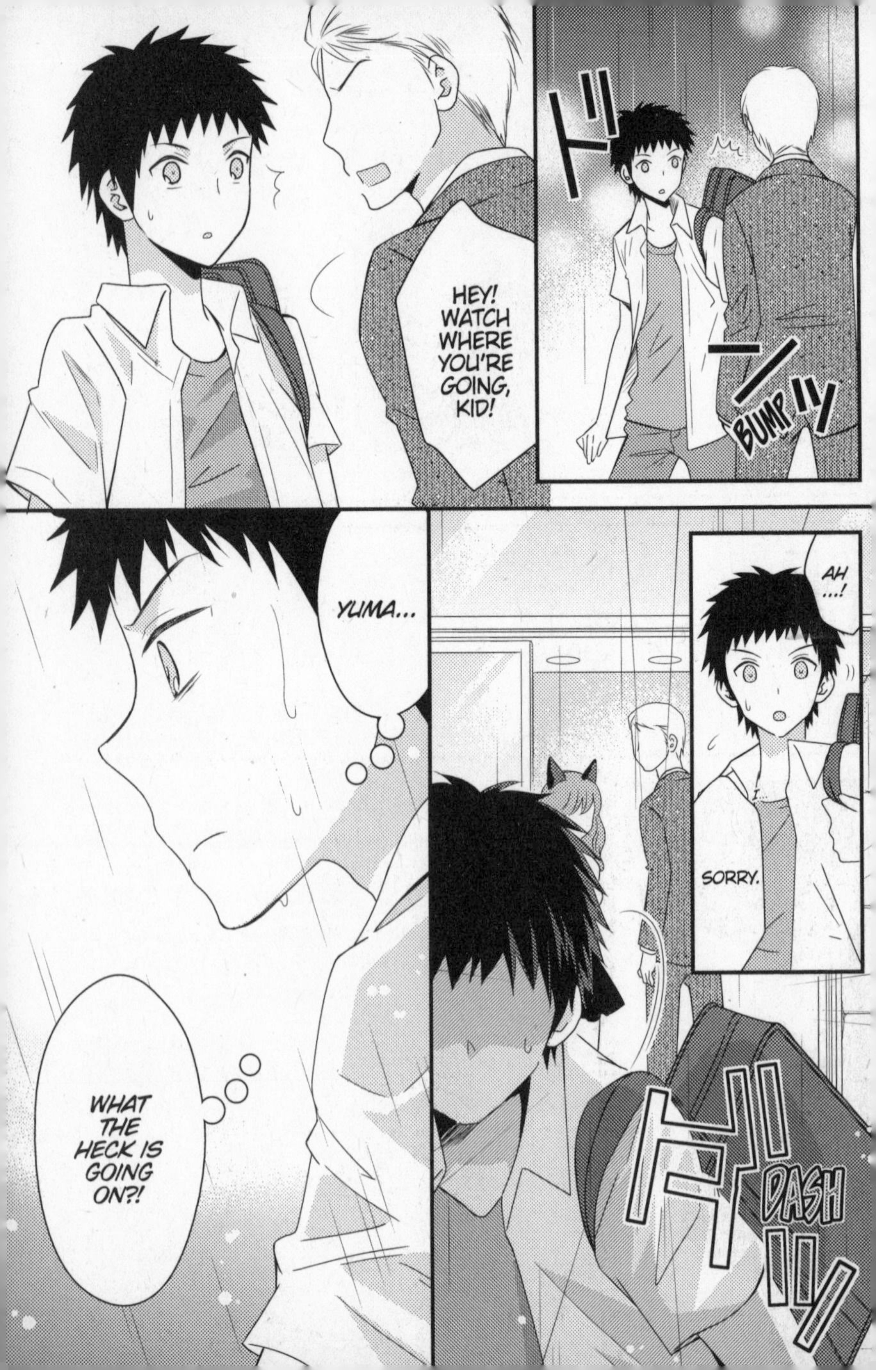
BUMP
HEY! WATCH WHERE YOU'RE GOING, KID!
AH ...!
I...
SORRY.
DASH
YUMA...
WHAT THE HECK IS GOING ON?!

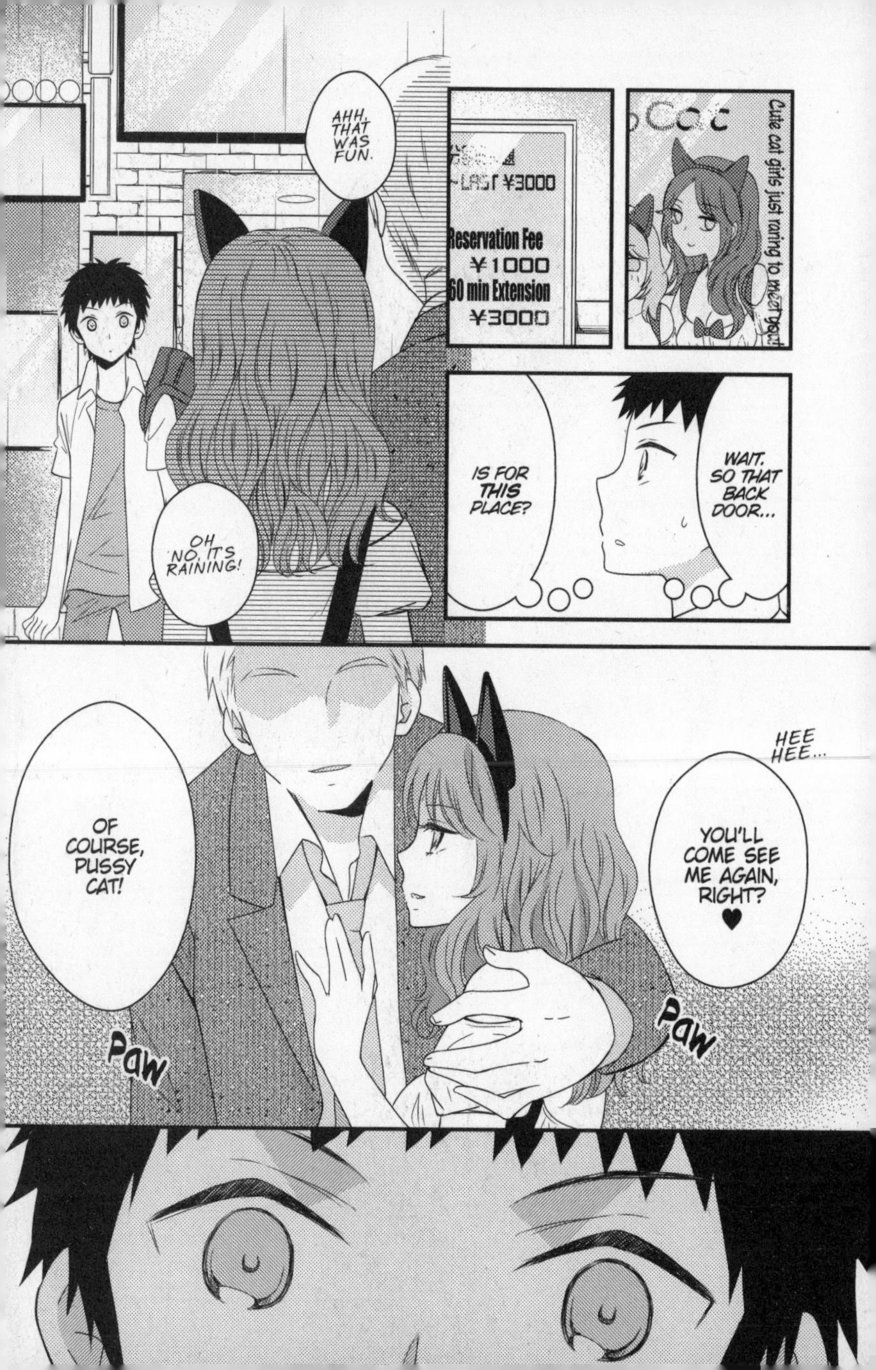
Cute cat girls just raring to meet you!
~LAST ¥3000
Reservation Fee ¥1000
60 min Extension ¥3000
WAIT. SO THAT BACK DOOR...
IS FOR THIS PLACE?
AHH, THAT WAS FUN.
OH NO, IT'S RAINING!
HEE HEE...
YOU'LL COME SEE ME AGAIN, RIGHT? ♥
Paw
OF COURSE, PUSSY CAT!
Paw

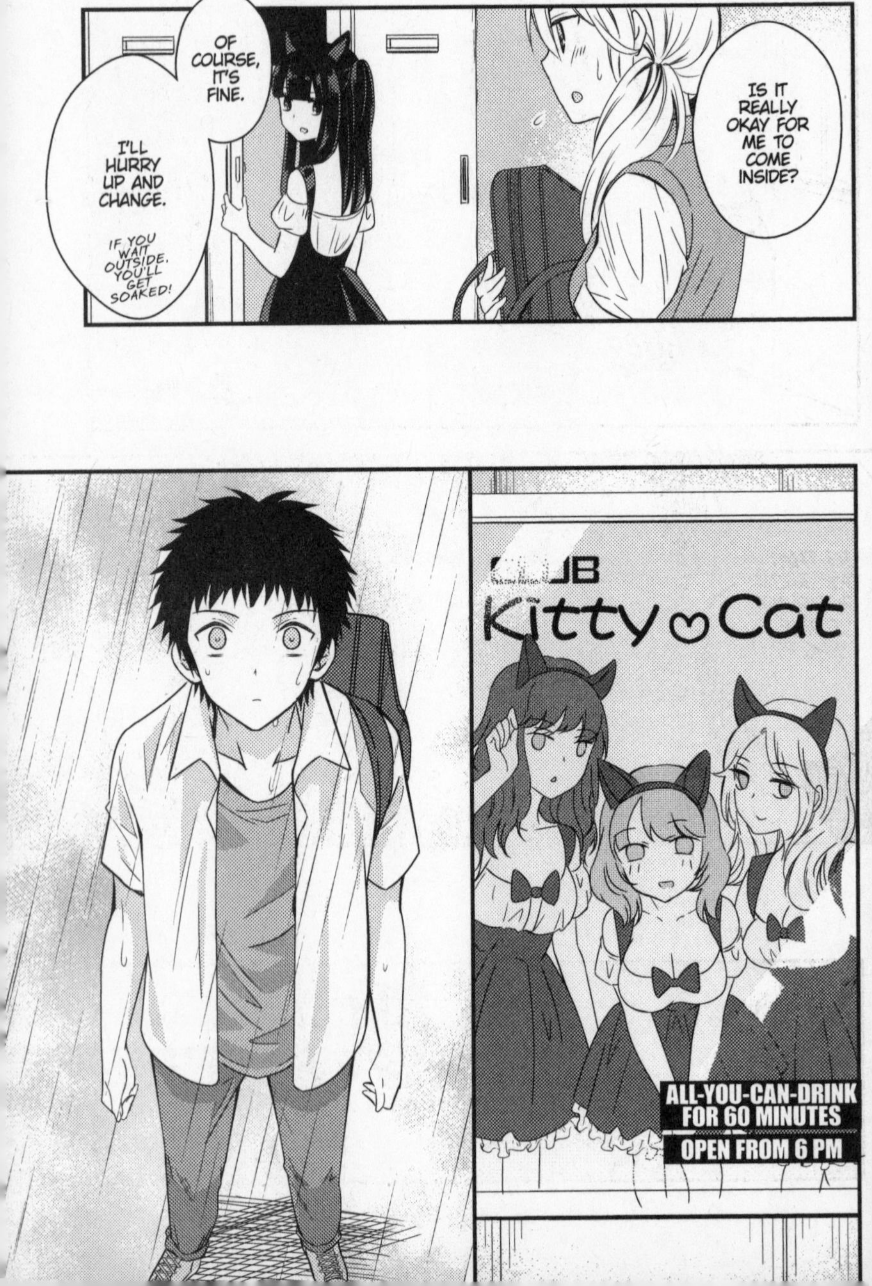
IS IT REALLY OKAY FOR ME TO COME INSIDE?
OF COURSE, IT'S FINE.
I'LL HURRY UP AND CHANGE.
IF YOU WAIT OUTSIDE, YOU'LL GET SOAKED!
Kitty♡Cat
ALL-YOU-CAN-DRINK FOR 60 MINUTES
OPEN FROM 6 PM

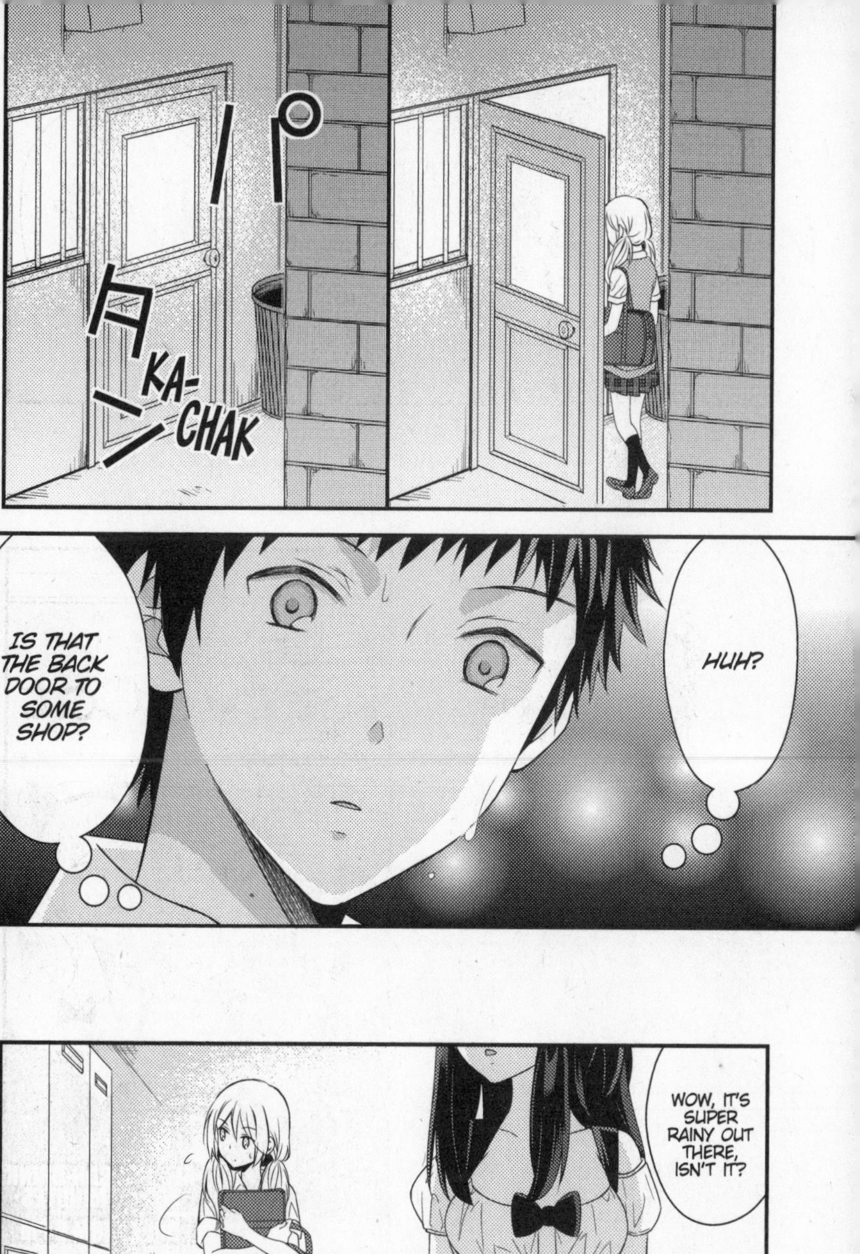
KA-CHAK
HUH?
IS THAT THE BACK DOOR TO SOME SHOP?
WOW, IT'S SUPER RAINY OUT THERE, ISN'T IT?

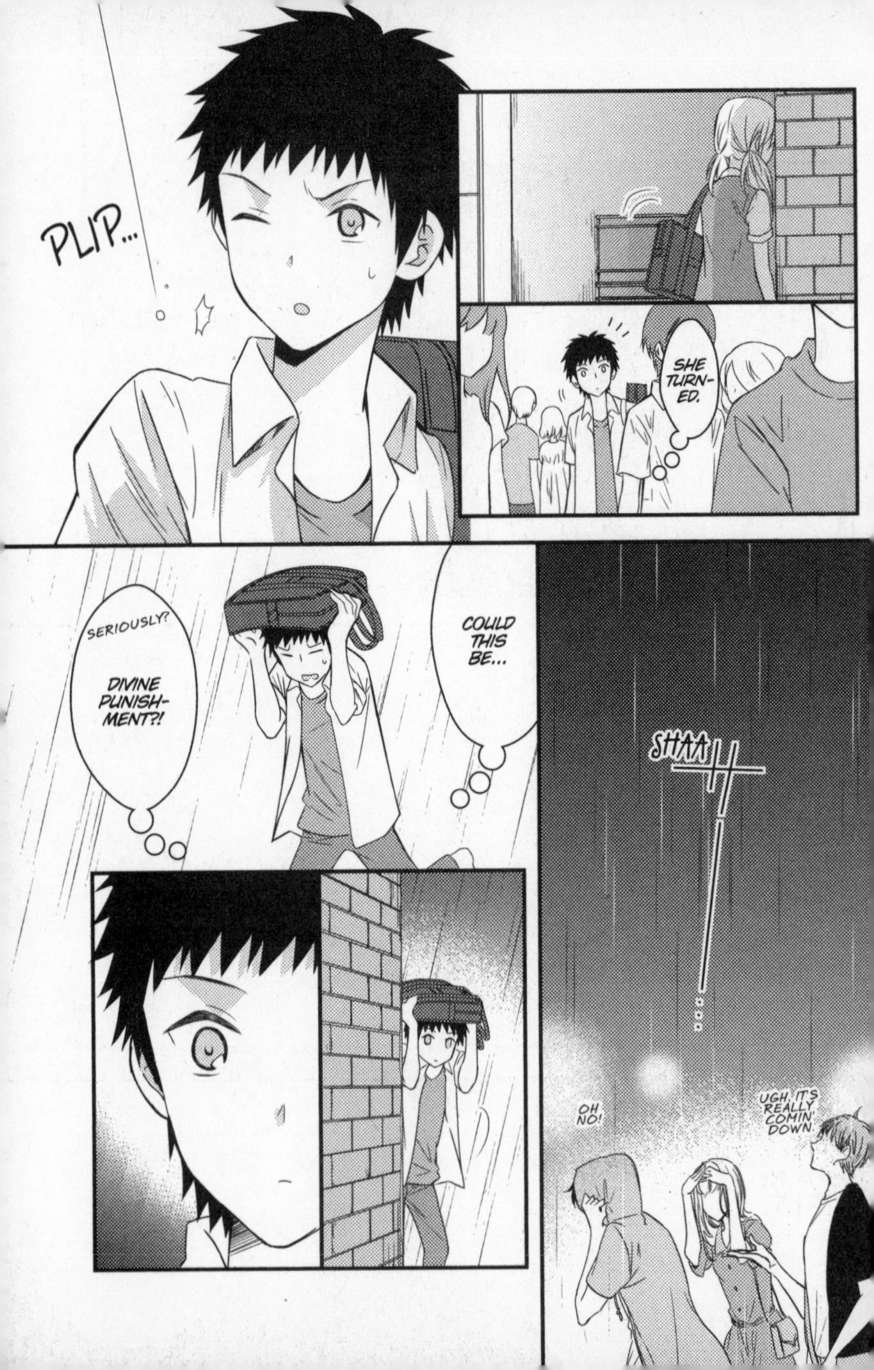
SHE TURNED.
PLIP...
SHAA...
UGH, IT'S REALLY COMIN' DOWN.
OH NO!
COULD THIS BE...
SERIOUSLY? DIVINE PUNISHMENT?!

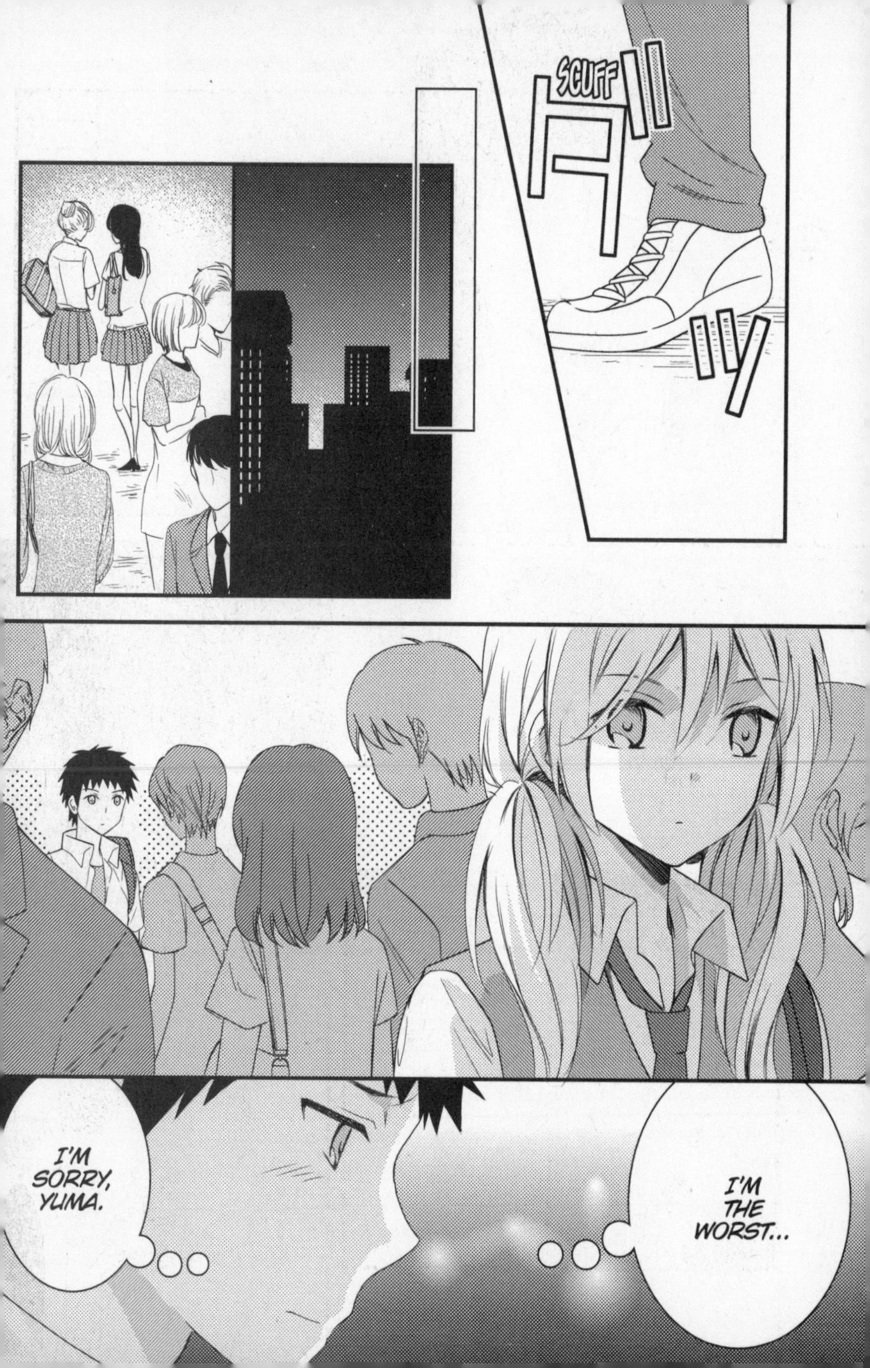
SCUFF
I'M THE WORST...
I'M SORRY, YUMA.

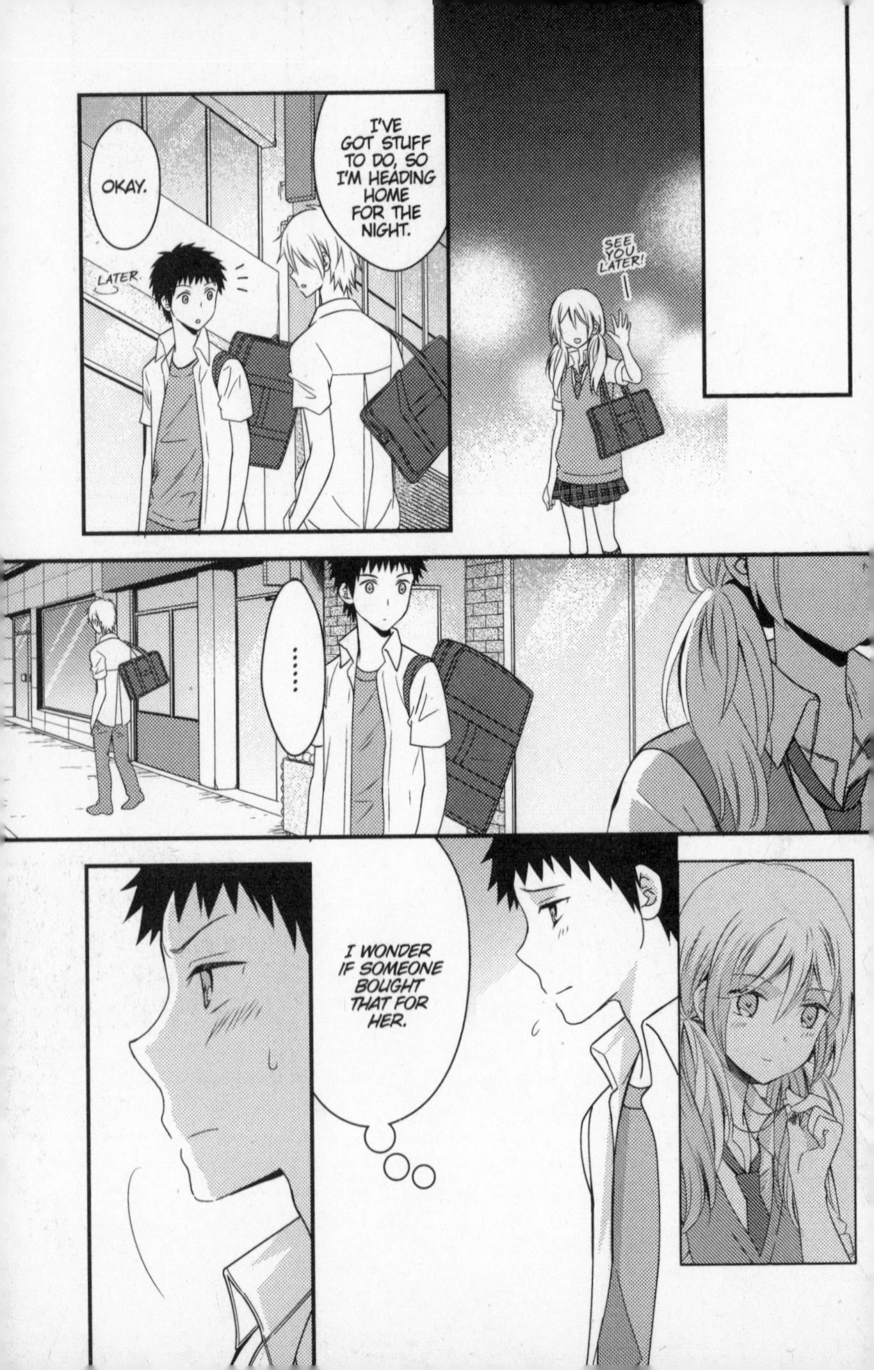
SEE YOU LATER!
I'VE GOT STUFF TO DO, SO I'M HEADING HOME FOR THE NIGHT.
OKAY.
LATER.
......
I WONDER IF SOMEONE BOUGHT THAT FOR HER.

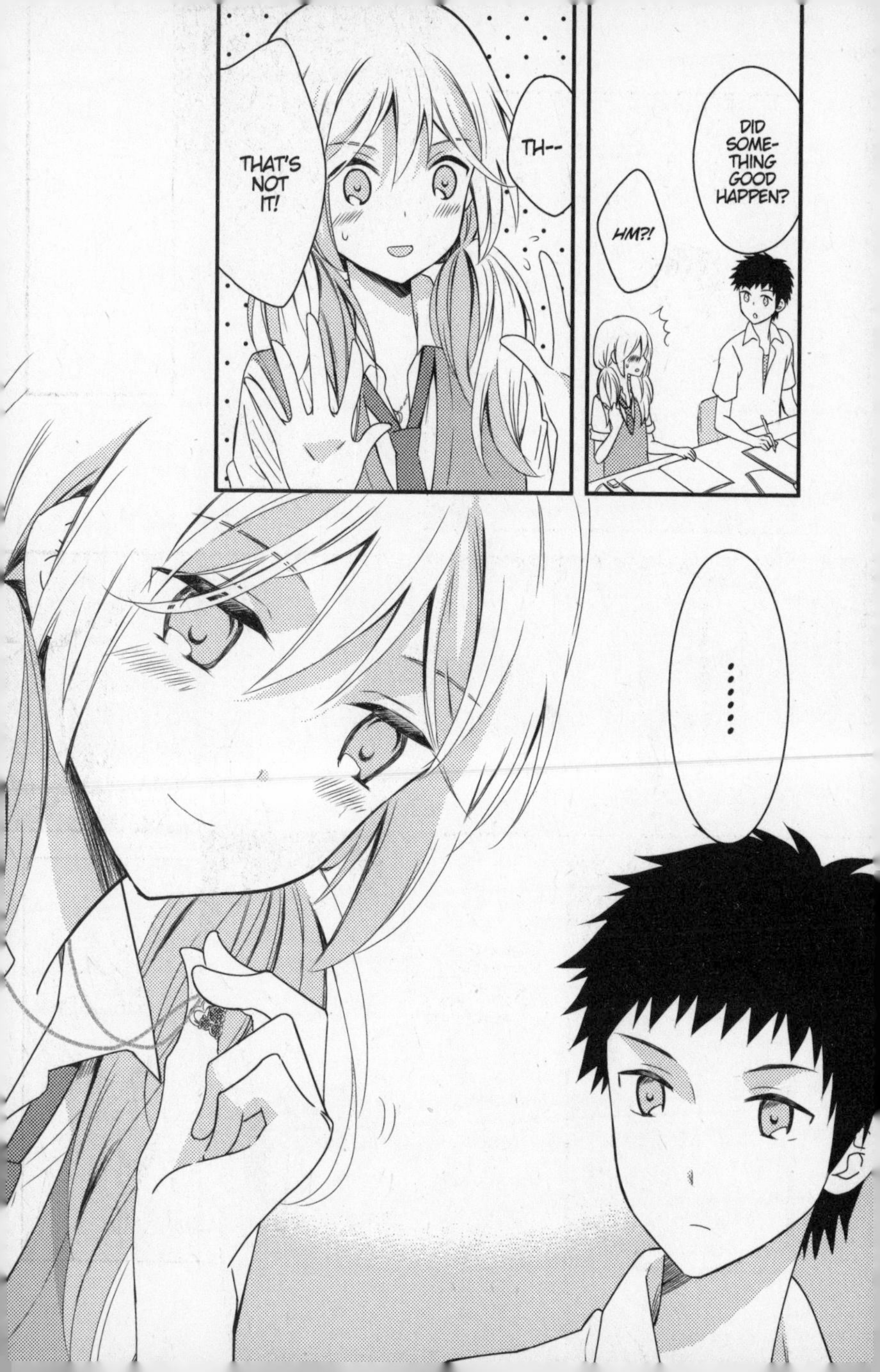
DID SOME-THING GOOD HAPPEN?
HM?!
TH--
THAT'S NOT IT!
......

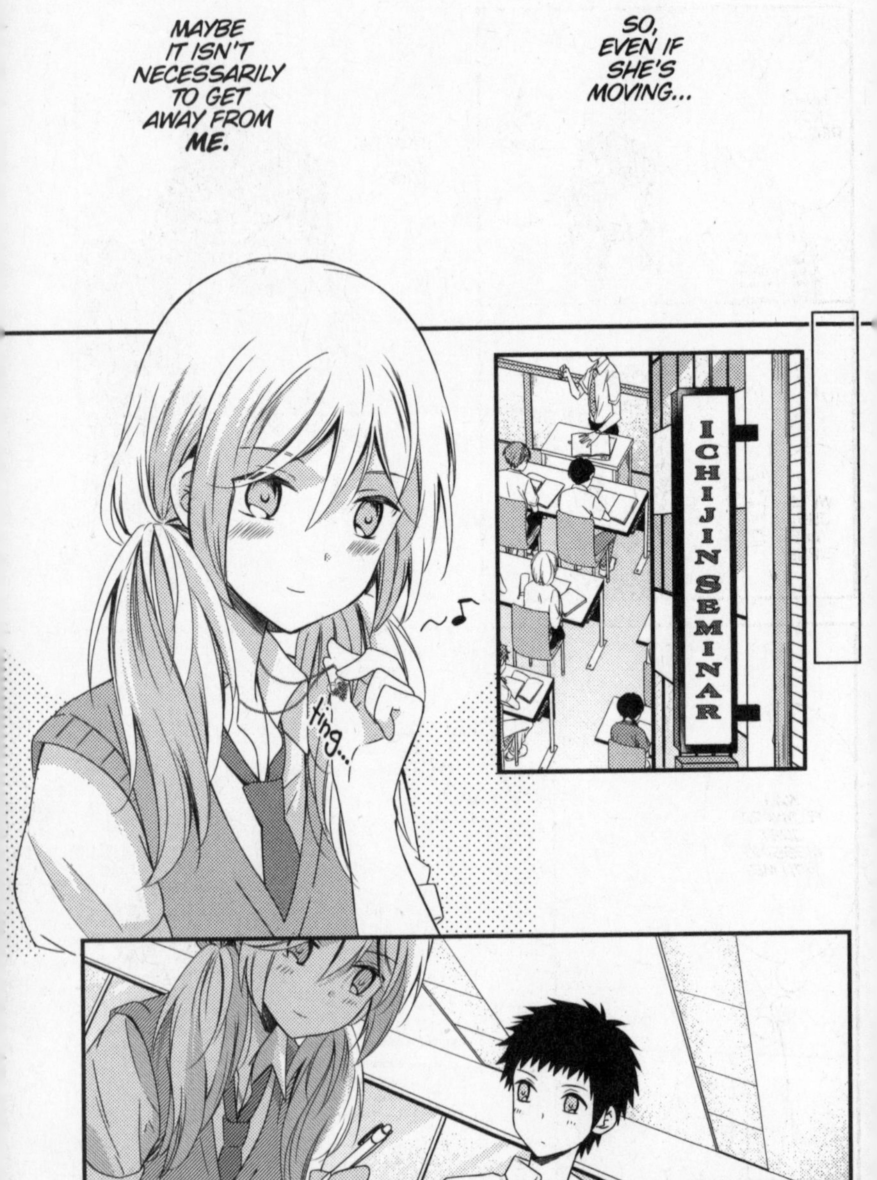
SO, EVEN IF SHE'S MOVING...
MAYBE IT ISN'T NECESSARILY TO GET AWAY FROM ME.
ICHIJIN SEMINAR
~♪
ting...

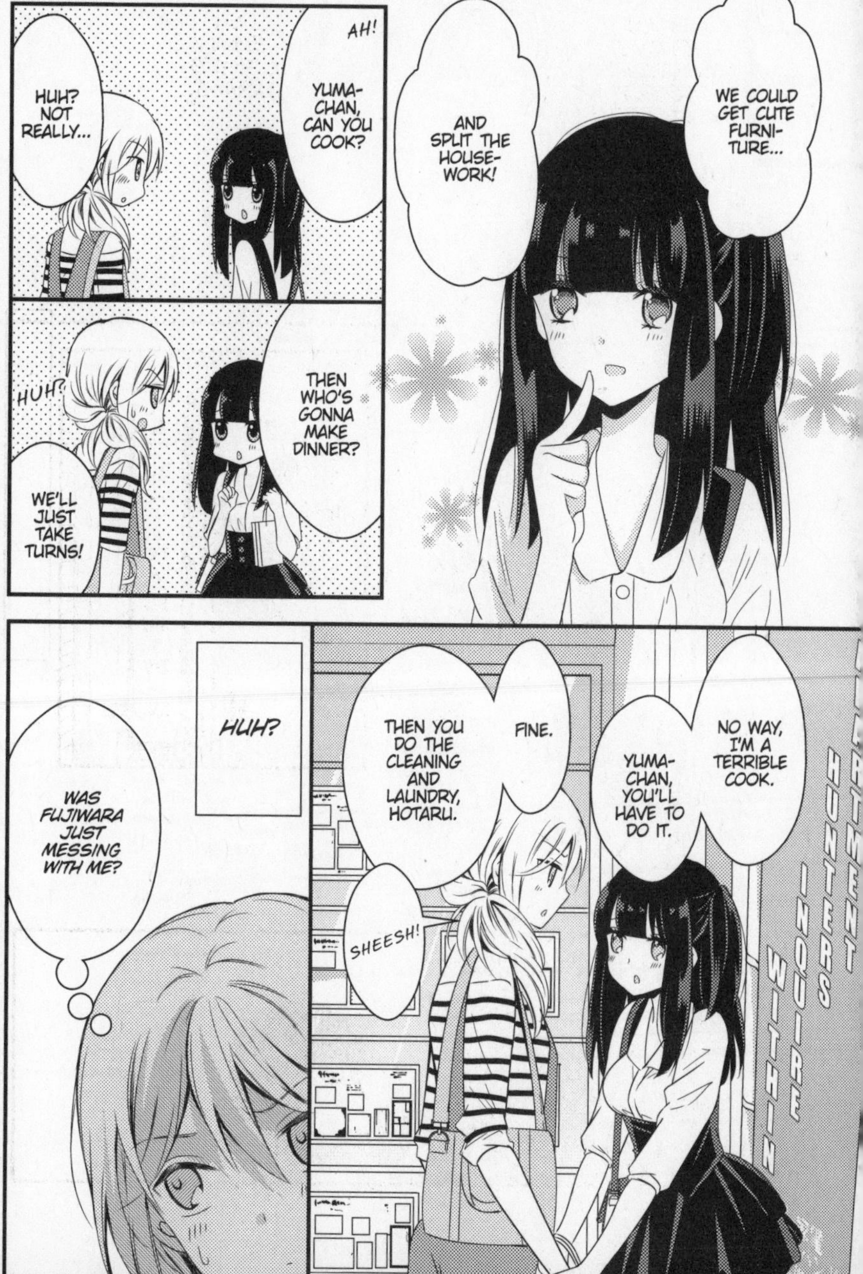
WE COULD GET CUTE FURNITURE...
AND SPLIT THE HOUSEWORK!
AH!
YUMA-CHAN, CAN YOU COOK?
HUH? NOT REALLY...
THEN WHO'S GONNA MAKE DINNER?
HUH?
WE'LL JUST TAKE TURNS!
NO WAY, I'M A TERRIBLE COOK.
YUMA-CHAN, YOU'LL HAVE TO DO IT.
FINE.
THEN YOU DO THE CLEANING AND LAUNDRY, HOTARU.
SHEESH!
HUNTERS INQUIRE WITHIN
HUH?
WAS FUJIWARA JUST MESSING WITH ME?

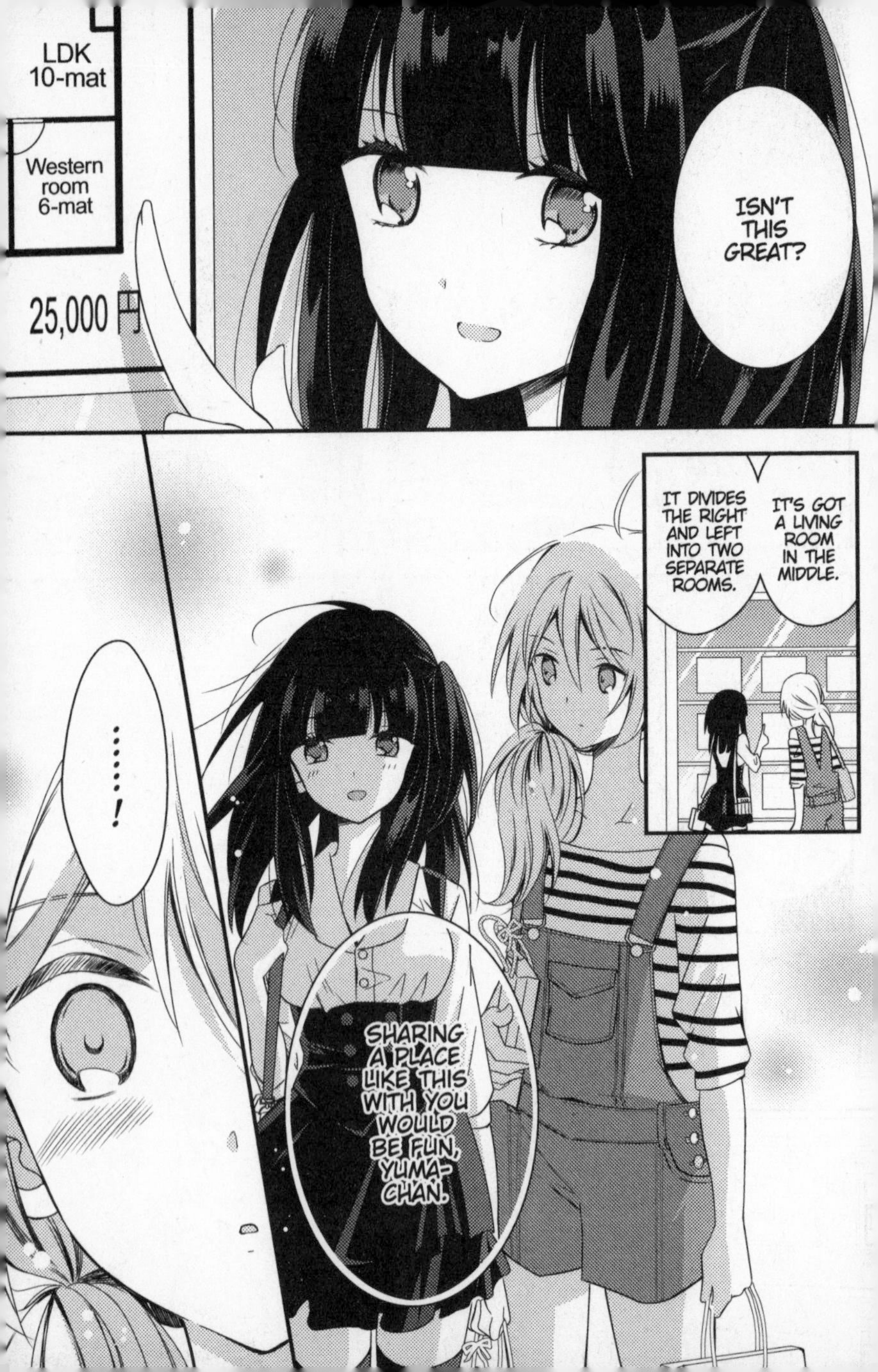
LDK
10-mat
Western
room
6-mat
25,000 円
ISN'T THIS GREAT?
IT'S GOT A LIVING ROOM IN THE MIDDLE.
IT DIVIDES THE RIGHT AND LEFT INTO TWO SEPARATE ROOMS.
SHARING A PLACE LIKE THIS WITH YOU WOULD BE FUN, YUMA-CHAN.
......!

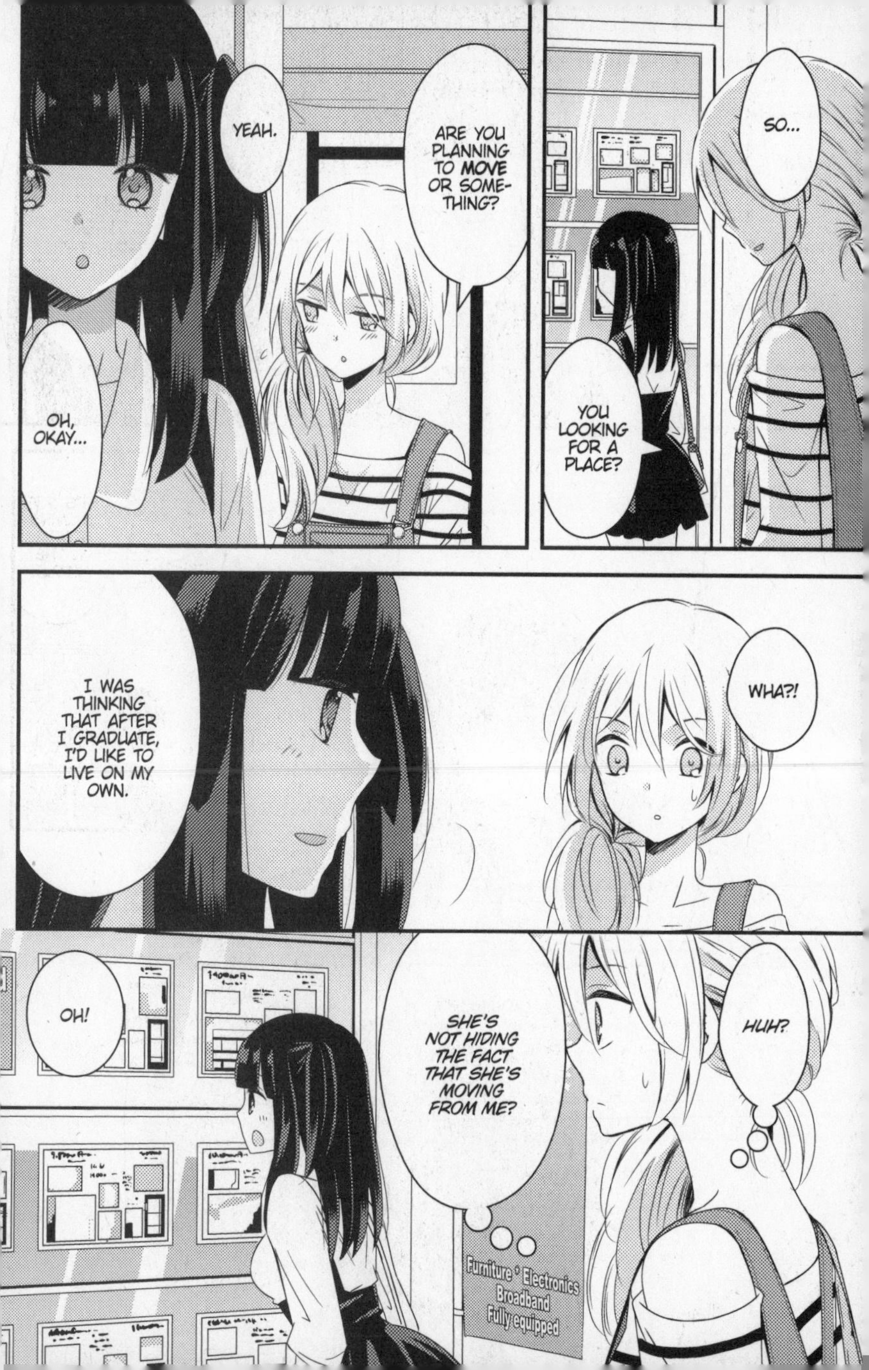
SO...
YOU LOOKING FOR A PLACE?
ARE YOU PLANNING TO MOVE OR SOME-THING?
YEAH.
OH, OKAY...
WHA?!
I WAS THINKING THAT AFTER I GRADUATE, I'D LIKE TO LIVE ON MY OWN.
HUH?
SHE'S NOT HIDING THE FACT THAT SHE'S MOVING FROM ME?
Furniture * Electronics
Broadband
Fully equipped
OH!

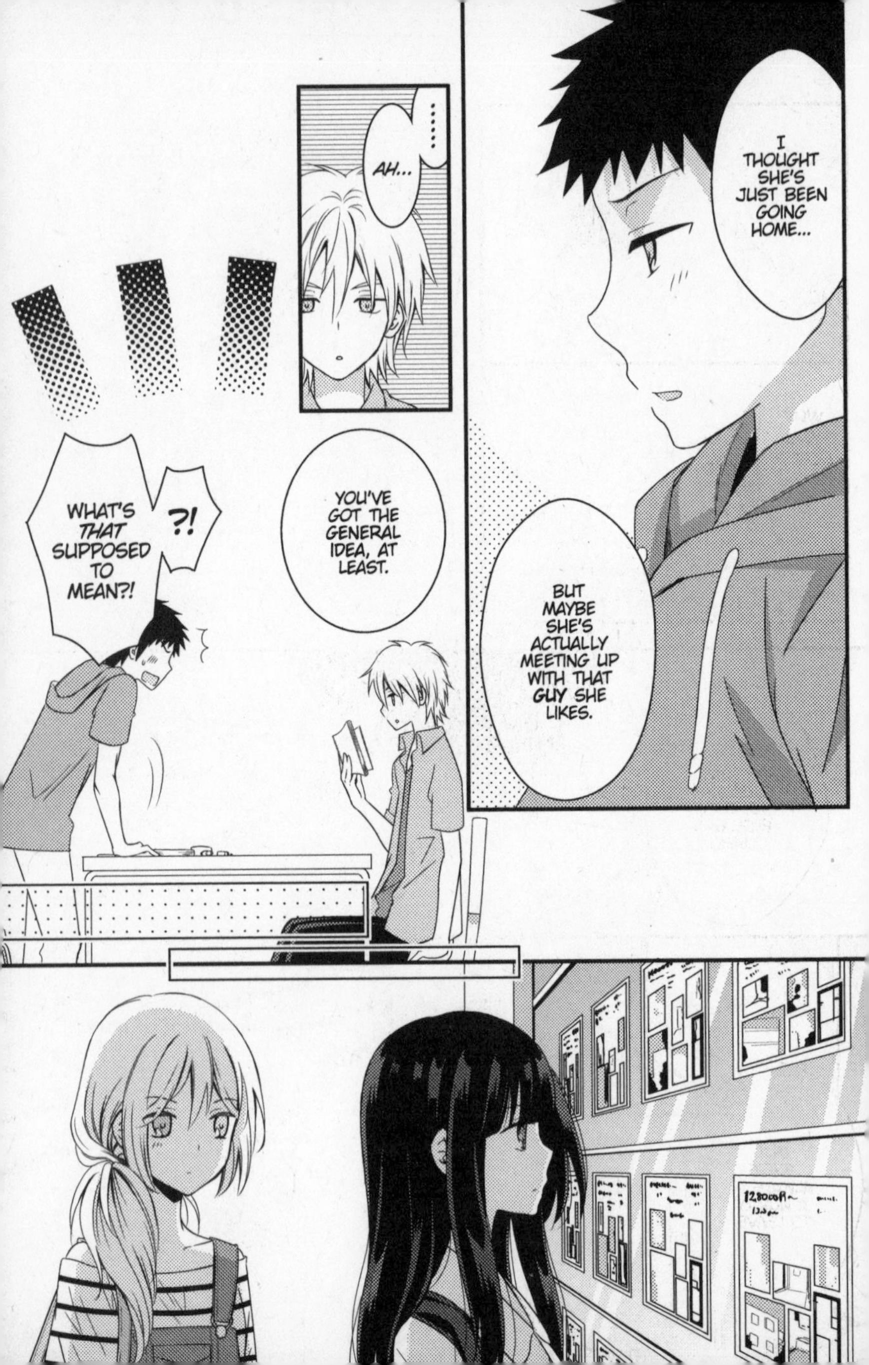

I THOUGHT SHE'S JUST BEEN GOING HOME...
BUT MAYBE SHE'S ACTUALLY MEETING UP WITH THAT GUY SHE LIKES.
......
AH...
YOU'VE GOT THE GENERAL IDEA, AT LEAST.
?!
WHAT'S *THAT* SUPPOSED TO MEAN?!

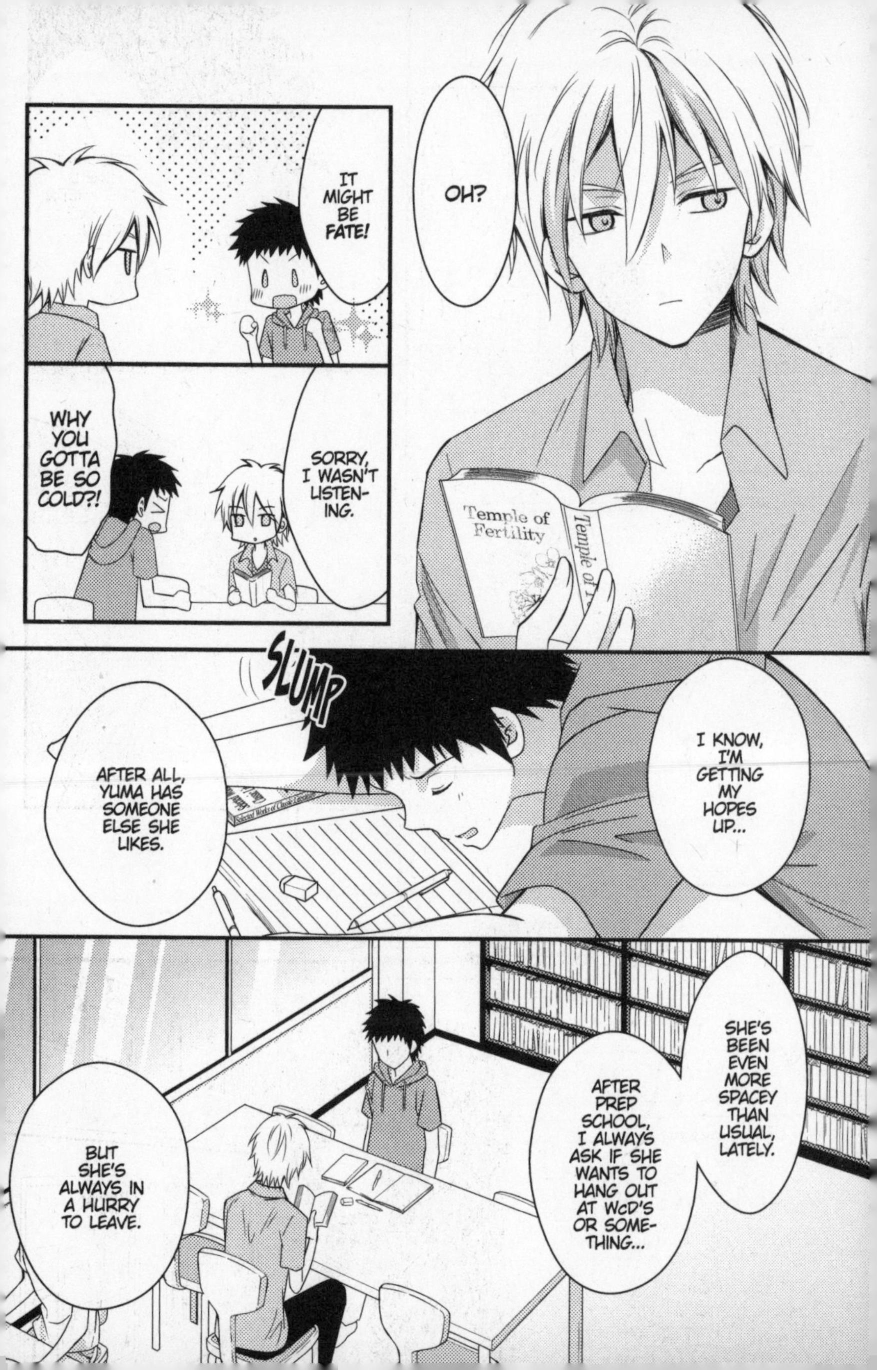
OH?
Temple of Fertility
IT MIGHT BE FATE!
SORRY, I WASN'T LISTEN-ING.
WHY YOU GOTTA BE SO COLD?!
I KNOW, I'M GETTING MY HOPES UP...
SLUMP
AFTER ALL, YUMA HAS SOMEONE ELSE SHE LIKES.
SHE'S BEEN EVEN MORE SPACEY THAN USUAL, LATELY.
AFTER PREP SCHOOL, I ALWAYS ASK IF SHE WANTS TO HANG OUT AT WcD'S OR SOME-THING...
BUT SHE'S ALWAYS IN A HURRY TO LEAVE.

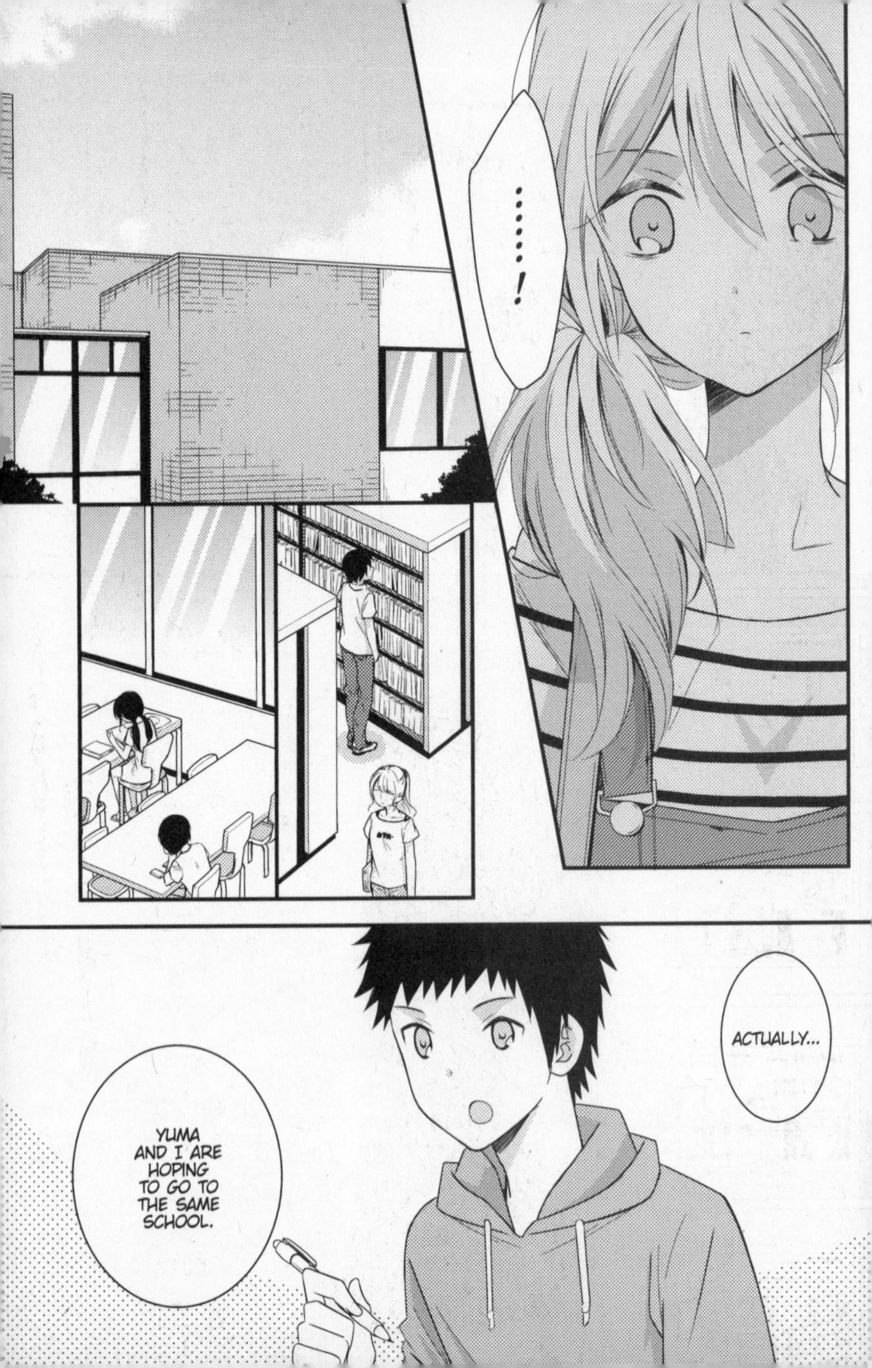
......!
ACTUALLY...
YUMA AND I ARE HOPING TO GO TO THE SAME SCHOOL.

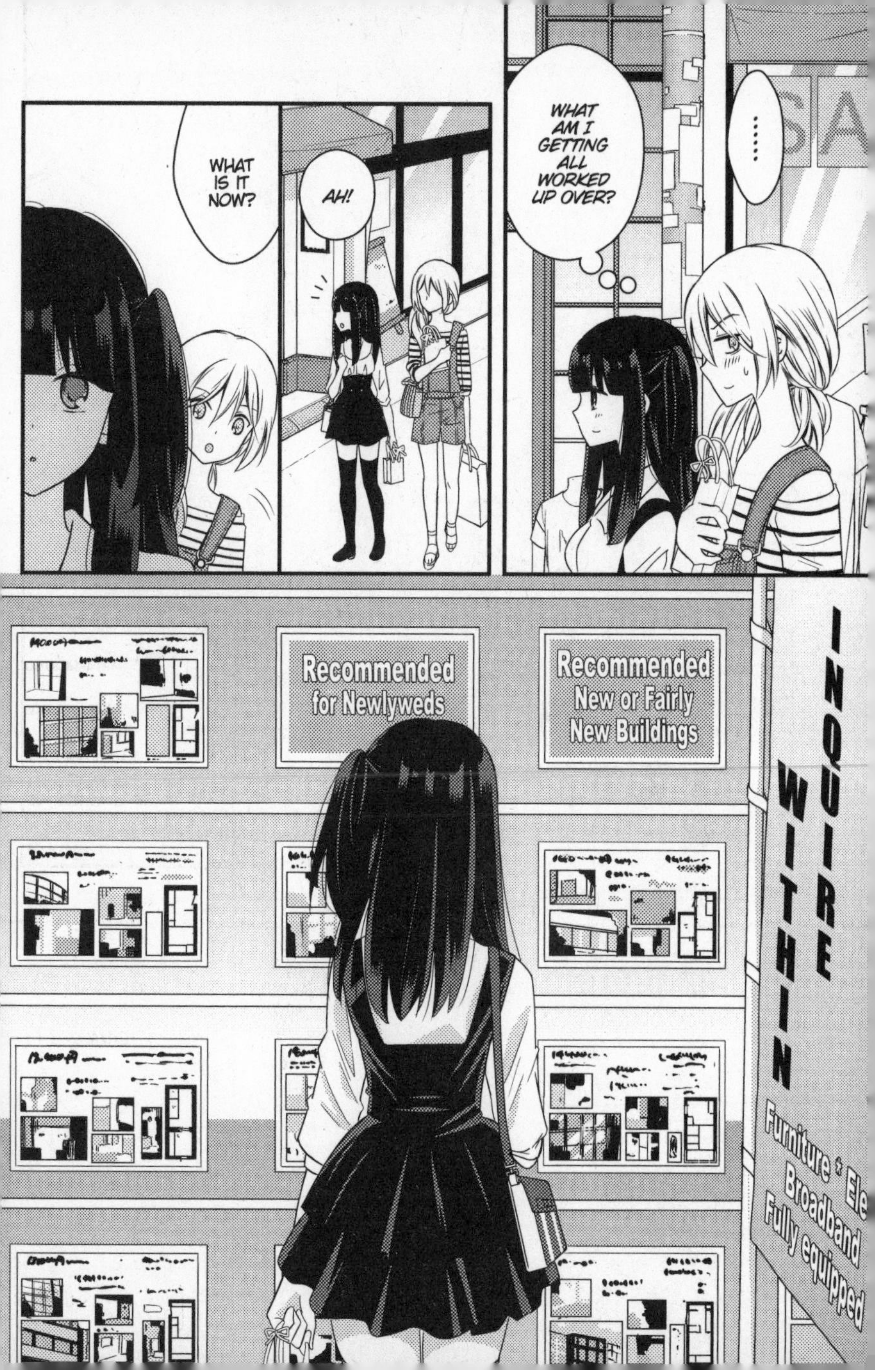
......
WHAT AM I GETTING ALL WORKED UP OVER?
AH!
WHAT IS IT NOW?
INQUIRE WITHIN
Furniture * Ele
Broadband
Fully equipped
Recommended New or Fairly New Buildings
Recommended for Newlyweds

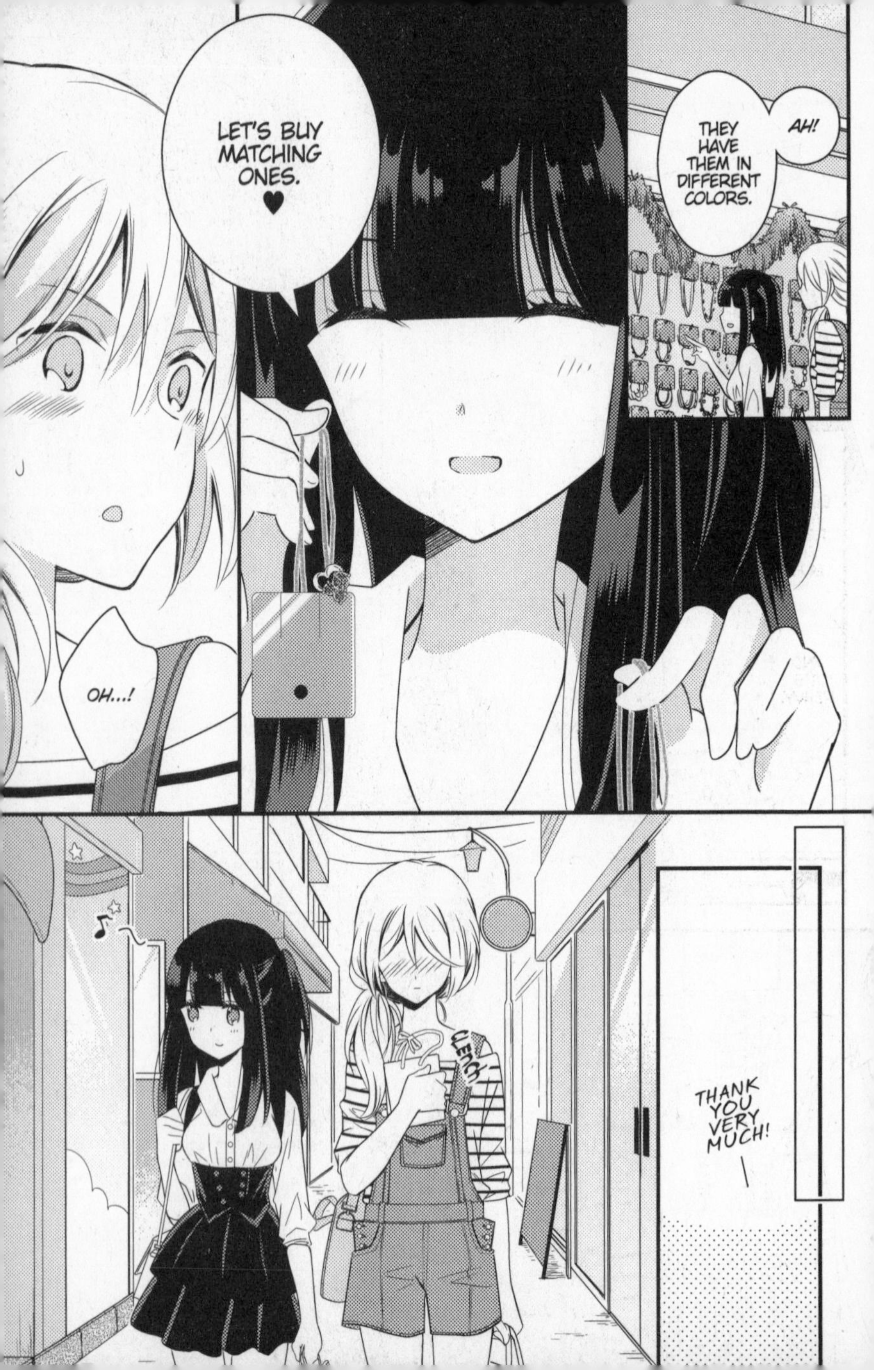
AH!
THEY HAVE THEM IN DIFFERENT COLORS.
LET'S BUY MATCHING ONES. ♥
OH...!
THANK YOU VERY MUCH!
CLENCH

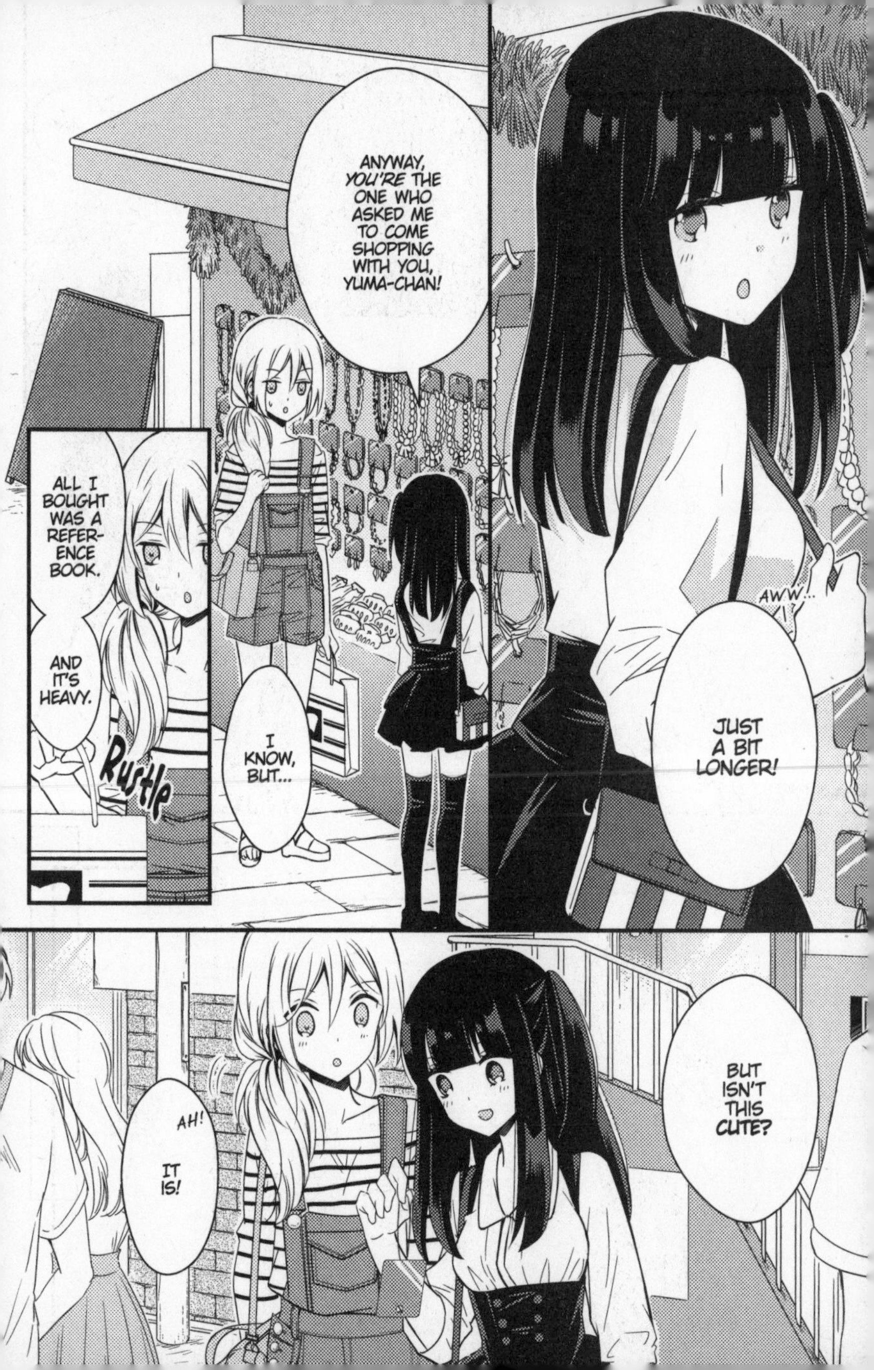
AWW...
JUST A BIT LONGER!
ANYWAY, YOU'RE THE ONE WHO ASKED ME TO COME SHOPPING WITH YOU, YUMA-CHAN!
I KNOW, BUT...
ALL I BOUGHT WAS A REFERENCE BOOK.
AND IT'S HEAVY.
Rustle
BUT ISN'T THIS CUTE?
AH!
IT IS!

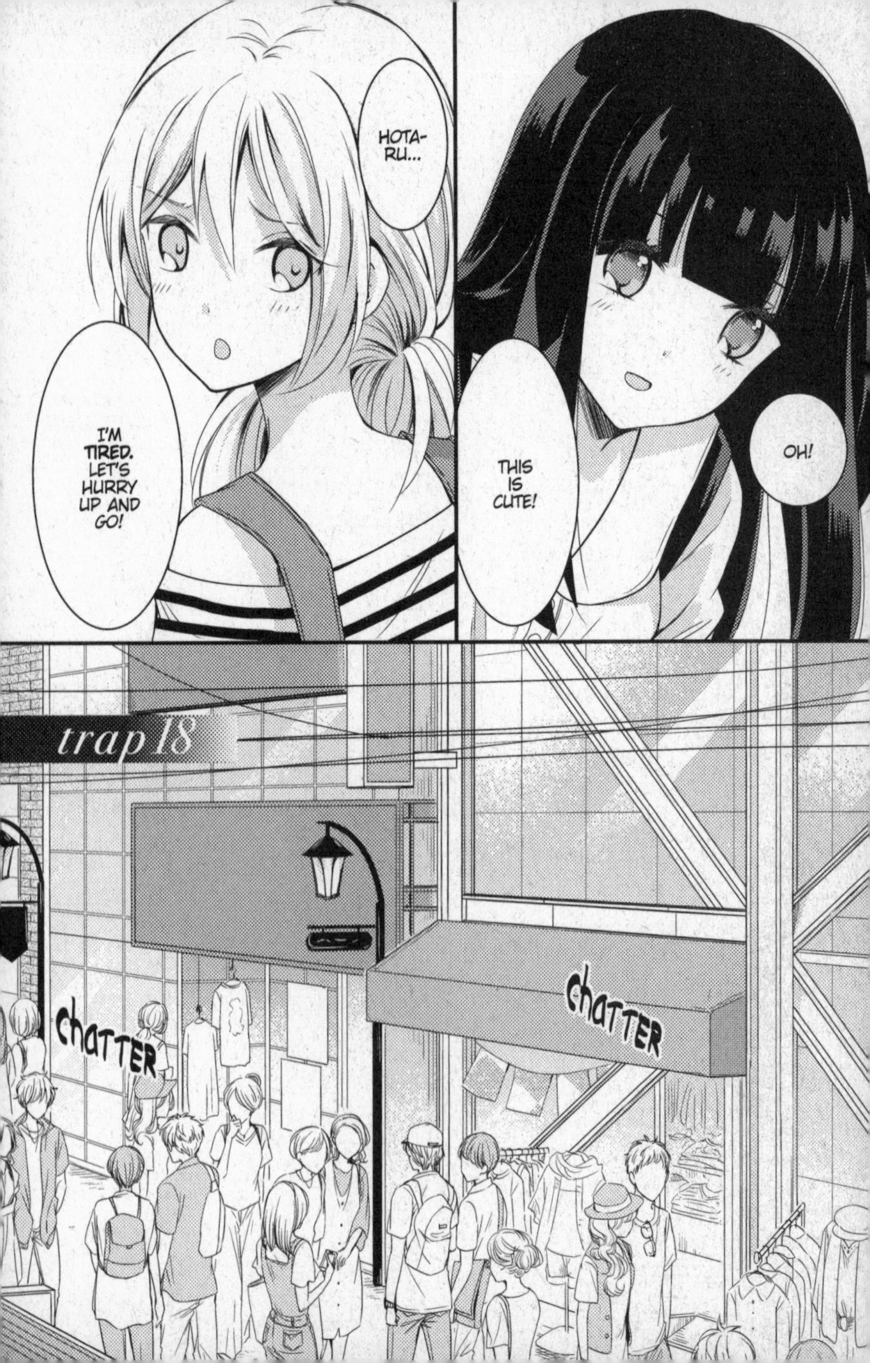
OH!
THIS IS CUTE!
HOTA-RU...
I'M TIRED. LET'S HURRY UP AND GO!
trap 18
CHATTER
CHATTER

Netsuzou TRap -NTR-

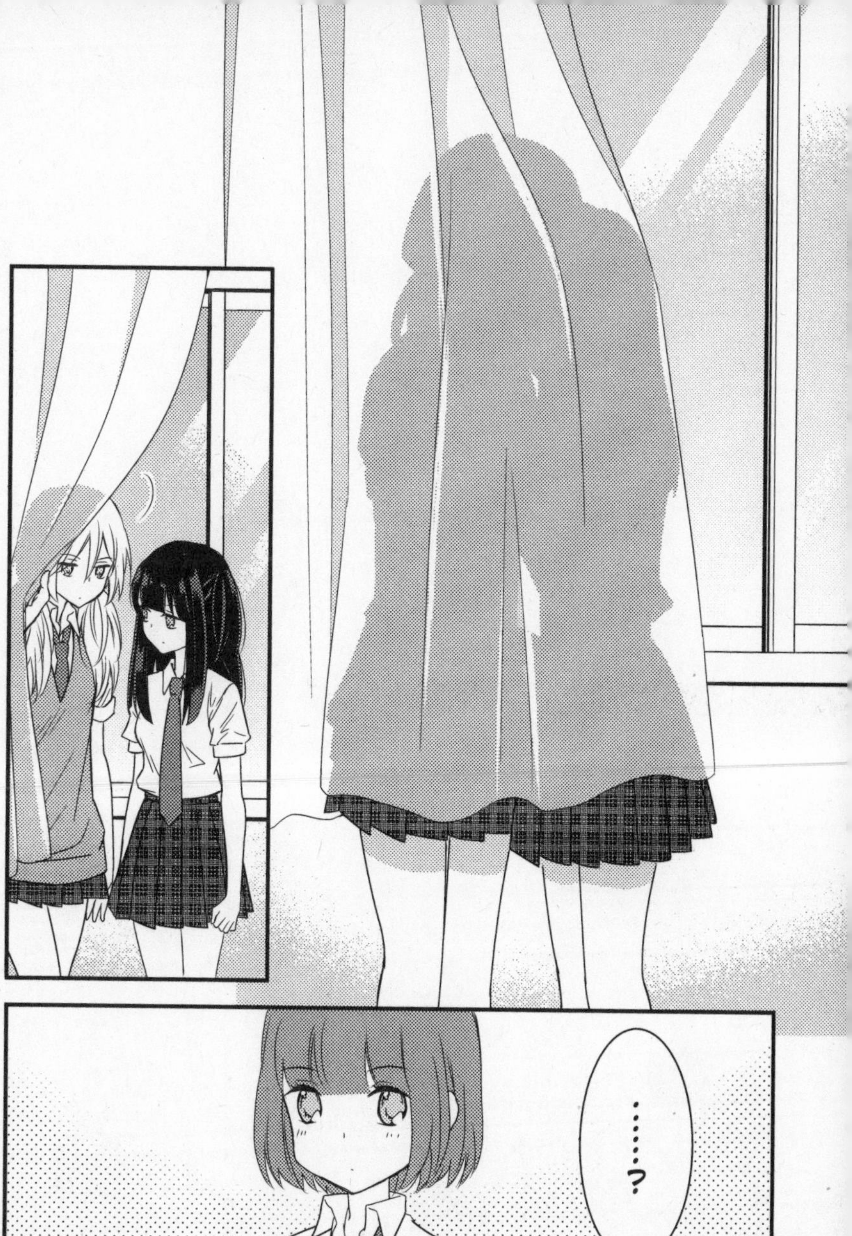
……っ

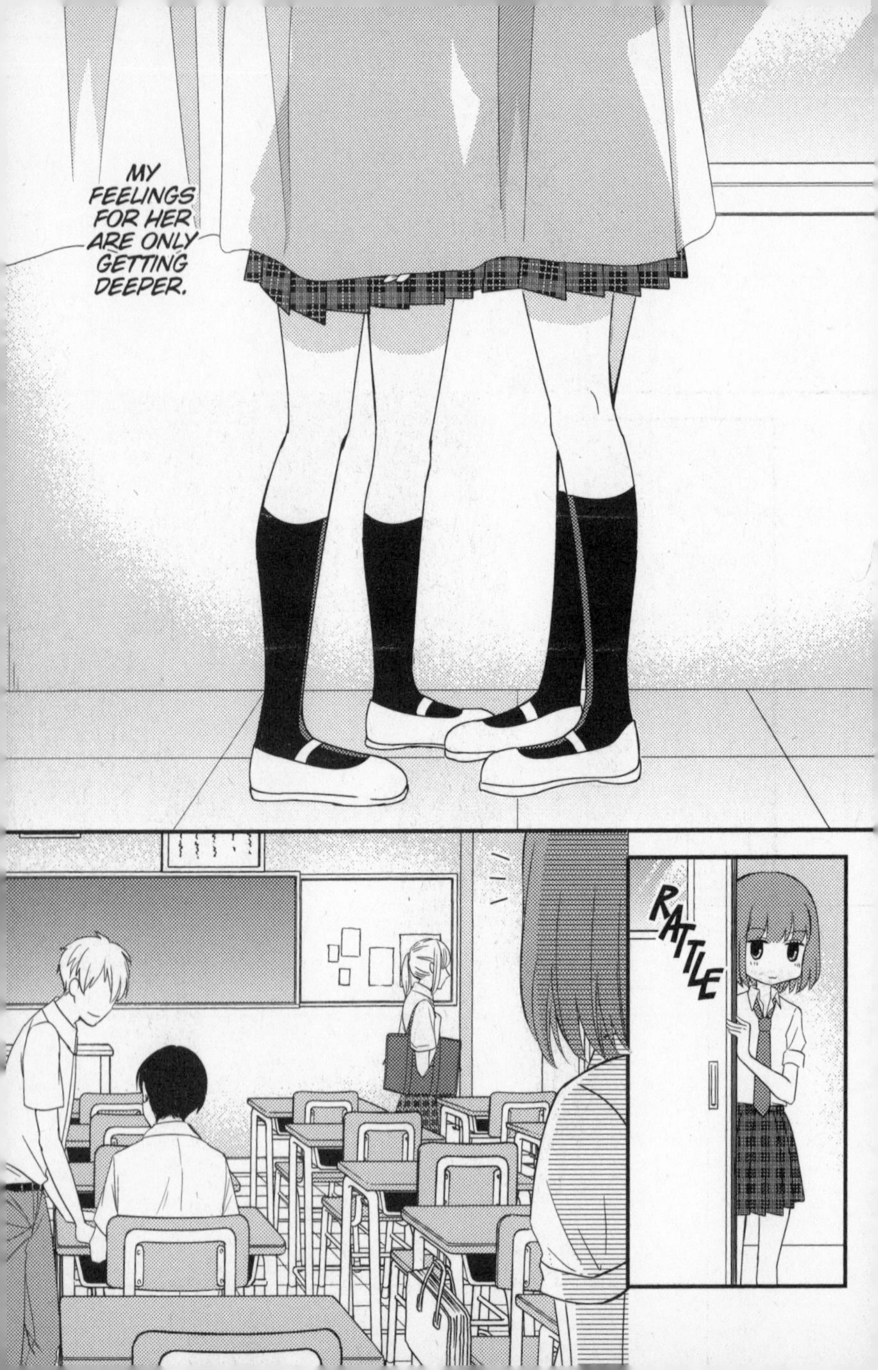
MY FEELINGS FOR HER ARE ONLY GETTING DEEPER.
RATTLE

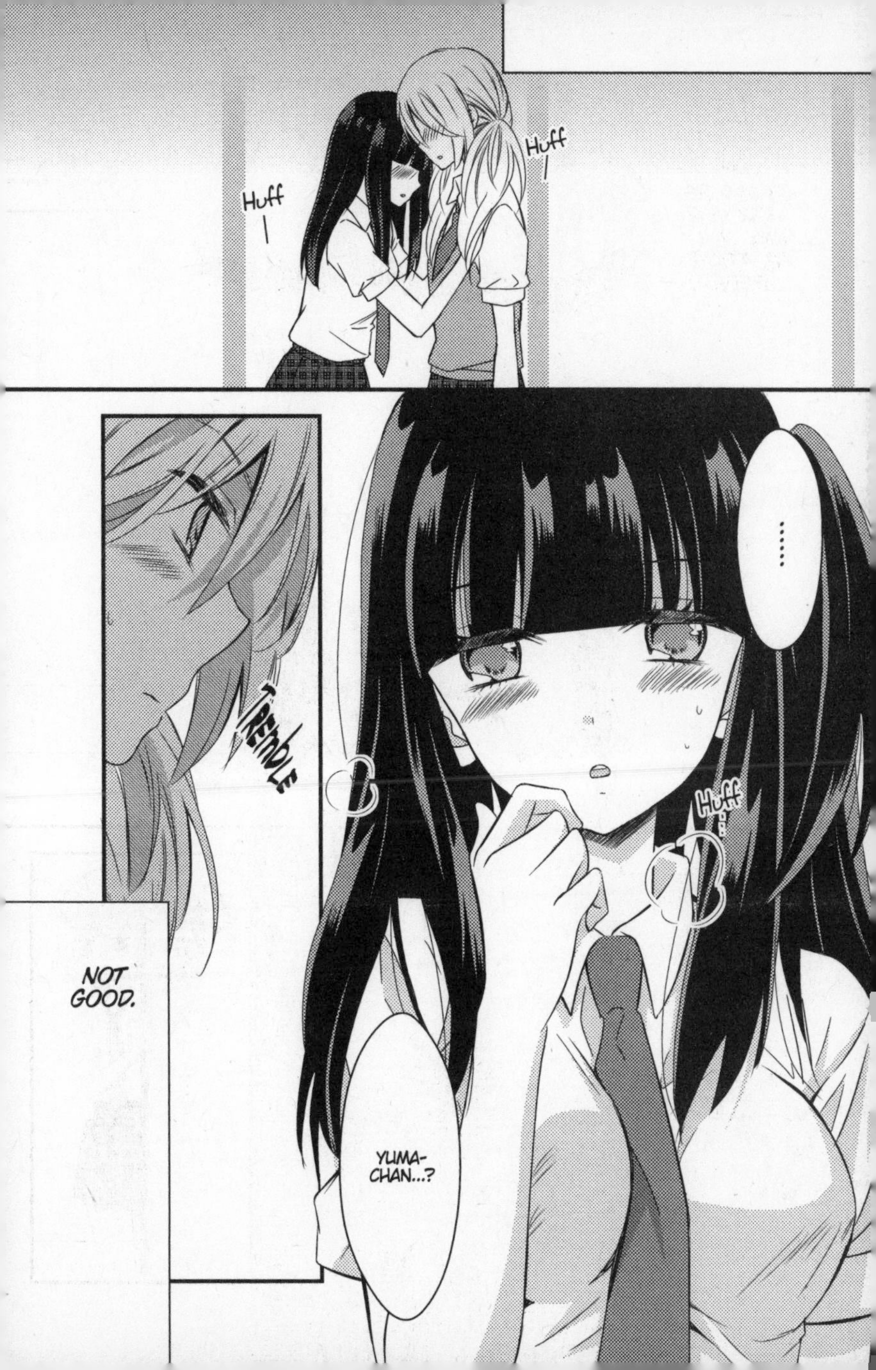
Huff
Huff
......
Huff...
YUMA-CHAN...?
TREMBLE
NOT GOOD.

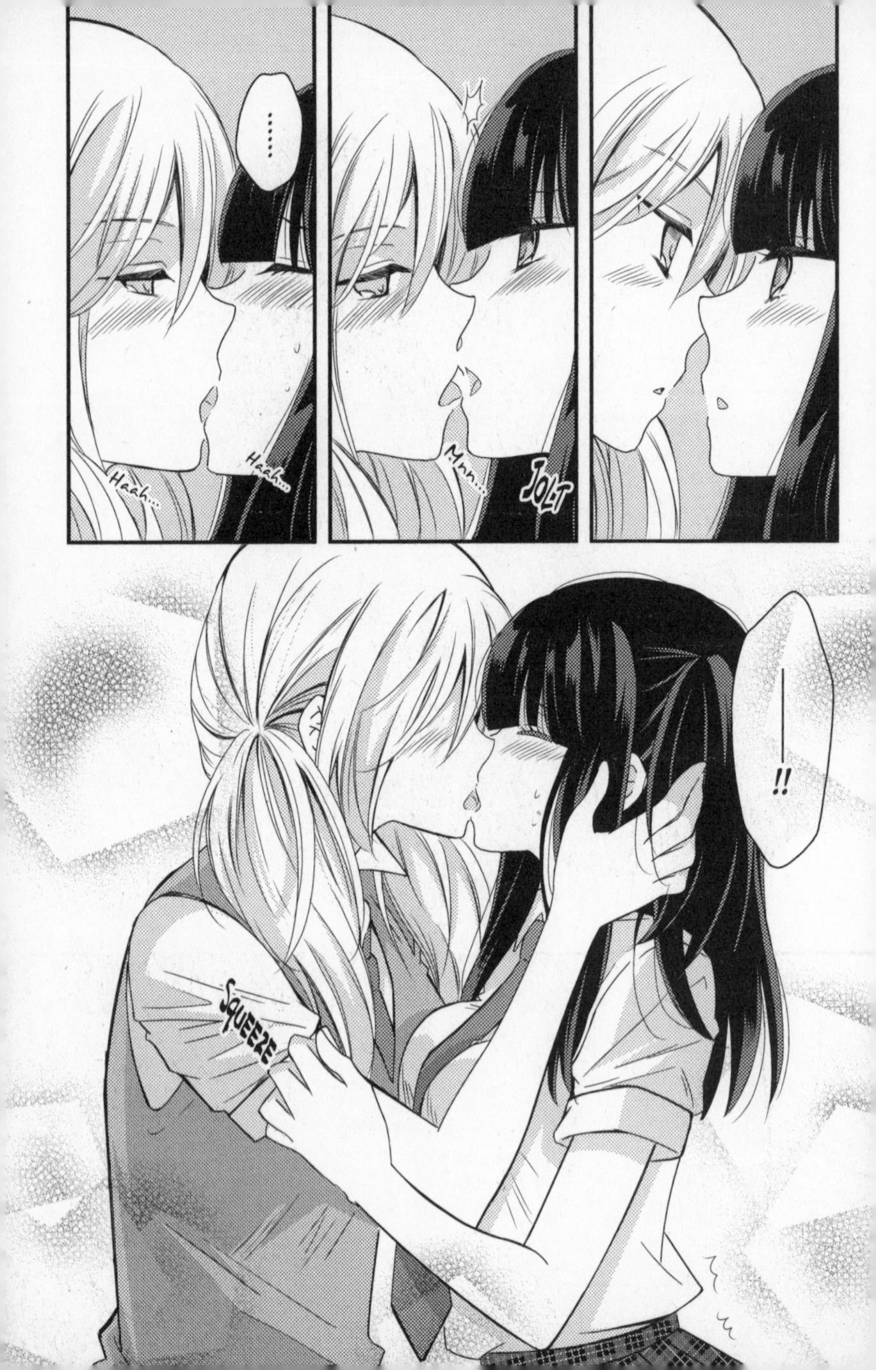
JOLT
Mnn...
......
Haah...
Haah...
——!!
SQUEEZE

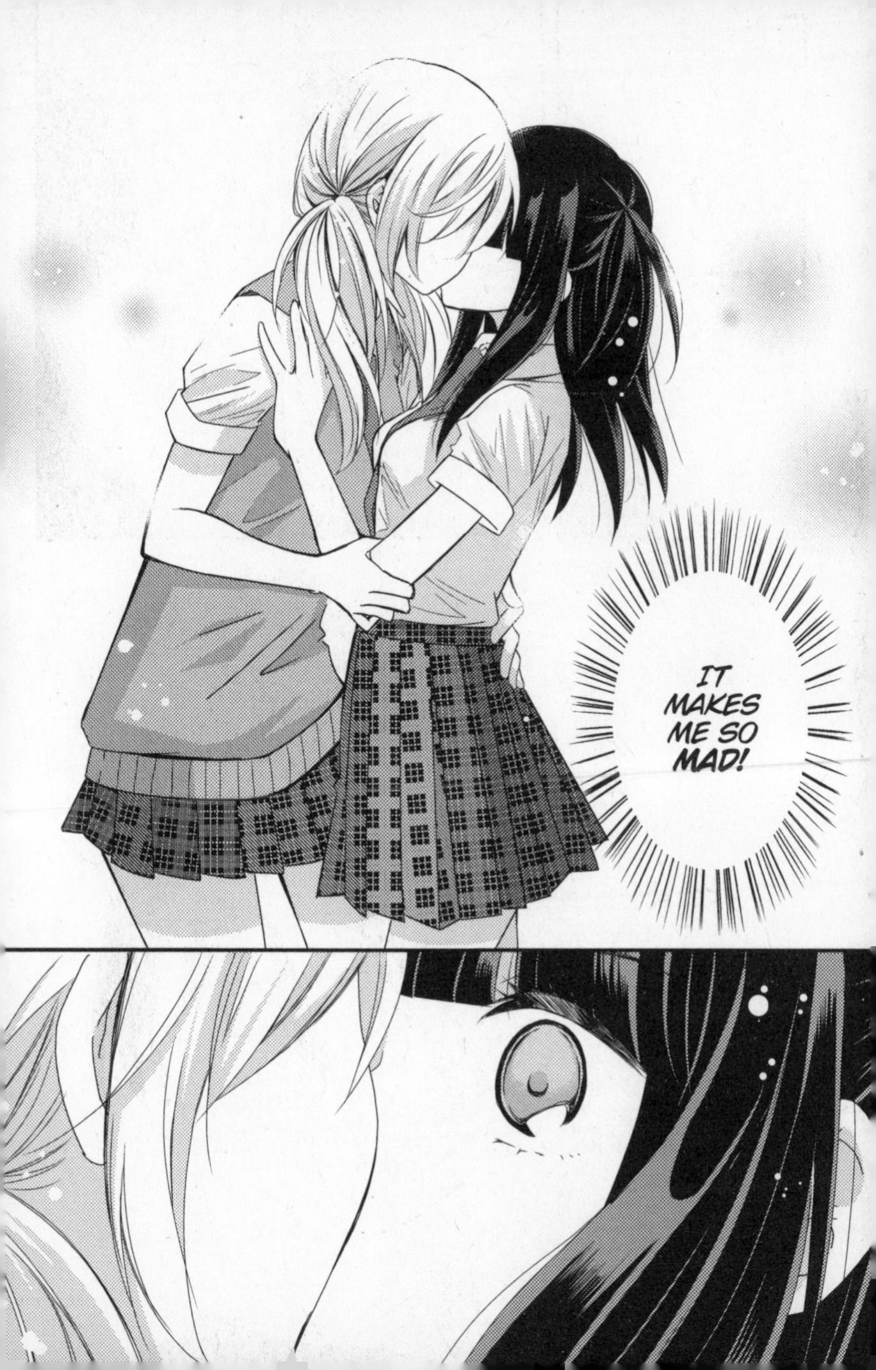
IT MAKES ME SO MAD!

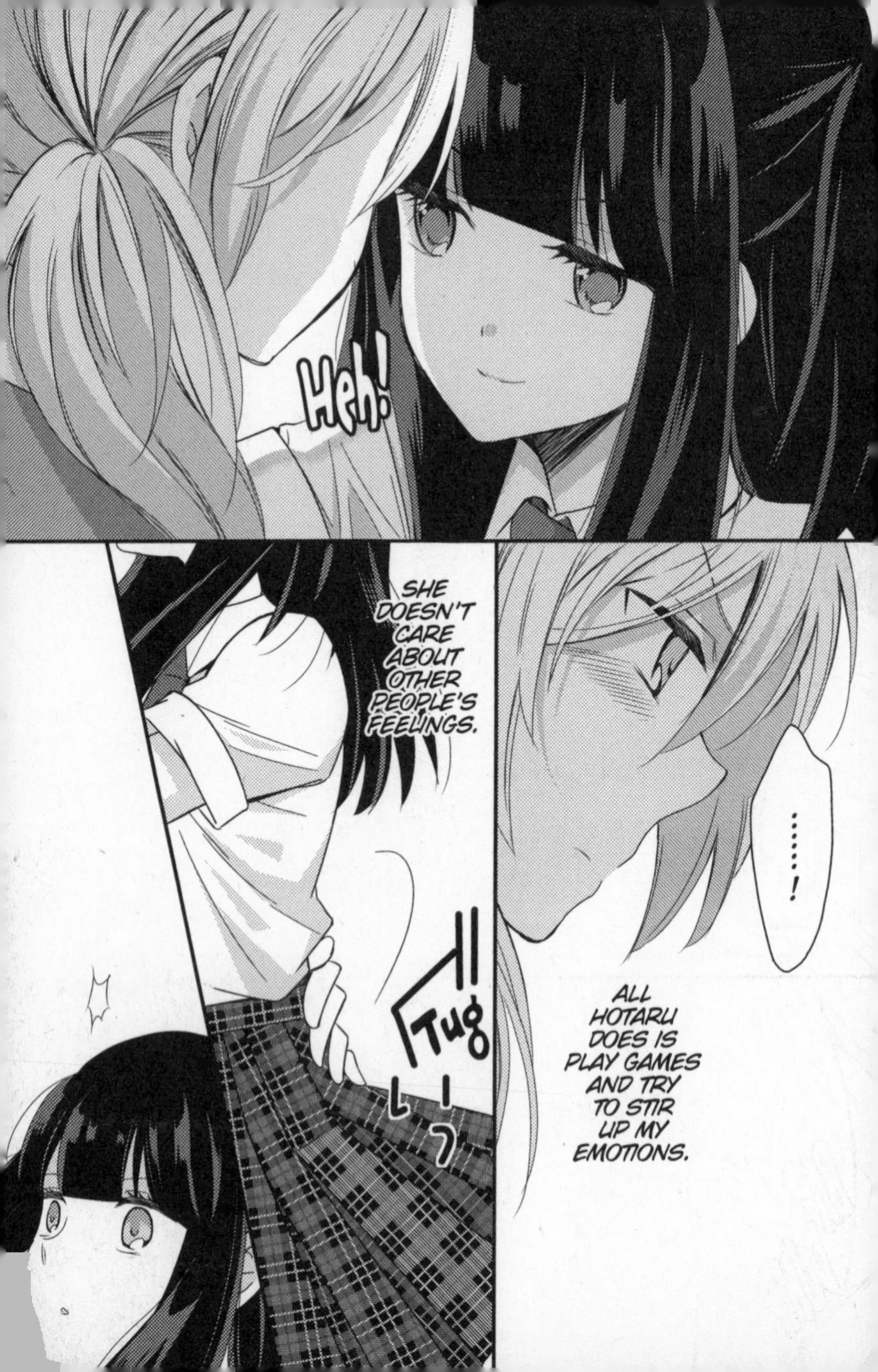
Heh!
......!
ALL HOTARU DOES IS PLAY GAMES AND TRY TO STIR UP MY EMOTIONS.
SHE DOESN'T CARE ABOUT OTHER PEOPLE'S FEELINGS.
Tug

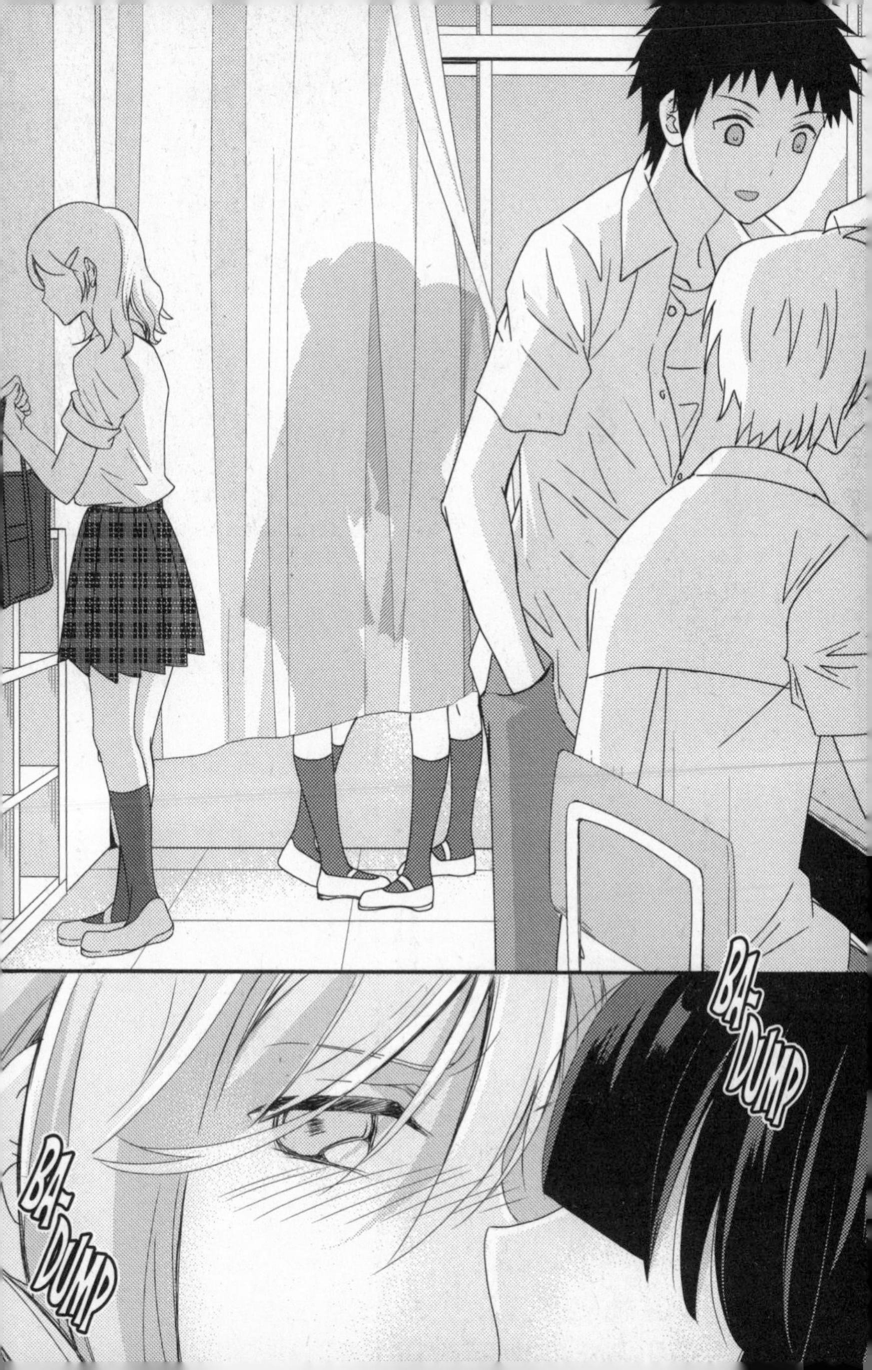
BA-DUMP
BA-DUMP

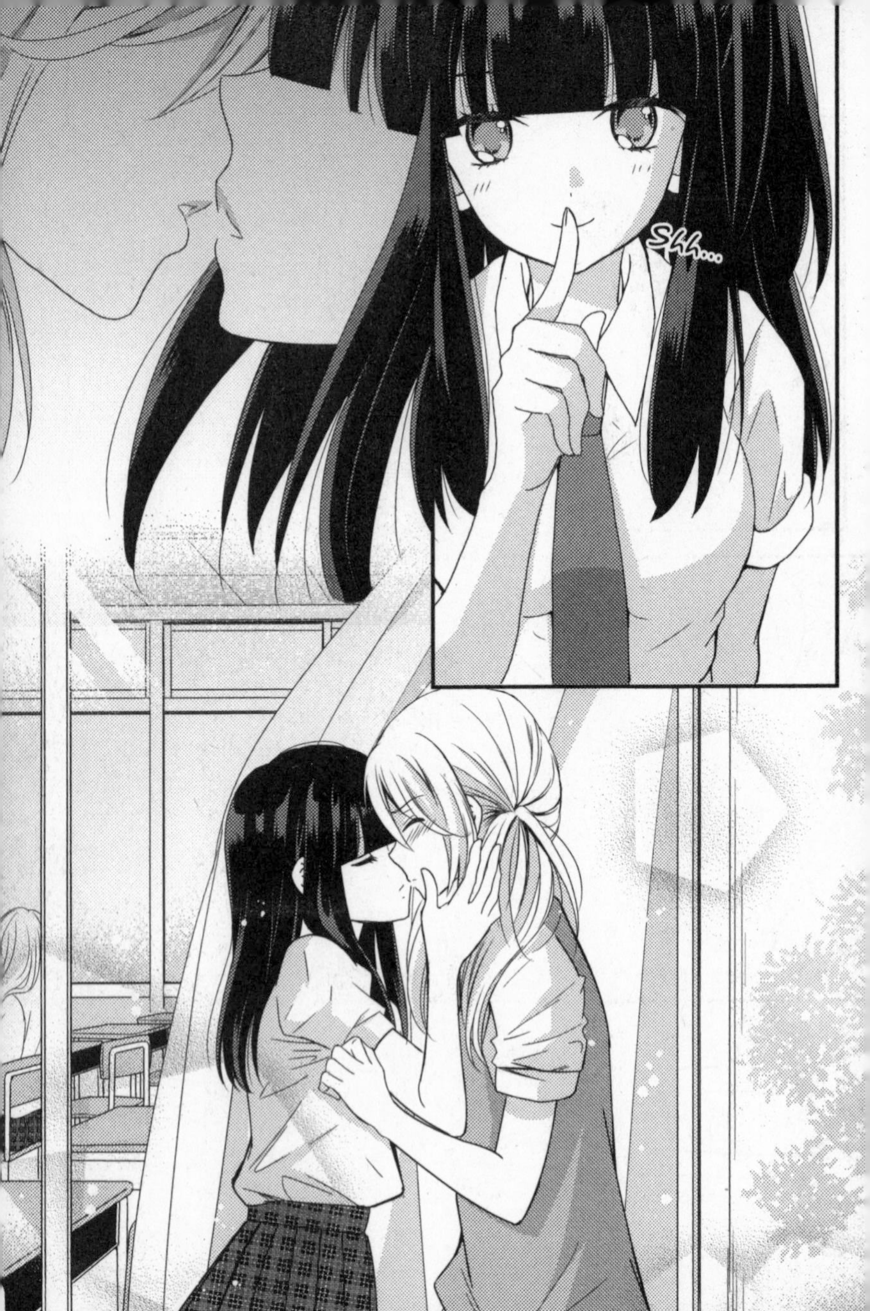
Shh...

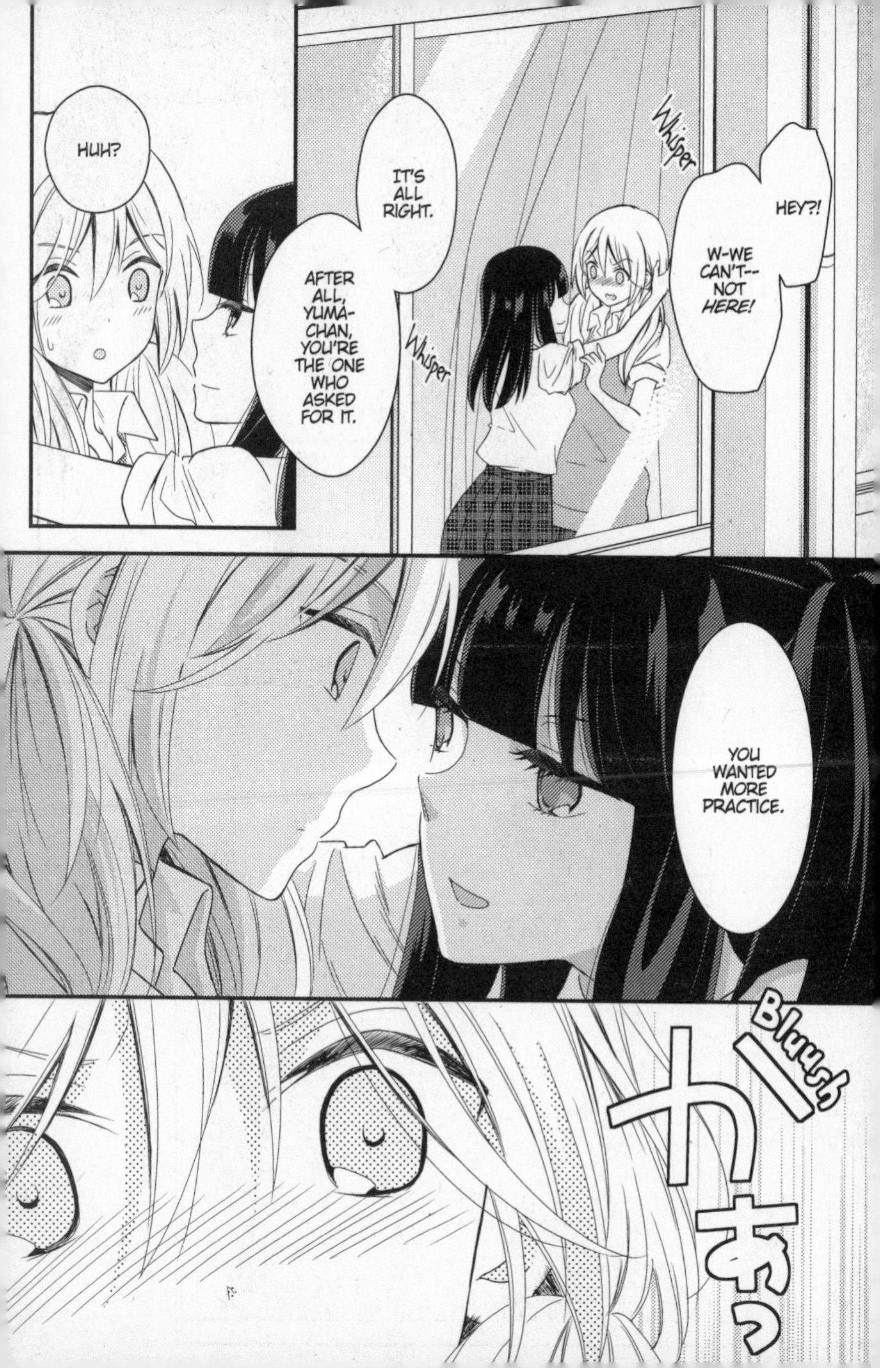

Whisper
HEY?! W-WE CAN'T-- NOT HERE!
IT'S ALL RIGHT.
Whisper
AFTER ALL, YUMA-CHAN, YOU'RE THE ONE WHO ASKED FOR IT.
HUH?
YOU WANTED MORE PRACTICE.
Bluush
わぁっ

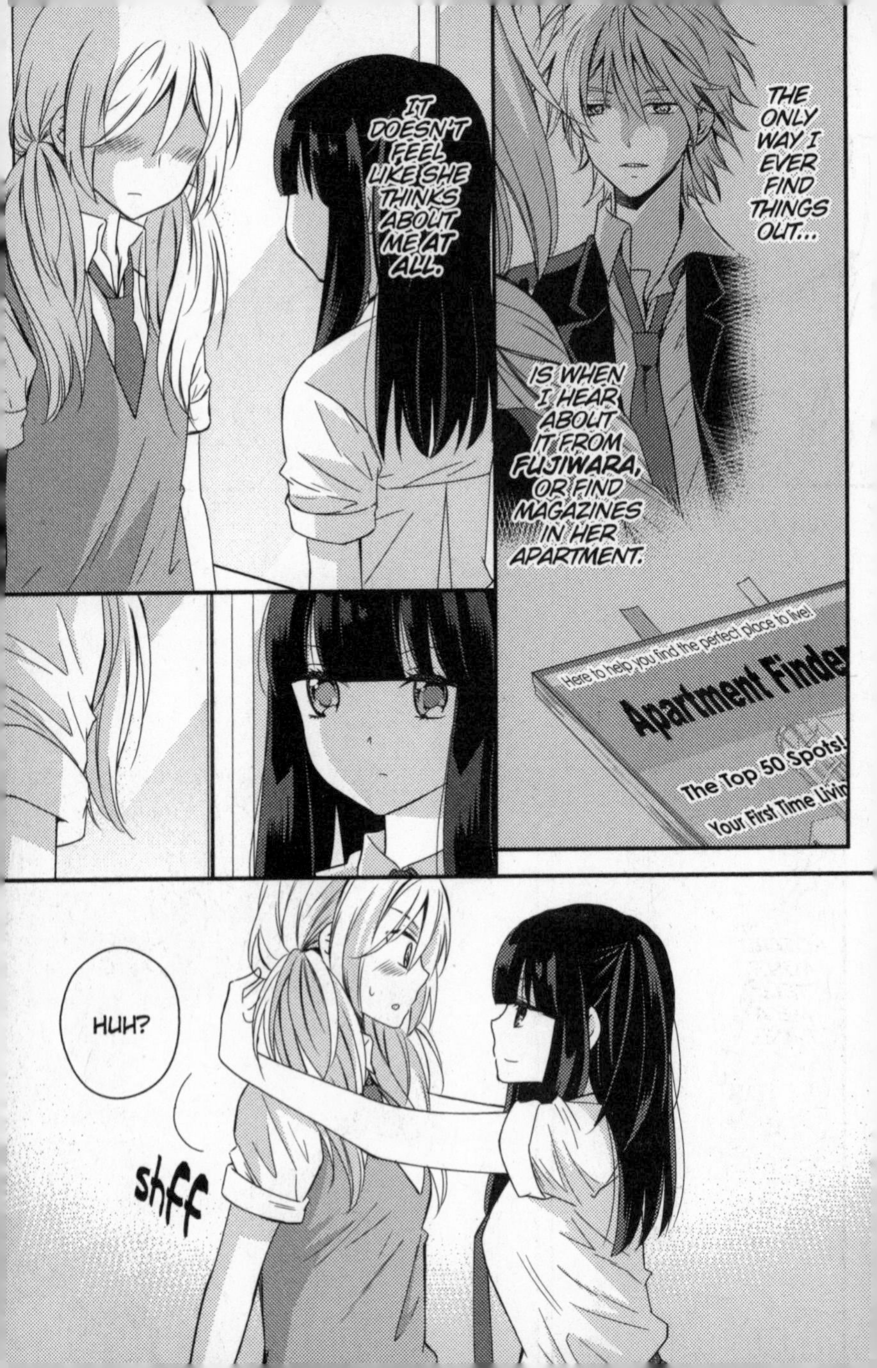
THE ONLY WAY I EVER FIND THINGS OUT...
IS WHEN I HEAR ABOUT IT FROM FUJIWARA, OR FIND MAGAZINES IN HER APARTMENT.
Here to help you find the perfect place to live!
Apartment Finde
The Top 50 Spots!
Your First Time Livin
IT DOESN'T FEEL LIKE SHE THINKS ABOUT ME AT ALL.
HUH?
shff

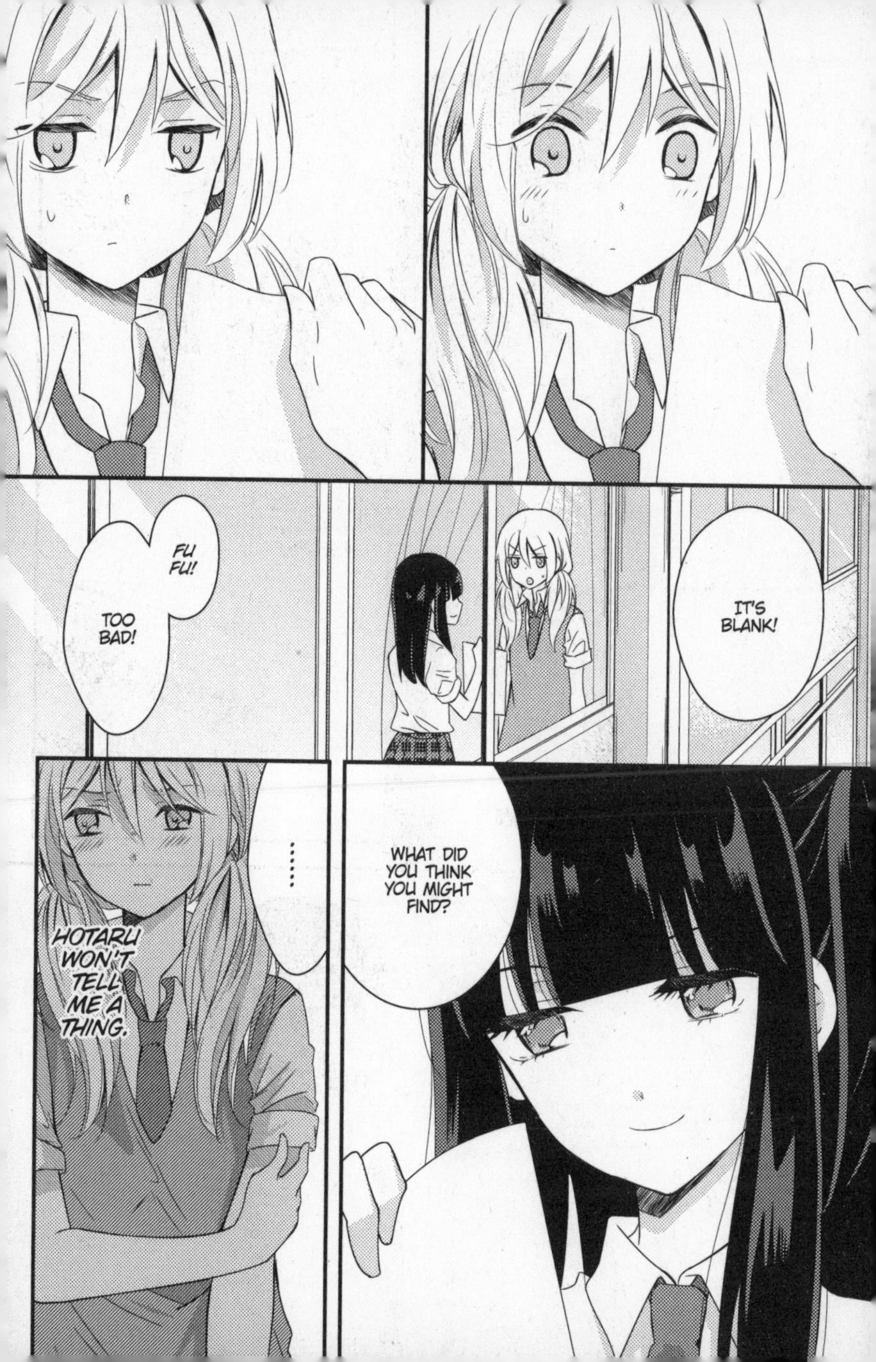
IT'S BLANK!
FU FU! TOO BAD!
WHAT DID YOU THINK YOU MIGHT FIND?
......
HOTARU WON'T TELL ME A THING.

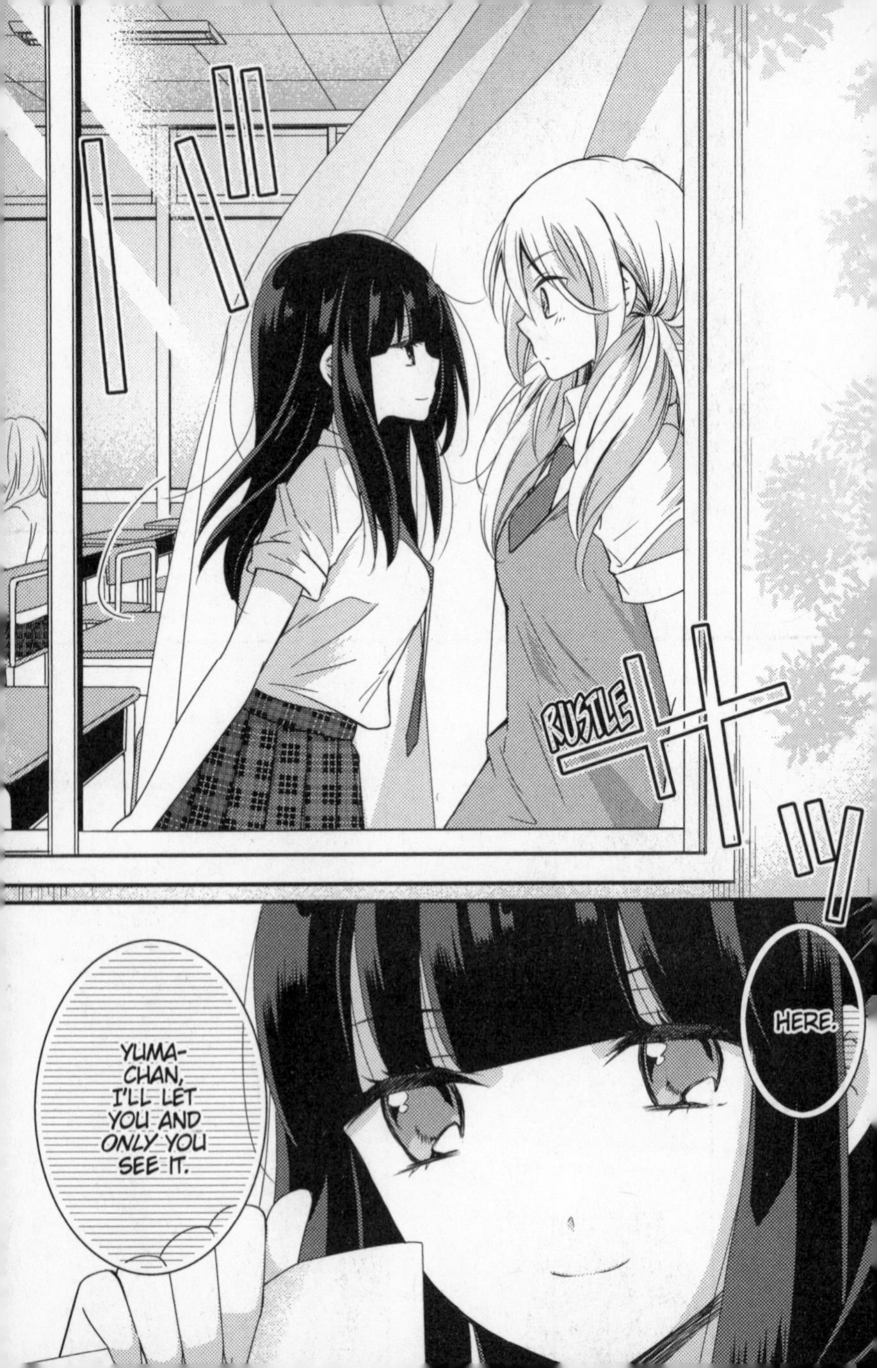
RUSTLE
HERE.
YUMA-CHAN, I'LL LET YOU AND ONLY YOU SEE IT.

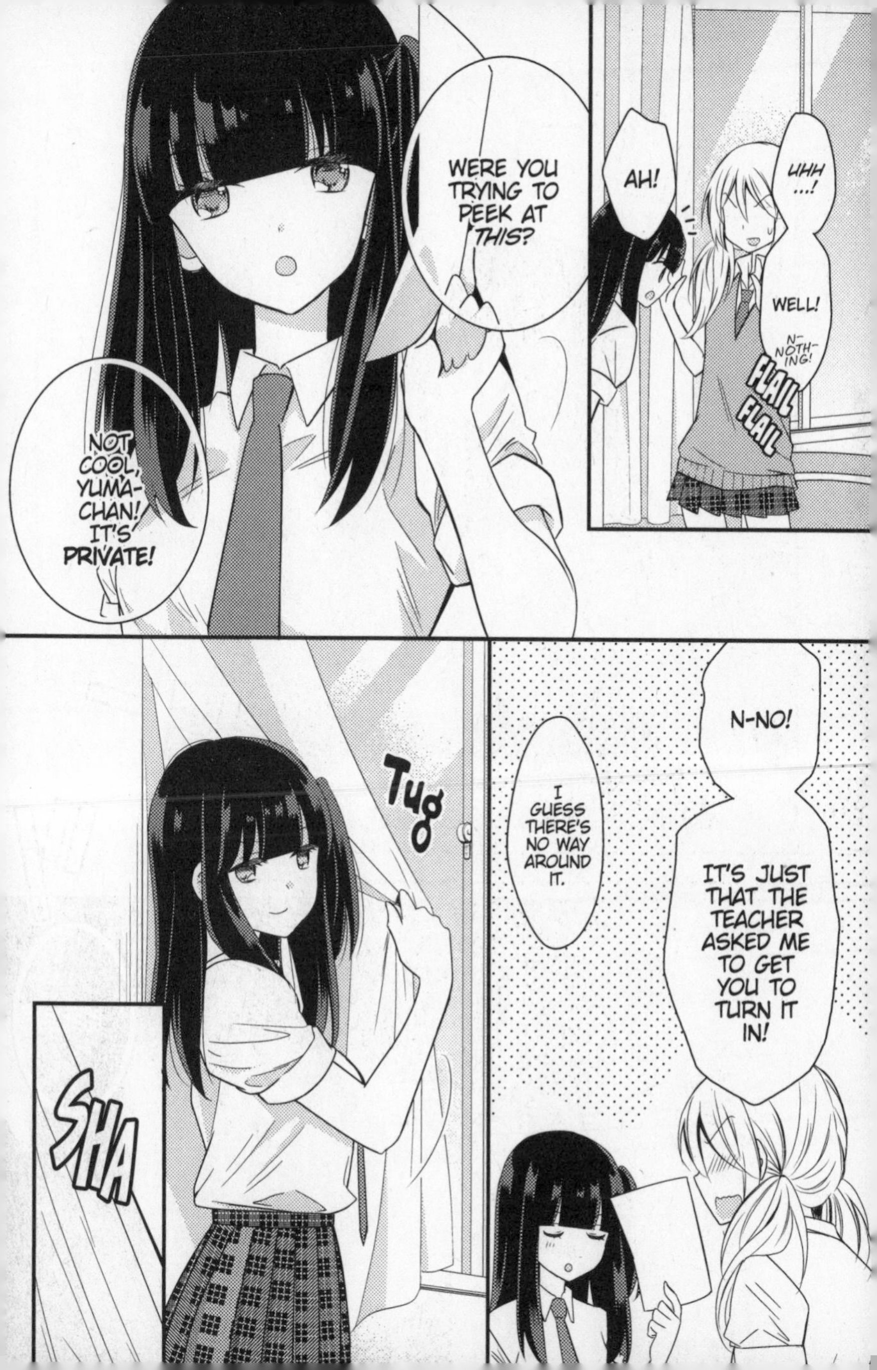
AH!
UHH ...!
WELL!
N-NOTHING!
FLAIL FLAIL
WERE YOU TRYING TO PEEK AT THIS?
NOT COOL, YUMA-CHAN! IT'S PRIVATE!
N-NO!
IT'S JUST THAT THE TEACHER ASKED ME TO GET YOU TO TURN IT IN!
I GUESS THERE'S NO WAY AROUND IT.
TUG
SHA

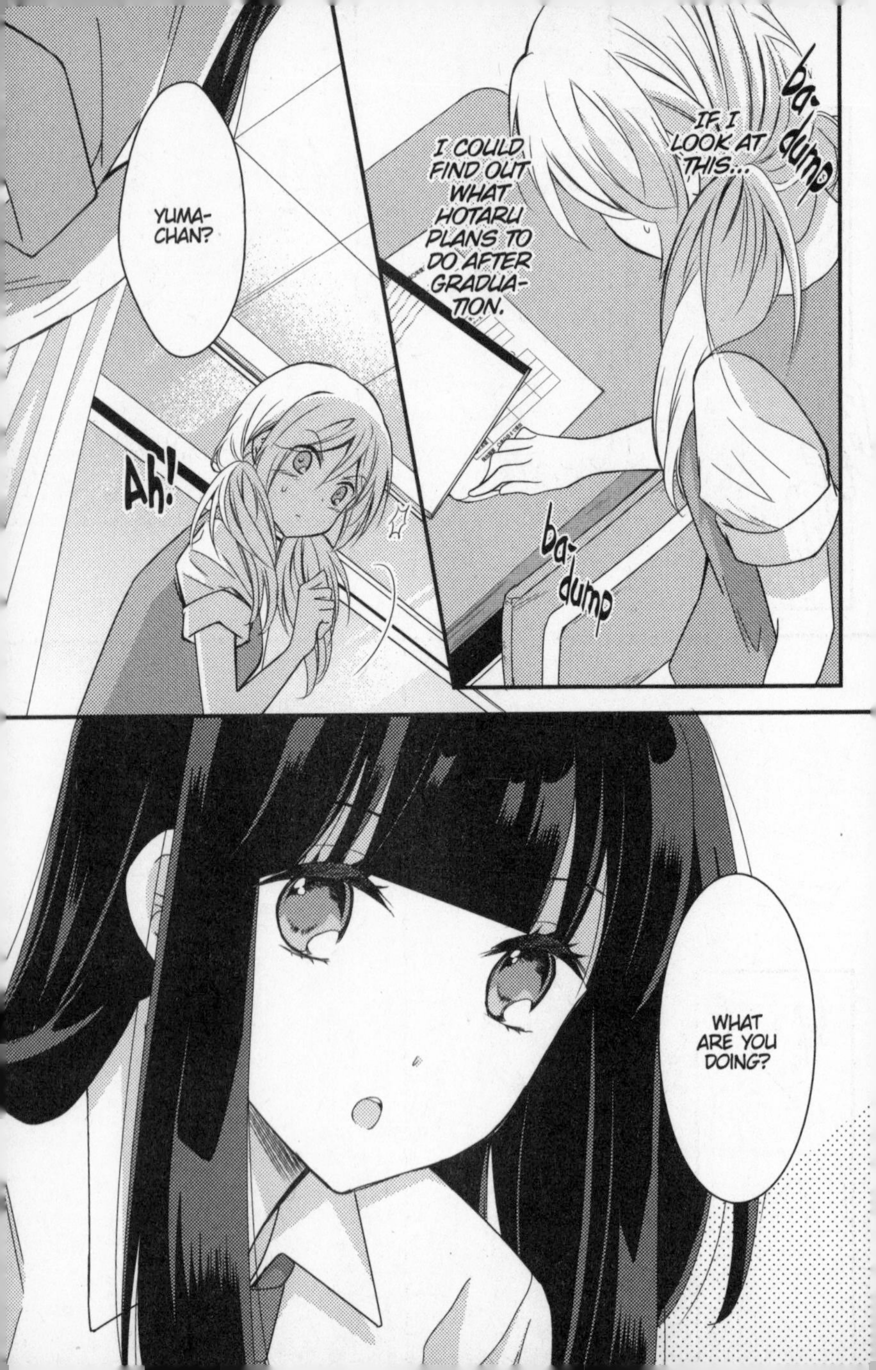
IF I LOOK AT THIS...
ba-dump
I COULD FIND OUT WHAT HOTARU PLANS TO DO AFTER GRADUATION.
ba-dump
YUMA-CHAN?
Ah!
WHAT ARE YOU DOING?

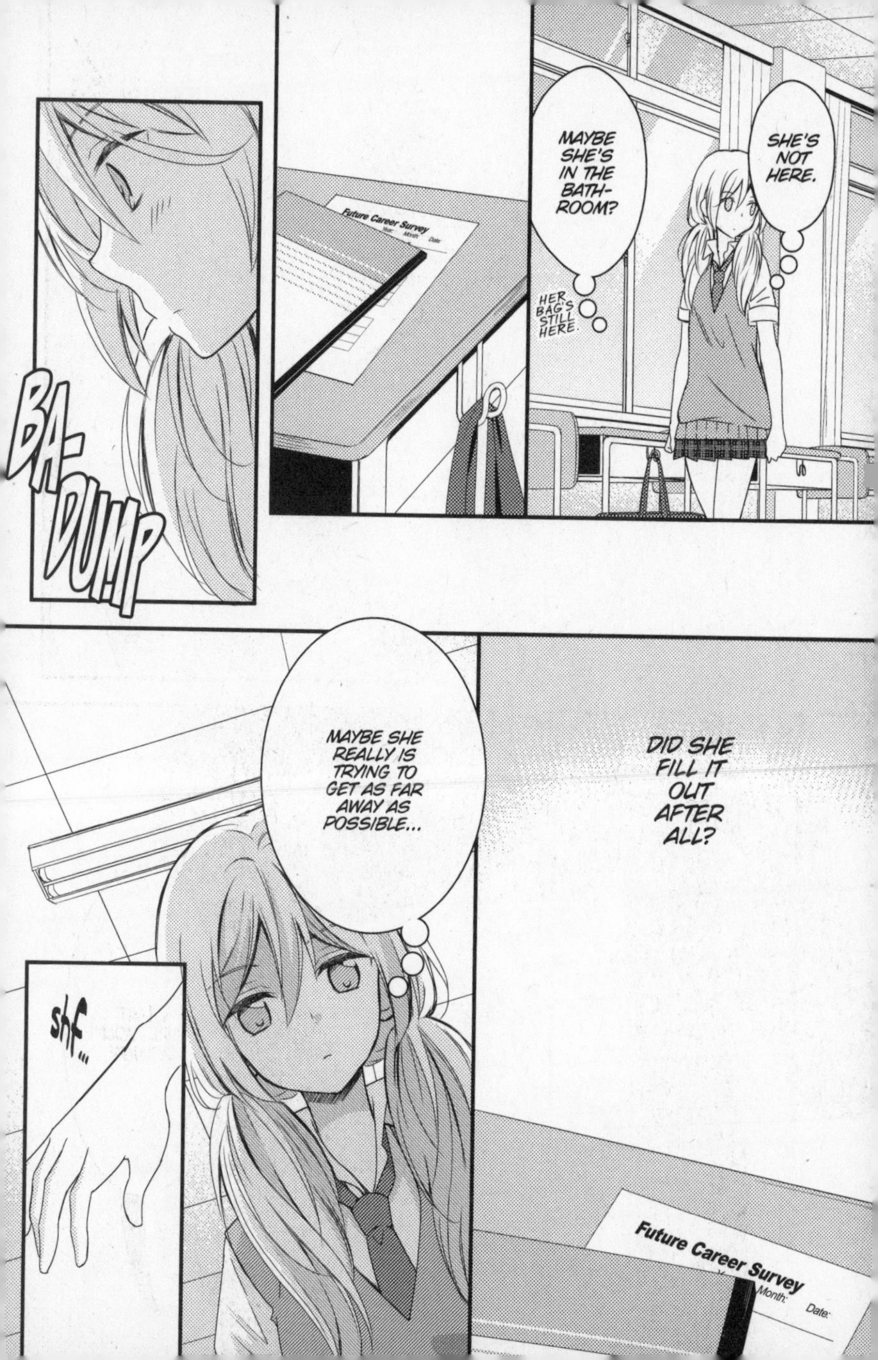
SHE'S NOT HERE.
MAYBE SHE'S IN THE BATH-ROOM?
HER BAG'S STILL HERE.
Future Career Survey
BA-DUMP
DID SHE FILL IT OUT AFTER ALL?
Future Career Survey
Month:
Date:
MAYBE SHE REALLY IS TRYING TO GET AS FAR AWAY AS POSSIBLE...
shf...

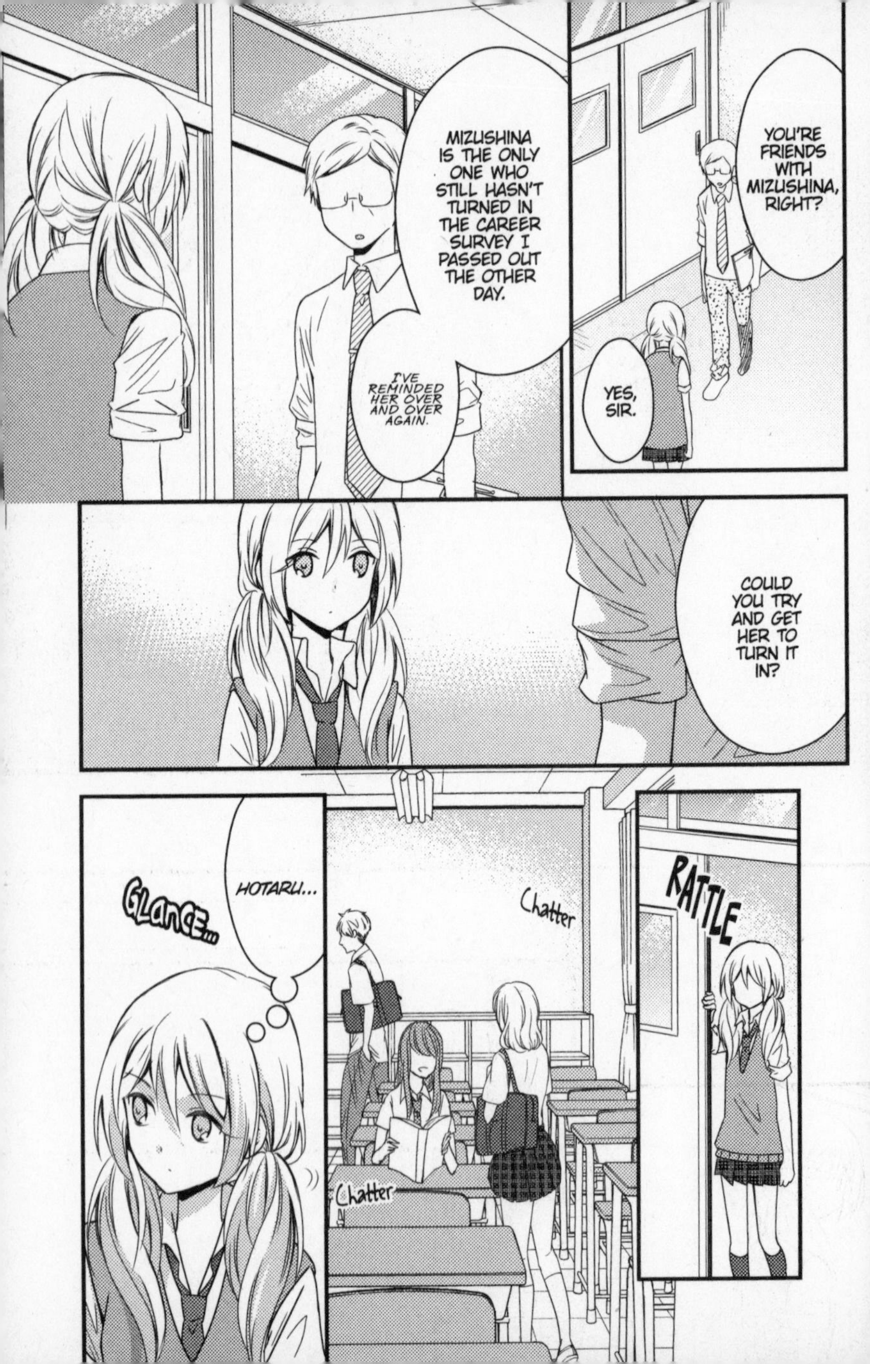
YOU'RE FRIENDS WITH MIZUSHINA, RIGHT?
YES, SIR.
MIZUSHINA IS THE ONLY ONE WHO STILL HASN'T TURNED IN THE CAREER SURVEY I PASSED OUT THE OTHER DAY.
I'VE REMINDED HER OVER AND OVER AGAIN.
COULD YOU TRY AND GET HER TO TURN IT IN?
RATTLE
Chatter
Chatter
HOTARU...
GLANCE...

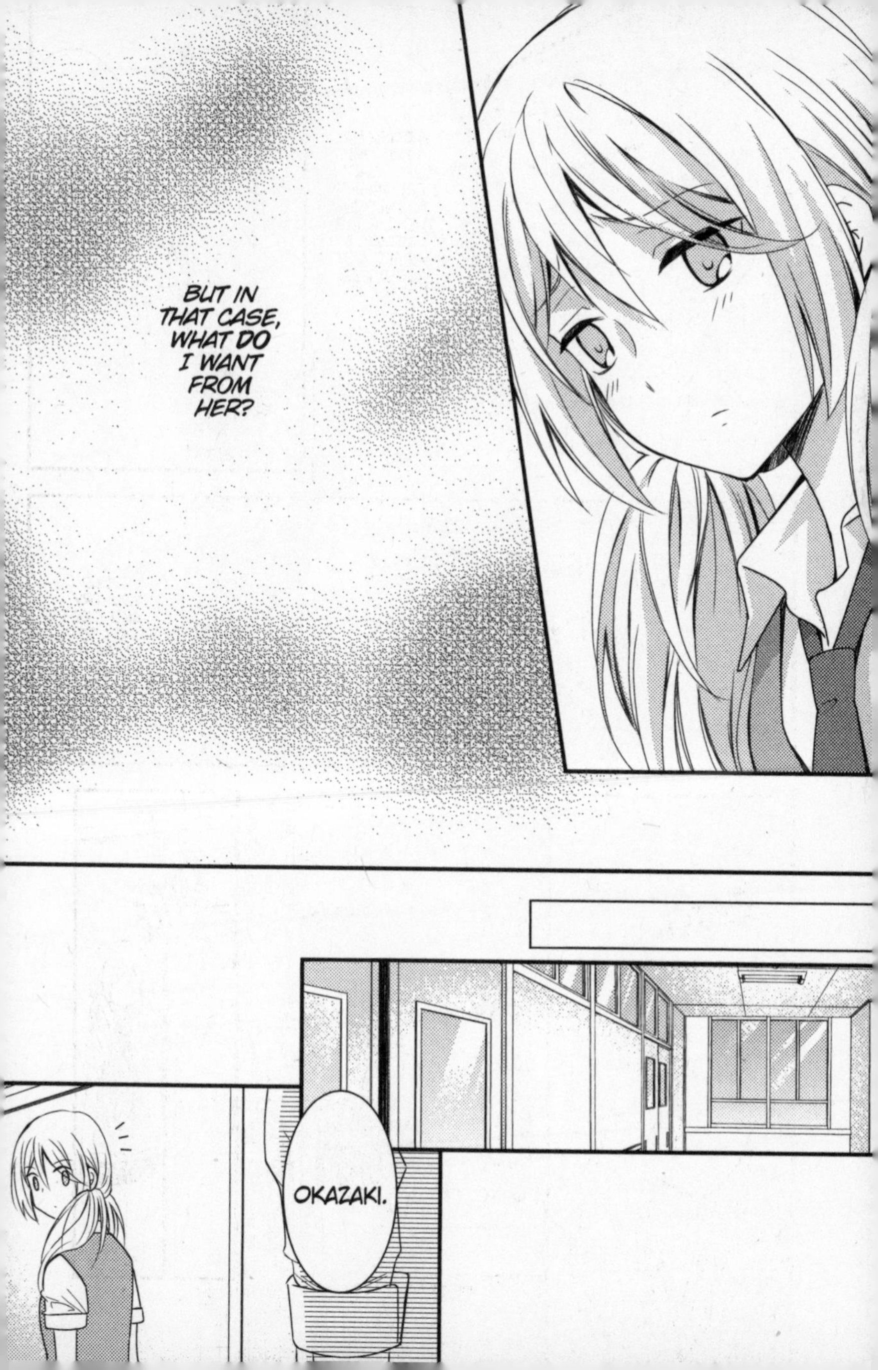
BUT IN THAT CASE, WHAT DO I WANT FROM HER?
OKAZAKI.

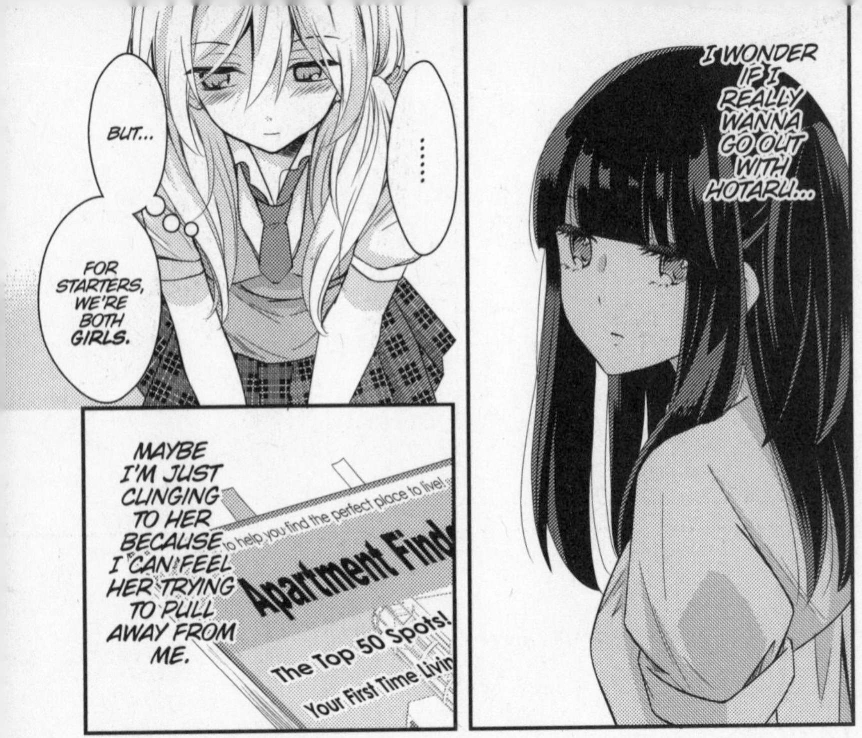
I WONDER IF I REALLY WANNA GO OUT WITH HOTARU...
......
BUT...
FOR STARTERS, WE'RE BOTH GIRLS.
MAYBE I'M JUST CLINGING TO HER BECAUSE I CAN FEEL HER TRYING TO PULL AWAY FROM ME.
to help you find the perfect place to live!
Apartment Find
The Top 50 Spots!
Your First Time Livin

OR COULD IT BE...

THAT MAYBE I'M HOPING FOR A DIFFERENT KIND OF RELATION-SHIP?

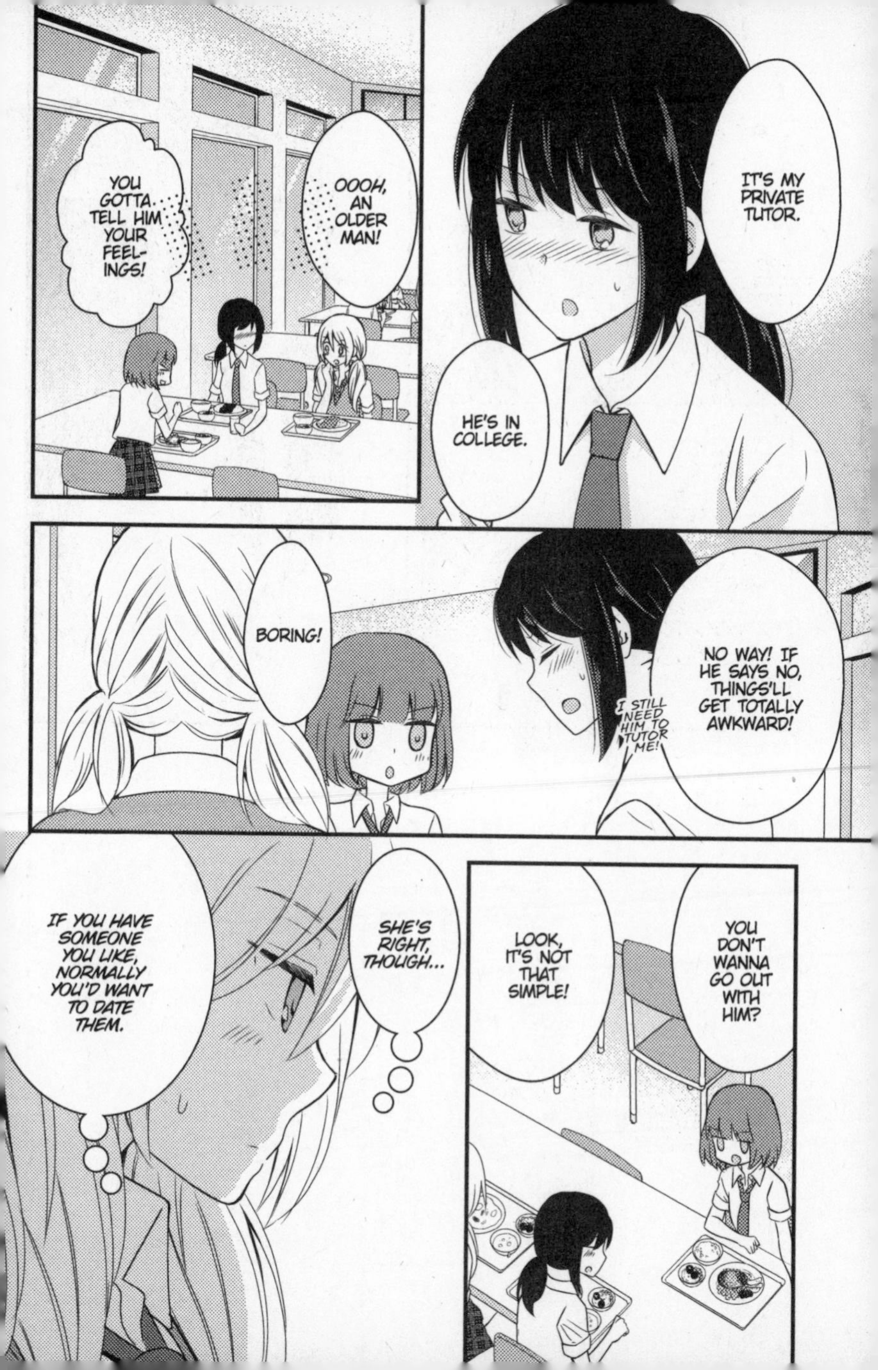
IT'S MY PRIVATE TUTOR.
HE'S IN COLLEGE.
OOOH, AN OLDER MAN!
YOU GOTTA TELL HIM YOUR FEEL-INGS!
NO WAY! IF HE SAYS NO, THINGS'LL GET TOTALLY AWKWARD!
I STILL NEED HIM TO TUTOR ME!
BORING!
YOU DON'T WANNA GO OUT WITH HIM?
LOOK, IT'S NOT THAT SIMPLE!
SHE'S RIGHT, THOUGH...
IF YOU HAVE SOMEONE YOU LIKE, NORMALLY YOU'D WANT TO DATE THEM.

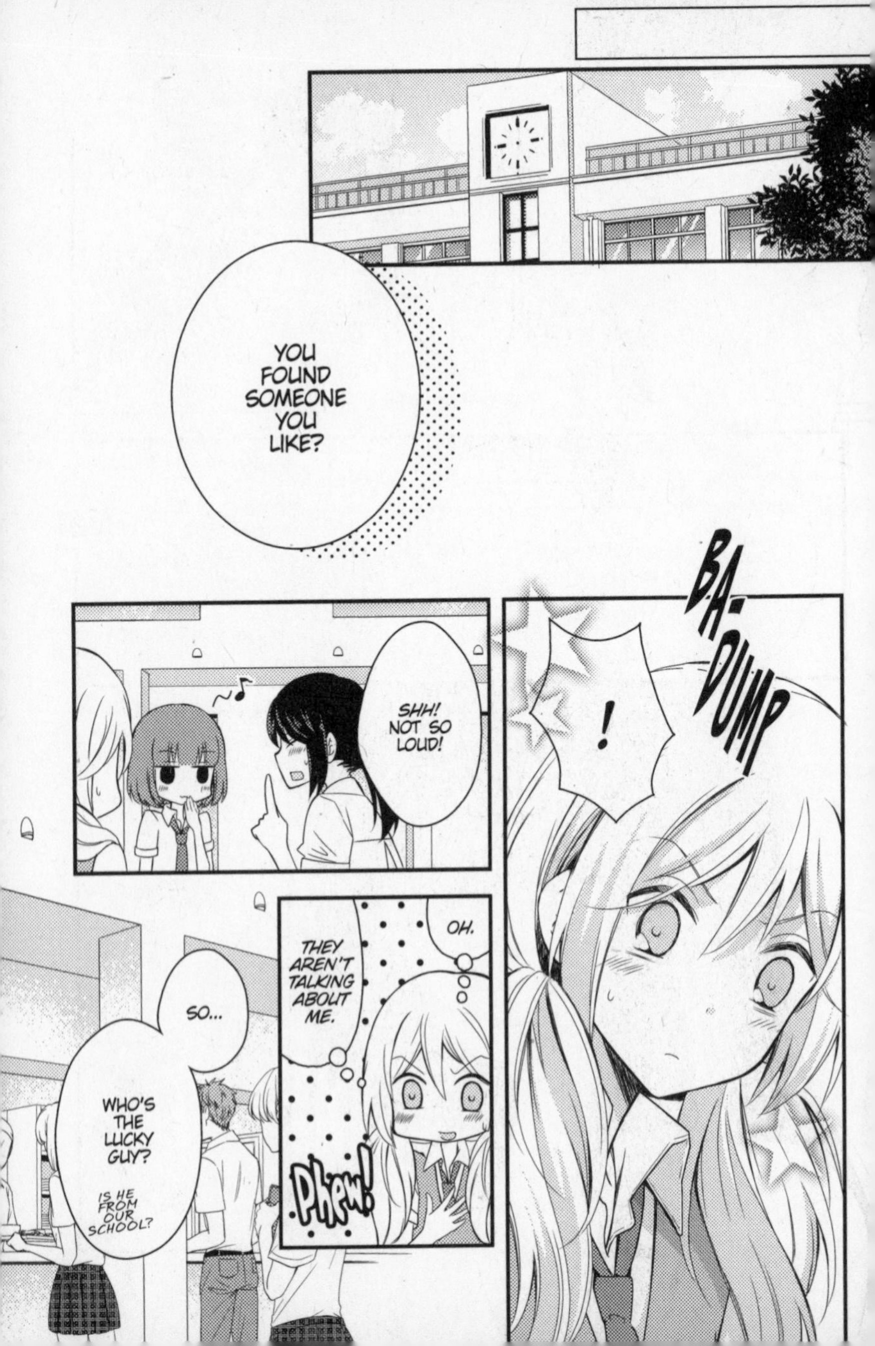
YOU FOUND SOMEONE YOU LIKE?
BA-DUMP
!
SHH! NOT SO LOUD!
OH.
THEY AREN'T TALKING ABOUT ME.
Phew!
SO...
WHO'S THE LUCKY GUY?
IS HE FROM OUR SCHOOL?

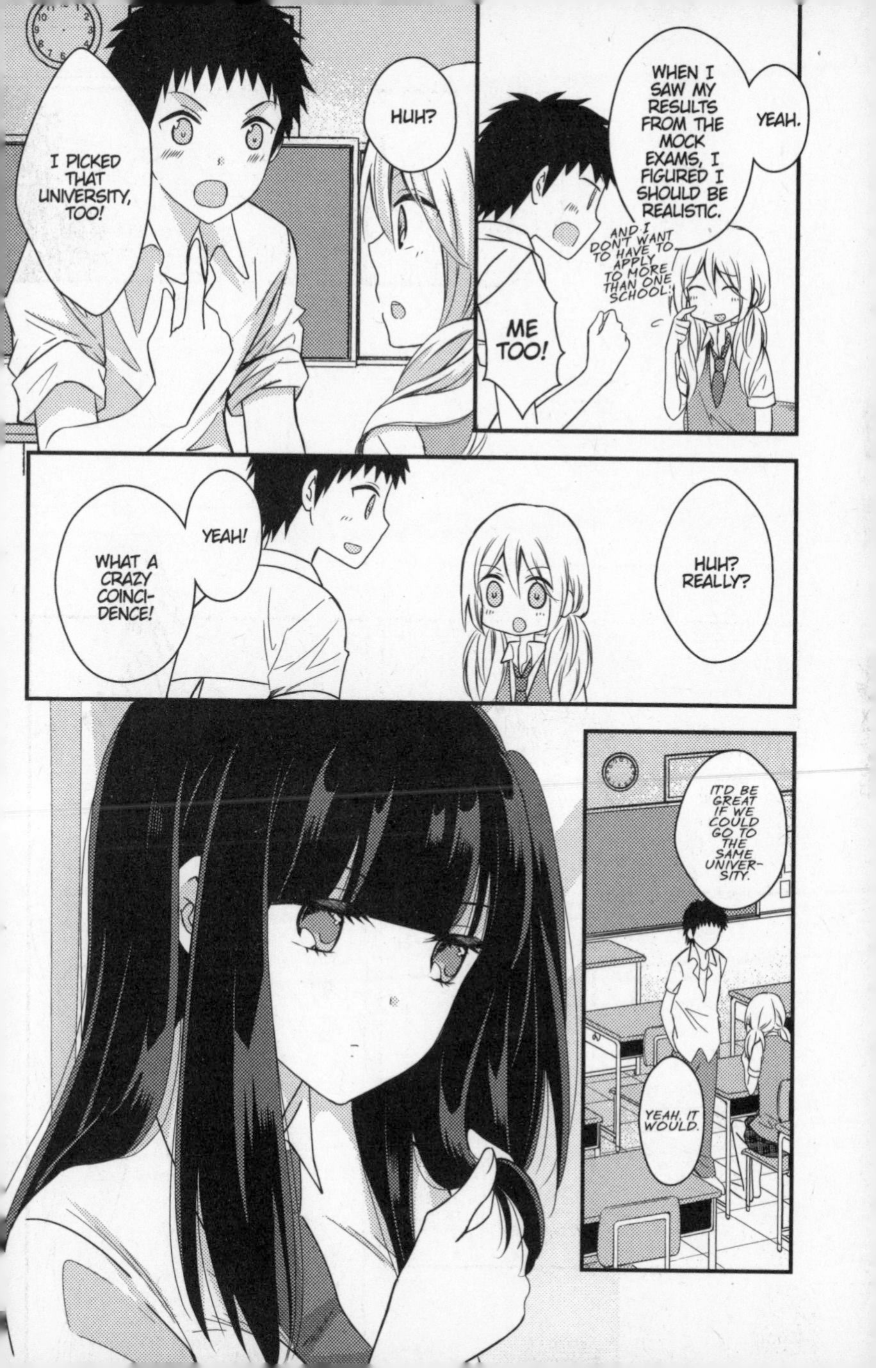
YEAH.
WHEN I SAW MY RESULTS FROM THE MOCK EXAMS, I FIGURED I SHOULD BE REALISTIC.
AND I DON'T WANT TO HAVE TO APPLY TO MORE THAN ONE SCHOOL!
ME TOO!
HUH?
I PICKED THAT UNIVERSITY, TOO!
HUH? REALLY?
YEAH!
WHAT A CRAZY COINCI-DENCE!
IT'D BE GREAT IF WE COULD GO TO THE SAME UNIVER-SITY.
YEAH, IT WOULD.

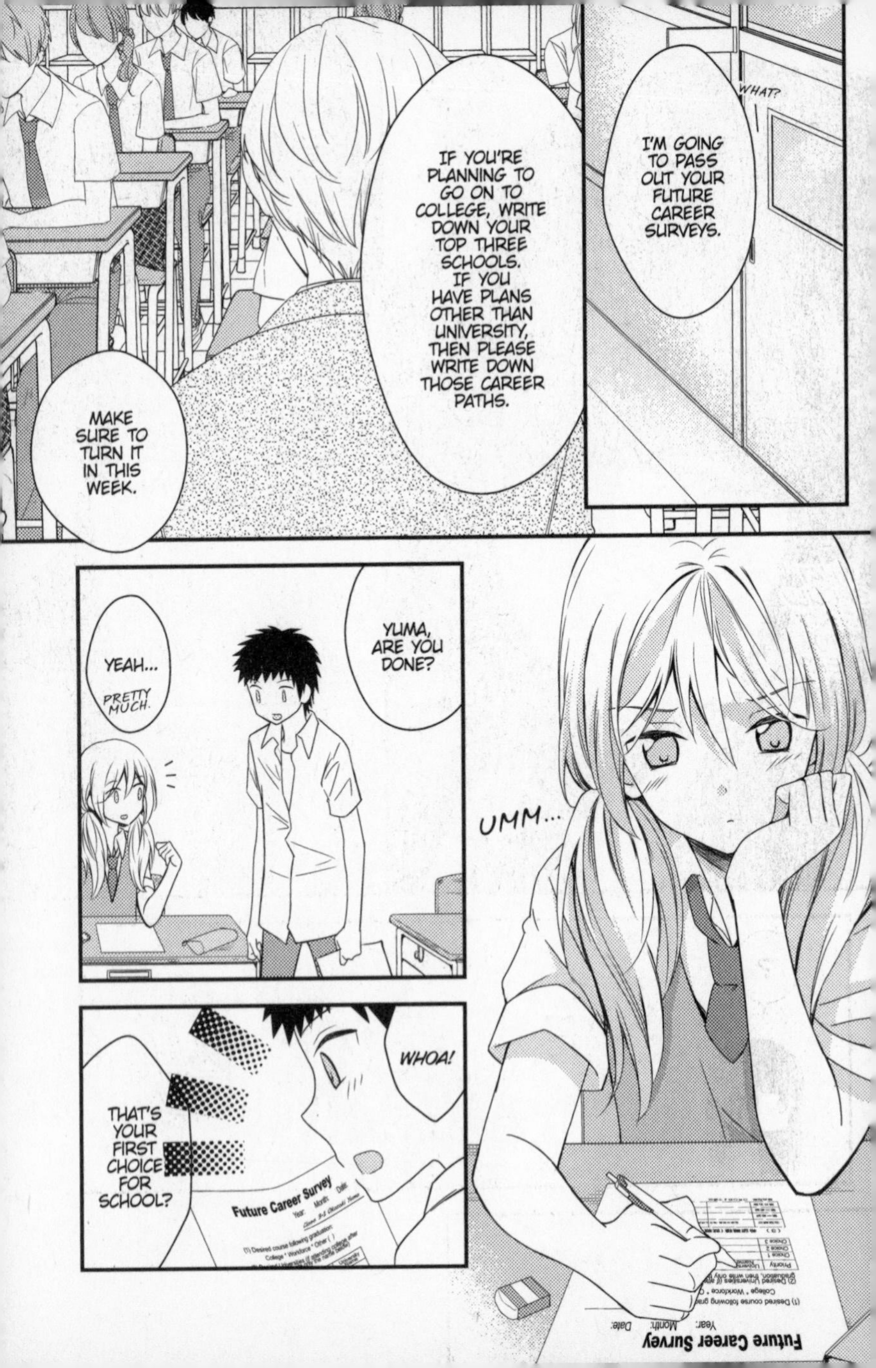

I'M GOING TO PASS OUT YOUR FUTURE CAREER SURVEYS.
WHAT?
IF YOU'RE PLANNING TO GO ON TO COLLEGE, WRITE DOWN YOUR TOP THREE SCHOOLS. IF YOU HAVE PLANS OTHER THAN UNIVERSITY, THEN PLEASE WRITE DOWN THOSE CAREER PATHS.
MAKE SURE TO TURN IT IN THIS WEEK.
UMM...
Future Career Survey
Year: Month: Date:
YUMA, ARE YOU DONE?
YEAH...
PRETTY MUCH.
WHOA!
THAT'S YOUR FIRST CHOICE FOR SCHOOL?
Future Career Survey

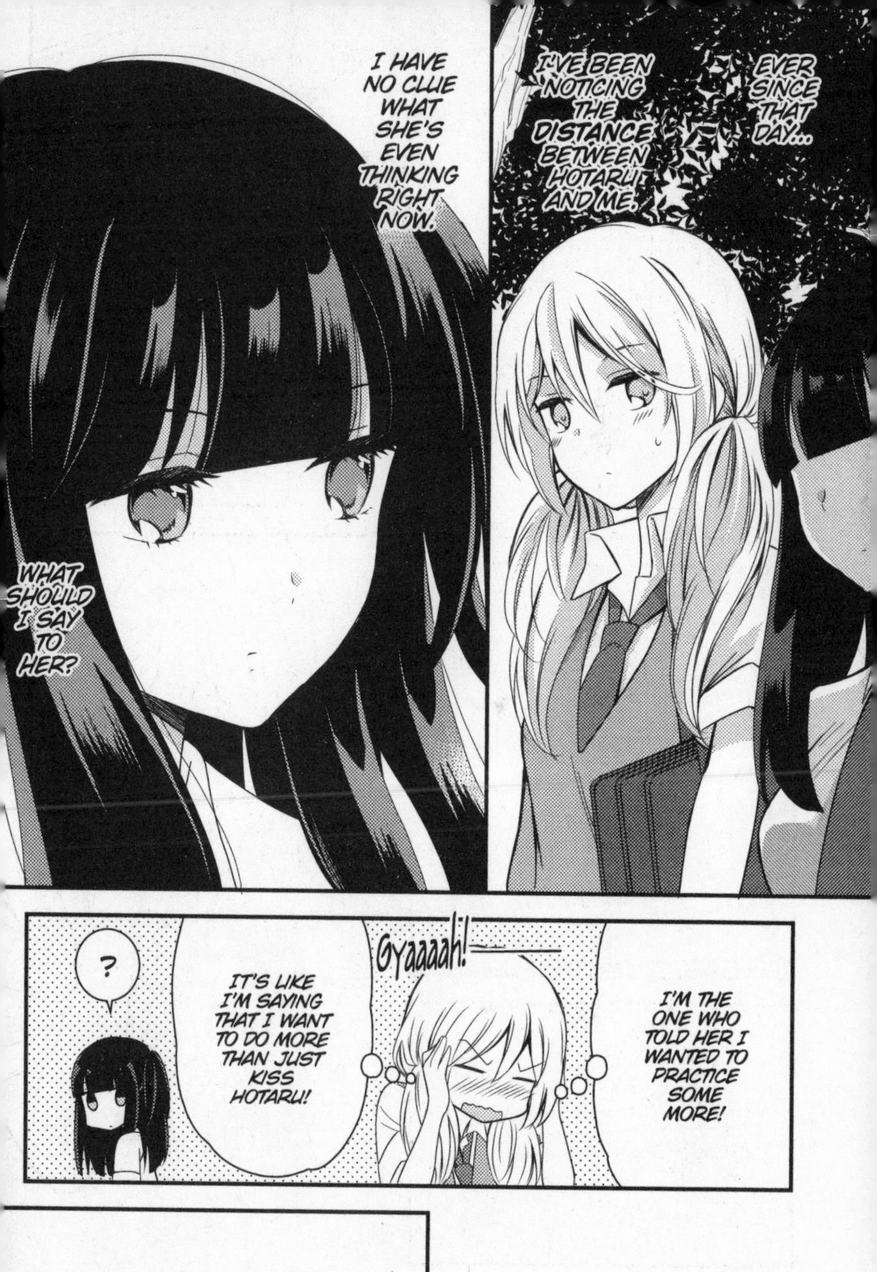
EVER SINCE THAT DAY...
I'VE BEEN NOTICING THE DISTANCE BETWEEN HOTARU AND ME.
I HAVE NO CLUE WHAT SHE'S EVEN THINKING RIGHT NOW.
WHAT SHOULD I SAY TO HER?
I'M THE ONE WHO TOLD HER I WANTED TO PRACTICE SOME MORE!
Gyaaaah!
IT'S LIKE I'M SAYING THAT I WANT TO DO MORE THAN JUST KISS HOTARU!
?

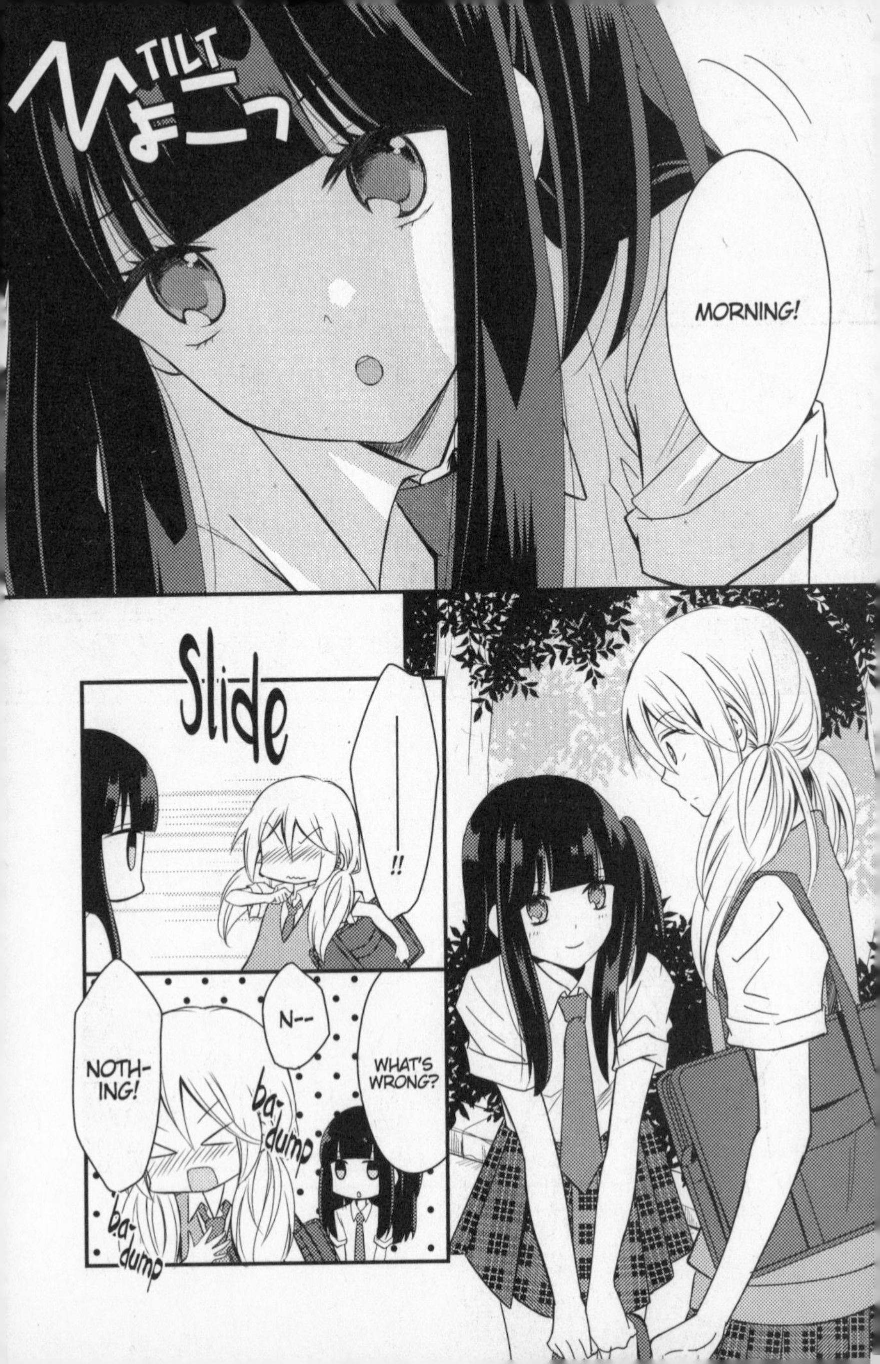

MORNING!
TILT
ひょこっ
—!!
Slide
WHAT'S WRONG?
N--
ba-dump
NOTHING!
ba-dump

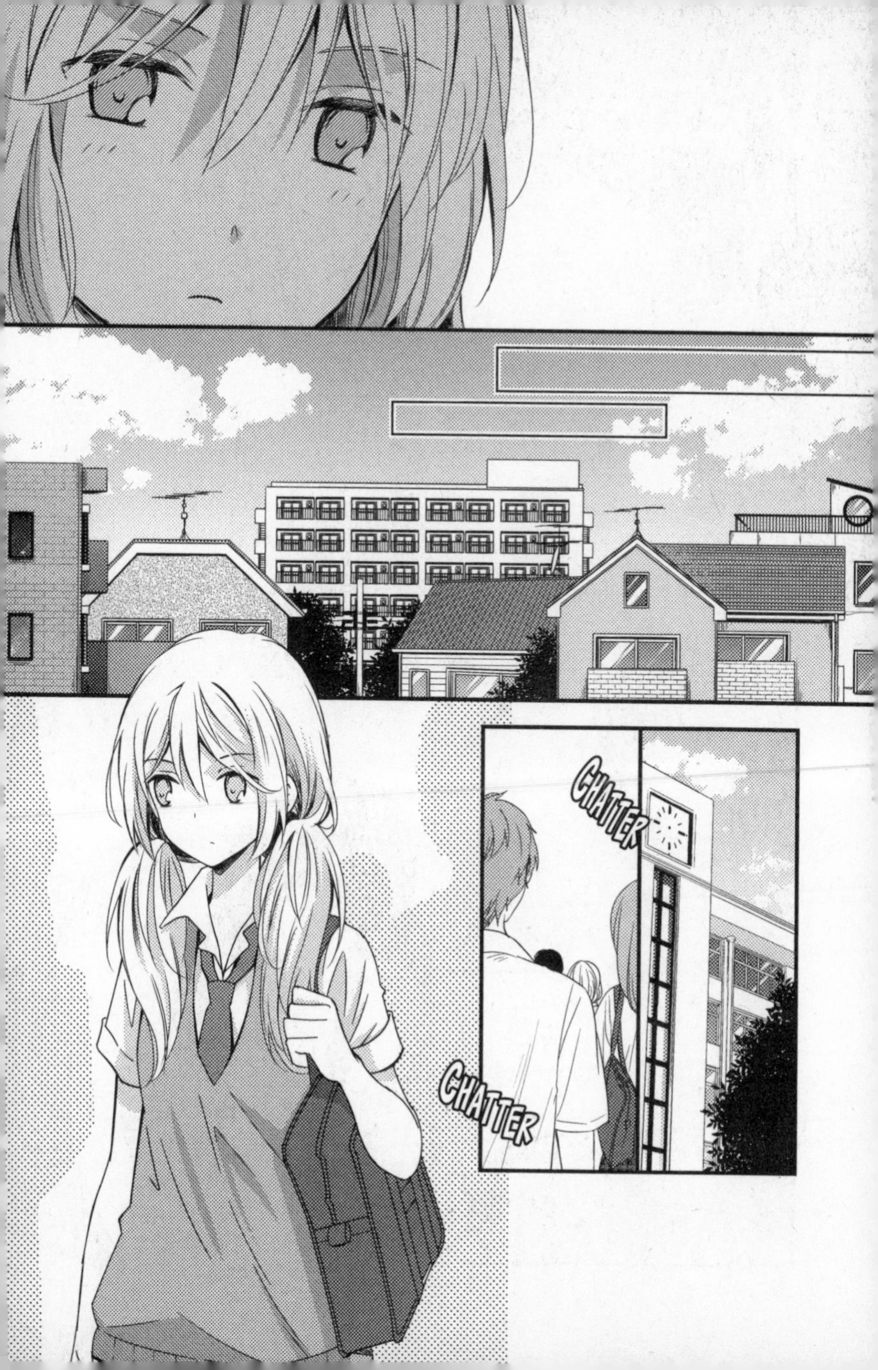
CHATTER
CHATTER

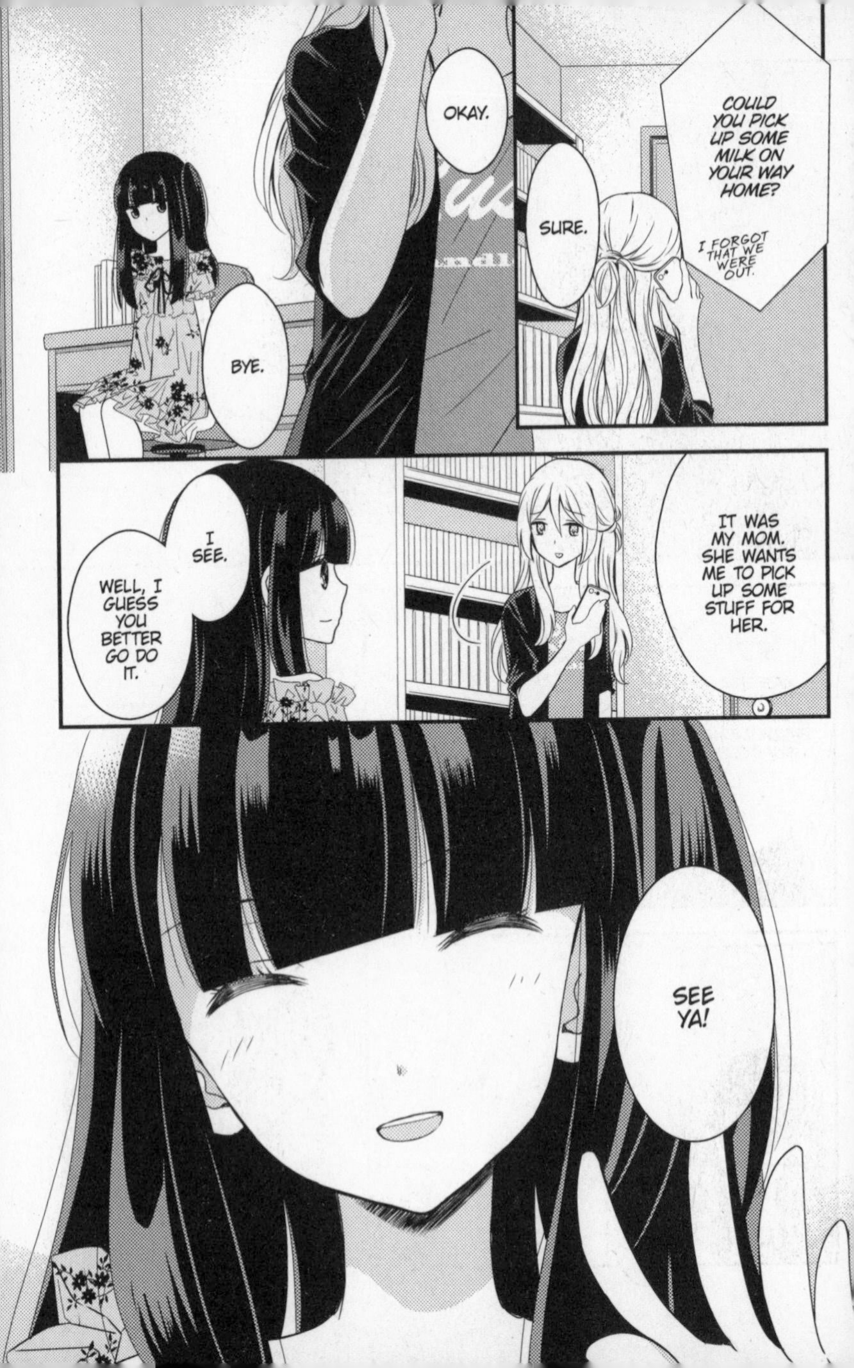
COULD YOU PICK UP SOME MILK ON YOUR WAY HOME?
I FORGOT THAT WE WERE OUT.
SURE.
OKAY.
BYE.
IT WAS MY MOM. SHE WANTS ME TO PICK UP SOME STUFF FOR HER.
I SEE.
WELL, I GUESS YOU BETTER GO DO IT.
SEE YA!

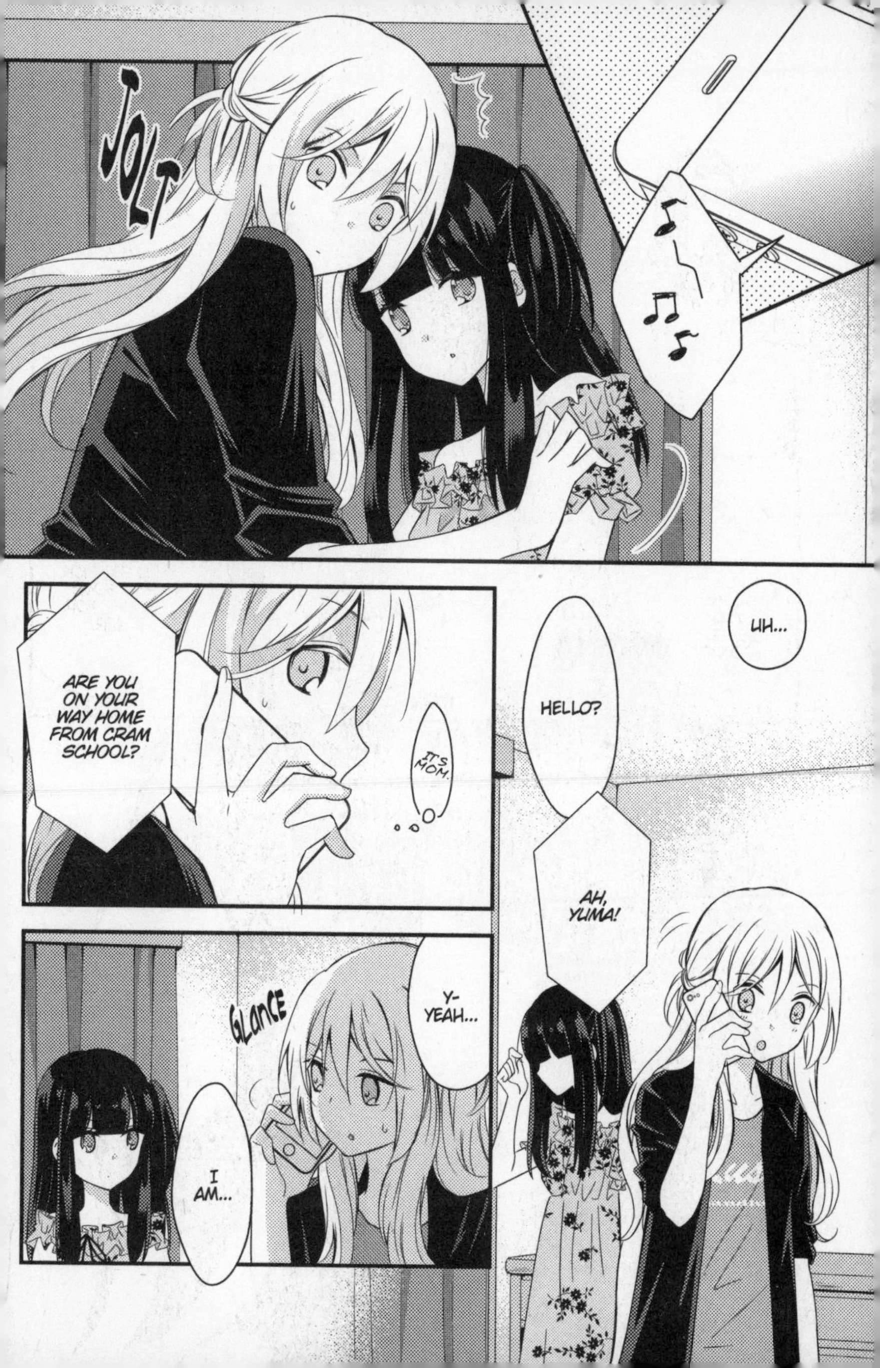
JOLT
UH...
HELLO?
AH, YUMA!
IT'S MOM.
ARE YOU ON YOUR WAY HOME FROM CRAM SCHOOL?
Y-YEAH...
GLANCE
I AM...

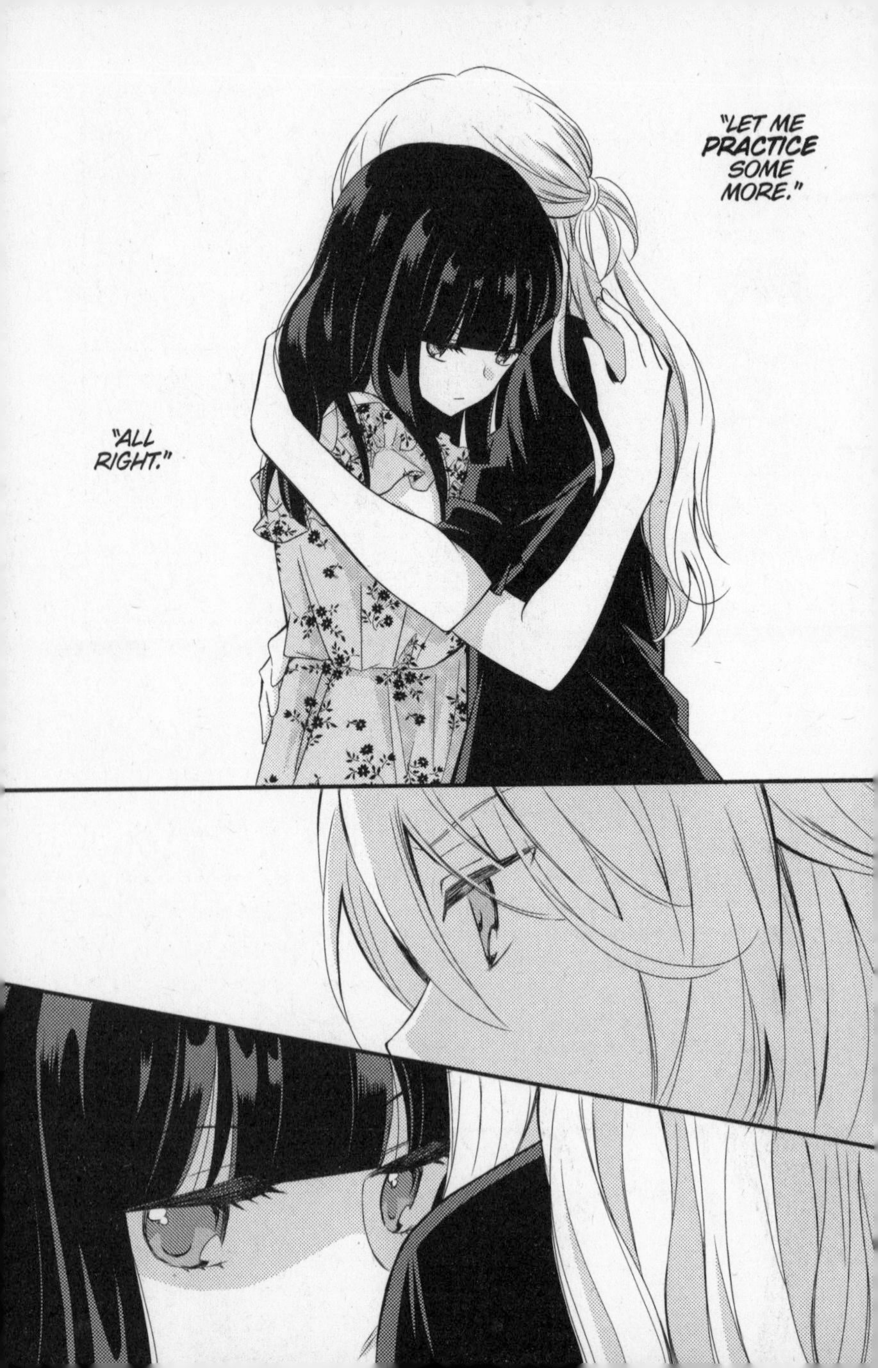
"LET ME PRACTICE SOME MORE."
"ALL RIGHT."

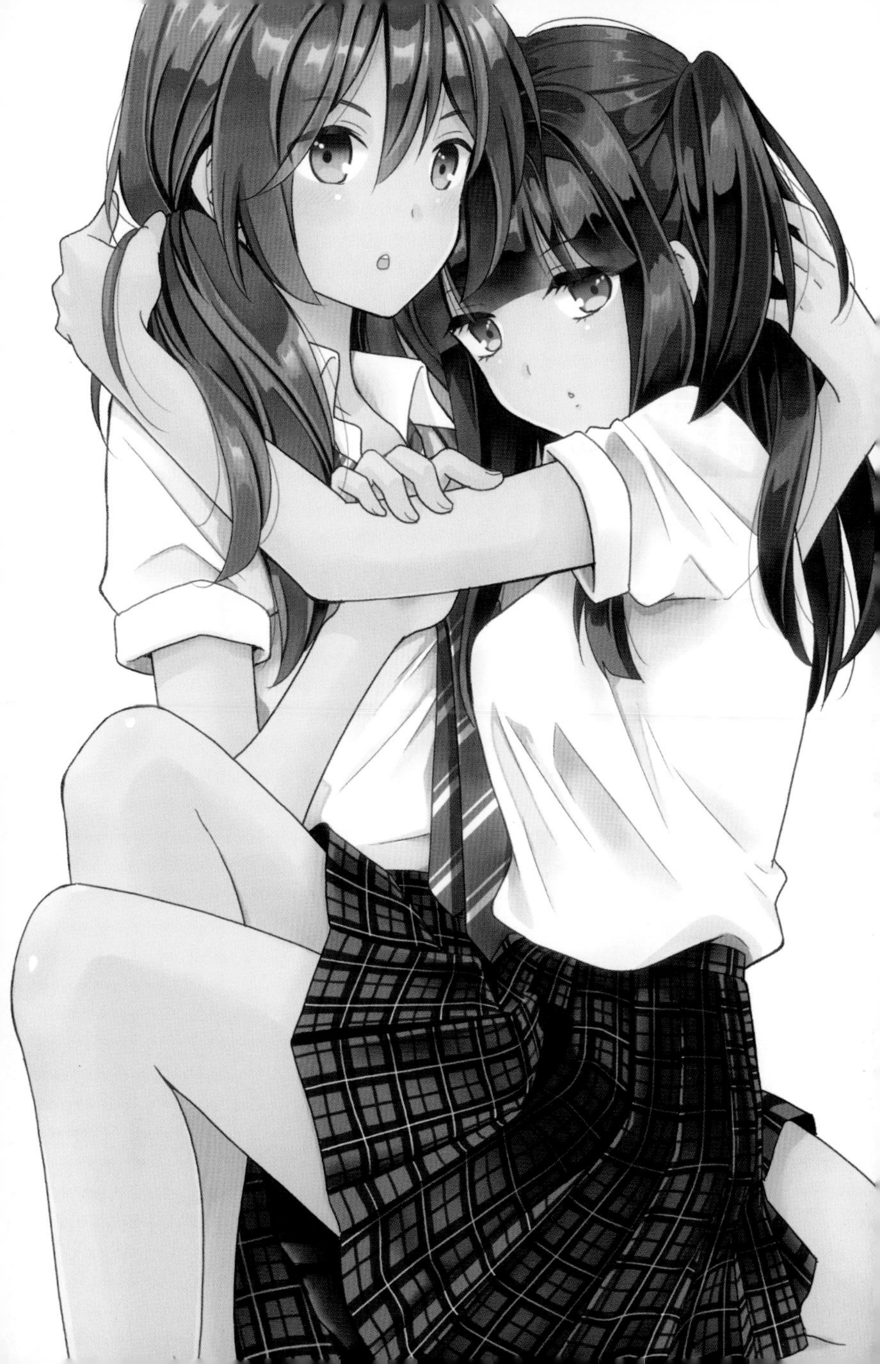

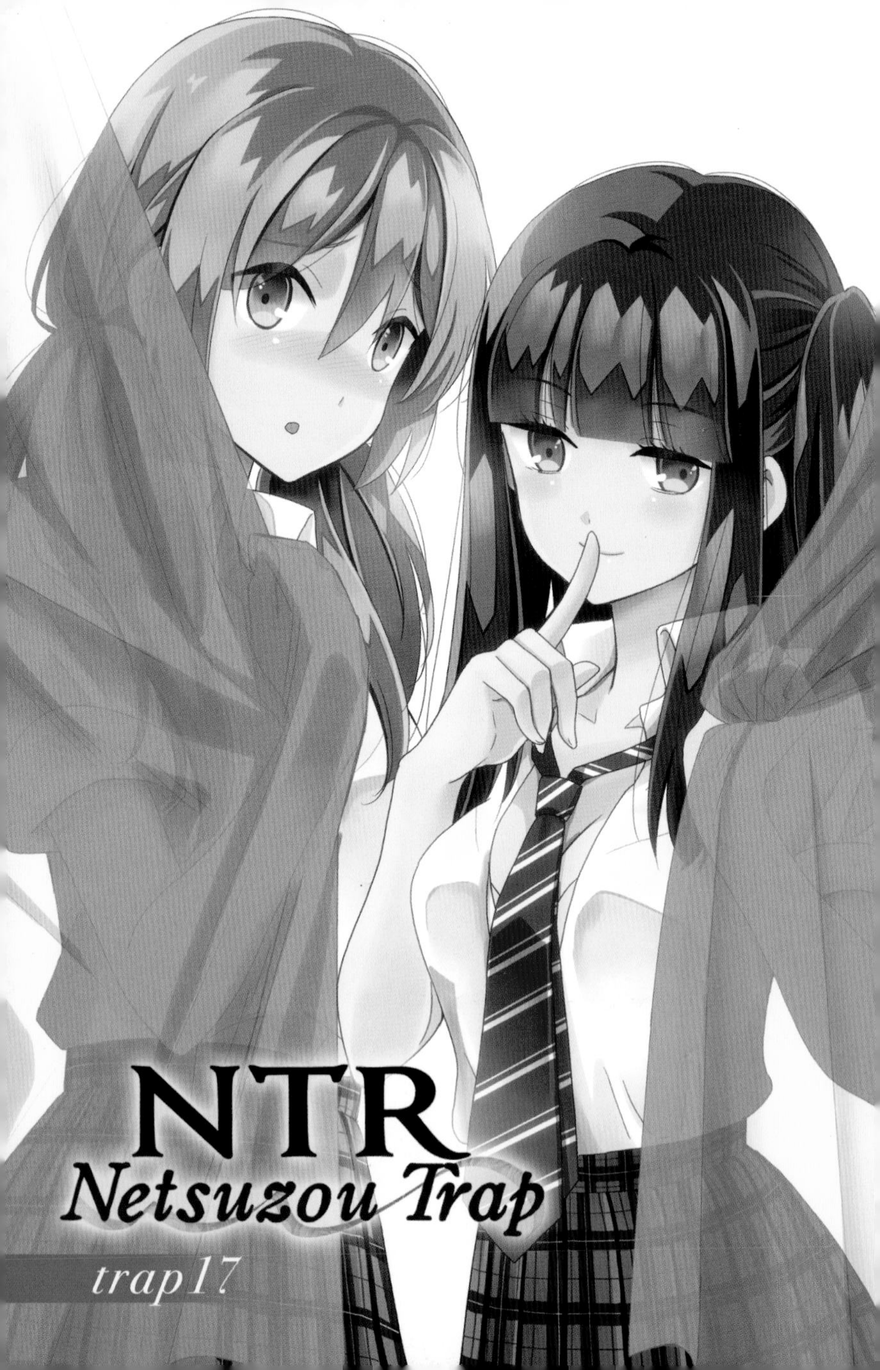
NTR
Netsuzou Trap
trap17